MARY ELIZABETH
SARAH ELIZABETH

MARY'S
Dedication

For everyone who is or has ever been Dusty or Bliss.
Love is knowing.

SARAH'S
Dedication

For trouble, whose cup I tender as dearly as my own.

CHAPTER
thirty-two

I'm sorely acquainted with the hardships that come along with being Thomas' safe spot.

Stretching out on my back, I slide my arms and legs between cool sheets that still smell illicitly sweet but bring no comfort. Wasted words and meager memories hold love's place around me, and I've given up on trying to sleep. Switching to my side, my restless eyes find red alarm clock numbers that are the only light in this room and torture to my heart.

Every minute that passes is the new longest he's ever been gone.

Three days.

The late nights I used to spend here waiting for trouble to come home before sunup are nothing compared to now. I choose my battles with him, but one's never lasted this long, and the uncertainty, the disconnect and unending, unavoidable doubts that are starting to creep in—

I close my eyes and focus on my heart, but it only makes me wonder how his is beating.

It's not unusual for Thomas to spend two or three nights in a row out with his friends, especially during the summer, but this isn't that. I haven't seen him since our fight in the driveway Thursday night, and I haven't heard from him since Saturday.

Come back, I texted.

I've been clinging to *soon* since that afternoon. I thought he'd be home that night. I thought he'd stumble in and kiss me awake with lips that are drug-dry but more comforting than these sheets. I thought this was just another battle, another hardship, another wound that would scar but pale in the warmth of love returned, strengthened by enduring.

But this meantime is stretching into oblivion.

I go back and forth between scared and hurt and angry, but they all feel like falling. My stomach bottoms out every time my mind circles back to the same stress-thought I've carried since I was thirteen years old, and my pulse doesn't know what to do. It's too fast, too slow, too shallow, inconsistent and lost without Dusty's. My body's tired from anxiety straining through my limbs all day, and my head's a mess of constant replays, countless insecurities, and a thousand reasons to get out of this bed and never come back.

Because, how do you do this to someone you love?

He didn't like hearing me and Becka talk about California, but he knows I can't go anywhere without him. Love knows, but I turn my face into his pillow and fight tears.

Because, what did I expect?

This longing, this hidden inconsolability, heartbreaking with no clear end in sight, is who we are.

It's who we've always been.

I love a boy who can't get his shit together, but without him I can't breathe. Thomas is love to me, and this love runs deeper than my blood and stronger than my own sense of instinct and survival. This love is forever-bound.

Pursing my lips, I exhale slowly, steadily emptying my lungs.

I'm here.

I'm exactly where I'm supposed to be.

Why isn't he?

I don't care where he's been or what he's done. I'll love bloody knuckles and a filthy conscience just as much as clear blue eyes and the warmest laugh. High as a kite or in tears on his knees, he can be gone as long as he's right here. I don't care.

I just want him back.

Pressing red-flannel-covered fingers to my lips, I dig for strength and assurance. I close my eyes and concentrate on breathing, slow and steady, but my inhale carries notes of vanilla and Tide that are far too cruel to be kind.

Alone in Thomas' bed for the third night in a row, I hide my face under his blankets and cry.

I can't help it.

CHAPTER
thirty-three

My alarm wakes me at 5:15.

Glowing blue before-dawn light surrounds me.

Love does not.

Before my eyes even open, hurt hits me like a brick wall. A pattern that should be natural, struggles and a practice I now have to constantly measure out, takes over.

Slowly, steadily, cautiously, I pull air through my nose. Sadness and frustration make oxygen feel like fire, but I take in a little more burning.

Slow.

Steady.

My eyes burn behind my lids, heavy and harsh with the weight of abandonment. My chest pangs with panic and desperation, but I concentrate on careful breaths. It's all I let myself focus on.

I don't think about how I wish the air filling my lungs was shared, tinted with Doublemint and true love instead of leftover smoke and fading soap. I don't think about what could be or should be. I don't even think he has to be okay, because I can't.

Love has burned down to learning how to breathe.

Over.

And over.

And over again.

Reaching for my phone, I know before I look—

Nothing.

It's Monday morning.

Thomas is still gone.

And I have to go home today.

Pushing blankets away and getting up, I swallow sadness. Resentment rises with sunlight that rubs salt into my wounded heart, and I throw his flannel back onto his bed.

Come home, I text him, burying bitterness and blame between my lungs as I leave his room.

Becka's on her stomach with her arms out when I open her door. Dirty bare feet stick out from her sheets and summer-sun-bleached blond is everywhere as she snores lightly. Ever the heaviest sleeper, she doesn't budge when I crawl in next to her, tug half of the twisted blankets over myself, or wrap my arms around her skinny middle. But when I pull her near and give a little squeeze that's meant to wake mascara-smudged sleeping beauty, she hums and wraps around me, too.

Familiar-sweet between coconut-verbena soap and the scent of a weekend spent outside, she's best-friend safe and the closest thing to what I want most.

"He texted me," she says.

I know by her dreamy smile she means Smitty.

"While you were in the bathroom just now, he said he wants to see me."

Things have been sort of stilted, basically fucked-up since prom, and not just with Dusty. What happened with my best girl and his closest boy has been unforgettable for everyone. Oliver and Smitty came over Thursday night, but the two-ton elephant in the room didn't leave much space for making-up or carefree ease. We tossed quarters until drunkenness led to dramatics, and Smitty wasn't having it. Oliver was apologetic, but they left, and for days my girl's been all bitten-down fingernails, hiding her busted heart in reckless pink wheels and bruised elbows.

But here and now, tangled close, I can feel how full of hope her strongest muscle is. She made a mistake, but she loves Smitty. He has to know that.

"He has stuff to do with his dad this morning, but later," she says, finally opening eyes that match her brother's.

Forcing a smile, I hide my face in her neck.

FALLING BACK asleep, we don't stir until there's a knock and Tommy's opening the door.

"Rebecka, Bliss, I'm sorry," she says, leaning against the frame.

My sore eyes strain under the wall of waking, but I don't let suffering or frustration show.

Sitting up, Becka rubs her face and I lean onto my arms. Late morning sunshine pours in around the edges of the Mexican blanket hanging in the window, lighting Tommy's nightgown with a harsh glow.

"Have you heard from your brother?" Concern she's trying to cover with nonchalance comes through all too clearly.

My heart cracks around a buried beat while my girl shakes her head.

"Nope," she says, sounding less sorry than annoyed.

Tommy closes the door again, and Becka shakes out sleep-knotted hair.

"He's such a dick." She pulls a tie from her bracelet-covered wrist.

I nod.

Heading to her desk, she sits with a yawn and pulls beat-up and Band-Aided knees under her chin. The lines around her eyes give away thoughtfulness she doesn't share out loud, and when I sit up, she throws a paper plane made out of a detention slip at me.

"Let's go to the beach," she says.

My hidden heart wants to stick around the house in case Thomas returns, but stronger spite outweighs teenage longing. Dusty's pushing me every minute he's gone, and what's he doing while I'm here covering hurt I'm not allowed to nurse and reminding myself how to breathe?

What's more important than this?

Let him come home and not find me.

Let him know how much it kills to have to wonder.

Bikinis on under shorts and tanks, we head to Agate Beach in Becka's new Jeep with a cooler full of fresh peaches, sunscreen, and all the beers it can hold. The sun shines June-noon brightly and the breeze swirls hot around us with pop music she turns all the way up.

Monday morning makes it easy to find a spot for our cooler and blanket, but we don't lie down. We swim and float together in the summer-warm salt water. We're quiet for a long time and it's nice. Easy waves and sun rays calm in a way that cool, trouble-scented sheets don't and comforts me deeper than my best friend can. It almost feels good.

"My parents are fucking crazy," Becka says after a while, sliding her hands across the surface of the water and her thoughts through my reverie.

"It's their fault, you know? That Dusty's so messed-up."

I listen.

"He's being stupid, though," she continues. "Petey doesn't even know where he is."

"You talked to Pete?" I ask, a feeling like jealousy winding around my exhausted nerves.

"Yeah." She shrugs. "It's whatever. I mean, it's Petey."

Her tone is warm and forgiving, and when I look over, her shoulders are slack and her face is worry-free.

"You just get caught up sometimes," she says, moving her arms through the water, closing and opening her hands. "Shit happens."

Mistakes in the sand aside, drunken apologies and confessions aside, this is Rebecka and the boy who always pushes her. There's naturally easy loyalty there that nothing else can compare to. It doesn't negate what she has with Smitty, but it also isn't going anywhere.

Squinting my eyes against the sun, I look closer at my friend and catch a glimpse of uncertainty in the set of her lips that makes her look exactly seventeen.

"They have a game Tuesday." She glides onto her back. "He's not going to miss that."

"Yeah," I say.

My girl dunks under the surface and I follow, physical burdens lifting as I dive. I chase the weightlessness for the few cool seconds I can hold my breath before coming back up, sparkling and soaked.

On the shore, Becka's phone rings, and I recognize the chorus of "Down On The Corner" as Smitty's call.

The swim back to the beach leaves me tired and dazed. I focus on the simultaneously cool and warm wind on my bare skin as I watch hopeful-hearted answer the one she betrayed, and everything between and around my bones aches. My stomach knots around sour envy, and there's tension in my limbs that's taxing to fight. My stupid heart beats yearning and worry, and it's not fair.

I miss him so much and I can't have him no matter what. I have to hide all of it, and I'm fucking drained.

"They'll be here in a little bit," Becka says, tossing her phone to the blanket.

We spread out our towels, and I fold a smaller one for my head, lying on my stomach while she relaxes on her back.

Behind my sunglasses, between the sound of the waves, I measure my breathing. I draw circles in the sand in front of me and concentrate on tiny grains between my fingertips, listening to the seagulls call to each other while overtired tears swell behind my shades. I fixate on the sunburn spreading from my neck to my shoulders, down my back and legs, beating hotter with every minute. Worn out under ultraviolet heat and love's torture, my breaths shallow and slow down as I hold my tears back.

I'm close to passing out when the sound of a car tugs my attention.

Looking up, I find Oliver's old blue-and-white pickup. Dizziness and weight bear down on me as I sit up on my towel, and in my peripheral vision, Becka sits, too.

Across from us, Oliver gets out first. With a sucker in the back corner of his mouth, he hooks his keys on his back belt loop and presses his hands casually into the front pockets of his jeans.

All my weary muscles go weak. Standing tall and straight in suddenly clouded-over sunlight, the boy I know that wants to be more than friends looks like cool comfort: strong, effortless, and needed.

Smitty opens the passenger door. The only one of us not wearing shades, he keeps his eyes on the ground as they walk toward us. Next to me, Becka's trying to hide it, but she's shifty in her want to be forgiven, just like her brother.

"Go," I prompt under my breath, impatiently combing my fingers through water-wavy, semi-dry hair.

Black bikini-bottomed and hot pink-topped, suntanned and platinum blond leaves her clothes and everything else behind as she makes her way to the one with bare eyes. He doesn't unpocket his hands as they walk away together, but she keeps hers free as a white flag between them.

Letting go of salty red-blond ends, I look at Oliver. He smiles as he walks toward me, and it's mercifully simple.

"Hey," he greets.

"Hey," I say back, and as he looks around, I notice it's grown gloomier. Behind him, the sky's full of oncoming dark, and beach air has thickened with humidity. There's a tinge of electricity in the breeze and it makes my skin prickle.

"It's a few hours away, but there's a storm coming," he says, the sucker stick still tucked between his back teeth, shifting as he speaks.

I push all my hair over my shoulder as he nods toward the horizon.

"Want to go for a drive?" he asks.

"Yeah," I say.

And it's the easiest thing I've done in three days.

Dusting off, I leave my shorts and flip flops by my towel, but tug my white tank on over my baby blue two-piece as we walk to his Chevy. I hang back while Oliver opens my door, and the scent of bonfires and hot chocolate surrounds my senses as I get in. I breathe a little deeper as he gets in, storm-tinted air that smells sweet and clean coming with him, and it consoles my raw nerves.

He sits down, and I feel as safe as I knew I would.

It's a different kind of security than I have with love.

This is total. Steady.

Thomas would shield me with his life from anyone and anything, but he can't protect me from himself.

The boy in the driver's seat, though, the one checking all his mirrors and buckling his seat belt before he turns the ignition, the boy with streaks of scarlet and white on his so-faded Levi's, with his eyes on East Coast art schools and his kind heart consistently wide open...

This boy would never hurt me.

Oliver's a lot of things, some similar to and some so the opposite of Thomas, but there's one thing he is most of all that my heart and soul never is:

Dependable.

Buckling my belt, too, I look over. Guitars and a 1960s harpsichord flow from the stereo as he starts the truck. Oliver keeps his eyes forward as he drives, and we don't go far, just a few minutes up to a higher spot where he backs into a row of spaces facing west, and from here, the storm is fully visible.

It creeps up on me out of nowhere, but dark, over-weighted clouds roll our way like they've been building for days. Some of them are almost black and others are greenish-gray, and they're all filled to the brim with a current I can feel in the air.

Leaving The Doors on, Oliver cuts the engine off, and I lean back as he does, crossing my bare legs.

"So," he starts, taking his sunglasses off and setting them on the dash. I push mine to the crown of my head. "Is Becka going to take him back?"

I laugh before I can help it. "What?"

Oliver furrows dark brows over darker eyes, sincere and benevolent, but confused. He's seriously asking if Rebecka is going to take back her true love.

"Are you kidding?" I ask.

"No." He pauses and smiles a little, taking the sucker out of his mouth. "No, Smitty—I mean ... what happened doesn't exactly convey that she wants to be with him, you know?"

I shrug. Lightning crawls through the clouds in front of us, and thunder, so far away I barely hear it, follows, and when I look over, his brows are lifted in wait.

"I don't know," I say.

Because I don't.

If I'd have said yes to Thomas on the beach or at any point over the last few months, if I'd have *conveyed* that I wanted to be with him, how different would things be now?

Bitter that I wasn't thinking about Dusty and am now, I pull a deep breath and push love out with my exhale.

"Of course she wants to be with him," I say. "They're so meant to be it's insane."

Uncrossing my legs, I stretch a little. The soft-rough multicolored fabric on the seat brushes my sun-sensitive skin, giving me a different sensation to focus on, and with another breath, I feel light again.

"How long has it been?" I ask. "Ten minutes? Fifteen?"

Low and assuring, Oliver chuckles, stretching and leaning back like me. It brings us closer, leaving just a few inches of space on the bench seat between us.

"Give or take," he says. "Why?"

"They're probably already having make-up sex."

He exhales a full laugh into his chuckle and I turn to face him. Near enough that I feel his shoulder rise with his intake and let go of air, I rest my head on the seat and can smell his mountain spring clean fabric softener, and the slightest hint of strawberry as he slips the sucker back into his mouth. Outside, clouds grumble louder and roll closer, but they're still far away. It'll be evening before they're on top of us.

I bring my knees up and we're quiet in this shelter. Meadowlarks and seagulls and low, psychedelic blues keep us company while the breeze blows through our open windows. Solid reliability invites and promises. Depleted inside and out, everything in me that aches gives in. My eyelids slip and sink in the comfort that comes with this closeness, and solace finds me quickly. I sleep so deeply I don't hear the rain start to fall or the thunder growl. I don't dream or yearn or wonder or worry. I just rest.

But not so deeply that I miss him shifting next to me.

Blinking, I open my eyes enough to find Oliver reaching over me to roll my window up, but I don't wake all the way.

"It's okay," he whispers, shifting back into the position I didn't realize we were in until he left it: in the middle of the seat with my head on his shoulder.

His sucker is gone and as he rests his left hand on his stomach. I curve my left arm around his right, pressing my hands together between my mid-thighs. I let my eyes close again, and he lays his hand over the outside of my knee.

His smooth palm and carefully strong fingers feel warm and trustworthy. He doesn't stroke his thumb or slide or push or circle his touch. Oliver just holds onto me, gently and barely, but there, soothing.

I nestle a little deeper into his stability.

"Is this alright?" I ask, but I'm already almost back to sleep. I hardly hear his answer.

"Yeah." Air-light and utterly genuine, his voice drifts between the sounds of the storm, and all I feel is safe.

"You can sleep, Bliss."

I WAKE to Becka knocking on my window. There's no light left outside. It's gone from raining to pouring, and this girl is laughing while she soaks it up.

"Wake the fuck up," she taunts, drenched and beaming. "Don't you know it's raining out here?"

Behind her, Smitty holds his hands over her forehead to keep the rain from her eyes, and I catch the corner of his grin as I sit up, cracking my window.

I feel rested, but the immediate weight of love's absence is excruciating beneath my smile.

"What's up?" I ask, drowsy and disoriented. "What's the plan?"

"We're starving!" She reaches behind her to touch Smitty. "And we want real food."

"Make-up sex will do that," Oliver says, quietly enough that only I hear. I don't look, but his voice is enough to still the moment.

Nodding, I roll my window closed. As they jog down to the beach, I breathe slow and steady through secret misery and turn in my seat.

His hair is cut too short to be too messed up from sleep, but Oliver pushes his hands through it anyway. Rubbing his eyes with his palms, he yawns. It makes me yawn too, and the deep intake of air feels like relief in my chest.

"I guess that answers that," he sort of says, kind of asks as he tucks his sunglasses into the collar of his tee.

He reaches for his keys and I raise my eyebrows, not sure what he means.

"Becka and Smitty," he continues, concealing his subtle smile behind his hand.

"I guess so."

Reaching for his seat belt, he looks left and right and into the rearview. He glances straight and flips the headlights on, then the wipers. Starting the truck, he looks both ways again, turns the music up and shifts from park to drive, but doesn't actually start to move until I reach for my seat belt too.

"WE DON'T need to call it anything," Becka says, lining her bottom lid with black pencil while I pull clean jeans on.

We're back in her room and I'm staying the night again since Mom doesn't want me out in the storm. I tug my best friend's hoodie hood up over my still-damp hair. My skin burns warm underneath sweater cotton, but Tommy has the air conditioning on high. It's all but freezing in the Castor home.

"It doesn't matter what we call it," Rebecca continues, tossing eyeliner to her desk and pulling a sweatshirt on. She nudges UCLA blue cotton off her showered-clean sun-kissed shoulder and shakes her hair out. "We still are what we are."

The difference doesn't escape me.

Not what they were.

What they are.

Downstairs, the couple-not-a-couple sits side by side on the loveseat and he writes lyrics on her shoe. Laughing low and talking with their eyes, they're together, but it's not the same. It will never be what it was before, and what stands out most to me is that it wasn't sex that took that innocence away.

It was a mistake.

Drunk. Thoughtless. Easy.

I lean my head back onto the overstuffed couch while next to me, with more than a few inches between us, Oliver does the same, but the comfort from this afternoon is gone. It's more than awkward in this living room, and it isn't just the boy and girl across from us.

Eerily loud thunder cracks outside and rain falls in dangerously thick sheets. Lucas sighs in the recliner, trying to cover the storm with the too-loud television. In the kitchen, his wife tries to cure her worry with made from scratch lasagna.

It's not working.

Lightning strikes, making me jump. Ron Burgundy cries out loud in a glass case of emotion, and my phone vibrates in my back pocket. My heart holds its beats, but when I look, it's just my mom.

"Are you okay?" she asks when I answer. "Is everything alright there?"

Nodding, I fib. "Yeah, I'm fine. We're just watching a movie."

"Safe and sound, Mrs. McCloy," Becka chimes in.

"I just wanted to be sure," Mom replies. "I'll come get you if you like."

I want to scream.

"Becka can bring me home tomorrow."

"Baby—"

"Mom," I interrupt. I don't want to fight. I don't want her to come get me. I just want Thomas. "You can pick me up tomorrow."

"Okay," she says, softer. "I love you."

Just like that, I go from frustrated to wanting her to make everything okay, because that's what moms do. It's what they're supposed to do.

But nothing can bring Dusty back except Dusty.

"I love you, too," I say.

Repocketing my phone, I force a smile when I sense Oliver glance over, but I keep my eyes on the television and dig my cold toes under sofa cushions, popping them out of sight.

Lucas gets up and comes back from the kitchen with a torn off piece of bread. He smiles when I look, but worry's sunken deep in his blue eyes. He holds the bread out to me in offering, but I shake my head politely. I'm starving, but the thought of putting anything into my wound-up stomach makes me feel sick.

It's been four days now.

Four.

Days.

Without a single sign of any kind that he's okay.

That he's coming back.

That he didn't just fucking leave—

Panic clenches my lungs.

Fueled with the fear I've carried since the first night I got out of my best friend's bed and snuck to her brother's room, worry takes over everything else. And if I wasn't frozen in place by it, I'd run upstairs to see if anything's missing from his room.

Because what other explanation could there be?

He's finally done it.

And he left me here.

For a second, there are no words for how sharp the agony in my heart feels.

Then it beats.

And another possibility splits me in half.

Burying my hands into sweater pockets, I brace myself as fiercely as I can while all my pain and dread disintegrate. They leave only two acutely clear likelihoods behind, and neither hurts less than the other.

Either Thomas has left without me, or something is very, very wrong.

The four letter word that starts and ends with D and haunts my consciousness, turns breathing into impossible torture.

I'm only able to because Tommy steps into the room, and I have to.

Wiping her hands on a dish towel, she smiles and it's made of desperate effort.

"Dinner's almost ready," she says.

Lucas smiles back, and their daughter gets up. She follows her mom into the kitchen and comes back with a piece of cheese. The house phone rings, but it's just the neighbor from down the street, asking if we still have power, and it's all I can do in the world to make my lungs work.

Slow and steady, I struggle silently around an inhale that burns to take.

"You okay?" Oliver whispers, his voice barely coming through.

I meet earnest auburn eyes and the kindness in them pits my anguish deeper.

"Yeah," I lie. "I'm fine. I just don't like storms."

He doesn't say anything else.

Thunder roars with rain and clashes with lightning, and it feels like everything I am stands on end. Becka turns the movie up, adding to the disquiet inside and out. Lucas remains as silent as Smitty, and I can't think. Terror cripples and crushes me, and in this moment, I hate the person I love most for inflicting this on me.

The corners of my eyes water and I look up at the ceiling. Swallowing, I beg a god I rarely talk to for mercy, strength, *please*—

I clench my hidden fists and concentrate harder, but this is bad.

This is pain I never, ever expected.

He's supposed to take me with him.

He's not supposed to leave without me.

Straining against the pressure of my next inhale, my chest throbs. I close my eyes again and hear Tommy in the kitchen, the sound of glass on glass as she pulls plates from the cabinet. Digging my fingernails into my palms for hurt I can measure and control, I listen as she sets the table, but nothing helps.

I rub my eyes to catch helpless, stupid tears, and I remember the first night Thomas shut the light out and wrapped his arms around me. I remember feeling like my heart was going to pound right out of my chest, and inside I crack open. Under my skin and between all my ribs, I sob and scream and plead. I curse and bargain with God, and swear in secret that I'll do anything.

Just bring him back.

The sound of glass shattering on kitchen tiles tears my lids open.

The storm pours and the too-loud movie echoes, but for a second, everyone freezes.

My skin heats and all my knots and nerves unravel lightning quick. My blood courses quickly, hot and heedless through my veins, while my pulse rushes harder.

In the next second, Tommy's heels clack over broken glass and she whips around the corner.

Outside, a key turns.

The weight on my chest lifts.

My heart flies, and before the door is even all the way open, Tommy pulls her soaking wet son inside.

Everything in me falls apart.

Taller than her and completely soaked, Dusty wraps an arm around his mother and she clutches onto him. With her face buried in his chest, her words aren't words. They're foreign cries that warn and threaten and promise and love.

Thomas just holds her, one-armed, dropping his keys and pushing wet hair from his forehead with his free hand. His cheeks are sunken thin and his skin is pale, and when he looks up from the top of his mother's head, there's no blue in his eyes. Just black.

Ice cold.

Marble hard.

Black.

In my blurry peripheral vision, Becka stands up and walks out, and I know I'm supposed to follow my friend.

Smitty does.

Oliver shifts slightly, but stays.

And I have no framework for this.

There's no precedent for this absence or return, and my head spins with the chaos that's home again. My conscience quavers while my heart beats pure yearning, and I look at Thomas again.

Every part of me aches toward where he stands, but there is nothing familiar about the boy in front of me.

This isn't trouble that kissed my head and reminded me we don't promise.

This is a person who could leave me behind.

And did.

Following careless all-pupil eyes, I find Lucas staring back at his son. While Tommy continues holding on, her husband stands from the recliner, shaking his head.

The whole room moves with him.

He doesn't say a word, but tension feels like doom as he shuts the television off.

Sudden silence, save for rain, bears unflinchingly down, and as Tommy steps away, damp-shirted and red-faced, father and son hold eyes. Neither backs down, and Dusty's so-spun blacks look like they could swallow everything.

Anxious in the wide-open exposure of his little white secret, my heart races. Uneven, discordant, and desperate, it trips over the sound that sets everything off.

Thomas sniffs.

CHAPTER
thirty-four

Everybody handles Thomas' absence differently. Tommy drinks, Becka's angry, I teach myself how to breathe, and Luke stands superior in the face of complete fear and gross disappointment.

"Bliss, go upstairs," Lucas says with fisted hands in his pockets, and dim eyes, aimed at his only son, ready to shoot.

"Okay," I say, standing up. Lightning flashes from outside, momentarily illuminating the room in silver-blue light. Cracking thunder follows the bolt of electricity, mimicking the sound of my breaking heart.

"The boys need to leave."

Oliver waits patiently at my side.

"Stick around, princess girl," Thomas adds sarcastically. Water drips from the ends of my boy's dark blond hair to the floor around his feet. Drenched clothes hang off his body, eyes as dark as the sound of his bitter laugh. "You don't want to miss this."

Dusty drops onto the couch where Oliver was just sitting, and Tommy wipes tears from under her eyes. In an attempt to help, the sweater giver takes my hand and laces his fingers between mine. With a soft pull I'm led toward the stairs.

"The seat's still warm," Thomas comments as we walk away. "Thanks, motherfucker."

Thunder crashes and windows quake, and it's like Thomas is the cause—of the lightning, of the rumble, of the rain.

Oliver follows me to the stairs, but I turn and face him, removing my hand from his. "Wait down here."

Brown eyes downcast, he presses his lips together before asking, "Are you okay?"

I look past my skater boy; Thomas sits on the couch, head back, legs relaxed—a dark silhouette. Indifferent to the emotional massacre he continues to inflict upon us, he yawns and stretches his arms above his head. As badly as I want to run to him and bury my face in his chest, I have to act as if my best friend's brother doesn't have my heart jarred up.

"I'm fine," I answer with a slight smile.

Swallowing hurt, I leave Oliver behind and run up the stairs. My bare feet beat into hardwood, and my face crumbles as I allow myself one second to feel the pain plaguing me. Stinging sadness burns my eyes, but when I reach Becka's closed bedroom door, I pull my hood up and wipe my face clear of Thomas-evoked tears.

I knock before entering, and thick tension in the room chokes me. Rebecka sits in the center of her bed, hair up and eyes focused, texting on her phone. Smitty, her not-really boyfriend stands against the furthermost wall with his arms crossed over his chest while his girl types away.

"If he knew where Dusty was, Bliss…" She falls short.

She doesn't have to say exactly who *he* is; Smitty and I know.

My best friend's phone rings once, and she answers it before it sounds again. Lacking consideration for me or the boy leaning against the wall, Becka shuffles from her bed and walks past both of us and says into the receiver, "Thomas just walked through the door, Petey."

She goes into the bathroom and closes the door.

Smitty and I shift tension into unease as he stands up straight and I avoid eye contact.

"Lucas said you have to go." To avoid seeing my own pain mirrored in his expression, I pretend to look for something on Becka's dresser while he takes in my words.

"Tell her to call me," Smitty mumbles as he exits the room.

I follow behind my childhood friend and take a seat at the top of the stairs in time to see him and Oliver open the front door to leave. The storm has calmed, but mugginess and humidity enter the house from outside with the scent of rain water and wet dirt. Within seconds, the warmth of my hoodie intensifies my discomfort.

As the back of my neck warms, I pull my knees up to my chest and inhale steadily. Luke watches impatiently as they leave, rocking back and forth on his heels. Tommy gives a sad attempt at normalcy by smiling at our departing guest.

The second those boys are out the door, this place will be a war zone.

"Bye, Mr. and Mrs. Castor," Oliver offers politely.

"Goodbye," Tommy replies in a hollow tone.

Becka comes out of the bathroom with puffy eyes as the front door closes, and she sits beside me with her phone in her hand. She doesn't ask about Smitty or explain why it looks like she's been crying.

"Petey swears he didn't know where Thomas was," my best girl explains. She pushes damp hair behind her ear. "I don't know if I believe him."

While I keep half of my life concealed from her, I've never once contemplated that Becka might keep secrets from me, too. She doesn't cry. Not often. Never in front of the boys. But five minutes on the phone with Petey, and Rebecka returns having bared her soul to someone other than me.

Studying the tattered ends of my hoodie, I brush my fingertip back and forth over frayed cotton to keep from looking at the girl sitting next to me. Her right arm lightly touches mine, and the almost non-existent contact makes me want to push myself up against the wall to put space between us.

From my peripheral vision, I see Becka sit up straight and wipe her eyes on the sleeve of her sweater, packing up the vulnerability she gave my boy's best friend behind closed doors.

As much as she feels like betrayal to me, the pull on my heart from the troublemaker downstairs trumps.

Love is picking and choosing.

And I've already chosen him.

My relationship with everyone besides Thomas has an expiration date.

Including my friendship with Rebecka.

I've put my entire life and everything in it on the line, and when my secret with Dusty is out, I'll be the liar and backstabber. But he'll get to keep them all, because no matter what, Becka will always be his sister, and Tommy and Lucas will always be his parents.

Resentful doesn't begin to describe what I feel.

"Are you crying?" Rebecka asks. Her tone is almost wary.

"No. I just yawned." I shake my head and smile.

Without warning, the fighting starts.

"Get up," Lucas orders. His anger echoes off the walls.

In one swift motion, Lucas reaches for Thomas by the front of his shirt and jerks him up from the couch. As if his son isn't over six feet tall, he shoves Dusty back, knocking him into the end table, bumping everything on its surface. Love's foot gets tangled in a white lamp cord, and when Luke shoves Thomas a second time, it crashes and shatters against the floor.

Father and son crush glass beneath their shoes as Dusty retreats and Lucas advances.

"You got something to say?"

He pushes Thomas back again, and this time he almost falls. Struggling for his footing, my boy, rain-soaked and lit, catches his balance by grabbing the staircase banister before his dad shoves him into the wall. It feels like the entire house shakes with the impact.

Unable to help myself, I cry out.

"Lucas, the girls!" Tommy calls out, stepping into view.

Despite his wife's pleas, Lucas doesn't back down. He presses his forearm into Dusty's chest, giving his kid no place to go.

I hold my unsteady hands over my mouth to keep from crying out, and Becka grabs onto my arm.

"Do you have any fucking idea—" His voice breaks, but his authority is iron-like.

Thomas sniffs.

Lucas takes a step back from his only son, but points his finger in his face. "You disgust me." I almost expect him to spit at Thomas' feet.

"Where were you?" Tommy asks, sounding small in this house full of hostility.

"Gone. I don't know," Thomas answers, straightening out his shirt. He isn't as cocky as he was before. "I lost track of time."

"Not good enough!" his mother yells. "I was afraid you were—"

Thomas scoffs. "What? Dead? Don't be dramatic."

"Did you forget who I am?" Lucas asks. His hands are in fists again. "What I do?"

Dusty sniffs again.

Lucas scoffs. "Did you think I wouldn't notice? Did you think you'd walk in here and I wouldn't know you're dirty?"

My boy lowers his eyes.

"I've dealt with the weed and the drinking, but coke? Are you fucking stupid?"

"It's not a big deal, Dad," Thomas replies. He sounds bored and tired and uninterested. "My phone died, and I lost track of time."

"You're grounded." Lucas sounds blank, unsure of his own conclusion, like he doesn't know what to do. He defends for a living; he doesn't know what to do when intimidation doesn't get the job done.

But he's grounded?

Thomas should have been grounded years ago when he started ditching school and missing curfew. Luke and Tommy should have put Dusty on restriction when he started getting into the liquor cabinet or when they found his bag of pot.

They shouldn't *ground* him for coming home high on cocaine.

They should intervene.

But the Castors have never gotten this part right.

Thomas laughs. "You can't ground me. I'm almost eighteen."

"You're seventeen for the next four weeks. No car, no phone—nothing." Lucas runs his hand through his hair.

"Fine." Thomas gives in. He drops his cell phone, his keys, and his wallet to the floor and starts climbing the stairs.

For the first time since he walked through the door, I get a good look at trouble. Beginning to dry, his hair sticks to his forehead, and his gray shirt is darker in some spots and not others. He's noticeably paler than he was the last time I saw him. As my heart races, our eyes meet, and his are nothing less than disturbingly dark.

He stops his ascent. "What?"

Rebecka gets up and goes to her room. The walls rock again as she slams the door.

A contradiction to everything, he smiles at me. I don't know if he expected me to welcome him home with open arms and a soft heart, but it's not happening. Standing up, I turn and follow Becka's steps—only I don't slam the door.

He doesn't get my anger.

The one who ran away deserves nothing more than my silence.

Becka's in front of her stereo, scrolling through her iPod, distracted by these worries. Chewing on her thumbnail, she absentmindedly bites away chipped nail polish and peels away cuticle and skin until she bleeds.

"Shoot," my friend mumbles, sucking the bead of blood.

I walk over and circle my arms around her stomach from behind and lay my forehead on her shoulder. "I'm sorry he did this."

"Me, too," she answers.

After Becka chooses a song, and the stereo begins to play a slow melody and soft-spoken lyrics, contradiction strikes again from down the hall.

Rebecka walks out of my arms as the uproar of Thomas destroying his room vibrates through the wall. More glass shatters, and the sound of a blunt object hammered against the wall over and over sounds as if the house will collapse.

Lucas and Tommy rush up the stairs.

"What's happening?" I take a slow step forward toward the door where Becka stands.

She opens it as her parents sprint by, Tommy behind Luke.

"Let me in, Dusty." Once disgusted, Lucas sounds nothing less than frightened for his boy. He tries the handle, but the door is locked. He tries knocking, but his son isn't listening.

So he breaks it down.

Becka and I move into the hallway as the frame splinters and the door opens.

"Get out! Get the fuck out," Thomas yells. Another break. Another crash.

I start the short walk I usually experience in secret toward love's room, determined to do something, but Rebecka jerks me back by my hoodie. It's a sudden reminder that it's not my place to *do something* for Thomas. I'm only supposed to be his little sister's best friend.

"Stay with me," she whispers, hiding behind my body.

My mouth goes dry, and pent up anxiety tightens my throat. I tug at the neck of my sweater, helpless and hopeless, unable to do more than stand back and listen while the boy who made it a rule that I have to smile whenever he is around makes it near impossible.

"Dusty, don't!" Tommy yells.

Becka and I both cower as his computer chair comes flying out of the wrecked doorway. It hits the wall and shatters, destroying plastic and metal and paint and plaster.

Followed by Thomas' body-rocking cries, desperate and throaty, the next one comes out louder than the one before it.

"What the fuck is wrong with me?"

REBECKA AND I have surrendered under her doorway. With her head in my lap, I run my hands through her long blond hair while she quietly weeps. Lucas and Tommy sit in bed with their son in his room. The house is quiet-still, destroyed but cleansed.

"You don't have to stick around for this," Rebecka reminds me again. "Someone can take you home."

"It's okay," I tell her, leaning my head back against the door frame.

She turns her head, and I watch sadness fall down her temple, into her hair. "My family's crazy, right?"

I smile and shake my head.

She sits up and rubs her face dry with her hands. "I need a sleeping pill. Want one?"

"No."

"Your loss," she says, lifting to her unsteady feet and stepping past me in the direction of her parents' room.

I hang out under the doorjamb, waiting to hear Thomas' voice again, or to see him walk out of his bedroom. Instead, his parents do, tired-faced and defeated. They're expressionless, until Lucas spots me and smiles.

Bending down to my level, Lucas' hair is uncharacteristically unruly.

"I'm sorry this happened while you were here, princess," he says.

"It wasn't your fault," I lie, looking down.

"My son makes some bad decisions sometimes, but ..." He pauses, tilting my chin up so I have to look him straight in the face. "We'd like to keep this within the family, Bliss."

The head of this household can be intimidating, but he's tender. It's in the careful tone of his voice and the blue eyes he shares with his children. It's the polite way he's holding his wife's heels in his hands regardless of everything that's happened, and the consideration he had to kneel to my level instead of towering over me.

"I understand," I reply.

Lucas leans forward and kisses my forehead. "That includes you, Leighlee. You know that."

"I know."

"You girls should get some sleep. Where's my daughter?" Tommy asks, barefoot behind her husband.

"In your medicine cabinet," I say.

When Luke and Tommy chase after Becka, I get up and go to bed.

Not the one my heart calls to, but the one I have to force myself into.

"Look."

Peeling back my eyes, Rebecka stands beside the bed with a small white pill in the palm of her hand.

"Mom said I'm not old enough for sleep aids. Meanwhile, my brother is coked out of his mind."

Becka drops it on her tongue and smiles as she swallows.

"Smitty and I fucked at the beach today," she says, jumping into bed next to me. "I missed him."

Sleep heavy, I fall deeper beside her, hoodie warm and best friend safe. I didn't like the feeling I had with Becka earlier. I don't like being detached from this girl. That's our future, not our right now.

"Tell me what it felt like." I roll onto my side and snuggle my face into her neck. "Tell me what he sounded like … and tasted like. Tell me."

"It was like the sweetest, hardest Christmas explosion ever."

She's asleep in no time at all.

After I slip out of bed, I cover up my girl. Sleepyhead is dead to the world and snoring. Her room is lit, and the stereo plays the same song over and over while the ceiling fan spins. The scarves hanging from the blades coat the walls in pinks and greens, and oranges and purples. The rope lights Smitty bought her years ago, sparkle and shine even though a few of the bulbs have burned out.

I change into one of Becka's band tees and turn the lights down before I leave the room. Tiptoeing down the hallway, I carefully step over broken pieces of plastic and drywall: a reminder that we're not the only things damaged in this house tonight.

Approaching the room with no door to open, I don't hesitate, and my eyes fall on Thomas right away. Taking a deep breath, filling my lungs with the scent of vanilla and delinquency, I lean my right knee against his mattress and carefully climb on the bed beside my sleeping boy.

"You're always supposed to tell me where you are, remember?" I whisper into his ear. The warmth of his body is on my lips. "What's the point of these stupid rules if we don't follow them?"

Dusty's eyes open slowly, baring black irises. He reaches up with an unsteady hand and touches the side of my face.

I kiss the inside of his palm.

Love is so fucking tolerant it makes me sick.

"I hate you," I whisper into the dark.

Trouble places his cold hand over my mouth. "Tell me you love me, Bliss."

I shove him away. "Like I could ever not love you."

It's the morning after Thomas returned home, and I'm in the living room watching Dora the Explorer while Lucas and Tommy are at the hardware store, purchasing a new door for their son's room and Becka's in the kitchen on the phone, begging Smitty to forgive her ... again.

My head is lack-of-sleep heavy, and my eyes sting every time I blink. Exhaustion is set deep within my bones, aching and sore.

Love comes downstairs, during the backpack song, in a pair of cutoff sweats and a white tee, with wet hair and the same black eyes. My heart stops.

"Morning," he mumbles, taking the seat next to me on the couch.

I turn the volume up like I give a shit about Dora's bag.

"You're going to ignore me?" my boy asks. His tone is rough, like it hurts to speak.

He reaches for my hand, and it takes everything in me not to reach back and smack him. Looking into his dilated eyes and sick, grayish skin, there's no sympathy for Thomas in me.

"I said I was sorry," Dusty's lips are tinted blue, and his hair is overgrown, covering the tips of his ears. Rib bones show through his thin tee. Anxious or frustrated, his knee bounces up and down, shaking the entire couch.

I scoff. "Actually, you never did."

Thomas sits forward and scrubs his hands up and down his face. His spine is visible through his shirt, too.

"I didn't do anything, Bliss. I—"

"He forgives me." Becka comes in from the kitchen, cutting her brother short, ignoring his presence completely. "Smitty said he gets it. I think we're going to meet up tonight. Can you come?"

"I have to go home," I tell her.

Dusty gets up and heads back toward the stairs.

"So, do you want to talk about you and Oliver?" my best girl asks, rolling her eyes as Thomas walks past her.

I can't help it. I smile. "Not really."

"You suck," she says, sticking her tongue out at me.

An hour later, I'm in the car with my mom, driving away from the Castors' house. Her curls are frizzy, and the skin around her eyes is starting to wrinkle, but the high smile on her face is genuine. The woman who gave me life is happy I'm coming home.

She's so unaware.

How many lies have I told her this week? This year? Since we've moved here?

I tell myself I'm dishonest because if she knew the truth, what would happen to *me*? But when she finds out, because she will, what will it do to *her*?

Compared to all the lies I've told her, this newest secret seems to be the worst of all: Thomas is on drugs.

His family knows.

And they're not doing anything about it.

"How was your weekend?" Mom asks, making conversation.

"It was good." Lie.

"Did anything exciting happen?"

"No. We watched movies." Lie.

Mom laughs. "For four days?"

"Yep." Lie.

"Was that a door Lucas was carrying into the house?" she asks, turning onto our street.

"Yeah." Not a lie. "He was moving new furniture into his office and busted a hole in the old door." Lie.

Mom nods. She believes me. Because I would never lie to her.

Lie.

The house is bright and morning-lazy when I walk through the front door with my mom behind me. All of the windows are open, and the curtains blow from the breeze. My dad sits in his recliner watching TV, wearing pajamas with a cup of coffee on the table beside him.

"Have a good time, Bliss?" he asks.

"Yeah, Dad." Lie.

"You look tired, kid."

"I slept all night." Lie.

At the Castors' house, everything's comfortable because everything's oversized. At my house, everything's comfortable because it's all lived in. The moment I sit on our couch, I succumb to the lack of sleep and yawn until my eyes water. Mom runs her fingers though my hair, and with the sunlight warming my skin and my dad's laughter in the air, I fall asleep thinking, *it's okay to be taken care of.*

When I wake, the sky is dark, and I'm in the living room alone. Light from the kitchen dimly illuminates the area around me, casting shadows on the walls. My parents keep their voices low, but I can hear them whispering about me. When I hear my freedom threatened, I get up.

"I'm only saying that maybe we shouldn't let her stay over there so much," Mom suggests as I intrude on their conversation.

Side by side at the kitchen table, Mom's hovering over a mug of tea, and Dad's beside her, twirling the end of his mustache. I grab a bottle of water from the fridge.

"What are you talking about?" I ask as if I didn't overhear what was said.

"You slept for six hours," my dad says.

"I was tired." Not a lie.

They're so cut and dry, so black and white, so predictable. I can't even take a nap without them questioning why.

"You know I like you in bed at a certain time, Leighlee." Mom taps the spoon in her mug against the rim before setting it on the table.

"It's summertime," I answer weakly. Condensation from my water pools between my hand and the bottle.

She scoffs. "You're not one of those girls who stays up all night and sleeps all day. I don't know what kind of home Tommy runs, but—"

"Teri," Dad warns.

"Maybe we need to keep you home more this summer." Mom lowers her tone, but she's still just as condescending with the small smile on her lips and the judge at her side.

"I took a nap!" I yell, covering my mouth with my hand the moment I do. "I'm sorry. I didn't mean to yell."

My mom's cheeks burn red. I can practically see the lecture building. But Dad pats her hand, and the fire in her eyes dims.

"Until Leigh gives us a reason not to trust her, you don't have a reason not to," he says, ending the conversation.

LATER THAT night, I'm in my room wide awake while the rest of the house has been in bed for hours. Too lazy to get the polish remover from the bathroom, I peel away purple polish from my fingernails when my cellphone rings.

And I know it's him.

"Where were you, Thomas?" I answer.

"In Portland with Casper."

"Why?"

"Why not? I—" He stops, breathing heavily.

"What is it?"

"It's not as easy to kick as I thought it would be." He takes a breath. "I'm talking myself out of not using again."

"I didn't know where you were."

"Baby, I didn't know where the fuck I was half of the time. It won't happen again. I won't leave you like that."

I want to ask him to promise me. But I don't. I know he'd break it.

"Can I come over?" he asks. His tone is low, and he's asking as if he's uncertain of my answer.

"Of course."

"Then come open the door for me, girl."

I don't bother tiptoeing down the stairs, and I don't care about the way the metal clicks as I unlock the front door. Old hinges squeak, and my heart skips a few beats. I listen for my parents, but their TV is louder than I am.

Warm and muggy, midnight-summertime air fills the living room. The stupid dog next door is barking again, wary of the tall, beautiful boy walking up my driveway in black shorts and a white tee.

Every house on the block is sleep-dark and quiet as I step onto the front porch. My bare feet cause the old wood to creak while humidity prickles my skin, leaving me feeling sticky-sweet. Pushing my hair off my neck, I wait on the top step for love.

When he's finally in front of me, Thomas takes a step up so we're the same height.

This boy wraps his arms around my back and pulls me to himself. I inhale vanilla-trouble until my eyes water, because that's all there is. No pot, no booze … Just Tide, Dove, and vanilla.

All Thomas.

He lifts my chin. "I'm sorry."

I lead the way to my room. Our left hands hold while we take one careful step at a time. I peek back and trouble smiles, but his look is shifty, and his hand trembles in mine. When we pass my parents' room, I hold a finger to my lips. "Shh."

He winks.

When we finally reach my room, Thomas goes straight for my bed while I close the door, not releasing the handle until it's all the way shut. As quietly as I can manage, I turn the lock.

Thomas toes off his shoes and tries to remove his shirt. It gets stuck on his shoulders, so I help him, and then I press the palm of my hands between his shoulder blades where I can feel his swift heartbeat the best.

"Are you okay?" I ask, scratching my nails lightly down his spine.

With the left side of his face hidden in my lavender pillow, he shakes his head.

I curl up beside him, pressing my cheek to his soft, warm skin. After a few minutes, Thomas turns in my arms. His tired eyes are glossy, but they're returning to blue.

"Take this off," he says, tugging at the end of my sleep shirt.

I toss it away, leaving myself bare-topped in cotton shorts. My boy pulls me beside him and scoots down a little before laying his head over my chest and wrapping his arms around my back. I light up everywhere our skin touches.

"Stay like this all night. It's a rule."

Love is mental.

THOMAS WAKES me up a little before four in the morning with kisses down my throat. "I have to go, little girl," he whispers, pressing hot lips across my exposed collar bone.

"Just stay," I say breathlessly, rubbing my thighs together.

Dusty pulls soft skin between his teeth before pulling away and getting out of bed.

The early morning air is crisp and clean, and the rising sun has turned the sky blue-orange-purple. Our neighbor's sprinklers are on, giving the air the most invigorating scent. We're quiet as we walk to the side of the house, hand in hand like we have been all night.

When we reach the side gate, I don't want to let him go. Thomas hugs me tightly, lifting my feet from the cement.

"Don't leave me," I say quietly, looking over his shoulder at nothing.

"I'll be back," he says. The color of his skin hasn't returned to normal.

I wrap my legs around his waist and grip hard with my arms. My chest presses against his, and my lips find the soft spot below his ear.

"You're making this so much harder," he says, letting me down.

When he leaves, I cry.

I can't fucking help it.

I'M HERE.

Texting with one hand and brushing my teeth with my other, I reply, *On my way.*

Wiping my mouth, I flip off the light and carefully open the bathroom door. I avoid every floorboard that creeks and close my parents' bedroom door before I rush down the stairs, two at a time.

I unlock the deadbolt without making a sound and open the front door quickly so the hinges don't squeak.

Love stands in front of me, tall, strong, and smirking like he was never sick at all.

Like his trembling hands and too-hard heartbeat were all a figment of my imagination.

Like he didn't come home last night dope-sick and helpless.

All of the blue that returned to his eyes is gone. His posture is straight and his composure is steady. The color in his face is normal, and when he says, "Are you going to let me in or what?" It's completely typical: arrogant, challenging, and smug.

There is something calming about it, though.

It's familiar.

It's what I know best.

It's our deal.

CHAPTER
thirty-five

"Are you nervous?" I ask.

Becka's eyes meet mine in the bathroom mirror, blue-devil and leading. "What's there to be nervous about?"

I shrug, rubbing the soft cotton towel through her wet hair. A few pink strands show, but I'm careful to keep most of it covered. "It's a big deal."

Her lips spread high into the curviest smile; she looks so much like her brother sometimes. "No way. This is going to be awesome."

I lower my lips to her triple pierced ear. "Ready?"

My girl closes her eyes and holds the deepest breath in her little lungs. She nods. I close my eyes, too, and drop the towel to my turquoise painted toes.

"Don't look yet," I say. "Let's save this." I wrap my arms around her chest from behind and set my chin on her shoulder. Soft, soothing drum beats and lower-toned lyrics caress our eardrums from her open door down the hall.

Between *Long beach* and *L.A.*, Becka says, "Can we look now?"

"On the count of three," I say. "One … two— I can't wait!"

Our eyes open at exactly the same time to find me and a different girl looking back at us.

"It's amazing," I say with a smile.

Becka sinks her fingers into her newly light-pink colored hair. She holds wet-wavy, long and rose-tinted ends right up to her face. "Holy shit, I can't believe we did this." She drops the locks and places her hands on the bathroom counter, leaning toward the mirror to get a closer look.

I pick the towel up from the floor and rub my hands, trying to wipe away pinkish shine. Color is buried in my nail walls and in between my fingers, because we forgot to get gloves at the beauty supply store. I can't bring myself to care. Not when my girl is high smiling and pink sparkling.

She looks to me over her shoulder, practically vibrating with excitement. "Do you love it, or what?"

I nod, rubbing harder.

"Chop it off," she says, holding her hair out. "All of it. Cut it off."

I drop the towel and shake my head. I'm a firm believer that all girls need to have long hair. Even flower-colored skater girls. "No way, Rebecka."

She rocks her head back and forth, shaking her hair dry like a puppy dog. Pink water drops sprinkle my clothes and face, for sure ruining her white Lydia shirt I'm wearing.

"Fine, sissy Bliss baby."

My best friend blow dries her tresses, and I sit on the counter beside her, rubbing alcohol into my hands to get the color off when Tommy comes upstairs to see what we're doing. Tall in a pair of red-bottomed heels, she's perfect.

"For the love of God, Rebecka, what have you done to your hair?" Tommy stands with her palm on her forehead. "You're going to look like that during your brother's birthday?"

Becka turns the heat off, smiles, and says, "It's pink. I thought you liked this shit."

BECAUSE DUSTY swears there's nothing better than breakfast for dinner, his mom makes pancakes, bacon, and scrambled eggs, with a special order of sunny-side eggs for me. We sit around the table, drenching our meal in syrup and butter, and eat until our stomachs feel like they'll burst.

Popping bottles of sparkling cider, Becka and I are high on sugar while my boy is high on his vice, and Tommy is drunk from the bottle of Moscato she's polished off.

She starts to cry around 11:55 when we're all in the living room, waiting for midnight.

"Crazy boy," she says. Tommy pushes the hair out of her son's face, revealing the light sheen across his forehead and the entirety of just how dark his eyes are tonight. "Why did you grow up so fast?"

Because you let him, I think to myself.

Buried in the corner of the Castors' oversized couch, my fingers smell like maple syrup, and my lips taste like apples. My heart beats in sync with the clock on the wall as the minutes tick by, forcing time we don't want to pass down our throats. Rebecka jumps up from the floor to grab pots and pans from the kitchen she can bang together the second her brother officially turns eighteen. Her mother wipes sadness from beneath her eyes standing with Lucas. He slides his arm across her shoulders and kisses her temple.

And Thomas sits beside me, holding my hand under the blankets that lie across our legs.

I watch in disbelief as time turns my boy into a man.

Nineteen, eighteen, seventeen … sixteen … fifteen …

At ten Thomas looks over at me and smiles.

At *seven* he squeezes my hand.

At *three* he leans over and whispers, "Be my girlfriend."

At *one* I say, "No."

At midnight Rebecka bangs metal together, and Thomas is eighteen.

"WAKE UP." Thomas smells like beer, his hands firm on my hips. He left after we celebrated his birthday. I came to his room to an empty bed. "I need to show you something."

I curl into a sleepy ball and turn away from my rude awakener. "Leave me alone," I whisper playfully.

Home from wherever it is he went, Dusty slips into his bed beside me. Shirtless and burning, he presses kisses and his drunk smile into the side of my neck. Turning to face him, I lay my cheek against his too-high heartbeat, and melt.

Nothing compares to *this.*

We're together almost every night. If I'm not here, he's sneaking into my house to be with me. But it's five minutes later each time, lessening our moments together as the warm season passes.

Thomas and I have a way of adapting to the things we put each other through: My boy never lets me go, and my grip on him is as tight as ever. He blames a lot of his crazy on me and my refusal to be his girlfriend. And I'm on the receiving end of late night phone calls that are usually him in a rage, locked in someone's bathroom, somewhere I don't want him to be.

Summertime has turned my boy into a monstrosity, but he's *my* monster.

I need Thomas' sureness, and I crave his late night calls that last for hours but make no sense. I accept his drug-induced bullshit, because buried in that craziness is our own kind of love.

Nothing compares to that.

But love is battling cocaine for love's attention.

She's created a trio out of our duo. His drug is the other girl. The lipstick on his collar. She makes Dusty so unpredictable. But She's nothing I can't or won't handle.

"What is it?" I close my eyes so I can imagine his are still blue and not deep-dark black.

"Everything."

I give in and look up. Thomas smirks, pushing blond-red hair out of my face. *He isn't really here,* I think to myself. He's in this bed with me, but his eyes are wild.

"How long has it been since you slept?" I ask, rubbing my thumb under purple-blue bruises beneath his eyes.

He doesn't answer me with words, but with an envelope addressed to *Thomas Levi Castor*, delivered on his birthday.

"My dad gave it to me before dinner." His eyes are on my hands, on the letter … waiting.

"Are you going to open it?" Thomas asks, pulling me away from my thoughts. He stands up and pats a cigarette out of his pack.

I slip my finger under the off-colored seal flap, tear it open, and pull the papers out and set the high-grade envelope to the side. Trouble lights his nicotine, and I look up as the cherry burns orange. He smiles, encouraging me to read. As I unfold the papers, my eyes fall on a number.

A huge number.

It's the trust he inherited when his nana died, and he hasn't been able to touch it until now.

"Insane, right?" He laughs, blowing smoke out the window.

"This is all yours?" I've never—not ever—seen anything so incredibly unreal before. "What are you going to do with it?"

"Buy my girl something pretty," he answers. The right side of his devious mouth curves up.

"Thomas, I'm serious."

"I don't know, Bliss. I'll keep it. It's for us … When we leave."

"You can go to college," I state the obvious.

He rolls his hooded eyes. "Yeah, I know."

"You can be anything you want with money like this."

The richest boy I know flicks his half-smoked cigarette out the window and walks over to me. He takes the paper from my hand, the scent of nicotine lingering on the tips of his fingers, and just says, "I don't want to be anything but with you."

Love is endless possibilities.

I WAKE up in Rebecka's bed after noon. The yellow sun shining in through the cracked-open window is too bright, and my best friend is wide eyed and buoyant.

"What?" I ask, rubbing my eyes, warm under thick blankets.

"You're in love," she says, holding up my phone.

My heart stops, and I grab my cell from her, hoping she didn't see anything from her brother.

"Were you trying to keep it a secret from me, Bliss?" She nudges me with her elbow, bouncing with her knees on the mattress.

My heart jump-skip-beats, pounding against my diaphragm as I touch-slide unlock my phone. But when my screen lights up, relief has never felt so good.

It's a text message from Oliver.

Hey, it says.

I take a much needed breath and fall back with my phone over my heart.

Becka laughs. "You have it that bad, huh?"

I shake my head and sigh. "Stay out of my phone, Becka."

"Sorry," she says, rolling out of bed. Her new pink hair is up and mid-morning tousled. "It went off and you didn't wake up. Tired much?"

"I didn't sleep well."

She pulls the blanket off of me, replacing body warmth with freezing, conditioned air. "Well, get up. We have a party to get ready for."

She tickles the bottom of my feet relentlessly before I finally crawl out of bed. I take my time finding my bra and raking my fingers through my strawberry-blond sunup mess. My eyes won't open, so I keep them mostly closed as we head downstairs. Becka thinks it's funny and takes a picture of me all zombie apocalypse-like.

"I'm so sending this to Oliver," she says.

My eyes snap open. "You better not!"

I chase her down the stairs, and as she turns the corner to run into the kitchen, she runs straight into Petey.

He catches her before she falls.

"I like it, pretty in pink," he says, twirling a lock of her ponytail around his finger.

This girl smiles and acts bashful and embarrassed by the compliment, but that's not her style. I'm not surprised when she reaches for his hair, pulls, and says, "Thanks, dumb in blond."

His smile is lopsided, so-in-love-with-her sneaky.

She makes him beg for mercy, and he does, but I'm over their flirting. I quietly move around them into the kitchen where the java is hot and ready, squeezing my way through the caterers to get to the coffee pot, but even then, all the counter space is being used: appetizers, main courses, desserts. Italian's on the menu, and the house smells so good.

When the dessert guy isn't looking, I steal a chocolate cannoli from his tray and dip it in my coffee.

"I saw that." Tommy struts by, winking right before she orders one of the workers setting up the tables outside to—not so kindly—move the stack of chairs away from her new gazebo—now.

"Leighlee, do me a favor, baby," she calls over her shoulder. She's at the back door, hanging up a birthday banner. It's crooked, but she'll figure it out. "Go wake up Dusty."

I shove the rest of the cannoli in my mouth and nod. The dessert guy gives me a dirty look.

My best girl and her hush-hush love sit on the bottom step of the stairs talking. I walk between them. Becka grabs my ankle, and I almost fall. "Where are you going? I thought we were going to raid the dessert tray."

"I already did." I slip her the napkin-wrapped cream-puff I snatched. "I have to wake up your brother. Your mom needs his help."

"Ha! Good luck," she yells. I'm already down the hall.

I open the door expecting Thomas to be laid out in bed, but he's fresh out of the shower in front of his closet with a gray towel around his waist and another draped over his shoulders. His window is open, but his room still smells like bad habits mixed with hot water and soap. The air is thick from the steam, and when I close his door and slip into bed, his sheets are cold, like he hasn't been in them since I left.

"We can ditch this party," he says without looking over. He searches through his hangers before pulling down a white tee shirt. "And never come back."

He drops the towel. Unfortunately, he already has a pair of boxer briefs on.

"And miss out on panna cotta? I think not."

Thomas turns around, slipping the shirt over his head. "You would choose sugar over love."

I smile. "Sugar is love."

My boy pulls down a pair of cargo shorts and steps into them. I pout, and he laughs. "You want some of this?" He jokes, cupping himself.

I slump into the pillows, laughing. I have to hold my stomach and bite my lip.

"Is something funny?" he asks playfully, pulling the covers from me like Becka did earlier this morning. "You think my dick is a big joke, sunny side?"

"It's big, but it's not a joke." I slap my hands over my mouth the moment the words pass my lips. Thomas' dark eyes widen before he leans his head back and laughs, holding his hands over his stomach.

He falls into bed beside me and chuckles. "You're killin' me, Bliss."

I push myself against his side, laying my head on his chest. I've grown accustomed to his accelerated heartbeat and used to the darkness of his eyes, because like his blues, his dilated blacks show me so much. He's in a good mood now, so the black is soft, maybe even happy. But when he gets upset, the black is devilish, too bottomless-gone and untouchable.

"You're not afraid of it anymore?" I ask softly, holding my hand over his heart, wishing I could slow it down myself.

Thomas takes a deep breath and sighs. He knows what I'm talking about: what no one else in this family is brave enough to bring up. "No."

My boy doesn't just smoke a little pot anymore. He's in deep.

"Will you stop when school starts again?" I ask. We're only six weeks into summer, but it feels like it's been months. These ups and downs are hard to keep up with. I can't imagine dealing with this between classes and homework.

"I can stop whenever I want." His smirk is delicious, and I want to smack it off his face. He must notice, because he smiles higher and slips his arm under me, holding my sides with both hands. In one swoop, I'm straddling his hips. "Come on, Bliss, it's my birthday weekend. You have to be nice."

I roll my eyes. "You don't think we've outgrown the rules yet?"

Recklessness slips his hands under my sleep shirt and circles his thumbs slowly on my stomach. "You're only fifteen. You haven't outgrown shit."

I playfully punch him in the chest once, twice, three times. He grabs my wrist and flips us over so he's on top, in between my thighs.

"Don't fuck with me," love whispers against my skin, softly kissing my neck. His throaty tone makes me wild, and the rumble in his chest makes my skin light up, sensitive and alive. His hands are on his mattress at the sides of my head, holding himself up, and it's killing me that he's not touching me somewhere … anywhere.

He's being too careful, too slow.

In my need for more, I pull my shirt over my head and toss it to the side. Dusty palms my breast and kisses my lips. He tastes like mint and smells soft and soapy clean.

I reach down between us and unbutton his shorts. Thomas rests his forehead on mine with pouty lips and slightly flushed cheeks. His black is so sweeping, all fucked-up and honest.

When I have him out, I wrap my hand around his base and move as slowly as he kissed me, making his eyes close and his lips lift at their corners.

"Too slow?" I whisper.

Crazy-love shakes his head, but covers my hand with his anyway. He strokes faster and harder, but his grip is gentle over my own.

I love the faces he makes.

I love making him feel good.

Love is slow-hard strokes and knitted eyebrows.

"You have to hurry," I say quietly, leaving heavy kisses at the side of his mouth, soaking in his sweet, warm breath.

Then I have an idea.

This time I'm flipping him, and he falls back on his elbows with wide, glossy eyes and the sweetest swollen lips. His hair is still damp and pushed up where my fingers were.

"What's wrong?" he asks, breathlessly.

I bite on my bottom lip and crawl between his knees. I have no idea what I'm doing, or how to do it, but Becka talks about it sometimes. She said it makes Smitty feel crazy good when her mouth is on him.

When I wrap my hand around his length and push my hair to one side of my shoulder, Thomas catches on.

"Wait … wait—Leigh, no." He tries to pull himself away, but I hold on, and now we're in this weird struggle over his penis, and it's so funny we start to laugh way too loudly.

Then there's a knock on the door and everything is real again. We're a secret, doing secret things, in his bedroom on secret stolen time.

"Dusty," Tommy says from the other side of the locked door, "get up."

"You're fucking nuts." My boy slips himself back into his shorts and buttons them before I get any more ideas. He gets out of bed. "You stay over there."

"You would have liked it," I say, staring because he's still showing through his shorts.

The boy who denies me simple pleasures lights up while I redress myself with a contagious smile. Fully clothed, I jump onto his computer desk and sit beside him while he smokes. We talk about normal things—school, friends, family—and it's good. So good, that when Becka and Petey knock on the door, Thomas lets them in and our conversation carries on for over an hour.

It's so okay, that I think, *maybe.*

Just because we're having a good time doesn't mean Tommy is. She's been trying to get her only son out of his room for a couple of hours and grows incredibly frustrated with her birthday brat.

"Dusty, get your ass down here before I beat you!" she yells from the bottom of the stairs.

Becka and Pete laugh, and in their distraction, I lean in and whisper, "Are you ready to party, party boy?"

"BIGGER, BLISS. Make it bigger!" Becka takes the teasing comb from me and dives into her huge pink hair. "My goal is Amy Winehouse, not J-Woww."

When it's as big as she wants it, I help pin it back, leaving her side bangs down and softly curling cotton-candy pink ends.

"Your turn." She laughs, coming at me with the tube of lipstick.

My long strawberry hair is board-straight and pulled back into a tight ponytail. My makeup is light and natural with the exception of my matches-my-best-girl's red lips. My parents are going to be here later, so while I want to be dressed up, I have to keep it toned down until they leave.

"Why'd you invite them?" Becka asks, slipping out of her gray cotton shorts and into her denim boyfriends.

I carefully pull my black tube top over my hair and down my chest, slipping on a cream-colored sheer tank top over that. "Your mom did."

The party's in celebration of Thomas turning eighteen, but it's also a pretty important event. Lucas invited co-workers and distinguished clients. Rebecka and Thomas have family coming in from all over the place, and it's all that anyone has been talking about for the last couple of weeks. My mom actually questioned me about the party before I even brought it up.

My parents have to be here, so I *have* to be on my best behavior. They have to see that I'm the same girl at the Castors' that I am at home. I follow rules. I'm innocent.

"Maybe they won't stay long," Becka says, slipping her feet into a pair of simple, black platform heels. After she has on a tube top that matches mine, she helps me squeeze into my black super-skinnies. "You need to lay off the fucking Twinkies, princess."

Downstairs, Tommy did a really good job about keeping the party outside. The kitchen crew is still completing the finishing touches on dinner, and the dessert guy is MIA, so I take the opportunity to snatch a few more cream puffs.

"I saw that," my teenage dream whispers to me from behind, caught for the second time today.

I turn around ... and melt.

He's beautiful.

Black slacks, black shirt, white skinny tie; my boy is to die for. He's even wearing dress shoes. Thomas's hair is gelled and brushed over, like Jack Dawson, only better. His eyes match his shirt, and he smells like mischief and bad intentions.

I bite into my puff when he smiles. It's all I can do to keep from jumping him in front of his family and the caterers.

"Are you sure you don't want to ditch this place?" he asks very quietly, reaching over my shoulder to steal a chocolate covered strawberry.

"Leigh, let's take a shot before your parents get here." Becka fist pumps from the other side of the kitchen island, showing up out of nowhere.

Ben and Petey follow in after her, looking like clean and proper versions of themselves. Lucas strolls quickly through as his daughter pours rum into glasses.

"Judge McCloy is going to be a guest," he reminds us before walking out the back door after his wife, who is stunning in a floor-length charcoal gown.

My cheeks burn. My dad ... *The fucking party wrecker.*

The guests, including my parents, arrive and the party starts, beginning with a sit-down dinner in the backyard. The table I share with my parents is right beside the Castors'. Rebecka and I make funny faces, and she shows me her chewed lasagna.

The backyard is crowded with people. The low beats of *"Let It Be"* swim in the warm summertime air. Forks and knives scrape across plates while laughter floats from different corners of the yard, and my boy sneaks a look that makes me blush.

Two tables over at my left, Oliver sits with Smitty and his family. He smiles, and it's enough to warm my cheeks and lift my lips.

"This is a nice party," Dad says. "Kind of a big deal for a teenager."

"He's eighteen, Dad." I take a drink of my water. Thomas' entire table erupts in laughter; I look over in envy.

"It must have cost a fortune," Mom adds.

I slide asparagus around my plate with my fork.

After the tables are cleared and the music plays a little louder, no one at the party is drunk enough, or brave enough, to dance yet. All of the suits are still suiting, and Thomas is smiling, playing the perfect son for his father's acquaintances. Mom has a drink at the bar with Tommy, and Dad gets with Smitty's father to talk about boring dad stuff, thankfully leaving me to do my own thing. I still can't drink, but Becka has a few.

"Dance with me," she begs, pulling me to the dance floor by my wrists.

From the bar, Tommy is all smiles, happy to see us happy, but Mom's eyes are looking a little harder. I don't know if she can tell if Rebecka has been drinking, or if she doesn't like the way my hips sway, but it's suffocating under her microscope.

And as I kind of, sort of look around, Teri and Tommy aren't the only ones staring. With sunglasses on his face and his hands shoved in the pockets of his slacks, trouble's attention is on me. So is Oliver's, from the table he hasn't moved from since he got here.

Their stares pull me in three different directions, and they all want something different: the uncorrupted daughter; a told secret; more than friends.

It's almost too much to handle, but I know freedom comes with nightfall.

AN HOUR later, my parents stand with me in front of the car.

They want me to leave.

"Leigh, I don't know those people. There's going to be drinking …" Mom trails off, waiting for Dad to finish.

"You can come back in a couple of days," he says dismissively.

I cross my arms over my chest and bite my tongue. "Mom, I've been looking forward—"

"I understand, Leighlee," Mom replies tightly. "But it's time to go."

Dropping my arms to my sides, my eyes water as I say, "I need to get my things."

"Everything okay?" Tommy asks, suddenly beside me. She's my saving grace.

"Leigh wants to stay, but I'm not comfortable with the drinking," Mom answers. She doesn't sound aggravated with Tommy for involving herself, which is a surprise.

Mrs. Castor puts her arms around me, hugging tightly. "Oh, let her stay, Teri. The party's almost over anyway."

Dad looks at me as if he's checking for a crack, an imperfection, a sign that I can't be trusted. It's his job to seek untruth in people, even in his own child.

I resent him for it.

I'm the liar, but I detest him for knowing what to look for—for making my life harder than I've already made it myself.

Tommy sweet talks and fake smiles well enough for my parents to let me stay. But I know she's drowning in wine. It's why she sneaks inside every fifteen minutes. In the house, up in her room, probably in her dresser, is her hidden bottle.

We're both good deceivers.

"Call me if anything happens," Mom says. She kisses my forehead and hugs me tight.

Tommy and I wave as my parents reverse out of the driveway. Mom flips down the visor, and the orange-yellow light from the mirror illuminates her as she wipes mascara out from under her bottom lashes. Dad doesn't take his eyes off of me until he puts the car in drive and slowly moves down the road.

A few other people make their way out as Tommy and I stroll back to the party. She stops to say goodbye, but I keep going. I walk until I'm at the back door, through the kitchen, and up the stairs. Once I'm back in Becka's room, the first things I change are my shoes. Brand new heels make me three inches taller and ten times more comfortable. I reapply red lipstick and tighten my ponytail. I smile and mean it.

Even though guilt decays my insides.

I push it away, deep down with regret.

Pink hair isn't easy to miss. The sun is completely down and the twinkling lights around the party set the mood. Thomas' slacks sag and his tie is undone. His hair isn't so perfect. The same goes for the few suits who stay with Lucas; they're not so pristine anymore, but laid back and carefree.

"Let's get drunk," I whisper into my best friend's ear.

Liquored up, we toast to birthday fun and sweet summertime nights.

I feel weightless after a few drinks. My lips are numb, my eyelids heavy. And I have to pee.

While my best girl gets down on the dance floor, I head toward the house, walking past Thomas' table and his glare. My heels tap on the wooden porch, and when I go to grab the handle to the back door, I miss it the first time.

My balance is shifty, so I decide not to climb the stairs to use the restroom and use the half bath next to the garage. But the door is locked.

"Hello!" I shout, knocking on the door. "Can you hurry up?"

It opens, and Valarie stands on the other side.

"Little sister," she says. "Why didn't you say it was you?"

She pulls me in.

The small bathroom is filled wall-to-wall with Sluts, giving me a space big enough to pull down my pants to pee. I sit on the toilet with my knees pressed together and my eyes wide. They act like I'm not here listening in on their conversation.

Valarie has her face right up to the mirror, rubbing lipstick out from under her lip.

"You can't keep it, obviously." She rolls her dilated eyes.

I pull toilet paper from the roll.

Val scoffs, "It's not like Casper would ever be around."

Mixie sniffs.

"He's a fucking lowlife," Kelly adds.

Katie, leaning against the wall across from Mixie, shakes her head. "You guys don't know that."

Kelly finally looks at me as I pull my pants back up. I'm quickly overlooked, and they continue their conversation.

"He didn't care when you told him," Valarie points out, turning away from the mirror only long enough to look at Mixie.

I kind of step between them to wash my hands, but I'm still invisible. That's until Val says, "Cute shoes, little sis."

I nod, pumping soap into my palm.

"I don't know." Mixie finally weighs in, sniffing. I turn on the water and lather my hands. "I don't know if I can do it."

"You don't want a kid with him, Mix." Valarie's tone softens, like she might actually care. "Trust me."

My hands stop moving. My heart doesn't beat. Air catches in my throat.

"Would you do it?" Mixie asks her, tears falling from her eyes. "If Thomas or some shit got you pregnant, would you do it?"

Without hesitation—without a second to think—Valarie hands me a towel to dry off my hands, not looking up as she says, "Yeah."

CHAPTER
thirty-six

I can't get out of the bathroom fast enough.

Only to run right into Thomas.

"What the fuck, Bliss?" he whispers harshly, puling me deeper into the hallway leading to the garage where the Sluts spoke so freely and easily about the most serious of issues.

Suddenly this boy's life is bigger than mine. More disgusting and real. It's a firsthand encounter with the results of his ugly ways. And it's more than superficial shit: jealousy, secrets, and habits. What's happening to Mixie is life altering.

And Thomas could be putting himself in the same situation.

"Did you know?" I ask, pulling my arm free from his grip. I do my best not to slur. I keep my footing still and ball my hand. I punch Thomas in the chest. "Did you fucking know about Mixie?"

"Know what?" he asks through his teeth, capturing my fist.

"That Mixie is pregnant. That she's getting an abortion." I pull my hand loose and walk away. He lets me. I move past the bathroom, and before I turn the corner into the kitchen, I say, "If you get Valarie pregnant, she'll do the same."

Love is revoltingly blind.

I DON'T know how much time has passed since my run-in with Thomas. I just spin, spin, spin my finger around my cup, wondering why I do this to myself. Wondering what Thomas hasn't told me. What he hides.

Because he does hide. I know he does.

Oliver's warm palm glides up my spine before settling on the back on my neck. I look over at him and smile. I blink for what feels like the first time in an hour. My eyes are dry. I close them and shake my head. I sit up and stretch my arms. I look around and notice that the party has thinned considerably. It must be late, because the air's crisp, almost cold. The music is still on, but not as loud.

"What time is it?" I ask anyone.

"Twelve-thirty," Oliver answers.

Valarie's obnoxious laughter grabs my attention. Mixie, who was not so long ago crying in the restroom, acts like nothing is wrong. Too many empty glasses to count, sitting in front of them.

The birthday boy sits at his table with Petey and Ben, quietly sipping from his drink. There's an energy around him that vibrates and sparks and burns, warning me not to fuck around, because he will not be fucked with.

I smirk.

Up from my seat, knowing his eyes are on me, I say, "What happened to getting stupid drunk?"

Becka's smudged red lips spread into the biggest smile.

A few shots later, Becka's in her bra and underwear, swinging her hips, standing on the edge of the Jacuzzi. With her arms extended and wide, like she wants to fly, she screams, "I fucking love you!"

I'm beside her, dying from laughter.

"Rebecka Castor!" Lucas shouts from the porch where he's sitting with his wife. Thankfully all of his co-workers and clients have left. The only people still hanging around are the boys, the Sluts, and Smitty and Oliver. "Put your clothes back on!"

She flips her dad off, drinks the rest of her drink, tosses the glass, and jumps in. Water splashes all over me, but I don't give a fuck.

This is how Thomas must feel all of the time, about everything.

I just don't give a single fuck.

I don't care that Oliver and Smitty are looking at us like we're two girls that they don't know at all, or that Lucas is running toward us, or that Thomas just pushed his chair back, watching me with the anger of the entire world in his stare.

"I don't fucking care!" I shout to the stars.

My voice echoes off the house and trees as my girl rises from the water. She reaches out and grabs me, stripping me from my top, leaving me in my black strapless bra. I step out of my shoes just as Becka pulls me into the warm water with my pants on.

When I come up, Luke's pissed and yelling, "Have some respect!"

We sink back under.

Only to be pulled out by her older brother and his friends.

I laugh as Thomas grabs me by my arms, pulling me over the edge of the gazebo. He shoves a towel into my chest and says, "You're a Slut now, or what?"

Overcome with anger, I throw my towel in his face. Then I pick up one of my heels and chuck it at Valarie. My aim's for her face, but it collides with her chest.

"Fucking leave!" I scream in her direction.

"You have got to be kidding me," Lucas mumbles. He starts to laugh, so he covers his face with his hands.

Father of the year.

Frustration I've kept hidden for years surfaces. Bathroom gossip and *"I told him I loved him, but I didn't mean it,"* send me into a rage not even Thomas can hold me back from. Liquor-brave and love-scorned, I run.

Just as Val starts to cower and the other girls move away, Thomas swoops in and wraps his arm around my torso, spinning me around. He carries me kicking and screaming toward the house.

"I hate you!" I shriek toward my worst enemy until my voice breaks, fighting to break free from love. Val stands straight, expressionless. "I hate you so much!"

Thomas drags me up the porch and opens the back door with one hand while holding me with the other. He pushes me inside and slams the door shut behind us. I don't try to shove past him. It would be a wasted effort.

Never taking his eyes from me, he unbuttons the rest of his dress shirt and tosses it in my direction. It falls to my bare, wet feet.

"Pick it up, Leigh," he says with a finality that leaves no room for argument.

I take my time buttoning each button with quivering hands and heavy deep breaths. My jaw aches and my eyes sting, begging to let go of this resentment in the form of tears.

Unstill, mischief moves his hand through his hair, pats his pockets for his cigarettes, and paces. Tension is thick between us, but as I button up love's shirt, the door opens, and Lucas walks in with Tommy and everyone else behind him. We do a good job at pretending like nothing is happening. Thomas opens the fridge and tosses me a bottle of water; I take it. I even say thank you.

"I didn't know you had it in you, Leigh," Lucas says with a sarcastic smirk.

My cheeks warm, and I somewhat smile as everyone laughs at my expense. Occupying bar stools and chairs at the table, the party goes on as if I didn't lose my mind.

"You don't leave until you get fucked, or what?" Becka asks the Sluts and pulls out a seat beside Kelly.

Disregarding the people who don't take me seriously, I go right to the boy who gave me his sweater when I was cold and let me borrow his bike because I can't skate.

"You okay?" Oliver asks quietly. He scoots over to give me room to lean beside him against the counter.

"Yeah." I nod and smile, taking a sip of the drink he's had all night.

"Are you going to apologize?"

My heavy eyes snap up at him. His soft expression and all-over goodness make me feel like I don't have a choice.

"My shoe wasn't supposed to hit your chest," I say. It's as close to an apology as Valarie's going to get from me.

Thomas scoffs, smiling into the neck of his beer. He takes a drink before setting green glass on the kitchen table. "Princess Bliss had too much to drink tonight," he says.

JUST LIKE that, the incident is forgotten, and Valarie forgives me.

"I know how it is." She turns her attention to Mixie, who is still drinking. "Remember that one time—"

And nothing I did matters, because I'm just the little fucking sister.

SOBERING UP and sleepy, I'm rocked away on the front porch swing with my head on Ben's lap and my feet on Thomas. The familiar sound of Petey and Becka's skateboards rolling up and down the driveway is a lullaby pulling me under.

The air is soothing cool, filled with sounds of crickets and breezes through the trees. The occasional car drives down the highway in the distance, and the swing has a tiny squeak that sings softly every time Thomas and Ben move us with their feet. My breathing slows and my eyelids grow heavy. I'm almost asleep with thoughts of skinny ties and monumental birth days.

Until perfection is interrupted by a crash and break.

Becka's board is on its deck, and its pink wheels spin. On her bottom, Becka holds her wrist, and Pete bends down in front of her.

"Let me see it," he asks softly.

"It hurts!" she cries, cradling her arm close to her chest. Tears roll down her rosy cheeks.

The front door bursts open, and her parents run out, sleepy faced and in pajamas. "What the hell is going on now?" Lucas asks, disoriented.

Pete explains that he and Rebecka were skating when she jumped on his back, and he lost his footing. They went down, and he fell on her. She tried to break the impact by putting her arm out, but they both landed on her wrist and heard a snap and ... and—

He's scared.

"She has to go to the ER, Lucas," Tommy says, taking a look at Rebecka's wrist, which swells fast.

He runs his hands through his hair like I've seen my boy do so many times before. "Let me get my shoes."

Becka cries soft little tears while I put her socks and shoes on for her. I think we all should go, but no one agrees. It's decided that Lucas, Tommy, and Petey will go to the emergency room.

"Stay here and get some sleep for the both of us," Tommy says, coming down the stairs in a hoodie and leggings.

"Your dad doesn't need to find out we had you at the ER at three in the morning, Bliss. Stay here with Ben and Thomas," Lucas says, grabbing his car keys.

"Are you sure?" I ask Rebecka, feeling terrible. I want to be with my friend.

She nods with a quivering chin. Thomas sits beside her, not saying a word. When Becka stands, he stands with her and walks his sister to the door. Everyone rushes out, but I stay on the couch and pull my knees up to my chest. Ben sighs, sitting up from the loveseat across the living room.

"I'm going to take off," he says with a yawn. "I'll see you, princess."

"Bye, Ben," I whisper.

Engines start and headlights illuminate the inside of the house through the windows. When the cars have pulled away, Dusty comes in and locks the door behind himself.

"Come on," he says.

I follow him upstairs, keeping my footsteps careful and noiseless. I'm not so brave anymore. I care now. And I don't want to fight.

His room is warm, like home, and I'm surrounded by the sweet smell of our secret and a darkness that keeps us hidden.

My boy steps out of his shoes with his back to me. He takes off his undershirt and unbuckles his belt, finally turning to give me his eyes.

Three steps is all it takes to reach me. Thomas wraps me in his arms and carefully lowers me to the bed, climbing between my legs.

He reaches under me, unhooking my bra. Sugar-sweet and feather-soft lips slowly move from my mouth to the side of my neck. I close my eyes and curve into him, begging with my body.

He doesn't leave marks. Or use his teeth. It's all mouth and tongue and whispers so low I can't make out his words.

Then he's up on his knees, slipping his fingers into my sweats, pulling them down my legs. I kick them off my feet and lean on my elbows. Thomas' eyes match the room: dark and full of feeling. His skin is warm, and when I reach for his wrist, wrapping my fingers around until I find his pulse, it races.

"Calm down," I whisper. "Calm."

His pulse is too quick, his breathing too demanding. I bite my lip, giving him what he needs—surrendering my body to his too tense touch.

"Thomas," I whisper, kissing the side of his face while he kisses the side of my neck. "Thomas."

Without words, the assault with his lips stops, and his uneven breath is right above my ear.

"Let me," I say, climbing onto his lap. Pushing him back, I place his arms on the mattress over his head. "Keep these here."

"Leigh," he pleads.

I kiss hot skin easily from the hollow point of his throat to his navel, dragging my nails down his sides. Love's chest rises and falls as I lower his zipper one notch at a time. When he doesn't stop me from going further, I pull his slacks to his knees and stand on the floor.

Pushing my underwear down to my feet, cool air touches where I'm warmest as I part my legs and straddle my boy again.

With his grip on my sides, I move up until his hard length isn't in me, but against me.

I gently circle my hips, as if I know what I'm doing.

Slow, slow, slow.

Steady, steady, steady.

Dusty shifts under me with hazy eyes and heavy breaths.

"Show me," I say lowly. "Show me how to do it."

He rolls me over, pushing my legs open with a hand on my knee. When I'm wide enough, lost and in love handles his cock, slowly guiding his tip to where I hurt for him so sweetly. And I want it. I want him there. Inside me.

I hold onto his biceps and arch and moan and spread wider.

"You'd let me?" he asks. His voice is rough, thick.

I don't answer. He pushes in more, giving just a little more than the tip, splitting me open.

"Why? Because you think this is how I want it?" he asks.

I open my eyes and try to find my boy in his face. It's hard, but he's there, behind Her. Thomas is in the freckles on his nose and the small ring of blue around black.

Thomas is in his unmoving hips, no longer pushing, because he knows.

He pulls himself out and pushes against me like I had him before he rolled me over: between and against. His thrusts are hard and strong, with his hands gripped into bed sheets beside my head, powerful with frustration and denied need.

"I don't want you partway, baby," he says. "I want all of you, Leigh."

Tears slide down from my eyes into my hair. "You have me."

I clutch onto his moving hips, falling into tingles and explosions and constricted muscles and stuck voices. I move with him, rocking while I come. My cries and heavy breaths fill his room, and he leans in, hovering his lips over my open, moaning mouth, taking my air as I exhale.

Just as I'm coming down, soaring, he whispers, "If that were true, you would have already said yes."

CHAPTER
thirty-seven

"Sweet, sweet Jesus ..." Becka's bottom jaw is slack. Her sunglasses are 1970s huge and the lenses are almost opaque dark brown, but I know she's staring.

It's taking effort on my part to not stare, too.

Lifting her candy necklace, she gets it halfway to her lips before she stops, staring so hard she actually forgot what she was doing.

"Seriously?" I ask. Sitting up a little straighter on the bottom back porch step we're sharing, I nudge my girl's shoulder. "Earth to all gawking Martians."

Becka catches her balance and leans back on her elbows, letting her pink cast-covered wrist rest between us.

"Go ahead," she dares, her smile taunting and totally disbelieving. "Act like you don't see it."

Smiling, I look down at my feet instead of what she's referring to.

My toenails are peaches and cream, and my feet are bare on Smitty's sidewalk. We're in the shade, but at the end of August, every day is the hottest day ever. Concrete is warm under my soles, and I can smell charcoal fires and just-cut grass in the breeze. Mariachi music carries from a few houses down, and while robins chirp to each other above us, panted-chuckling and shoe-shuffling echoes from the driveway.

"Liar," my best friend says. "Tell me this isn't the hottest thing you've ever seen."

Rolling my eyes, I rest my phone in my lap and unbind my hair from my ponytail so I can pull it higher off the back of my neck.

"They're just boys," I remind her.

"Lies," she declares.

I pop my toes.

"Oliver looks damn good today, and you know it."

Across from us, damn good looking jumps, blocking a lay-up and sending the basketball to Smitty. It bounces once before it's in hands that were made for talking, and then through the basket.

Trash-talk and easy laughs fly in front of Smitty's garage hoop. Stephen, his brother, is home from college, and other boys from around the neighborhood are here too. We've been watching them play for about an hour now, and Becka's right.

My shelter from the storm does look good.

Turning to watch his best friend's shot, the person I've only ever considered as a comparison has his back to me. His tee shirt isn't really tight, but his shoulder blades stand out underneath gray cotton, and I like it.

It couldn't have happened over night. Backs don't broaden and jaws don't square in the blink of an eye, but when Becka and I pulled up today, and I saw quietly reliable turning and reaching and playing in the sun, that's exactly what it was like.

Bam.

Oliver isn't just an alternative to my boy.

He *is* a boy.

"Have you finished your paper yet?" I ask, rerouting my train of thought.

"Of course," Becka answers. "Like, a month ago. The whole idea of summer homework is twisted, but you might as well get it done and out of the way."

The sound of high fives and Oliver's upbeat, deep laugh drift from the driveway. Glancing, I catch his grin and the line creases around the corners of lit-up dark eyes.

My brain says looking's okay.

My heart beats no way.

Pausing for a drink of water, Smitty holds the ball between the inside of his forearm and his hip while Oliver lifts the front of his tee to wipe sweat from his face. His stomach looks smooth and strong in the sunlight, and there are these two sort of dips, like muscle lines–

I brush my hands down the front of my little pink dress and look over at my friend. She's not even trying to hide her ogling at this point.

"What book did you read?" I ask, tugging her candy necklace for a bite.

"*1984.* Julia is a badass motherfucker."

In my lap, my phone vibrates with one new message from Dusty.

Ain't no sunshine when she's gone.

"What about you?" Becka asks without looking over.

Looking up from Bill Withers' lyrics, I shrug. "I don't know."

"You haven't started?" She studies me through oversized lenses. "There's like, three days of summer left. Have you even picked a book?"

My heart beats, but I shrug again.

"Slacker," she says, pulling baby-bright pink hair over her shoulder and looking back to the boys. "Just read *Catcher in the Rye*. It's an easy A. Oliver can help you."

Back in my lap, my phone vibrates again.

Are you coming to the game?

I glance from love's question to his sister, to sharp shoulders, and then back to my phone.

Let me talk to Becka about it.

Dusty's reply is immediate.

Come on your own.

A few minutes pass.

I can come get you.

Guilt and nervousness pinch my heart while longing-love pulls at it.

We'll be there, I tell him before returning my phone to my lap.

The boys have stopped playing and talk about heading in. Smitty's mom wants her sons to stay home for dinner, and I think Becka will want to stay if he does.

Tap-tip-tapping my feet on warm concrete, I choose my words carefully.

"Don't Dusty and Pete have a game tonight?"

"Yeah." She nods. "At eight."

Half playing my part, half deciding how to ask if she wants to go, I'm cut off when she stands up.

"Come on," she says. "Let's go home and change."

BACK AT her house, I trade my dress for a tee and short-shorts while my girl doesn't change a thing.

But she grabs her board.

I SPEND the next night in Toledo, dancing with my girl under the full-moon light.

Smitty, Stephen, and a few other boys pile driftwood together and set fire to it. Flames crackle and climb as Becka and I kind of sway, sort of stumble toward the bonfire, and when I hold my empty red Solo cup up to Oliver, he smiles.

Skater-strong and quietly-kind looks good in firelight.

"Wow, Bliss," he says, his subdued smile growing as he reaches out. "An empty cup. For me? That's so thoughtful."

I'm not too drunk to misunderstand his teasing, but the warm tips of his fingers brush the backs of mine as he takes my empty, and I giggle.

"Fill it up," I tell him.

Oliver's eyes glint. He takes a drink from his own red cup and next to him, Jackie passes a bag of marshmallows to Laura, who passes it to the boy in front of me.

"How about this instead?" he suggests, sitting down beside me with the bag. He gets two skewers ready, but on my other side, Becka's a step ahead.

"You have to get closer than that," she says, I think to Smitty, or everyone. Anyone who's listening. "Otherwise it won't melt all the way through."

Her first marshmallow falls off the skewer.

Her second catches fire and burns black before Smitty can blow it out.

Laughing, I keep my own mallow a cautious distance from the flames.

A few minutes pass.

A few more.

Oliver laughs.

"You're never going to get anywhere like this," he finally says, pulling his marshmallow away from the fire and offering me crisply toasted golden goodness.

Readying a fresh one while I savor summertime Heaven, he passes me the skewer and shows me where to hold it relative to burning warmth.

"You do have to get a little closer," he tells me, low and deep between flicker-pops from the fire and the echo of waves lapping against the beach.

With his help, I toast the perfect one.

And then two more.

"So," he says, sipping from a fresh cup. He offers me a drink, but I'm content with toasty vanilla sugar. "Becka said you read *Catcher in the Rye* for the banned books assignment?"

"Becka lies," I reply, kidding without thinking.

Oliver kind of smirks.

"I'm going to read it," I clarify. "I just haven't started yet."

"It's an easy read," he says, his smile effortless on his lips. "You could finish it in a day."

"That's good." I nod. "Considering there's only like, a day left."

"Well …" Oliver takes another drink. The fire in front of us crackles higher, and his tan skin glows, smooth and soft and inviting. It's hard to not want to touch him.

"I could help you if you want. I read it last summer. If you finish the book tomorrow, I could help you with the paper Sunday."

"Yeah?" I ask.

"Yeah. I mean, if your parents are okay with that?"

Looking down, I hide my sad laugh in the back of my hand.

"Yeah," I say again. "My parents will be fine."

"Do YOU guys want anything? I could order a pizza. Are you hungry?"

"We're okay, Mom."

"Are you sure? I just brought some zucchini and tomatoes in from the garden. I could whip something up–"

"Mom," I look up from where Oliver and I sit at the kitchen table and repeat myself clearly. "We're okay."

Nodding, she gives her biggest, warmest smile and finally leaves.

"Sorry," I offer, opening my laptop.

Oliver shakes his head like it's nothing. We work quietly and well together, and after a while, I hear Mom go outside.

While he reads over my final conclusion, I sit back in my chair.

My mother has no reason to be more wary of Thomas than Oliver, but I know she is. Both of my parents are, and it makes me sort of worry they notice more than I think. Not only was Mom fine with Oliver coming over, she's been practically floating since he got here, and now they're both outside leaving the two of us in privacy like some kind of sign that's supposed to show they trust me, but it's not about me at all.

They'd never leave Dusty and I alone together.

Like love just knows, my phone vibrates in my pocket.

Baby, baby, baby.

My heart flutters and pangs at the same time.

The most I've seen my boy was two days ago on the field. He didn't come home, and I know he's out with Her.

"Alright," Oliver says. "I think you've got it. This is good."

I smile tightly as he passes my laptop back.

"Thank you," I manage.

He glances at me with eyes that I can't deny are beautiful.

But have no effect on the precious pain in my chest.

"IT's HIS birthday, and his mom probably won't remember."

On the other end of the phone, Dusty sniffs, but the silence in the background matches the silence in my room, and all I can think is at least he's home.

"She asked Mixie for pot last week."

Poor Petey.

"Why would she ask Mixie?" I ask, curling up in my bed.

"I don't know. Can I pick you up tomorrow?"

"Thomas …"

I'm cut off by a knock on his door and I hear his mother's voice.

With no summer left, I'm up past one in the morning with spun-love, thankful we were interrupted so I don't have to tell him no again. We've been on the phone for a couple hours and he's with me, but he's all over the place. Tomorrow's the first day of school, and at this rate, neither of us is going to sleep tonight.

"Sorry," he says, sounding tired as he returns to the phone. "She keeps printing out all these admissions applications and bringing them to me. She leaves them on my desk when I'm not here."

Brushing the sleeve of his baseball hoodie across my lips, I stare up at my ceiling in the mostly dark.

"She just loves you," I tell him. "She wants what's best for you."

"You're what's best for me," Thomas replies.

Behind faded-soft navy cotton, I smile.

"So let's do it together," I say. "Where do you want to go?"

Trouble sniffs again and I hear him shifting, opening his window. I catch the spark of a lighter and his words come out with smoke.

"I don't know, Bliss. When can I see you?"

Under covers I wish were his arms, I sigh.

"We'll be at school tomorrow. We'll see each other–"

"No." Love stops me with strained desperation in his tone. "I need to really see you."

HALFWAY THROUGH the school day, my whole body starts to lag.

Running on almost no sleep, my limbs weigh like dead weight and my eyes sting under shimmery shadow. My patience dwindles while my mood unevenly swings, and my heart drags, sore for much needed closeness.

On my way to English, I square my shoulders and make my way through the hall crowded with commotion and full of every face except the one I want to see. As I turn the corner toward the stairs, I see Ben, but he's alone. We smile, but inside, all I want is love I can't help.

As I enter the classroom, I see Oliver turning his paper in.

"Hey," he says.

"Hey." I bring my binder closer to my chest.

Once the lecture's started, my tired mind wanders. It's almost lunch, and the possibility that Dusty maybe skipped altogether seems more likely with each slowly passing minute. I want to text him, but my seat isn't inconspicuous. The more I think about him ditching, the more frustrated I get.

Isn't seeing each other just a little bit better than nothing at all?

When the bell rings for lunch, I'm the first to stand up.

I walk with Oliver, but when I spot pastel-pink hair, I step ahead and reach for my girl.

Groaning dramatically, she leans her head on my shoulder. "Could this day drag on any longer?"

"Tell me about it," I say, curling my fingers between hers, resting my palm on her cast as we head to the cafeteria.

Conversation-busy and laughter-loud, it smells like baked hash browns and cinnamon rolls. I scan the long, table-lined room as we get in line, but still don't find tall, dirty-blond and delinquent.

While Becka grabs a chocolate milk, I take a white, and Daisy strides up with an orange. We walk to the stairwell that leads to the commons and sit on the bottom step, the skater-tomboy, then the girly-girl in the middle, and nerd-fabulous on my right. She tells us about her new boyfriend, and B shows off the purple T-Rex Oliver drew on her cast. Keeping my knees pressed together under my dress, I stretch my legs out and talk about perfectly toasted marshmallows when my best friend insists. Mostly though, I drink my milk and just listen. In between frustration and frayed-short nerves, I kind of relax into the moment, and I'm overcome inside with never wanting to forget this.

A cotton-candy knockout, a strawberry sundae sweetheart, and a vanilla soft-serve misfit, we're undeniably different, but we complement each other, and there's comfort in how we fit. We live in a world where innocence is stunted and short, but there's strength and acceptance here.

Cafeteria commotion grows louder, and I glance up from my open-toe heels. Students file down the stairs across from us, and just like that, my pulse recognizes love's proximity before he's anywhere in sight. Beats like butterflies rush against my ribcage, and in the same second, at the top of the steps, I see black on black Converse and bare ankles, then strong calves and knees under black cutoffs. Dusty's wearing Petey's Motion City Soundtrack tee, and as this boy comes into view, he flashes his most defiant smirk.

With the chaos of a hundred or so other kids between us, all my heart wants finds my eyes for a single, insubstantial second. His smirk curves into a smile, and my blood tingles through my veins.

Blinking, I look away and breathe secretly, deeply. Pushing impatient fingers through my curls, I slowly exhale.

This is a different kind of learning to breathe.

While all my exhaustion and missing and bitterness melt into pure want, I concentrate on not giving away this love that still feels so much like a crush.

There is nothing in me except how much I want Dusty's teeth and lips on my lips right now.

It's not even fair to want someone as heavily and wholly as I crave this person. I feel too small to contain it, and all he did was look at me.

Quick with my eyes, I take in the whole picture.

Strolling next to Pete, he stops at a table full of people. Valarie calls my soul's name, and my chest caves in when he looks at her. Low-fiving Tanner and pocketing his hands, Dusty's nothing but instigating grins and rebellious black, and I look back down at my pastel-painted toes. I focus on what Daisy's saying about some upcoming election, but I feel love's look all over me.

Glancing up again, I meet careless eyes for another fragment of a second.

I dare you, his look says. *Come on, girl.*

Helpless, my skin warms and my cheeks blush. I give my full attention to Daisy to distract myself, but my legs tremble to stand and run to the source of my longing.

Harsh and hated, the bell rings, and I despise having to leave with my friends. I shoot Thomas one last glance, but he's not looking anymore, and nothing about love is easy.

It's stubborn and unfair.

Love is forcing myself to not look over my shoulder as I walk forward. It's returning to the third floor empty handed, starving for skin on skin contact and deepest wholeness. It's taking my place next to altruistic dependability when all I want is a self-indulgent monster to kiss me until I can't breathe and bite until he breaks skin.

Carrying the burden of yearning in my already worn-out limbs, I fill my lungs with measured breaths and suffer through the rest of class. There's only one left, and I have to go home after this, but at least alone in my room I won't have to fight or hide.

Sociology is my last stop, and I slump down in a seat in the back.

Not staring at the minute hand on the clock takes conscious effort.

After about twenty minutes into reading requirements and extra credit possibilities, between soft tingles and instinctive warmth, my phone vibrates in my lap.

My pulse thunders under my skin.

Come out here, princess pie.

Exhaling a slow breath, I look around and think quickly about how to exit.

I know it's the first day of school, and I know the boy waiting for me is a bad influence to say the least, but knowing doesn't assuage my yearning or lessen the pull I feel toward the hall. Knowing doesn't stop me from closing my notebook or slowly raising my hand.

"Leighlee?" Miss Carson meets my most unimpeachable look.

"May I be excused?" I quietly ask.

When she nods, I stand. Leaving my notebook so it looks like I'm just going to the bathroom, I head toward the door and turn its heavy handle.

Frenzied and strung-out, the muscle that wants nothing more than what's meant to be floods me with beats as I enter the hallway. I glance left and right, and when I don't see Thomas, hesitation twists my stomach, tightening around my conscience until he steps around the corner.

Messy dark blond is summertime overgrown, curled a little at the edges and falling into eyes I can't find any blue in, but when love looks, I see him.

Seeing only me.

I all but sprint to him.

Dusty grins, taking confidently slow strides in tandem with my quick-clicking heel steps.

"Don't fall, baby."

Reeling, I reach for his hand the second we're close enough, and my rebellion interlocks our fingers, warm and tight and right, as he kisses the top of my head. I pick up my pace to keep up with his as we walk, and he leads us down a back set of stairs toward the school's basement.

Outward from where his hand holds mine like a magnet, eager anticipation flows through me. I don't know where we're going, but I'd follow this feeling anywhere.

Lit with old fluorescents that shine half-burned out, the hallway he guides us down grows darker as we go, and every step I take is somewhere I've never been before. I squeeze love's hand and pull myself closer. He glances down at me, and high eyes glint gritty light.

"You scared, Bliss?"

I smile. "No."

Within a few more steps, he opens a door leading us into a pitch-dark room that smells sort of like pot, but more like rust and machine heat and years of abandonment.

"Where …" I start to ask, but stop when Thomas flips a switch. Yellow-orange bulbs flicker over our heads, but their glow is minimal and dust-hindered, and they're so old I can hear them buzz as they strive to function. There's a furnace in the corner and boxes piled high against the wall to our left, but I don't notice much more before I hear the door close.

Turning to the boy whose hand is still wrapped around mine, I step closer so that we're face to face, save for the few inches of height he's always had on me.

"Hi, girl," he says, like I'm the only one in the world.

"Hi, boy," I whisper, lost in his.

Bringing my other hand to his side, I take another step closer, basking in his warmth in the mostly dark. Soaring on love and harder drugs, Dusty grins higher and brings his lips to mine.

He kisses me and my heart goes wild.

We bend and move together, burning up. We cause and affect, pulling strings and pushing buttons, kissing so deep I can't catch my breath even when my meaning lifts to let me.

Leaning into and depending solely on each other, we turn and turn. We stumble but don't fall, and I don't want to ever not be kissing him. His kiss is so full, so passionate, I feel it in my knees. I grab onto him for life and his hands grip and slide everywhere, up my sides, in my hair and down my back, picking me up and pressing me into a wall I didn't know we were near.

Breathless and dizzy, I'm unable to contain small sounds as love steals kisses down my neck. Pushing and pulling my dress and bra strap out of the way, he kisses my shoulder and chest and I lean back, up and into him. Reckless footing shifts, and I go totally soft when I feel how hard he is. I moan in the dim light and he pushes against me.

"Hold on," Thomas whispers, starting to move. "Hold onto me, Leigh."

I lift into him and cross my ankles around his back, tilting for more of his kiss as my dress rides up between us. Tinted with dank vanilla and Doublemint and heavy with consequences, solid strength and uncontrollable need surround me. Starting between my legs, desperation opens and aches and tingles deeper with Dusty's rhythm. Telltale sparks tighten and thrill, and delicate tension yearns for more pressure, more weight, more of him.

Smiling in my neck, love moves with intent.

My skin heats and my heart flies. My breaths sound like pleading around us, and he's low-toned and short of breath when he speaks.

"I've wanted you so long," he says, lips and teeth and breath under my ear, undoing me. "I think about you all the time. I can't stop thinking about you …"

Gripping the back of my thigh, Thomas raises me up, moving harder where I need him most.

"You're in my chest," he whispers, lost and on edge sounding. "You're here. You've always been here, Bliss. Always …"

All my muscles strain to hold on as Heaven lights up behind my eyes, and I clutch onto love so tightly it hurts. I come in waves, the force of life coursing through me so sweetly I moan out loud. He drags his teeth over my skin as we move together, and I know he wants to mark me. I want him to. I want this boy's mark all over me.

Leaning back, letting him hold me up, I reach between us for his buckle, but he catches my hand. My heart pounds as I fight back, frustration and deeper want flaring between my ribs as trouble I've always loved locks both of my hands under his. Old brick grazes my knuckles and he presses all the way into me.

The room spins, and I push and pull against his grip.

His laugh is so low I feel it in my bones and I tighten my hands into fists. The impulse to hit him only grows as I open my eyes. Messy and beautiful in dirty basement light, my bad decision smirks and coke-filled blacks taunt my codependent heart.

Dusty's worst habit is all over him, slick under his skin and fucking with his pulse, and I hate Her.

I fight harder, digging my knees into his sides, making him groan and curse under his breath. He pushes heavier against me; heart to mad-heart, we both slip.

Thomas is stronger than me, but no more in control than I am.

It's in the sounds he can't help and the way his uneven breathing shallows. It's the slide and press of his fingers between my legs, handling me when he can't steady himself.

That's the thing about this love.

It's a thousand times stronger than both of us, even together, and the deeper this boy pushes, the better falling feels.

Thomas turns me around, and my legs nearly give out as he presses both hands between them under my dress. His chest swells against my back as he slides lace aside, giving me his fingers, and I bite my lip to keep from screaming.

I love when he touches me this way.

"Stop pushing me," he says, his voice quietly pleading and rough without air as he curves his fingers, pressing and filling until I see stars.

My fight gives out and I melt for him. I shake through coming so hard I leave the basement and school and whole world behind for a moment. Love holds me up, covering me as I fall apart until I'm nothing but his.

Love's.

Loved.

Love.

My heart beats his name and there's no part of me that doesn't feel it.

I've just changed into sleep shorts and a tank and am looking in my dressing table mirror at my right arm. There are light red marks on my hands and elbows from fighting against a brick wall today. They might be bruises by morning.

"I won't be able to wear short sleeves for a week," I inform love, phone pressed between my ear and my shoulder while I rub lotion into my arms. "People are going to think I'm crazy if I wear cardigans in August."

"You are crazy," Thomas replies easily.

Putting lotion away, I glance at the clock.

It's almost one, and I said goodnight to my parents hours ago, but I can still hear the television going. They're rarely up this late, and they're making my boy wait.

"I'm sorry," I say into the phone. "I don't know why they're still up."

"It's okay," Dusty says. He sniffs, but his voice is brittle sounding and unrushed, and I know he hasn't used since I saw him last.

Sighing and impatient, I shake out my towel-dried hair and turn off my light before opening my door. I strain my ears as I peek into the hallway, and I can make out voices but not words.

"Let me go listen for a minute and I'll call you right back," I tell Thomas.

Leaving my phone on my desk, I slink down the hall to the top of our stairs. A commercial for the History Channel echoes up, but their conversation is hushed and still too hard to decipher. Creeping down a few steps, I sit three up from the bottom and crane my neck so I can see my lifegivers' profiles.

Dad was just getting home when I was saying goodnight, and he's still in his work suit, but his tie's loose. His collar's undone and his hair's upset-messed, like he spent his entire drive home with his hand in it. Mom's in her fluffy ivory-white robe, and she has her head sort of tilted, like she's worried.

She says something I miss, and I scoot down a step.

"It *was* just pot," I hear my dad say, "but it wasn't just a little bit."

"Okay," Mom replies.

It's one word, but in that one little word I hear real concern and new knowledge, the pitch of protection, dip of nervousness, and glimmer of hope. It's a reminder of what sets people like my mom apart from the rest of the world. It's the sound of wanting to believe there is good in *everyone*.

"But that doesn't necessarily mean Thomas was connected to it," she insists gently.

My heart beats in my throat.

Dad shakes his head.

"They all run around together," he says, rubbing his forehead. "I told you I saw him with the boys last week. Dusty was driving."

Mom tucks loose hair behind her ear. She leans her cheek against the couch so I can't see her face anymore, but my nerves are all firing.

I'm pretty sure they're talking about Casper because he's the only one that would be carrying more than just a little bit, and I swallow uneasily, measuring my breaths.

Mom sighs as Dad drops his head back onto the couch, staring up at the ceiling and then at her.

"I mean... what kind of people are we letting Bliss hang out with?"

CHAPTER
thirty-eight

"Let me come get you."

"What about Petey?"

"He can ride with Ben."

"Thomas—"

"Come on, Bliss. I'm straight."

"Dusty …"

Baby sighs my name with regret in her voice, and I know I've lost. Cocaine tickles under my palms and incites from within.

Come on, boy.

"It can just be us," I say to my girl, pressing my phone between my ear and shoulder as I tie my shoe. "I'll skip the game. We can sit on your mom's couch and drink fucking apple juice. I'll talk to your dad. I don't care."

Love is silent.

It's like this a lot lately.

Since Casper got popped a few weeks ago, Leighlee's parents have cut back on the time she's allowed to spend with her friends. They're more watchful when she's home, and it's made her extra cautious about keeping everything concealed. We steal looks in the halls, but we're a world apart. I'm not fifteen anymore and I'm tired of being a secret.

Keeping the phone that might as well be connected to dead air pressed to my ear, I tie my other shoe and grab my keys. Desperation crawls under my skin and I think about saying *please, I need to see you*, but love speaks up just to let me down more.

"It's a school night, Becka." Her tone is hollow and her unwillingness opens painful frustration between my lungs.

Lust slinks inside and spreads Herself out where it hurts most.

I head downstairs and outside into the Lincoln while craving strokes every heartbeat, tugging and tempting. Knowing how much better She could make it just makes everything worse.

"You're not even trying," I say into the phone. My voice sounds pitted and thin, and I hate how susceptible and dependent love makes me. I know our chances are slim and the odds are stacked, but I didn't ask for the stars.

Silence lingers.

Reaching into my pocket, I find bittersweet consolation and my pulse rushes just to touch Her. I empty my voice out like none of this matters to me either. Like I'm not falling apart. Like I'm not about to get chest-deep into my second choice.

"Forget it," I tell Leigh.

Hanging up, I toss my phone to the passenger seat and use both hands to get inside bliss that never tells me no.

"DON'T GO," Love pleads, burying her face in my chest.

She curves small fists tightly into my unzipped hoodie, hiding from crisp, early-autumn wind. Her tears soak through my shirt and every drop cuts through my skin like a new razor, marking me with her cries.

"YOU'RE FUCKIN' up," Valarie scoffs, shaking her head.

Tossing messy black hair over her shoulder, she creeps her touch along my hips with backroom-temperature intent. She brings her mouth to my neck, but not even her breath has heat. Nothing about the devil is warm.

LET'S GO, cocaine whispers.

Hot in my veins and compulsive in my marrow, She fills and flows and pulls at me.

They can't love you like I do.

CLENCHING MY eyes closed, I grip with everything I have. I clutch onto soft limbs so tightly my knuckles ache and my muscles scream. I cough, and inhaling sets my lungs on fire.

"I can't—"

My voice breaks apart in the dark and I struggle, straining every raw nerve to just hold on. There's a loud choke sound cut in half by a too-sharp breath, like a sob, strangled and drowning and lost, and my chest feels carved out.

"It's okay," Leigh assures quietly, soothing and cool along my forehead.

Gentle as Heaven, her fingers console me in the burning dark. She feels and finds everywhere I need her and she touches so easy. Pulling me up and out of the fire, love gathers me to herself while I'm still in flames.

"I'm right here," my soul whispers, brushing reassurance with her lips and solace with her fingertips, fastening us together with strong softness. She's calming and clean and home, and *I can't—*

"I'm with you, Thomas. Be here with me."

PUSHING MY hand through hair that needs cutting, I drop my hat backward onto my head and unclip my keys from my belt loop.

"Rebecka, come the fuck on," I call from the bottom of the stairs.

"Chill out," she snaps from her room. "Ribbons are important. Why are you in such a rush?"

It's baby's sixteenth birthday, and I haven't used in over a week.

Standing around, waiting, *chilling out* is easier said than done. I shake my keys against my hand and rub my eyes. I mess with my hair and turn my hat around while my pulse beats unsteadily. Becka finally comes around the corner.

"Grab Mom's presents," she says, carrying a box that used to hold banana popsicles, now tied in rainbow ribbons.

I step into the dining room and shake my head. Gifts are piled two on top of three and bags sit in front of them. Mine and my sister's birthdays have always been like this, and as far as my mother's concerned, Leigh's shouldn't be any different.

Grabbing the pink envelope and the box right behind it, I leave the rest for her to open this weekend and head outside. It's early evening, but the sun's already setting behind gray clouds, and late October wind blows through layers of clean cotton, slightly calming my nerves.

Rebecka plugs her phone into the Lincoln's stereo, searching for music while I drive with love in mind.

Leigh shined at school today. She was surrounded by my sister and their friends at every turn, but every time she chanced a look in my direction, unallowed devotion and eager longing lit up her eyes.

Maybe she doesn't say yes to me because she's scared.

Maybe that's smart.

Whatever the reasons, love still won't try for me, but she'll lie for us without missing a beat. She sneaks and distorts and covers unflinchingly, and it's flawless now. It's laughable how unaware everyone is at this point. It'd be funny if I wasn't the secret.

Need thumps behind my ribs, weak and sore for my girl, while my sister presses play on a song Pete's had on loop for days.

Tightening my right hand on the wheel, I roll my window down with my left and throw my hat into the backseat. Fresh air that smells like cold concrete and dying leaves blows in. Tinted with the scent of fires and damp decay, it gives the slightest kind of comfort and keeps me from telling my little sister to cut it the fuck out with my friend.

I take a deeper breath and try to make cold air enough.

I want a joint, or a cigarette, something to cut the edge, but I don't need the judge or his wife looking at me with any more questions or assumptions than they already do. I want to be walking instead of driving. I want to be with Bliss. I want to walk down the street with her, but we can't, and I wish she'd just leave with me already.

Breathing out, my stale lungs ache and my sinuses feel brittle-unwell. My skin crawls under my sleeves, and inside, my heart's anxious for a rush. I sniff without thinking and Becka snorts under her breath.

"Don't fuck around," pale pink, pissed off and protective says. She doesn't say anything else, but I hear her wordless warning: Don't destroy my best friendship by being a screwup in front of her parents.

Don't take her away from me.

I turn onto Leigh's street and shut the stereo off. Unplugging Rebecka's phone, I toss her shit to her lap and shake my head like I'm the only one in this car keeping some damaging secrets. But I don't say that.

I say, "Alright, kettle," because we're all a bunch of hypocrites.

I say, "Sure," with a smirk, because there's no arguing with a mind made up and dead set on defending someone it knows as family. As love. As all that's good in the entire world.

I don't argue with my sister, because I know.

I love the same blissful wonder she does, and neither one of us is doing it right.

Parked in front of the little white house love lives in, I sit back while Becka gets out without another word. I fix my hat-matted hair and gather myself together.

I want to use so badly I feel it in my teeth.

As I get out of the Lincoln, Teri McCloy opens the front door with a welcoming smile.

"Come in, come in," she says as Becka passes and I approach with a nod.

Inside, love's lifegiver pulls my sister into a hug, kissing her pink hair and then hugging me too. Simultaneously strange and needy, her sincerity is warm and unconditional, and the second I come into contact with it, I feel undeserving and starved.

"Bliss is on the phone with her aunt," Teri says, gesturing for us to follow her. "She'll be down in just a minute. Do you guys want something to drink?"

While my sister accepts and they small talk, I hang back, filling my chest with the smell of vanilla-cinnamon candles and baking carrot cake. Simon and Garfunkel float from the record player in the living room, and laughter scratched by decades of lives well-lived drifts from the kitchen. We're about to turn the corner into it when the prettiest voice stops me.

"Hey," Leighlee Bliss calls from the staircase, smiling birthday-bright as she takes the last few steps.

For a second, she's the only thing that registers.

My heart beats, and everything I wanted before this fades out.

"Hey, birthday baby!" Rebecka bounds straight past me to wrap her arms around L, greeting her like they haven't seen each other in years instead of hours. My girl smiles from ear to diamond-poked ear over her friend's shoulder, and love courses through me as I look. Soul-deeply rooted rights flow with my pulse, and I'm jealous of acceptable contact, but it doesn't diminish the truth behind my ribs.

From every distance, regardless of what's between us, this person is mine.

"Hi, Dusty," she says, glossed lips curved up. Wrapped in skin-tight denim and a powder-blue sweater so oversized it hangs off her shoulder, she radiates excitement and happiness so warm I feel it where I stand.

"You got me something?" beautiful in blue asks, holding her hand out for the box and envelope I forgot I was holding.

"Um, no." My sister laughs derisively before I can answer. She tugs my girl's hand. "Those are from my mom," she says, leading love away. "Wait until you see what I got you."

I follow with longing tucked deep in my heart.

In the quaintest kitchen ever, I shake hands with Leigh's father's father and bend my knees even more than I do with her to hug her grandmother. Judge McCloy nods as he comes in the side door and I return the salutation, leaning back against the counter while my sister takes the last seat at the table. Teri pulls cake from the oven and while it cools, I sip from the mug of coffee she hands me, watching in hidden adoration while her miracle opens birthday gifts.

Between presents, laughter, and sweet gratitude, Teri ices the cake while it's still in the pan. Thaddeus gathers silverware and dishes, while his wife gets sixteen candles into place and passes me a lit one.

"Help me out?" she asks with a generous smile.

Setting the last few little fires, I step back and flip out the light when the cake is ready, and when Teri places it in front of her daughter, love glows.

It's perfect for a second before Rebecka starts to sing.

Everyone joins her, and after baby blows out the candles, I turn the light back on and we eat homemade carrot cake while the judge's mom tells us about when Leigh was little. High spirits, the scent of candles just blown out, and the sound of everyone my girl loves laughing and carefree are easy to get caught up in. Everything about the house around me feels like a home, spiteless and worriless, cozy with prudence and cherished memories.

Then the birthday girl and my sister head upstairs to a room that as far as everybody knows I've never seen, let alone made Bliss come and sigh and cry in.

Without her, I feel less at home and intensely out of place.

Thaddeus McCloy glances at me as he sits at the table. His look is quick, but loaded with everything it carries. It's a glimpse of the same way my dad looks at Smitty, but this is far less lenient. There's judgment in the square of his shoulders and decision in the set of his jaw, and in the two seconds he looks at me, there's warning.

Rights and defenses stand up under my skin.

Love is mine, but nothing stops cumbersome discomfort from sinking in.

I pocket my suddenly restless hands.

I'm the cleanest I've been in a while, but I'm certain in this moment that everyone in the room can see Her all over me.

Turning around, I put my dishes in the sink. I pick up Leigh's and place them there too. I think about washing everyone's just to keep from having to be still, but hands that look older than my own mother's stop me as I reach for my sister's saucer.

"Don't worry about those," Teri says.

Guilt hooks me.

I want effort from Leighlee. I want her to try, but the weight and threat of my choices and fuckups are tremendous and loud inside me here. In this perfect little kitchen, with her wholesome family surrounding me, I feel my unworthiness. Every shred of how undeserving I am of love bears down on me.

"You can turn the television on if you want," Mrs. McCloy offers. "You know you can make yourself at home here."

"Thank you," I say.

The judge looks over as he takes a drink of coffee.

Excusing myself, I step out the front door. Cold nighttime air greets me, and I push the heels of my hands against my eyes. Sitting down on the top porch step, I try to abide not smoking, but give in after a few minutes. My hands stop shaking, but smoke and the bitter breeze are painful in my chest. Every breath feels like a sharper edge, and it's unbearable to the point that I want to hide.

Love's sheltered here, but she's my shelter, and knowing you'd die without someone isn't romantic.

But I would.

Hopeless and homeless and wasted.

I blow poison into the air and reach for another cigarette as I finish my first one.

Craving tortures me from inside while cocaine calls to me from my glove compartment. Knowing I could have Her and that everyone inside would just go on with the conclusions they already assume anyway kills me.

Exhaling through my nose, I rub my eyes again and take another hit of dead leaves and most-sacred-day-of-the-year air. I hold it until my lungs burn and hurt invigorates.

Just two more years.

Less than that if we leave right after she graduates.

We just have to ride it out a little longer and we'll be free.

Stretching my legs, I shift my feet down a step and scuff a chip in the old wood with the toe of my new shoe. The splinter splits deeper and leaves a scratch on the white bottom of my black-topped Circa and I lean down, trying to rub it off when the side door opens and closes.

Teri comes around the corner and the porch light reveals upturned and undoctored wrinkle lines in her face from years of joy and worry. She waves and I watch as she opens the garage. My grin takes over when I see the old Volkswagen Rabbit parked inside. Grass green and modest and unconventionally conservative, it's nothing fancy, but it's safe.

I stand on the top step, laughing through my smile as the front door opens behind me. Leigh beams through the glass as she watches her mom back the car out of hiding and into the driveway. Out-loud excited and truly grateful, she beelines straight for the car as Teri parks it.

Strawberry-blonde looks so pretty behind the wheel my sore heart skips.

I can't wait to kiss her right there.

MY HEARTBEAT pulls me from sleep.

Before I'm coherent, I'm hard. Sunrise burns around my curtains and waking hits me with a solid mass of resentment. The fact that I saw love last night doesn't matter. Every morning I'm still a secret starts this way.

My phone vibrates with my alarm and my eyes sting as they adjust to semi-light. Showering and dressing quickly keeps thinking too much and jonesing too hard at bay, but not completely quiet.

Knowing She's ready and waiting for me in the Lincoln gets me through.

Downstairs, my family's already left, and outside, the sky's cloud-covered. Everything's damp brown and frostbitten gray, but I put sunglasses on.

Pulling my hood up as I get in the car, I turn the key and check my phone while I let the engine warm up. It's almost eight o'clock. If I left right now, I'd make it to first period probably just as the bell rang.

I pop the glove box and tug pure romance out.

I take a hit from my pinkie like it's nothing, and when She hits me, I feel it all the way down.

My blood fucking sings.

Lining up on the back of a notebook I keep just for this, I take Her swiftly deeper.

Left.

Right.

My pulse throttles me and my lungs open wide.

There you go, this slut coaxes, taking me too.

Give me more.

Left again.

Right again.

Left.

My whole body heats and my heart makes haste. I feel my pupils stretch, and unequivocal potential soars through me while the best-worst taste tingles on the back of my tongue. Cocaine comes apart hard in me and I fucking want it. Gratification after too long without drops my lids and my eyes roll back. My head hits the seat as She rides through my veins, tethering Herself around my muscles, and my chest heaves breathless beats.

Just like that, Dusty.

Rapt and lit, I'm late for school, but I take the rush of being selfish at heart two more times in the parking lot.

Inside, the secretary leers at me as I stride into the office unburdened and dauntless. Carelessness and cold wind cling to me, but all I feel is my pulse as I sign my name on the same clipboard I have a hundred times, just like all tardy motherfuckers are supposed to. Looking up, I give her a respectless smile and drop the ballpoint making it roll off the edge of her desk and hang from the chain it's attached to.

I abide the urge to knock off the pencil holder and stack of papers in front and show her both my middle fingers.

As I swing the door and walk out of the office, the bell rings, ending first hour and dismissing students to fill the hall. Leaving my hood up, I take my sunglasses off and head toward the stairs. I don't expect to see the only reason I come here until lunch, but my body picks up on love's nearness right before she turns the corner.

Binder held loosely to her chest, walking next to Oliver, L has a tight white sweater on and skinny jeans she looks poured into. Her smile doesn't slip when she sees me, but blue-greens flicker defensive bitterness as she takes in my black.

My blood beats a stolen split second faster, but my attention's pulled behind my back.

"Thomas!"

The instinct to haul off on baby's little skater bitch boyfriend seethes through me, but Kelly tugs my book bag. I turn, and her pupils are dope-wide.

"Have you seen Val?" she asks.

Reality checks me and I reroute my shit from impulsive love and violence to the question at hand.

"She won't call or text me back, and I haven't seen her since Sunday," she continues.

Leigh walks by without the slightest falter, and Kelly loops her arm through mine like I'm some kind of gentleman.

"I'm just worried," she says, walking and making me walk. "She's never disappeared for this long."

Between wishing she'd let go, pulling toward love, and flying high, I remember Valarie texting me Monday night, asking me to come out.

I never replied.

"Have you tried Cas?" My voice sounds ragged and I realize those are the first words I've spoken all morning.

Blond curls and cheerleading ribbons sway as Kelly shakes her head.

"I don't have his number. Petey—"

I know what she's going to say. I don't want my girl talking to him either.

But that's the thing.

Valarie isn't anybody's.

She can't be loved because she doesn't let anyone near her, and really, who cares about the devil?

Sometimes you just go nowhere.

"Don't worry about it," I say to Kelly, loosening my arm. "Val's where she wants to be."

Walking ahead, I type out two messages. One to Queen Slut:

Call your friend.

And one to Bliss:

Talk to me.

Ninety two minutes into chemistry, my phone vibrates with a message from the wrong person.

I'm fine. Come over.

I tap my pen against a blank page while another five minutes ticks by.

Ten.

Fifteen.

Sixteen.

My phone finally vibrates.

Don't be mad, baby says.

Looking up from the last seat in the back row, I sniff and think about walking out while cocaine tingles, indulgent for more under my skin.

Why? I text back.

A few seconds.

A minute.

Two.

It's just a show. It's nothing.

The bell rings, and I go straight to where I know she is.

Strawberry-blonde's easy to spot as she walks away from the French classroom. My steps remain even but my pulse doubles up, and I know love feels me. She looks up before I'm beside her.

I keep my eyes straight, walking with her until we're close enough to the library that I can reach in front of Leigh and push her inside.

I'm uneasy, but I don't give a fuck who sees.

Stuffy silent compared to the hustle in the hallway, the library's mostly empty. The girl who won't say yes to me doesn't push my hand away from her back as I continue pulling her left, then right, until we're out of sight.

"It's my birthday," she whispers spitefully over her shoulder. "We don't fight on birthdays, remember?"

Pulling her elbow down some forsaken back aisle, surrounding us with dust and dead poets nobody cares about, I stop.

"Your birthday was yesterday," I tell her. "What are you talking about?"

Princess-kid yanks her arm away and opens her binder to hand me two tickets to a show in Portland tomorrow night.

"I thought you heard," she says flatly, fixing her sweater sleeve. "Oliver was talking about—"

"Don't say his fucking name to me."

Taking a deep breath, my traitor starts over.

"It's just a birthday gift. You can't—"

"You're not going," I cut her off again, keeping my voice low.

"Yeah?" Love that's learned by example snatches the tickets. "Who's going to stop me? You?"

"You're not going with him, Leighlee."

"You knew I wanted to go to this show. I've been talking about it for weeks."

I laugh. Out loud. I can't help it.

"Please," I say, extending my empty hands in invitation. "Explain to me how that matters?"

When she can't, when all she can do is stand tall in her indignation, I place my hands on the bookshelf behind her, on either side of her face and lean in. It's softly raw, but her nerve is stunning as she tilts her neck, refusing to back down.

Brash, unhidden, and provocative, love goes an eye for an eye with me, measure for measure.

Love is the tables turned.

"Why don't you just say it?" I ask, dropping my stare from hers to the corrupted space between us. "You don't want this. Just say it."

She swallows hard. I see her throat work. I watch her fingers clench, unclench, and curl into fists at her sides. Between her teeth, Bliss grinds her whisper out.

"I'm dying for this."

I lift from her.

"Have fun with your boyfriend," I spit, turning and walking away because it's not the same.

Dying for this love isn't the same as wanting it.

THERE'S NO sun to find or follow as I drive north on I-5. I don't know where I'm going, but a glance at my tank assures me I'll get there.

Cracking my window, I light a cigarette. Tar coats my lungs with menthol and carcinogens while my head spins, but I can't think.

I can't do anything but feel love not want me.

Gripping the wheel, I sniff hard and press harder on the gas while my stomach knots and twists.

Time drifts, and when I still can't focus but need to fill up, I take the first exit I see. It's toward Tenino. I drive until I see signs for gas stations and when I'm finally off the freeway, I'm in fucking Aberdeen.

Pulling into the first run-down station there is, I park and head inside to the bathroom with my slut in my pocket. The door's barely closed behind me before I puke bitterness into a dirty toilet.

Clearer, I wash my face with cold water that smells like metal and lock the door. Fluorescent lights buzz above me, tinting the dingy all-white bathroom sickly green and making my hands unrecognizably pale as I open coke on the edge of the sink. Eager and greedy, She moans between impatient heartbeats.

Spreading Her shamelessly wide, I lower myself and take from this cunt until I feel nothing but numb.

The rush swallows me whole, and when I lift myself, She breaks my ribs open and sets my mad-beating heart free.

Hurt is a memory.

Futility and insignificance are rumors I've never heard.

Abandon fucking rings in me, and I swing the door open without a single care.

Back outside, winter-tinted wind blows against me, cutting through my clothes, but I don't feel cold.

I leave my car parked in front of the pump without half a thought and pull my hood up. Sliding my hands into pockets that carry all I need, I step onto the sidewalk and head toward what looks like a main street.

Passing failing mom-and-pop shops, ten-story banks, and private practices, I fall into stride beside the consumption-driven and the unsheltered hopeless. I step on trash, through traffic and across neatly kept lawns with struggling-against-the-frost flowers.

Starving stems don't bend.

They break under my steps.

Everything I set my eyes on gleams perfectly clear for seconds at a time and then blurs away. Nothing is actual in this town. Every face is forgettable. All the trees are dead or dying, and I have to keep turning because every street leads nowhere.

Just like Heaven, She whispers, pleased and pulsing around my heart.

As gray daylight starts to fade, I head west. My phone vibrates in my back pocket for the first time since I left and it pulls me back to myself.

But who I am is worthless.

I keep walking, and what's left of late afternoon fades into nighttime. Eventually, I'm back at the gas station where my car's parked, but I still don't know what I'm doing.

Heading inside the broken-down excuse for a building, I'm bombarded by the jingle of bells against the door and the stink of incense, beer, and bleach. The gritty light's too bright, and my stomach twist-turns. I want to spit, but my mouth is dry.

"Hey!" the attendant yells from behind cigarette-sticker covered glass. "Take off your hood. You can't wear that in here."

I push my hands into my sweater pockets, causing the hood to tighten over my head and cover more of my face because fuck him.

Fuck everything.

Filling half a Styrofoam cup with white cherry slush, I walk to the counter and pull out my wallet. The man behind bulletproof glass punches numbers into the register and I glance through the windows at the Lincoln.

"Is that your car?" he asks.

Grabbing the cup, I pull frozen sugar through a purple straw. Ice-cold sweetness cuts the chemical taste dripping from my sinuses and stings my chest.

"You can't leave your car here," he says, picking up a cordless phone. "We're having it towed."

I leave a twenty on the counter and walk out.

I STOP and fill up at the next station.

I had to carry a key attached to an old hubcap to get into the bathroom, even though it's smaller and dirtier than the last one, but it doesn't matter.

This gutter doesn't mind.

My easy fuck is unconditional.

She loves it.

The wider I spread Her, the deeper I go and harder I take, the sweeter She sings.

Somewhere between lines, I hear the the sound of the door chime. A group of girls enters the station and muffled giggles float through thin plaster walls.

Baby's laugh swims through my lake of fire and for a second, I wonder what time it is. If she's at home or if she's with him. How her heart is beating while mine's here pounding.

Don't stop, cocaine pleads, wet and wanton inside me. *Don't stop now.*

I take two rails back to back without a breath, and I hope wherever Bliss is, her chest lights up.

SUNRISE COMING in through my lids burns.

Pressing my hands over my eyes, I curve onto my side and bend my knees up to my stomach. I fight waking, but reality setting in is brutally relentless.

I don't know where I am.

Memories open up like clouds and blur together into one long, convoluted nightmare. I remember dirty bathrooms and frozen sugar, everything looking the same, and driving and walking.

And walking.

I remember the shitty broken-brick hole in the wall club that smelled like cheap bourbon and sweat, a sea of unforgettable faces and how easy the Xs on my hands were to scrub off. I remember the filthy but private little bathroom stall, and finishing Her straight from the bag, rubbing what was left into my gums.

My stomach twists around barbed wire, and my eyelids pang with my pulse. My whole body tightens with hurt while my head throbs with retrospect I do not want.

The giggle that stood out in the crowd and drew me near last night echoes in my sore eardrums. It fades from me, but leaves a pink dress, soft but wrong-colored curls, and small curves in its wake.

"You think you're a princess?" I asked this stranger that reminded me too much of love.

"Don't lie." I dug at her in front of her friends before I lowered my lips to her ear.

"Your dress covers up some ugly truths doesn't it, liar?"

I curl tighter in on myself, into my hoodie and an unfamiliar couch. My mouth tastes like dirty iron and misplaced hate, and when I swallow, the left side of my jaw is sore because it worked. The slut-wannabee-princess found some douche-fuck to come to her rescue, and that was what I wanted.

Pressure from leftover violence weighs heavy on both of my temples and my hands ache. My knuckles might be broken, but I remember it not being enough.

I remember standing over her knight and walking away, and then it comes back to me.

I'm on a different girl's couch. She wanted sex and when I didn't, I laid here for hours, stuck on what it all comes down to.

The tuth is excruciating.

Because I'm fucked.

I'm so goddamn fucked.

"Hey."

Breathing in stings as I open my eyes to purple terry-cloth and all wrong knees.

"You have to get out of here. I have class."

Blinking, I bring damp blond hair into focus as she walks away and closes her door.

Sitting up, I rub groggy and wayward coke-sleep from my eyes while my entire diaphragm pulses, bruised inside and all throughout. Early morning shines in through translucent curtains, stinging my still-dilated pupils and illuminating a living room I don't recognize for shit. Magazines, keys, an agenda for Grays Harbor College, and a pair of heart-shaped sunglasses lay scattered across a coffee table, and I grab the white plastic sunnies, leaving before the girl who let me stay comes back out.

Even with my hood up and stolen shade hiding my eyes, morning glows too bright and too cold, unmerciful and disorienting. Nothing about the street I'm on is familiar, and craving makes everything worse, but as I start to walk, my body recalls steps my brain cannot. My feet know where to find my car.

Alone in the front seat, I kick on the heat and drop my hood. My head swims as I push my hands through my hair, trying to fully wake up. I reach for my phone.

Friday, October 25th, 7:49 a.m.
Fourteen missed calls.
Eleven voicemails.
Twenty-nine new text messages.
Nothing from Bliss.
Closing my eyes, I clench screaming fists until raw pain is all there is.
Opening my eyes, I glance at the gas tank.
If I left now, I could make it to school in time for the second half of the day, in time to see all I want lit up like a candle for the first boy who ever gave her his sweater. I could walk by and make like she's not killing me, or I could walk right up to her in front of everyone.
I could call her right now.
But love takes two.
Tapping out a message to someone I'd rather chew glass than let Leighlee talk to, I drive south, but not toward school.
When's our girl coming by?
Casper calls instead of texting back.
"She's on her way."
Music thumps and sluts giggle in the background.
"We're at this chick's house," he says, giving me the address. "Come on over."

A few miles outside of Newport, I'm in a cramped house that stinks like sex, flat beer, trees, and drywall. Unconcerned with bass beats and blaring pandemonium, a spider crawls in the corner of the smoke-stained ceiling, and Pete passes me a bottle.

I drink without knowing or caring what's in it or which way is up from down.

I've done nothing but line after line since I arrived.

I see laughs. I hear smiles. Everyone around me is high-lidded and forgiveness-forbidden. We're all lost, and I fit right in.

After another drink, I pass the bottle to Ben and he hands me a blunt. I pull smoke while Valarie looks at me with eyes I refuse to meet, and there's no shortage of girls slinking in and out of the semicircle I'm standing in with my boys.

Fuck 'em.

Fuck all of 'em.

I'm six feet deep in fuck-Bliss mode, which translates unmistakably into fuck life and every meaningless aspect of it.

Taking another hit, I glance down as a blonde I don't recognize slides up next to me.

"Can I hit that?" she asks like we're some kind of friends.

I blow smoke in her face while I pretend to think about it, and then laugh as I pass the blunt around her to Katie.

Someone ups the volume on down-tempo rhythms that sound spun under water, and across from me some brunette blows a raspberry on Ben's cheek. Pete passes the bottle back to me, and he's laughing.

Everyone is.

The young and doomed don't have a care in the world.

Turning, I head into the heart of the party and everything deepens. A hundred hard-beating, out of sync pulses surround me, and when I close my eyes, I can't tell my own from anyone else's.

Rubbing my eyes, I find myself in a girl's room. Mixie's next to me and we're both face down in Her.

I smoke a cigarette on the front porch.

I knock a family portrait off the wall.

I climb the staircase, and fingers slip pills over parted lips in plain sight. Hands grip and hips grind. Red-shot eyes look to empty eyes for guidance and assurance and for clean towels for bleeding noses. We pound on death's door, but find only each other.

Breaking into a master bedroom, I lock the half-bathroom door so I don't have to share Her with anyone.

The bedroom's full when I open the door, and my phone vibrates in my pocket, but it's the wrong girl again. It's two in the morning, and there's still nothing from Leigh.

My chest caves in around unstoppable beats as I move through the crowd.

I try to remember where I am and sort through where I've been, but all that comes through is not knowing where love is, where she's been. Dope-tilted and fearful, my mind tortures me. The only thoughts that ring clear feel like heart attacks back to back.

His arm around her birthday-happy, high-shrugged shoulders.

His hand in hers, wrong fingers and wrong palms pressed to skin I'm addicted to.

The pride in his eyes the night she gave him her kiss.

Coughing to clear my sinuses, I open and close my lids against tears so hot they're sharp. I push my fallow, good for nothing, constantly and inconsequentially breaking heart back down my throat and make my way downstairs, searching for a place She can spin me numb again.

"COME SMOKE this," someone says.

My eyes don't want to focus. I don't try to make them.

Sinking down, I lean back into the worn-out love seat by myself. The music's still going, but not as loud now. Or maybe I'm used to it.

My foot taps and I pat my knee, my whole body coursing energy even as I smoke. I feel the devil's eyes on me but I don't give her mine. I hit the joint and hold it in my chest, seeking disconnection.

Across from me on the couch, Pete's phone goes off. Twice. I force my vision to focus long enough to see lines crease his forehead. He rubs his chin and I look away because Kelly's here. Somewhere. And I know who the fuck he's talking to.

I stare at the cobweb in the corner of the ceiling while my gut kicks with want for free rein. Val's eyes burn holes in my skin, and Petey's phone goes off with another message from my sister.

Who may or may not be with my girl.

Who doesn't really want to be my girl.

Synth beats blend with melodramatic minor chords, and I stand up. Making my way from the living room to the kitchen, I head out the back door.

Save for the faintest hint of slivered silver moonlight, it's practically pitch-black outside. Freezing sleet rains down on all sides of the rickety awning above me, and when I stop to let my eyes adjust, I notice her.

The stranger to my right is a burning cherry and rising smoke, but I know she is a she without seeing any more of her. She's nothing but silent, spindling toxins, and I want that.

I want to be that.

The weight of how much absolutely nothing matters makes me forget what I was doing, and I step toward the girl I can't make out.

"Can I have one of those?" I ask.

Abstracted and almost invisible, perched on the corner of the porch railing, she blows smoke up. Between darkness and my own haze, I scarcely bring a pale neck and pink glossed, poison breathing lips into focus.

"Sure," faceless says, pulling a pack from somewhere. She passes me a stick and sparks her flame, and the curve of her cupid's bow stands out in the glow.

As I lean in, I catch her scent in the cold, wet air. She smells like the drywall inside the house and like cough syrup, like rust and spoiled apples and nothing good.

Giving my lungs cool smoke, I step away not to be further, but in effort to better see her.

I can't, though.

All I see is her mouth, full of smoke.

It's so easy, I laugh as I turn.

I step to the edge of the porch, not to get away, but to ignore her, because it's the last thing a girl wants. Her silence says she doesn't care, but as wind blows between us and right through me, I hear her shifting. Illusory like a shadow, the sound of bare legs uncrossing and crossing again fills my ears.

With all thoughts of leaving this place long forgotten and the cigarette almost gone, everything in me scrapes and claws and demands something stronger.

But this moment is all there is.

And I want to be buried in it.

Flicking the dead stick, I blow smoke into the night. Behind me, mostly invisible exhales and sends her own little ember flying into the darkness too. More shadow-shifting sounds fill the silence, and they're less elusive this time. Less a sound, more the feel of simple instinct, the whisper of bare legs uncrossing and remaining uncrossed calls to me before she does.

"Come here."

Her voice scratches the moment, but I step toward where she is. Bare feet and ankles sway slowly as I approach, and when I breathe her in again, she smells sterile and filthy at the same time, like rubbing alcohol and squalid regret. This girl smells like the ebbing of life and makes me want to know what the valley of the shadow tastes like.

"Give me another cigarette," I tell her.

Sliding the sole of her foot against my leg as light as dust and ashes, she takes her pack back out. As she reaches to hand me one, I stand still, just feeling blind fingers brush my stomach and side through my clothes as she searches for my hand.

When her creeping fingertips touch my thumb, I take the stick from her and light it.

Standing still between bare knees, I exhale smoke through my nose. And when I inhale again, her scent hits like megadeath in my chest, and I feel her pulse, working without wanting to. Every beat reverberates in the air like an atrocity, and I take a step closer to the heart mimicking my own.

Naked knees press and brush against my hips as unfit for goodness shifts. Pink lips open and I purse my own over them, breathing formaldehyde-filled breath across her mouth as I lean down.

This kiss is an open grave, worm-eaten and welcoming, and I tilt her head back because I want nothing more than to tuck myself into it.

I want to drown, and this girl is all-encompassing.

My cigarette is gone and we're moving, stumbling, and falling. Her clammy hands go from my neck to the door behind me, but I press her against it and myself against her, and snow-bitten fingers return to me. They slide under my hood and push it off while her legs wrap around, and the heart of darkness burns me, but I can't lift from her mouth. It's bottomless and dangerous feeling, but when she bends to kneel, I welcome her descent.

Throbbing to the agonizing beat of a purely self-seeking heart, her pulse covers my own as her mouth covers me, and I drown in every slide and swallow. I want to disappear, and she's oblivion, opening.

The breath I take when she lets me up tastes frost-burnt and dirty.

No longer cold hands move all over me as she stands, dragging greedy teeth and a sticky tongue along my neck. We fall together onto a couch, and the scent of mildew and wet ashtrays rises as we sink. Shadow weight rolls fire into me with her hips, but I want more. I want inside, and I know she'll have me, because suicide is like this.

Salacious.

Profane.

But we all die.

Sitting up, I push her down my thighs and reach for my wallet. My trespass doesn't make a sound as she takes the condom from my hands and puts it on me with her mouth.

Fever-hot and hemming me in tight circles, she moves with me inside, and I ride enfolding wrongdoing just as hard as she rides me.

Every time she lifts, I breathe pitch-black. Every time she comes down, my stomach coils like wires, and my connection to everything not slick and sinful falters. Every push twists and thrills, filling me with miserable, insatiable lust, and I cut myself adrift inside the girl with pale ankles and a mouthful of smoke.

She moans as she takes me deeper, and her voice is the only part of her that's not welcoming. It feels like fiberglass in my ears, clearing my clouds, and I hear my own moaning too. She slides, God-awful and slow, and when I turn her, she moves compliantly.

Pushing her into the couch, I rise behind her, and when I slide inside, my name pours obscenely from her.

"Dusty ..."

My knotted-tight stomach turns.

Pressing a face I've never seen into dirty cushions, I clench my eyes and fuck just to come. I move with desperate intent to forget, to disappear, but she moans and shakes and pleads for more.

She comes.

And I hate it.

But I move deeper, harder. I press down on her skinny spine, right between glinting shoulder blades and grip her bony hips so tightly my busted knuckles burn fresh. I fuck with all of my muscles, but anger rises in my throat, overriding everything because I need this, and I can't—

Hatefulness consumes me and I push nameless and faceless away, cursing and stumbling as I pull myself back, kicking everything nearby off the porch and into the night.

I follow it all.

"Do Mom and Dad know you're here?"

Pink from the cold, Rebecka's face gives away everything I knew I'd come home to: sick and tired unease, resentment, and disgust.

They enter the kitchen together, but I don't look at the girl standing next to my sister. The one making my worn-out pulse race and ache. The one who can come to me every bit as easily as she thinks I can go to her. The one who kept me in the dark for days.

"What do you think?" I answer, filling a cup with crushed ice. Tipping it back, I crunch pieces between my back teeth and walk past them.

Not acknowledging love is easy.

It's not kicking the island over, grabbing her by the arms, and jerking an honest explanation out of her that's difficult.

What keeps me in check is knowing.

My pulse isn't the only one affected. Just like every time we see each other in the halls, just like when I pulled her out of her princess-bubble and into the street light, just like when I brought that stupid lizard to her and Becka at the picnic table when we were kids—

Bliss and I have never not been heart and soul attached.

I realized it first, but I knew she felt it too, even then, because the same cadence flows through us. We're cleaved at the heart, bound by rib-caged, fist-shaped muscles that beat out blood to the same tempo.

Love will come to me.

In secret, because that's what she wants.

And when she does, she can work for her shakes.

She can earn every ounce of forgiveness, just like she makes me.

PUSHING A hand through my second-shower damp hair, I cut Her into two skinny lines on my bathroom sink. Lust that's never enough hums through me as I sniff, and as I stand straight, I hear my bedroom door open and close.

Laced with dirt, my codependent pulse pulls toward love.

Rubbing what's left of Her along my gums and the tip of my tongue, I wash my hands and glance at my born-in-black eyes before opening the door to my ends and means.

Leighlee's back is to me while she looks through a mess of unfilled-out applications on my desk. Red-blond pulled messy-high, she has on a sleep tank with tiny flowers all over it and the top of her gray sweats are rolled down, showing skin she knows I crave. For a second, all I want is to wrap around her.

For just a single second, I just want to be held in love.

But then I remember, *"It's a school night, Becka."*

And *"I don't want to be with you anymore."*

And *"I deserve more than you are to me."*

And his name on her lips and every *"no"* she's fed me, and I'm right back to fuck this.

She doesn't move as I step behind her, but as I stand there, I can see her chest moving with deeper, quicker breaths. My fingers close at my sides, containing the urge to reach and hold while my arms sting, sore to encircle and fold closer, and my stupid, stupid heart...

It hasn't learned or doesn't care that baby's a liar and a fake.

My hopeless, defiant heart flutters just to be near her.

Turning slowly, Leigh looks up at me. She stares right into me, because chemically numbed as I am, I'm still ripped wide open.

But love's defenses are cruelly high. She's miles from backing down, and I break our three-day silence with a snort.

"This is fucking stupid," I say, walking around her and sitting down because she didn't come here to say she was sorry, or that she wants this. I pick up the first book my hand finds and she just stands there, and I feel how stupid we're being this time. I feel how stubborn and wasteful we are, but I don't look up.

And Leigh leaves without a word.

Sleeping with Her is fickle.

It's impossible to know how long I've been in or out of consciousness, because it always feels like just a few seconds. I have no idea how long I've been drifting when I hear my door finally open.

Just like I knew she would, my girl creeps into my room and crawls to me on her knees.

Love's a glowing outline as she climbs on top of me.

In the barely illuminated hours before dawn and through the dizzy haze of coke-sleep, I breathe in the sound and scent and feel of her, all honey-dipped tea trees, pajama softness, and needy little inhales from my neck.

"I'm sorry," she whispers, kissing my chest through my tee. She pushes it up my stomach and her tears cut through my skin, but these razors are the first things that have felt right in days. "I'm so sorry, Dusty."

I groan as she kisses my stomach. It twists and turns audibly for nourishment, and love cries harder. She wraps around me, and this life goes from high stakes and bottomless pains to totally effortless.

Pushing her shirt up and off too, I let my hands find her full little curves. Baby presses and slides and rocks easily, sweetly perfect and home to me, and need I've carried longer than I can remember aches hard against precious softness.

"You know nothing happened," she whispers. Her tears have stopped, but her voice is broken.

I drag her along myself and groan again, rolling my hips up and into her. Leigh whimpers through bite-to-keep-quiet lips and leans down to hold onto my shoulders.

"You know I love only you. You know it," she says, grazing her teeth over my chin. "Tell me you know it."

I turn my face away, not ready, and impatient love sits up. I think she's going to let me feel her. I think about the rest of our clothes coming off, and my body throbs at the thought of sliding along where I need so badly, but she doesn't take anything off. She shifts lower, dragging her open lips down my stomach. She kisses my belly button and lower, over the waistband of my boxers.

My pulse dips and I'm deaf to everything for a second.

Then it picks up twice as hard, and when this girl wraps her hands around me, my whole body lights and lifts for her touch.

Lush and penitent, she kisses everywhere, from my hipbones to the base, and I lean up. Replacing her hands with my right, I hold my cock for love's amends-seeking mouth, and her lips are the softest, sweetest sensation ever.

Beyond gentle and so warm, Bliss opens and kisses with eager, effortful sincerity, laying all her yearning bare and making my fingertips tingle. Exhausted muscles and bones melt, and my ragged-raw nerves surrender. My sore heart unwinds, calming and collecting its beats between baby's lips.

Loyalty and her apology and shared yearning flow through her as she learns me and shows me all the devotion there are no words for. She kisses me as deeply as she can, and when she leans up for a breath, meeting my eyes in the almost-light, she smiles, first-time shy and blushing in love.

My chest fills and I love the pressure. Nothing compares to or comes anywhere close to this. I've never, ever felt like this, and I love how baby gets me.

Tucking stray strawberry-blond hair behind her ear, Leigh gives me more, and when she hums around my cock, I almost fucking come. But she takes me deeper. And sucks so Heaven-soft I could die.

My spine burns and hot chills slide down the back of my neck. I shake inside and open my eyes, finding made-for-kissing lips wrapped so pretty around me, vulnerable and unselfish in this moment. She swallows around me, taking all of my doubt and beleaguerment and ability with her, and my vertebrae liquefy one by one. Ache dissolves into euphoria, and I hear my voice.

"Baby, baby, baby …"

She hums again, and everything in me stretches, straining, and when she slides her lips to the head of my cock, covering me with soft kisses, everything ignites. No one's ever touched me like this or loved me like this or can be this—

"Bliss …"

Nothing hurts or has ever hurt, and as pure relief rushes from behind my eyes and down my back, it shakes my whole frame. Love adores me as I give her everything, and after I do, when her chest-swelling, heart-surrounding, soul-filled and high-spirited laugh resounds through kisses and into me, I smile for the first time in days.

I can't help it.

CHAPTER
thirty-nine

"Leigh, you have to push in the clutch before shifting gears," Thomas says.

"I did!" I stall the car and throw my hands up. "I give up. I can't drive."

"Calm down," he mutters, scrubbing the palms of his hands down his face. "Stop being dramatic."

"You calm down," I say quickly, squeezing the steering wheel. "You're making this hard. Maybe I should ask someone else."

Because I'll hit him if I look at his arrogant face, I keep my eyes straight ahead on the empty parking lot. We've been in the car for over an hour, exchanging digs and dirty looks. This isn't what I expected when he offered to teach me how to drive.

"Like who, Bliss?" Dusty opens the door, kicking it when the ocean wind shuts it on his leg. "Call that motherfucker. I guarantee he won't make it out of his truck."

He slams my door and walks away.

My car rocks, and the old windows rattle under the force of his anger. Thomas might not think much of my old Volkswagen, but this car is precious to me. He can treat his things however he wants, but I refuse to let him disregard mine.

I unbuckle my seatbelt and get out. Cold November beach air smacks me in the face, stinging my eyes and burning my cheeks, but the smell of driftwood and salt takes me back to a time before my boy was so intense and unstable, and a place for secret-stolen kisses and just us: our dock.

I should have known this is how my lesson would turn out.

Thomas paces with the wind blowing through his little-bit-too-long hair. He has a cigarette in one hand and his cell phone in the other, probably calling Casper.

"Hey!" I call, walking toward him.

Dusty hangs up his phone, looks back at me with sinister, deep dark eyes that match the night sky and lifts the hood of his hoodie over his head before turning away.

I lift my own hood from the sweater love gave me years ago. The cotton is worn thin, and Castor is faded on the back, but it doesn't mean any less to me. And when I'm in bed and Thomas is out doing whatever it is that he does, it's all I have to remind myself that he wasn't always this way. There was a time when we were innocent and genuine, and young, stupid in love.

"I'm not doing this with you," I say loud enough I know he hears me and head back to my car.

I wanted to do this together, but it's cold and well after midnight, and I didn't sneak out of my house to slam doors and chase him around. Risking everything for love is one thing, but this is a waste of time.

Fueled by stubbornness and back inside the comfort of my Rabbit, I recall what Thomas has managed to teach me and pray I can start this car on my own. With the clutch in neutral, I press in and start the car successfully.

I flip on the headlights, and a faded yellow glow illuminates the moonlit parking lot, lighting my path. I hold my breath and release the clutch, shifting the car into first gear. Four tires move five feet before the clutch pops and the engine stalls. Shaking and stranded, I hit the steering wheel with the palm of my hand, honking the horn.

My car door opens. "Get the fuck out, Leigh."

I try to close my door, but Thomas reaches over me and pulls the keys from the ignition.

"Get out of my car!" I hit and push, and grip and keep.

As if I'm not fighting him, he lifts the emergency brake and unbuckles my seatbelt. Trouble grabs me by the front of my sweater, clutching onto soft cotton and sweet memories, and pulls me out from behind the wheel. I scream, using lungfuls of salty ocean air for momentum.

"You're not driving my car!" I yell in his face, but my cries lack conviction.

"*You're* not driving," he snaps. Cold, white air blows from between his lips. Behind him, waves crash on the shore as the tide rises. Dusty walks me to the other side of the car and opens the passenger door. "Get in so we can go home."

I shove my hands into his chest, pushing him back. "I hate you."

As I'm getting into my Volkswagen, Thomas grips onto the back of my hoodie and pulls me against his chest.

"You hate me?" he whispers harshly, in my ear. "I wish I could hate you, Bliss, because this"—he squeezes me harder—"this is killing me."

Love's too dope-numb to feel, but I press my fingernails into his skin until it breaks and four crescent-shaped wounds bleed from his right hand.

"You're such a little girl," he says, letting me go with a small push.

Irrational anger straightens my spine and reddens my cheeks.

"You're a sixteen-year-old brat who has me stuck in this bullshit town." He spits on the ground and pats his pockets for his cigarettes. Thomas drops his pack of smokes, and instead of picking it up, he kicks it and throws his lighter into the sand. "Why are you doing this to me?"

I stand silent, breathing in through my nose and out my mouth. Tonight's argument is years of frustration stacked and hidden, too tall to push away anymore. A little trigger is all it takes, and we end up like this, saying things we don't mean, taking our aggravation out on each other.

My heart pumps misguided love.

"This isn't how it's supposed to be," it beats. *"But that's your boy—aimless and crazy for you."*

Knowing that I had a role on his spiral to the bottom kills me. As his parents continue to fail him, I should be the one that steps forward and says, "This is wrong."

But to do so at this point in his madness would be betrayal, and I have to handle his trust with care.

Inhaling an uneven breath, I watch him. His already pale complexion glows under the silvery moon. Icy wind blows my boy's white tee against his slender body under his unzipped hoodie, and his hands shake.

I place my hands on the sides of his cool face and whisper, "Tell me a secret."

His body relaxes.

"I don't want to be a secret anymore, baby."

This is the part where I should tell him, "It's too late. We're too wrong." Instead, I say softly, "Do you really wish you could hate me?"

His arm circles around my lower back, and Thomas turns his face until our noses touch. Gripping onto my sweater, it lifts and frigid air kisses my bare skin.

I slip inside of my boy's unzipped sweater, reaching around until my arms overlap. Tight and rock-steady, I bury my face into his shirt until the smell of salt water is replaced with vanilla and heartbreak.

Love is never breaking completely.

Thomas chuckles. "Do you really want someone else to teach you how to drive?"

SPINNING IN the cycle of dependence with Dusty, time takes on a different meaning. It's not kept in normal seconds, minutes, hours, weeks, months, or years, but in how many days at a time he's gone; how many hours it's been since I last spoke to him; how many minutes it takes him to apologize this time; the seconds until I see him next.

Seasons kind of, sort of blend. Holidays come and go.

October. November. December. January—I don't remember anything about the actual time passing, but I remember how many weekends I spent alone in his bed because he didn't come home. I remember the hours I spent calling his phone over and over until he answered, and I remember how many minutes those conversations lasted before he said he had to go.

His time away becomes more frequent.

Because I'm usually the only person who knows where he is, I sit back and watch his parents stress and his sister worry. He forces me to lie to them more than I already do, because when Tommy asks Rebecka and me if we know where Thomas is this time and I say no, I'm lying straight to her face, looking right into her blue eyes. When I hear her cry, I could so easily ease her concern … but I never do.

"Come over tonight and eat left-over spaghetti with me," I say softly, pushing pink-faded blond hair behind Rebecka's ear.

Three weeks into January, standing in front of the school that was dismissed an hour ago, my best friend's nose is red and her eyes water. Bundled up in a yellow hoodie under a black leather jacket, she types into her phone, mumbling under her breath.

I know who she's trying to reach.

He won't answer.

"Did you see him at all, Bliss?" Becka asks, shoving her phone into her pocket. She picks her backpack up from the ground and hooks it over her left shoulder. "Because he was here. He drove me to school."

I bite my bottom lip and shake my head. Lie.

I tighten my cobalt blue scarf around my neck and button up my dark-gray peacoat to keep my hands busy. "He wouldn't leave you here, Rebecka." Lie.

Disgust for my boy is all I feel when a lonely tear falls down Becka's pink cheek.

"I'll drive you home," I offer, pulling on her backpack.

She runs her hand through her long, three-day dirty hair, searching for a Lincoln that won't be pulling up. I hope for her and her family that this won't be another weekend they have to calls hospitals and police stations looking for their runaway.

And ten minutes later, Thomas isn't here.

Madness lurks behind their son's black eyes, and anything sets love off. He misses school … he misses meals. Trouble deteriorates right in front of us, thin and never sober. Thomas is eighteen, but I thought after the second time he took off, Lucas and Tommy would stop this from happening again.

I bite my thumbnail, about to offer my girl another ride home when Petey strolls out of the school office, high and wandering.

The moment Becka's cry-red eyes catch his pitch-black ones, she's up.

"Where the fuck is my brother, Pete?" she yells, shoving her hands against his chest.

Icy air bites my lungs as I chase after her, and my eyes water. I want so badly to admit, *he's with Casper!*

I reach for her hands as she reaches to hit Pete again. He puts his shades on and looks right at me when he says, "Why don't you call him?"

Becka frustratingly groans, breaking my hold on her. Petey's smile wavers, but he holds his stance—indifferent and protecting.

"This isn't funny anymore, Petey!" she cries. "You say things to me, but then you do this."

She walks away.

"Rebecka," he calls out. I walk past him after my girl. I don't look until he calls for me.

I only give him my eyes long enough to show disappointment.

In both of us.

THREE MORE weekends. Hundreds of phone calls. Too many seconds to bear. Countless minutes of asking myself why. More lies than I can count.

March.

"WHY ARE you here?"

"Leave with me."

I scoff. "No."

Thomas scoots his chair a little closer, pulling mine to the side until I'm between his knees. "Don't make me beg, princess."

I drop my pen and push my Calculus book away. I look over to him and try not to smile. His smirk is silly-high and contagious, like *whoa*. My boy smells like cinnamon gum and cigarettes and vanilla-delicious. He plays with the ends of my strawberry curls, reeling me in.

Keeping my voice library-low, I whisper, "I'm not leaving, because I have to study, and you're not leaving, because you have a game after school."

"I can make it a rule," he says slyly.

I smile back. "I like to break our rules."

"You like to break me." Thomas kisses from my wrist to my elbow. He rubs my arms when he gives me goose bumps.

I roll my eyes and look around, making sure no one can see us. "Anyone can walk back here, Dusty."

He pushes my hair away from my shoulder and kisses my neck. I turn in my chair, moving closer to him. My boy holds on to the side of my chin, pushing his thumb under my jaw to tilt my head back.

"Touch my cock, Leigh," he says loud enough to be heard. My eyes snap open and mischief laughs. "Do you think I give a fuck if anyone sees us?"

I make a noise of playful disgust and push him away. Thomas ignores me and shuts my book.

"Leave with me before I go to the lunch room and tell your boyfriend you like it when I finger fuck you from behind," he says.

I sit back in my chair and let him pack my stuff into a white with pink hearts backpack. I cross my arms and pretend to be mad.

"Come on." Thomas holds a hand out for me with my backpack over his shoulder.

Snatching his sunglasses from his face, I slip them into the pocket on his shirt and say, "I'm driving."

My boy drops his arm over my shoulders and leads us out the back. "Whatever you want, strawberry-blonde."

After a short drive, we enter his house through the kitchen door. All of the shades are drawn and the TV is off. Dirty cereal bowls from breakfast sit in the sink and someone left the coffee pot on.

Upstairs, my boy closes his bedroom door with us inside, and the comfort of our space makes it easy to forget how tricky we are being right now. We fall right into low hushes and soft laughs.

Trouble pushes my hair over my right shoulder and kisses my neck, walking us toward his bed. When my knees hit his mattress, his touches are tenderly firm and effervescently alluring, and I feel more alert than I have all day. My heart doesn't beat blood through my veins, but sparks and fire and tingles and Thomas.

Standing over me, my boy bends at the knees to look me straight in the eyes with his delightful, dark stare. Bent and sure, he presses his thumb against my lips. I kiss it. He pushes until he pulls my bottom lip down. I bite him. He laughs.

With a gentle shove, my back falls flat on mattress, and I stretch my arms above my head. Thomas takes my foot and unbuckles my right shoe. Then my left.

I wiggle and stretch my toes.

"Lift," he bids carefully.

I place my feet at the edge of the bed and lift my hips. Crazy love places a knee between my feet and reaches under my light teal skirt for my underwear. White lace brushes against my legs on their way down, and when they get stuck at my ankle, we both laugh. I kick, but they won't go.

"Stay still," Thomas says, gripping my calf, pulling and dismissing my unders with my shoes.

Disappearing below my skirt, he presses the palms of his hands to the insides of my thighs and opens me up.

"It's better like this sometimes," he whispers, slipping his leg off the bed until he's lower. "When I can't see everything, but I can feel."

Dusty tugs me to the edge of his mattress; above and between me, I can feel him hard under denim. His heart quick-beats beneath tee shirt cotton, and I slip my hands under it, sliding them up until he gets the point. His hat comes off first, then his shirt.

My stomach dips and somersaults, and my knees come up trapping him within me. I circle up against hard slim-straights and hold my arms around his neck. Thomas' tongue parts my lips, and he strokes so hard my entire body shifts up.

I hiss against his kiss and bite on his bottom lip until he groans and pushes again.

This boy reaches between us and brushes his knuckles over my center. The rumble in his chest curls my berry-pink toes and tingles the tips of my fingers. Standing, he pushes my skirt around my hips until he sees me and holds the top of my shoulder with his free hand. With his other, he presses two fingers inside. He isn't measured or soft or easing, but swift and heavy and unapologetic.

I cry out for his touch.

His hold on my shoulder prevents my body from moving up, forcing my middle to take the entire impact every time he pushes his fingers in.

My boy doesn't slow down once I start to come; he goes harder and deeper and rougher. While I rock and roll through waves he causes, I hear him whisper, "Your pussy is so fucking pretty, Bliss."

Tears fall from my eyes, down into my hair. It's too much. I feel him at my heat, in my ear, on my chest. He pulls my top down and bites my nipple until I scream and clutch and grip.

"I can't—" I begin, only to be cut off by his lips, and his tongue, and his hands.

Thomas pushes … So far, so deep, so into me. He touches and rubs and presses from the inside. He keeps his palm pressed hard against my clit, still and strong and bold, and so fucking certain. My hips keep circling, and my muscles still squeeze.

My lips shake and plead and beg. "Please don't stop. Please, Thomas, don't stop."

He drops to his knees.

Then his lips are where his palm was.

His tongue is where his fingers were.

My eyes open, and all I see is the ceiling. My voice is stuck, and my mind is momentarily clear.

Then I fall.

I reach down and tangle my hands into his hair. I hook my left leg around his shoulders, ensuring he never leaves … never stops.

There is nothing more beautiful than his lips on me.

He kisses my middle like he kisses my mouth: dirty, deep, and long. I can't keep still. I lift and push, feeling his chin and his nose and his laugh.

With his fingers back inside, he kisses between my folds. Soft and puckering, he tells me how good I taste between open mouthfuls. "You're sugar coated, baby. I knew you would be."

And with one more hard push and deep kiss, my world spins, and I arch.

CHAPTER
forty

On my stomach over his messy sheets, I'm spent, tired, and slack as he pushes my hair back and kisses between my shoulder blades. Thomas' hardness presses against my hip, but when I move, he says, "Stay just like this until we have to leave."

So we do.

We're content and quiet and close until I'm almost asleep and feel him get up and go into his bathroom.

With Her.

Curling up, I sometimes wish he would keep that bitch hidden from me like he does with everyone else, but there's comfort in knowing he uses around me. It's sick and contorted, and I wish I was brave enough to ask him to stop, but if he has to use, I want to know when and how and where. I want to be included, even if it's only through the door.

When he returns to his spot that has grown cold, I ask, "What if I used?"

Dusty kisses the top of my shoulder. "You wouldn't."

"But what if I did?"

Thomas rests his head in the center of my back. I bring my arms up and lay my head on my left elbow.

"I don't know, Leighlee. It's not something I can even consider. It's not you."

I turn in his arms and lean up. His dilated eyes shift away. "It could be me. It's not hard to get."

Love covers his eyes with his forearm. His bare chest rises and falls with steady breaths. His jeans are low, showing his boxer briefs. I have a silly thought about sticking my finger in his belly button. I want to touch the hair that leads below the waistband of his dark green Fruit of the Looms.

He smirks. "I'd find who gave it to you and break their fucking neck."

NOTHING ABOUT my boy changes as cold weather turns warm. The school year is almost over, and he still hasn't decided what he wants to do after graduation.

"I'm not going anywhere, Bliss. You still have another year of school, so I'll just play ball at the JC or something," he says. His pockets are fat, and he's having a good time; he's set. "You don't have to worry about this shit now."

Meanwhile, our friends' lives slowly come together.

Enjoying the near-summer night, Becka, the boys, and I are on the Castors' back deck, smoking a bowl and sharing a bag of chips and a two liter of soda straight from the bottle.

Passing the pipe to Petey with a lungful of smoke, Ben holds his finger up like he has something to say. He stands from his seat and reaches into his back pocket, exhaling as he presents a white letter envelope that's been folded in half.

"I got this today," he says, sitting down.

As he removes a sheet of paper from the envelope, Petey passes the bowl to Becka. Dense smoke hovers in the air above us, and the scent of marijuana taints the fresh smell of the water spraying from the sprinklers.

Weightless and past faded, when Rebecka passes the pipe to her brother, and he passes it directly to me, I shake my head. Thomas shrugs with a lazy smirk and holds the lesser of his evils to his lips with his lighter. Sparking a couple of times before the flame ignites, its orange glow lights up his face.

Ben holds up his letter with the fancy letterhead. "I got into Oregon State."

Excitement for the boy who once drove the getaway car bubbles in my chest and comes out as joyful laughter. Pete stands up and hugs his friend, and Becka goes right into how she and I are looking into UCLA, USC, UC Berkeley, San Diego, and Santa Barbara.

"We'll take whatever we can get," she speaks for both of us. "Bliss and I just want to go to California."

Dusty's expressionless, flipping his green BIC between his fingers. "Do you actually think your parents will let you off your chain, little girl?"

Playing indifferent, I shrug. "Mom says they've been saving so I can go."

California makes my stomach flip. When my parents get on my back about my future plans, I jump online and look at schools to appease them. I also send out for information to show Rebecka that I'm on the same page as she is for show.

Once we're both out of high school, we won't have to lie anymore. Then what? Will Thomas and I just take off like we've always planned? Where the fuck are we even going?

"What about you, Pete?" I ask to change the subject. "What will you do after high school?"

Lazy-faced and low-lidded, he answers, "There are no acceptance letters in my mailbox, little sister."

"Because you didn't apply," Becka teases. She bats her eyelashes before shoving a handful of chips in her mouth.

"But I got that auto body job in Toledo," he says.

As pretty in pink and dumb in blond bicker back and forth like we don't know what's going on between them, my boy's knuckles are white and his eyes are distant. I have no doubt California is on his mind.

"HE ASKED you?" Thomas takes a drag from his cigarette, staring into the forest of trees in front of his house. He's rooted, with the exception of his hand which flicks his cigarette, and his chest that inhales and exhales thick smoke into the evening air.

"Yeah. Earlier."

My parents are under the assumption that I'm at a late movie with Becka, but she's actually at Smitty's. With Lucas and Tommy out of town, Thomas and I were supposed to spend the entire day together, but he's lost in the hell he always loses himself in and forgot about me.

Instead, I spent time with Oliver at my house, in front of my TV, drinking fucking apple juice while he talked with my dad.

"You're not going." Dusty's dark stare falls on me.

I cross my arms over my chest and let my keys jingle from my finger. "I told him I wasn't going."

My boy drops his cigarette butt to the concrete driveway, and red-orange embers flake off. Burning nicotine doesn't go out right away, and the urge to step on it is almost as strong as the urge to tell him I wanted to say yes to Oliver.

"Did you think it would be okay?" He actually smiles, but it's delirious and dope-slanted. "Like the concert?"

"I told you I said no, Thomas."

I'm apathetic as he takes the few steps to close the distance between us and bothered when he grabs my chin and forces me to look up at him. Love pushes my head back and tilts it to the left and right, looking at my neck ... searching but finding nothing.

"Were you with him?" he asks, releasing my face from his smoke-scented grip.

"I just told you he came over." I slap his hand away.

Cocaine plays her tricks, whispering untruths into his ear, making him paranoid and disillusioned. She swims under his skin and slithers around his bones, overwhelming his heart, twisting his thoughts and actions against me.

"You know what I mean, Leigh." He grabs my wrist and pulls me close. Madness breathes in against the inside of my arm before burying his nose in my hair and inhaling.

"There's nothing to find, Thomas," I whisper softly, wrapping him up in my arm. "I don't want to go anywhere with him, but you're never here when I need you."

"Stop." He groans deeply, burrowing his fingertips into my back as he grips onto me.

"Where were you?" I ask, tied up with this boy. "Why are you always away from me?"

ALL RIGHT, I have chicken soup, cold medicine, and a temperature taker." Rebecka drops the grocery bag at the end of my bed; a can of condensed soup rolls out.

From under my heavy comforter and a couple of extra quilts, I smile at my best girl. "Thank you."

Her blue eyes cross looking at the tip of the thermometer. "I don't know how to use this thing, so maybe just stick it in your armpit."

Sweating under the amount of unneeded blankets I have on top of me, I hold my hand out and throw it across the room when she gives it to me. The only way I could get out of going to prom was to tell everyone I'm sick. My parents were easy to convince, but Becka won't let it go.

I swat at her, but she manages to press her palm to my forehead, as if she knows what she's looking for.

"Eww," Becka says, wiping her hand on her sweats. "Your head is sweaty."

It's all these damn layers I'm under, I think to myself.

My girl stomps her foot, fresh-faced with wet hair. "I cannot believe I'm going to prom and you're not. You suck."

I spend the entire night watching the clock. Rebecka texts perpetually, hoping to make me feel better about being left out with photos of all of our friends, of her and Smitty, of stupid things like the tacky disco ball that hangs above the gym floor, and the fake flowers the school used as table centerpieces.

The dance is over, and my phone is silent by the time love steps in quietly though the back door. We spend the night and early morning watching movies on his cell phone, eating ice cream bars and whispering not to wake my parents up.

Prom doesn't come up once, and I'm glad.

When school comes on Monday, it's hard hearing stories about the monumental school dance, and it's all anyone talks about. This person hooked up with this person, and that girl's dress was so ugly, and Oliver kissed Casey, the girl he went to prom with at the last minute.

"I mean, you guys aren't dating, right?" she asks. I didn't even know she was in my calculus class, but someone told her Oliver was mine, so she thought she'd come to me before I went to her.

"No," I say, shaking my head.

Casey is pretty-ish. Blond hair, brown eyes, she's simple and semi-popular, and until today, I never noticed her. Now, I see her all of the time. She wears the same jean shorts almost constantly, and has freckles on her nose, but nowhere else. Her locker is on the other side of the hall, five down from mine.

It's been two weeks since prom, and I still don't know how I feel about the Casey/Oliver kiss. Rebecka says she's a skank, but she's not. He's not wrong for kissing her, either. They're cute together, and it kills me.

Not that they're together. But his lips were on hers, not mine … and it's disorienting.

I'm in the lunch room at school, searching for light brown hair, black eyes, and a crooked smile. Instead, I find Oliver—tolerant and observing—waiting in line for lunch. When our eyes catch, he comes over and takes the chair next to my own. He smells like simpleness, like cut grass, grip tape, and Carmex.

"Hey," he says quietly.

Before I reply, my soul senses the one I was looking for. When he walks into a room, I know it. My body knows it. My heart and lungs and spine and nerves, know it. Everything sparks and straightens and comes to when my boy is near.

Thomas walks past me and kicks a leg of my chair, spinning and shoving me away from my skater boy. "Princess kid."

Oliver stands up, provoked. "What's your problem, Castor?"

Petey turns around and walks backward for a few steps and laughs, like he enjoys my torture. Dusty sits at a table on the opposite side of the cafeteria and ignores us.

"He's such a jerk," I say, brushing it off so no one thinks anything is out of the ordinary.

Oliver takes his seat after placing my milk in front of me.

Eventually, he calms, and when his eyes aren't so concentrated, I finally ask, "You kissed her?"

Oliver looks at me and pauses before nodding with an unreadable expression.

With his hand on the back of my chair, we leave it at that.

CHAPTER
forty-one

Despite how hard he made it, Dusty will graduate.

The thought of her first born out on his own crushes Tommy, no matter how many college applications she passes him. I have a sneaking suspicion she's relieved when she finds her efforts tossed in the trash. Lucas, on the other hand, lays his disappointment on thick, unamused by Thomas's lack of enthusiasm about life after high school.

"What are you going to do, Dusty?" he scolds his son. Our dinner table conversation flips from Dusty's new shorter haircut to college.

Mischief smirks. "I don't know, Dad."

Tommy tips her wine bottle upside down over her glass, capturing every drop, and Rebecka drops her fork—full. I keep eating my chili dog.

"You graduate in a week, and you've accomplished nothing." Lucas pushes his plate away.

I take another bite.

"I have an appointment at Oregon Coast in two weeks. I'll go there until I figure something out."

His confession surprises me more than the haircut does.

Lucas snorts. "Community college? You little, thankless mother—"

The argument lasts over an hour and results in Thomas's departure. But he comes back for me, and we sneak out into the night when the rest of the family is dreaming.

Thomas completing high school is the first step in the right direction—our designed path. One more year, and we'll be what we've always talked about being: gone and together.

"I'm nervous." Dusty smiles, lit by the moonlight.

From love's lap, I lean my head back against the car window and extend my legs out in front of me. Holding smoke in his lungs, he offers the blunt to me between his thumb and pointer finger and places it to my lips. It tastes like oranges and sour citrus, smooth and glowing.

"Don't be," I say, exhaling.

"You'll be there tomorrow." It's not a question. His hand slips between my thighs.

"Front row," I whisper, melting as his fingers push into me.

As the loud speaker announces, "Thomas Levi Castor," Becka and I hold up our handmade sign that boldly states the obvious: Dusty Delinquent.

My best girl and I jump up and down on the football field turned commencement venue and shout as trouble reaches for his diploma from the principal who has given him more detention than attention. Unmoved by accomplishment, love doesn't acknowledge the crowd or make a grand gesture like some have before him. Thomas walks off the stage and pulls the white cap with the tassel from his head.

"I can't believe he did it," Rebecka says with a slight smile on her dark red lips.

Before my guy even reaches his seat, Petey's name is announced. Dumb in blond accepts his diploma and waves it around, proud of his moment with a smile that steals the show. Ben follows as Pete exits stage left, receiving his certificate gimmick free.

Although I hate her, I clap for Valarie after her name is called, and when Mixie crosses the stage, blushing and wide eyed, I think about her stomach which never grew.

The florist I ran into before we got here said, "Peonies are a flower a boy can appreciate." So with a bouquet of sunset-colored peonies in my hand, when the ceremony wraps up, I run for her brother.

He's looking around from the middle of the field, not yet seeing his sister and me in a full sprint. The hem of my sweetheart dress skims my thighs, and my wedges sink into the soft grass. The smile on my face is the size of the sun and just as bright.

"Dusty!" Rebecka calls as we close in on him.

He sees us and his shoulders drop. Relieved, he takes a few steps in our direction, but we make it to him first—and jump.

Rebecka leaps in his arms, and when he spins her, I jump on his back.

"I'm proud of you," I whisper in his ear. My boy leans his head back, nuzzling his nose in my neck for the smallest of moments. But it's enough, and I know.

It's our deal, and love is the smallest of moments.

Our families show up, as do Petey and Ben. While Becka hops all over them, I give Thomas his flowers.

"They're from my family and me," I say, telling him the truth with my eyes.

Holding the flowers with the same hand he carries his cap in, Dusty reads the small card from the posy.

Ask me again, it says.

Between hugs and congratulations from all sides, he lifts his eyes from the card and keeps them on me. Unwilling to wait, he wants to do this now—ask me now.

I press my pointer finger against my lips.

Not in front of everyone, I say with my gaze.

Thomas' smile dims, and his mostly blue eyes darken. As if he's suddenly too restricted, he takes off his gown and untucks his shirt, taking a slow step back from everyone.

"Can we go?" he asks openly, patting his pockets for his pack.

With a nervous heartbeat in my throat, I turn to my parents and say, "I'm going to Becka's for a while."

"We have reservations at Franchino's. You're more than welcome to join us." Tommy slides her arms across my shoulders and tucks me into her side.

Dad smiles politely. "As good as Italian food sounds, I have some work to do tonight."

"We'll take care of Leigh. We always do." Tommy smiles.

Ben and his family, Petey and Rachel—who's in large sunglasses and baggy jeans—all of the Castors, and my parents and I walk to the parking lot together.

"Are you staying with Rebecka tonight?" Mom asks, twirling one of my curls around her finger.

"Yeah," I answer, looking around for my friend.

Off to the side with her parents and Thomas, Becka crosses her arms across her chest and rolls her eyes. Dusty lights a cigarette and blows white smoke over his shoulder while he speaks to his mother and father in a defensive posture. Lucas keeps up with appearances and projects calm and cool, but his false smile is weak.

Walking away from the people who gave him life, even as they call him back, love flicks his smoke across the lot. He approaches my parents and me with the scent of nicotine on his clothes.

"Can I ride with you?" His voice is short, and he doesn't look at me as he speaks.

"I guess," I answer with shrug.

Since we're all going to the same place, Ben and Pete ride with us, too.

"Drop me off at my house, princess," Thomas says from the seat beside me. He avoids my eyes, but his tone isn't so short.

"Mom's going to flip," his sister says from the back.

He looks over his shoulder and smiles, but it's untrustworthy. "I want to get my car."

"We're almost to the restaurant." I stop at a red light and look over at my boy. "Can't you get it after dinner?"

"No."

That's all he needs to say.

Since the top is down, Petey and Ben don't wait for the car to stop before they jump out once we're in the Castors' driveway. The Lincoln's parked in front of the house, and I secretly hope it doesn't start so Thomas can't go anywhere.

"Thanks for the lift, kid." He smirks, opening the car door.

"Bliss, I'm going to run up and get my phone charger. Wait for me." Becka jumps over the side, and I turn the car off.

Since we're alone, I ask, "What's wrong?"

Thomas gets out and shuts the door, leaving me inside.

"Nothing." He reaches in for the flowers and picks the card off the stem. He folds it in half and sticks it in his pocket. "Put those in water for me."

He leaves the peonies in the passenger seat and walks away.

In the time it takes Becka to come back out, the boys pile into the Continental. It starts, and when they drive away, it's in the wrong direction.

"TRY HIS phone again, Tommy," Lucas orders lowly.

I spin my fork into my spaghetti, keeping my eyes down.

"I've tried ten times," she says.

"Dad, he's not answering," Becka speaks up. She's annoyed, like her parents should get a fucking clue.

But no one will say what we all know: Thomas isn't coming.

Across the restaurant, Ben's family suffers from our same worries.

Rachel didn't come at all.

Another fifteen minutes pass before Lucas surrenders and pays the bill.

On the walk out, my girl takes my hand.

"I can't go home," she whispers into my ear.

It's not easy being the kid who's here while the other is missing … run away—whatever. Thomas doesn't see the sadness he leaves behind when he decides to disappear. He receives the anger when he gets back, but that's nothing compared to the hopelessness his sister lives in his absence.

"We can go to my house," I say.

"No." She shakes her head. "I already called Smitty."

IN A house more like mine than Rebecka's, the couches are old and the carpet's worn. Smitty's mother's coffee table is chipped and scratched from years of use. The air smells like laundry detergent, and the curtains over the windows, the clock on the wall, and the throw blanket over the arm of the rocking chair in the corner are all rooster themed.

"Want a beer?" Oliver asks at my side.

Becka's on Smitty's lap in the recliner beside the couch, hands linked and bodies completely touching. Her head leans back on his shoulder, and he whispers into her ear.

"Sure," I say, praying for numbness.

He gets up, and I check my phone.

Nothing.

I hear the sound of the refrigerator opening and the clink of metal bottle caps hitting the counter. I consider shooting Thomas a message, but Oliver comes back before I think of what to type.

Side by side, we drink our beers and keep our eyes on the TV. Oblivious, I'm back to the place I go when Thomas is gone. I count each inhale and pace my exhales and make sure not to breathe too hard or too deep or too fast.

Anxiety presses a hole into my chest, and when I think about Thomas, it constricts painfully. The empty spot throbs and beats, reminding me that my other half is away, and I don't know where he is.

I place my palm on my forehead and close my eyes. Setting my elbow on my knee, I hang the half-empty beer between my pointer and middle finger.

"Do you want to go upstairs?" Tenderness asks quietly.

I turn my head and look, unsure of how to answer. Oliver smirks, and his eyes shift over to our best friends. Smitty slips under Becka's shirt, and the recliner rocks back, and they laugh. I know they want to be alone.

My phone rings.

Dusty, the screen reads. *Answer or decline.*

Without thought, I stand up and press answer without greeting my caller. I take the stairs two at a time until I reach the only door I know.

"Where are you?" I ask.

There's muffled noise in the background—music, voices, and running water. I can hear Thomas moving around, but he doesn't answer.

"Thomas," I say a little louder. I leave the door and sit on the edge of Smitty's twin bed.

"I've been calling you," Thomas finally replies. His words are slow and slurred, like it's taking him a huge effort to speak.

"You haven't called me at all."

"Whatever."

My boy shuffles and shifts, curses and spits. He speaks in half-sentences and unfinished phrases, repeating the same thing three or four times before he switches to something else.

"Can you come here? Can you come get me?" he asks.

"Where are you?"

Nothing.

His mood shifts between sniffs. One second he wants to be found, and the next he wants to be left alone for good, forever.

"You're killing me, you know?" he argues. "Why did you call me?"

"You called me, Thomas." I breathe out.

"Because I love you so fucking much." His voice is desperate. "My chest hurts, babe."

With tears in my eyes, I ask, "Why didn't you come to dinner?"

"Because of you!" he shouts. "You and those orange flowers, Leigh. Shit."

I push my hand through my hair and stand up as panic devours my heart.

"Do you still want me to ask you again?" Thomas asks cruelly.

He sniffs.

"Not like this."

"Be my girlfriend, Bliss. Be my fucking hidden heart, baby."

Suddenly there's a voice on his end of the phone I recognize too well.

"Are you hiding?" Valarie asks, faintly at first. But as she get closer to my boy, my nightmare's slurred tone becomes crystal clear. "Come out here with us."

Bitterness creeps up my spine, and disappointment I never get used to feeling presses down on my shoulders. As the burden of our secret pangs, I ask breathlessly, "Who is that?"

Smoothly, he answers, "The devil."

I hang up.

In need of composure, I straighten out my dress, hold my shoulders back, and lift my chin. I transform myself into this Bliss—happy, secure, complete—and walk out into the hallway.

Oliver waits for me at the top of the stairs. His forearms are on his knees, and his head hangs low. I sweep my fingers across the back of his neck and sit beside him.

"Are you good?" he asks. I nod.

I lean my head on Oliver's shoulder and inhale until my lungs are full of air I've deprived them of.

Tilting my head up to find comfort in soft brown eyes looking down at me is simple.

Pressing my lips to Oliver's warm neck is easier.

When our lips almost touch, I close my eyes and settle.

He's slow and soft, but I press my hands against his shoulders and push Oliver's back against the wall. His head hits with a small thud, and we laugh, but for only a second before I cover his lips with mine again. I sit up on my knees, one step below where my skater boy is, and put my palms on his hips and slip my fingers inside the waist of his jeans.

"Bliss," he whispers, shuddering.

"Take me to Smitty's room," I say into his ear before pulling his earlobe between my teeth.

Oliver holds my face in his hands, and my stomach spins. To avoid watching him search for something he'll never find in me, I shift my eyes toward the ceiling. Careful and caring kisses the corner of my mouth as he rubs calloused thumbs across my cheekbones.

I bite down to keep from screaming.

"Come on." He stands up and goes into his best friend's bedroom.

I follow, swallowing sickness.

Undeserving of this boy's thoughtfulness, I don't give Oliver a chance to ask me if I'm sure about what's happening between us. I push him against the hollow door and dig my nails into his sides over his tee shirt, ignoring when he hisses. Harshly kissing up his throat, I reach between us and unbutton his Levi's.

"Um..." he starts, pulling his hips back a fraction of an inch. "Leigh."

"Shh," I smile, pulling the zipper down. "No talking, okay?"

When his pants are undone, I pull his shirt over his head and drop it on the floor. I bite my bottom lip and look at him through the dark.

Wrong chest. Wrong skin. Wrong person.

I touch his stomach and laugh when his muscles flex.

"Bliss, come on," he says softly, stepping away from me.

Indifferent to his conflict, I lift my foot to unbuckle my shoe, letting it drop to the carpeted floor. As I undo the second one, I turn around and say, "Unbutton my dress."

Silence.

"Oliver, help me," I say as the other shoe falls from my hand.

His hot breath tickles the back of my neck, and his fingers caress my spine as he undresses me. When my dress is loose enough, I curve away from a touch my body doesn't want and hide shame behind a deceiving smile.

What I need is to forget my life is fucked up for a night. I need this boy to prove to myself that I have choices.

And right now, I choose to forget.

I choose who really taught me how to drive.

My bra and underwear don't match, but when my dress comes off, he looks at me like I'm the most cherished thing he's ever seen. Tenderness reaches out and touches my hand and links our fingers before he pulls me against his body.

I'm shaking. Literally trembling.

He kisses me airless. He kisses me thoughtless and numb. He kisses me until I have to pull away and gasp, only to sink right back into his lips.

Held as if I'm made of glass, I say, "Tighter,"

He squeezes, but it's not enough.

"Harder," I groan, pulling the hair at the nape of his neck.

I step back until my legs hit the mattress and fall to my bottom. With his hands in his hair and his jeans undone, he looks good without a shirt.

I think about him kissing Casey like he kisses me.

I open my legs.

Between my thighs, he climbs over me before I have to ask. I slide my hands up his chest and use my feet to push down his denim. I kiss his jaw, nibble on his collar bone, and ask, "Do you like her?"

With his hands beside my head, dipping the old mattress, Oliver looks down at me. His eyebrows come together, and it's so fucking wrong.

"Who?"

"Casey."

"I don't know. No," he says. The sweater giver brushes his lips across my neck.

Closing my eyes, I whisper, "Why do you love me?"

Oliver just kisses my body softly, slowly, like he's making love to me. But this is too slow, so I reach down and hook my thumb into the waist band of my underwear and pull them down as far as I can.

He's on his knees right away, and he's hard. I can feel him against the inside of my thigh. His eyes follow while my hands lower cotton to my knees, but that's as much as he can take before he lowers his lids.

"Leigh—" He sounds unsure. His hand's back in his dark hair, and he's not looking.

Robbing him of choice, I sit up and push my underwear to my ankles and kick them off. I kiss his chest. "Will you look at me?"

I slip my hand into his boxers and wrap my hand around his length as my mouth pools with saliva repulsively. My jaw aches, and my stomach somersaults.

Oliver sucks in a sharp breath and tries to back away, but I grip firmer and stroke harder. His head falls back, eyes closed. His Adam's apple moves up then down as he swallows.

There's beauty in the boy who allows me to touch him without restriction, and it's freeing to know I could keep this easy affection just by saying I want it. To be cared for not only by necessity but because of sincere fondness is something I don't know.

This would be a love that doesn't only take.

When he finally opens his eyes and looks at me, I like his depth. I like his sincerity and openness. His soul is mine to have.

I lie back and open my knees and reach for his hips, pulling him over me.

"You get this from me," I whisper. My eyes fill and tears run down my temples into my hair. "You can have it."

"Leigh, we don't—"

I reach for him, wrapping my small hand around the base of his length. Unsteady and unsure, I guide him to my opening. I lift my hips, but Oliver pulls away.

"Why?" he asks in a shaken voice. "Why do we have to right now?"

"Just do it," I insist.

My escape gets off the bed and pulls on his jeans. "I'm not going to *just do it*, Leighlee."

I close my legs, but it's too late, I've already bared my sad, true self. The ache in my chest splinters and devours, hurting me until I finally sob.

Oliver slips my underwear up my legs and lies beside me. Once my tears slow, he whispers about things that aren't important, like how his mom accidentally washed all of his whites with a red shirt.

"Don't judge me if I'm wearing pink for a while," he says quietly.

Hiccups quickly turn into laughs. We don't kiss, or touch or go back to where we were, but we talk. We reminisce about peanut-butter-scented teachers and Sublime all summer long. Then he shows me his socks and they're pink, and it's so funny I laugh until I cry for a whole different reason.

"I GOT a summer job," Oliver says. His voice is loud in the early morning air.

It's a quarter past three, and once my tears dried, I needed air. After telling Becka I was ready to go, the sweetest sincerity lead me outside.

"You did?" I lean against the trunk of my car. He lifts me up, and I let him settle between my legs. He doesn't push or advance or take advantage. It's innocent.

"Lifeguard," he says shyly. "Me and Smitty."

I push dark brown hair behind his ear, and he relaxes his forearms on the car beside my legs, leaning his face between my arm and side. I rub his back, and we don't talk any more until our friends come outside.

"I didn't realize how late it was," she says, opening the passenger door and getting in. Smitty leans in and kisses her mouth.

Hopping off the car, I smile at Oliver as I walk away. Before I can get in, he reaches for my elbow and turns me around. He kisses me three times before his tongue parts my lips.

"I'll see you later," he says, letting me go.

Becka stares at me on the drive home.

She wants dirt.

I let her suffer a little longer, and when we come to a stop light, she squeals.

"Ask," I say, shifting the car into first when the light changes.

Her cheeks are freshly-fucked red, and her lips sweetly swollen

"What did his cock look like? Did you touch it?" She shakes my arm.

I tell her that he was nice and unselfish. "He has the prettiest lips."

"Do you love him or what?" Her eyes and ears are all mine.

I chew on the inside of my cheek but ultimately shake my head. I more than like Oliver. We have a simple, sweet history, and we could have a simple, sweet future. But I love Thomas—absolutely, utterly, completely—and it's all I have room for. He's all I want.

Love is that simple.

"You're stone cold, you know that?" Becka laughs and reaches for my hand.

When we get home, the Continental is parked in the driveway.

"Fucking asshole," she spits, pulling her hand from mine and unbuckling her seat belt.

I follow her up the front porch and stand behind while she unlocks the door. The entire house is dark and sleeping. The only sign of Thomas is his keys on the coffee table.

Becka and I quietly pass through the living room and up the stairs. Tommy and Lucas' door is shut. Blue-silver light from their television shines from underneath. She places her ear against the wood.

"My dad is snoring," she whispers.

My best friend and I are soundless as we enter her room. I sit on the edge of the bed and unbuckle my wedges for the second time tonight as I pretend my heart isn't about to beat out of my chest.

"Did you notice if Dusty's light was on?" she asks. "Should I talk to him?"

"No. It was off." Lie.

My girl lifts pink tresses into her hands and ties them up high with a black hairband. She shimmies out of black leggings and slips into bed wearing Smitty's shirt. I undress myself and fall in next to her, wearing the same underwear Oliver saw me in tonight. Holding my arms open, Rebecka clings close, wrapping her arms around my lower back, and I run my fingers through her hair until she's heavy and snoring.

I get out of bed and put on a tee shirt and a pair of gray cotton shorts and sneak out of her room and down to his door, but I'm afraid to go in.

My mind races. Everything Thomas told me on the phone, everything I did with Oliver, crashes down on me so fast that when I do open his door, I'm already crying.

Thomas stands in front of his TV. The remote's in his hand, and he's flipping through channels, fully dressed, down to his shoes, wearing exactly what he was at his graduation today.

"Hey," I say quietly.

"Tell me," he says. He turns off the TV and drops the remote but doesn't turn around. His head drops and his hands run through his hair. "Say it, Bliss."

"I was with Oliver," I cry softly. Tears roll down my cheeks.

The hole in my chest, which usually goes away when I'm with Thomas, burns and widens. I move my hands from my face to my chest and clutch my faded cotton shirt. I cry harder.

"Did you fuck him?" he asks. His voice is unstable and rough.

I shake my head. "No."

My boy finally turns and his eyes are darker than the forest outside. They're wholly black and entirely depleted.

I don't recognize this person.

"Why not?" He smirks.

I don't say anything. I don't move.

"Why didn't you, Leigh?" he asks again. The curve in his lips lifts slightly higher.

"I don't know, Thomas!" I yell, frustrated with his apathetic grin and broken glare.

Yelling doesn't make me feel better. It's like punching in a dream; no matter how much insistence and effort I put behind it, it's not enough.

But it's the trigger my boy needed.

Thomas pushes me against the door with his left hand over my mouth. With his right hand pressed against the side of my throat, his forearm presses across my shoulder. He's so tall, I have to stand on my tippy-toes to meet his eyes.

His eyes cry like mine do. His chin quivers. His teeth grind.

I hold onto his wrist. He isn't hurting me, but I want him to. I can manage physical pain much more than this … This is killing me. This I can't hold in.

"Shut the fuck up before someone hears you," he seethes.

I breathe too quickly through my nose. Salty water blurs my vision, and the tips of my toes hurt from standing too tall. My cheeks burn and my lungs sting. The hole in my chest, the emptiness of my guilt, becomes a vortex, with everything I own and feel and have, falling right into it.

I pull his hand away from my mouth.

"Listen to me," I cry out. I touch his face. I kiss the inside of his wrist. "Please. Please!"

I manage to lift away from the door, but Thomas pushes me back into it.

"No," he groans. I clear away his tears. My boy whimpers.

"It didn't mean anything. Listen to me!"

"Shut the fuck up!" he moans. "I can't—I can't do this, babe."

"I always forgive you. I've forgiven you for everything."

He closes his eyes and hides his face between my shoulder and neck. I feel his teeth on my skin, but he doesn't bite. I wrap my arms around him while he cries, and I feel the shortness of breath through his chest. His heart beats quicker than ever before. The capability of his anger and hurt literally ripples beneath his skin. Muscles tense and shift. His fingers squeeze and clench. He's keeping himself this close, but inside he's moving so far away.

He reaches behind me and opens his door. I try to close it, but he keeps his hold steady and secure. I turn between his arms so that my chest is to his back, and I try pull on his wrist from the doorknob with both of my hands, but he doesn't budge and the door stays open.

We scuffle and struggle and groan and cry, but eventually, I lose. He pushes me out and stands in front of the door so I can't come back in.

Defeated and tired, pathetic and heartbroken, I look up at my boy and wish

things were different. Not only this, but everything … From the start. I wish we would have done things differently

I walk away.

"Leighlee," he calls for me.

I go to his sister's bedroom where I belong.

I sit on the floor beside the bed, wrapping my arms around my pulled-up knees. When the crashing and breaking begins echoing throughout the house from the room next door, everyone wakes up. Becka jumps out of bed and opens the door.

Lucas runs by, sleepy faced and in his pajamas. Tommy's right behind him, tying her cream-colored silk robe with a panic-stricken expression on her face.

The sound of Dusty's fist going through his wall shakes my bones.

I cover my ears.

Every shout and struggle ricochets through the narrow walls in the hallway, intensifying the chaos. Tommy screams. Lucas fights back. Thomas storms past all of it with bloody knuckles and unfocused eyes.

His mother chases him, pulling on the back of his blue button up. The heels of her feet dig into the carpet, but it's useless.

And when he leaves—when the Continental roars to life and speeds out of the driveway—I know.

He won't be back.

CHAPTER
forty-two

It's like we're twelve years old again, sneaking sweets and telling secrets, hidden from the world in our own little existence built from imagination and, this time, desperation. We take every chair from the kitchen and every blanket from the closet. We strip my bed to the mattress and carry pillows, sheets, and stuffed giraffes downstairs. Mom calls us silly. Dad says we'd better clean up our mess.

Becka and I make a fort big enough for the two of us. It's quilt-draped and wooden chair sturdy, lit up by multicolored Christmas lights I begged my mom to pull down from the attic. They hang above and around us, twirl-tied around chair legs and in between layers of blankets.

We use flashlights from my dad's garage to read to each other. She recites *Pale Fire,* and I whisper from *The Fault in our Stars.* We take turns, page for page, reading chapters out of order until Vladimir Nabokov and John Green become the same person, and a new story is born from our favorites.

My girl eats banana chips, and I chew on taffy. She drinks water, and I stick to cream soda. Our legs tangle and our toes wiggle together. My left arm pushes against her right, and while I read, she leans her head on my shoulder.

"Okay, no more," she cries softly, wiping tears out from under her eyes. "I can't deal with fake funerals right now, Bliss."

I point my flashlight from the book to my best friend's face, and her tears reflect in the low light. She fills her cheeks up with air and exhales slowly, smiling sadly.

It's been a week, and she's been here every day since he left.

I search her face and look from her eyes to her nose to her lips and chin. Her hair is faded pink and clean, left down and fanned around her head and shoulders. She's in black boy shorts, and I'm in yellow. She's covered in an oversized tee, and I'm wearing a peach tank. Her eyes are swollen, bloodshot and red. Mine aren't.

Maybe having Becka with me every day since Thomas took off has kept me from crying, or maybe I just don't have it in me anymore, but since that night I haven't shed a single tear.

I can feel them building behind my eyes and pushing against my chest. My heart's wrapped in tears, floating in perfect heartache. My sadness is under my skin, between my toes, and in my hair. It's there when I go to sleep and on me when I wake up. My despair is vengeful, relentless, and mocking. It laughs in my face and says, *I told you so,* before clenching my heart in its firm grip knocking me off my feet.

Maybe I knew all along this would be our conclusion, and that's why I can't cry.

Becka's clingy in her grief. Her parents are their own kind of crazy, and I knew she needed to be out of her house until they calmed down.

Tommy's a mess and Lucas isn't any better. My judge father might be able to help them find their kid, but then my dad will know the truth about Thomas.

"I'll pick something else then," I say.

I set my book aside and sit up for another one. We have them all: fairy tales and classics, fables and fantasies, fiction and biographies. I toss *The Heroin Diaries* aside because of the too-close-to-home content, and pass *The Very Hungry Caterpillar* because we read that first. I hold up *Wuthering Heights,* and Becka makes a face.

"Boring," she says. I drop the book.

Scattered all around us, some books are in piles, but most are knocked over and open. The air in our tent smells like old paper, ink, and binding. Books are meant to be loved hard, used and abused. I'm not careful in my search to make this girl happy. I toss this book over there, and another over here. I accidentally rip a cover and get a paper cut.

"How about this?" I hold up a romance.

"No," she answers easily. "Gross."

"This?" Stephen King.

"Nah."

"How about this one?" I smile, showing her the cover to *Dirty* by Megan Hart.

Rebecka bolts up with huge open eyes and takes the novel from me. "Is this … *sex?*" she whispers.

I take it back and look at the cover. It's an image of a couple in a bathroom stall. All you can see is their shoe-covered feet and their position.

"I don't know where it came from," I say.

"I bet it's your mom's, Bliss. Under all of that floral print and Birkenstocks is a freak." She picks the book from my hands and lies back against our best-friend-made bed. "She probably likes Christmas Explosions as much as we do."

I slip in beside her with my elbow on the pillow and my head on my palm. I shudder. "Let's not talk about my mom and orgasms, okay?"

"Your dad's mustache probably tickles."

"Rebecka!" I let my face fall into cushy cotton.

"What?" She tilts her head back and laughs loudly, until her teeth show. Like his do. "Your dad's mustache is sexy."

I turn onto my back and cover my flushed face with both of my hands. "Can you just read?"

"Fine," she says, still laughing. "But if this gets me all hot and bothered, you might have to touch me after."

I hit her with a pillow. "Touch yourself."

"Or we can do that."

"Becka," I groan, beyond mortified and thriving in the first back-to-us conversation we've had in six days.

"Okay. Okay." She opens the book and reads.

WE READ from the book for a while, narrating the words in silly voices, trying to make it ridiculous. Rebecka makes sex sounds, and I blush like crazy. When she's sure she read every blow job, finger fuck, and love making scene, she finally puts it down.

Swimming in sexual tension, I bite my fingernails, and she rubs her thighs together. We avoid looking at each other, and it's awkward and funny and embarrassing, but normal. We're able to be ourselves for an hour. For sixty minutes, I don't feel the gaping hole in my chest.

"No more books," Becka finally says.

We open up the front of our tent and let out the scent of printed paper and turned-on teenager, and power on the TV. We watch *Fear and Loathing in Las Vegas* for about twenty minutes before the feeling of comfort shifts right back into apprehension. The hollow point in my body throbs, and my friend isn't smiling anymore.

"Do you think that's how it is for him?" she whispers. "Do you think he's lost like that?"

"He isn't looking for the American dream in the Great Red Shark, B. Thomas …" I swallow. "He's fucked-up. He's addicted. He's an addict."

It's like speaking fire and flame. The words burn, but we've spent years tiptoeing around the truth: Thomas has problems. Not once has anyone come out and said it.

Speaking the truth doesn't make us feel any better. Becka doses herself and falls asleep, and I'm wide awake, surrounded by children's books, in a tent lit by Christmas lights in June. My mind won't shut off.

Is he with Her?

Is he with Valarie?

Is he with anyone?

I worry until my stomach flips and tumbles and stirs until I clutch all ten fingers into my chest and try not to scream into my pillow. I kick my legs, pushing all of the blankets away, burning my knees on the rug. I bend my toes until they ache. I scratch into skin, trying to break through to the bone and blood and veins and arteries that's between me and where it hurts the most. My heart beats his name, his touch, his smell.

Cry, cry, cry, cry.

I'm sweating. My body is too warm. I breathe, in and out, in and out. My face tingles. My jaw hurts. I sit on my knees. My head hits the top of the fort. I shuffle over books and knock down one of the blankets that played our roof.

Out from beneath the covers, and away from the girl who laughs like my boy, I stand up and walk to the kitchen. Cool air touches my skin, forming goose bumps. My sticky feet form to unwarmed tile, making a soft suction sound with every step. I go to the sink and turn on the water. I hold my hair over my shoulder and cup my other hand under the liquid bringing a mouthful to my lips.

I rinse off my forehead and press wet hands against my panicked cheeks. I remind myself how to breathe: easy, steady, normal. Water drips from my lips, my forehead, my chin. I look at the clock; it's a quarter past four in the morning.

My phone rings.

I don't know if it's my legs or my heart that rush back to the fort. I stub my toe on *East of Eden* and catch my right wrist in holiday lights. My phone stops ringing.

"Shit. Shit … Shit." I untangle myself and push my pillow away.

Dope-sleepy blue eyes open a little. I look at her, but she isn't there. They close again. She's out.

My cell lights up.

Dusty.

Decline or Answer.

I silence the ringer and listen for my parents, but it's hard to hear over the echo of my heart's pulse.

"Thomas," I whisper into the receiver.

"Hi, baby."

Like nothing ever changed.

But then it happens.

I cry.

I bunch a sheet under my arm and bolt out of the blanket-made home. I step through the kitchen, unlock the backdoor, and walk out into the early morning night. Wrapping myself up, I sit in a cracked, sun-bleached green plastic patio chair while my eyes drip freely. My chin quivers. My nose stuffs up.

"Where are you?" I whisper, heartsick and moved.

"Princess girl … Baby, baby, baby," he says gently. His words are thick and drawn out. I don't hear anything on his side of the phone other than the sound of his breathing and soft speaking. "My girl."

I sit back, holding a hand over my mouth to keep my cries soundless. "Thomas"—I squeeze my eyes shut—"please come home."

"You're mine, right, sunny side? You'll always be mine?" Little tap, tap, taps litter the silence behind him, and I know She's there. He's cutting Her up into little lines.

I listen to him breathe cocaine in through his nose.

He groans.

He laughs.

Tap, tap, tap.

"I've been looking for you," he says.

"I'm where I belong," I answer, broken voiced. Pulling my feet up, I set my forehead on my knee and use the sheet to wipe my face. "It's you I can't find."

He laughs loudly. I think of Becka earlier with her head tilted back and her teeth showing. My face crumbles, and I sob.

"I'm right here, Leigh!"

"I'm supposed to always know where you are, Thomas. Remember our rules?" The stupid dog next door starts to bark.

"Are you smiling, baby?"

"No."

"Rule breaker." I can hear the smirk in his voice. I can see it in my mind, but it's blurry.

Then it's not so quiet where he is anymore. Someone's knocking.

"Give me a minute," he calls out absentmindedly.

Tap, tap, tap.

"Come home." I'm not crying anymore. I'm more desperate than that. I sit at the edge of my seat, biting my nails too low. I can feel my heartbeat in my face and in the tips of my fingers.

"I'll be home," he says, distracted.

"When?"

Thomas laughs. "I don't know. Whenever. Why?"

Let him go, my conscience whispers. *Tell him you don't need him. You don't love him. Lie to him like you lie to everyone else.*

"Because I love you. I miss you." Tears slip over my lips. I'm crushed, suffocating under the weight of our situation.

Tell him his degree of difficulty isn't worth it. Tell him his addiction is too harmful. Tell him you can no longer be what he needs you to be.

"I'll be your girlfriend, but swear you're coming home, Thomas."

"Yeah?" He's amused. "Just like that, Bliss?"

"I want you back."

"I didn't want you to fuck Oliver."

"I didn't." A feeling of being trapped creeps in. It's as if my arms are pinned at my sides and my ankles are tied together. I can't breathe out of my nose, and more air comes out of my mouth than in.

"You should have," he says in a calm, clear voice.

"I don't love him."

"Stop loving me."

"No," I answer, exhausted.

He's quiet, listening to me cry too hard, breathe too deeply, love too much. I can't take a breath. I can't catch up with myself. My tears drown me.

"Calm down," he says, sounding annoyed now.

I'm pouring. Draining. Depleting.

"Baby." He's a little more concerned. "Leigh, listen to me."

"I can't!" Not a lie. I can't hear anything over the sound of my own panic.

"Tell me a secret. Come on, little girl, tell me something."

I still don't know where he is or how to fix this. I don't know how to be without him. I need *our* secret. It's all I know. It's my backbone. This boy's my heart, and I'm alone.

So I say the only truth I know. "I'm scared."

"How LATE did you girls stay up?" Mom asks.

What she's really asking is, *what were you doing that I need to know about? Why did you sleep until three in the afternoon?*

Prying bitch.

"Late. We read a book, Teri," Becka answers. Her voice is uppity-happy.

I already know where this conversation is going, but I don't have the energy to stop it. Emotionally shattered after last night's phone call with Dusty, I feel like I'm looking through a fishbowl lens.

"You did?" Mom asks, disassembling our fort. She stacks my pillows on top of my comforter.

"I'll show you which one." Becka picks through our stacks of books on the coffee table. The one she's looking for is at the bottom of the second stack, but like my inability to interfere, I also lack the willingness to speak.

I fold the sheet I cried into all morning, while my best friend, who reminds me too much of my boy, taunts my mom.

"This one." Rebecka holds up the sex book. "Have you read it?"

Mom's face turns red. I toss the sheet I folded to the side with the rest and lie on the couch, heavy-lidded and weak.

"It was mixed in with my books." I curl up on my side and close my eyes.

"Leigh, were you crying?" Mom asks. Her embarrassed, defensive tone transforms into legit concern. It hurts my stomach.

I open up and both my mom and friend stare at me.

"Your face looks puffy, baby." Mom comes closer. She tries to touch me, but I sit up and run a hand through my hair.

The erotic book is forgotten because her blissful wonder hurts, and she doesn't know why. Brushing hair away from my forehead despite turning away from her, the woman who gave me life smothers me under her unwanted touch and intrusive eyes.

"Stop looking at me like that," I say, swatting her hand away.

Becka's eyebrows rise. She covers her mouth to keep from laughing.

"Don't treat me like that, Leighlee," Mom scolds. I hurt her feelings.

I scoot off the couch, step over blankets, and head up the stairs. "I'm taking a shower."

"I'm coming!" Becka shouts, following my lead.

"HAVE YOU talked to your brother?" Tommy's voice echoes through the speakerphone.

Two days have passed since Thomas called, and he hasn't reached out since. My best girl rolls her eyes. "No, I haven't."

"Neither have we. We call him every day, but—"

"I can't deal with all of this. I have a life and problems, too. Why don't you ever worry about me?" Becka falls back on my bed and blows overgrown bangs out of her eyes.

"Because I know you're safe," her mother answers sharply.

Becka hangs up the phone and turns the ringer off before shoving it under my pillow.

"We should do something today," she says. "Let's get out of the house and get sunburned. I'll call the boys."

Embarrassed with an unreasoning heart, I haven't spoken to Oliver since we hooked up. I'm too wrapped up in myself to deal with the other side of this sad, true love story.

I let him kiss my skin, and I dug into his. I wanted him so badly I begged. If Oliver hadn't stopped us, I'd have given him something that was never his to begin with.

But that's not the worst part.

I felt a flickering need for genuine kindness and care.

"What do you have in mind?" I sit up and hold a hand over my chest to keep from falling apart.

I look for my cell phone hidden in my sheets.

Tell me you love me, I text to Thomas.

"We should make a lemonade stand," Becka suggests. She goes into my closet and finds a piece of poster board left over from our science project last year. "Do you have any lemons?"

Don't make me, his reply reads.

"Umm …" I try to keep myself here with her.

"Is it a dumb idea?" She lays the white poster board on my bed, scented markers in hand.

I shake my head and smile, looking up. "No. It sounds fun. Mom probably has lemonade mix."

Tell me, I text him again.

"Good, because I can't stay inside anymore. It's summertime." Becka pulls her sleep shirt over her head, leaving herself topless. She goes through my closet, tossing a few tank tops to the carpet and searching deeper.

I wait for my phone to beep.

My best girl chooses a geo print tube dress her mom bought for me a few months ago. She lets her hair down from its messy ponytail and shakes it out.

"Get dressed, baby," she tosses a similar dress my way.

I hate the way she says baby. It's like he's here. Their voices are alike, and I can almost feel the way he would whisper it against my skin, in my ear … on my lips.

"Let's be barefoot, like we used to when we were little." She runs her fingers through washed-out pink strands and sprays beach waves on her ends. "Let's get dirty."

Thomas doesn't text me back, but reminiscing about unclean toes and playing outside until we smelled like puppies makes me smile. I open the top drawer of my nightstand, toss my phone in, and close it.

While I change into my summer dress, Becka separates my braid and smears lip gloss on my lips. She applies too much, and it gets on my teeth.

"Rebecka!" I look for something to wipe it off on.

She holds my face in her hands and presses our lips together instead. She opens slightly, but only enough to soak up shimmery color. It's sort of like him, too, but smaller and not nearly as deep.

It's over as soon as it started, and it's not weird or awkward or unusual. We're best friends.

Simple.

Maybe our time isn't running out.

In front of the mirror, Rebecka and I stand side by side. We're a fucking mess. Her hair is much worse than mine. It's higher on the left than the right, and she refuses to brush out the huge tangle at the back of her head. My hair is crimped at the ends from the braid, but the top is lifeless and flat. I have strawberry flyaways and too much static. But this is carefree and fun, and sort of who we really are.

This is how we started.

With the board and markers in hand, Becka opens my bedroom door and heads downstairs. I'm right behind her, until I hear my phone.

Standing in the doorway, I consider not answering it. I know it's him. Every part of me kick-starts and reaches outward for love.

I should keep walking—I should go and be and not think about him while we sell lemonade—but I don't. I turn and step toward my nightstand. I open the drawer and pull out my phone. I swallow my heart while I slide my thumb across the screen.

I love you. It's a rule.

"WHERE DID you get a slingshot?" I place my feet in her empty chair and extend my toes, soaking up the sunlight.

The air is noontime muggy and thick. We've had our lemonade stand up for a couple of hours, but the only people who've come by are my neighbors. We've made five dollars.

"Smitty bought it for me for my birthday." She rolls by on her skateboard, shoeless and sweaty. Her rumpled hair is in a bun, and she holds her dress up when she skates, showing too much thigh.

"Speaking of Smitty," she says with bad intentions in her tone, bringing her board to a halt behind me. She kicks it up into her hand. "He called me."

"Yeah." I tilt my head back and watch her upside down through green-rimmed, star-shaped sunglasses.

"He and Oliver are working at the beach all day. They want us to come by." She shrugs like she doesn't care.

"We should go," I say, not sure if I mean it or not, but knowing that I should.

My girl drops her board but doesn't jump back on. It rolls into my parents' lawn. Behind it, the willow tree branches are already so long, brushing a foot or two above the grass. Becka sits on my lap and looks at me, setting all playfulness aside.

"Do you think if we drive around ... Maybe ask Kelly or Valarie—"

"Becka," I stop her, even though the idea accelerates my heart pump.

She bites on her bottom lip and nods her head. "Let's go to the beach."

I can tell she doesn't really want to.

So I say, "Maybe tomorrow."

AFTER FOURTEEN days of silence, Becka and I have finally left the house. But being out in the open makes me feel so much more ... alone.

"Hey."

Pulled away from my thoughts, I look up at Oliver. He's a slight silhouette with the bright sun behind him. His rescue can is in his left hand, and he's in the standard orange-red shorts all the lifeguards wear.

I hold my palm over my brow and smile, grateful he can't see my watery eyes under my sunglasses.

"Hey," I say.

"I haven't seen you in a while," he says, shifting his footing.

I drop my hand and look out to the ocean. Becka's beside me, facedown, sun soaking. She turns her head at the sound of Oliver's voice and asks, "Where's your friend?"

"Around." He shrugs.

She leans up on her elbows. "With that girl Margo or what?"

He doesn't say anything until he looks over at me. "Can we talk?"

I snap the back of my girl's bikini top playfully and ask, "Will you be okay by yourself?"

She waves her hand, not bothering to look up. "Whatever."

We're quiet. Girls look, and it makes me smile because I know even surrounded by sun and sand, this boy is probably thinking about art or religion or something as complex.

Love.

"Do you know what you want?" he asks, setting his rescue can on the table outside of the snack bar. He searches the menu, contemplating.

"I'll get whatever you're getting," I say.

He waits for our food by the window instead of sitting with me while our fries cook. He says a few words to the girl who took our order. I try not to look at him. I stare at the graffiti engraved on the plastic table and at the people walking, riding, and running by the boardwalk. I definitely don't look down at the dock. But after a few minutes, my eyes naturally fall back on my skater boy.

There's a future with this person if I want it. Nice and neat, tied with a bow. Drug-free, drama-free, honest.

"I got you some ketchup." Oliver sets my fries and soda in front of me with a handful of packets.

"Thank you," I tell him.

He sits across from me eating his fries four and five at a time. He chews with his mouth closed and uses his napkin. He gets a drop of ketchup on his white tee shirt and curses.

"So, you want to talk?" I eat a fry. "About the last time we were together?"

He nods and takes a drink. "Yeah."

I eat another fry and wipe my hands on my thighs. "I was upset."

"I remember," he says.

"I shouldn't have taken advantage of you," I say, keeping my eyes down.

Oliver coughs on his soda. He wipes his mouth with his napkin and says, "Don't make me seem like I'm some victim," he jokes.

"I'm saving myself," I blurt out. "For marriage."

He nods.

That's it.

"I like you," I say. "But I kind of need some time. Maybe."

The right corner of his mouth lifts. He opens another packet of ketchup and squirts it on his fries.

"We've been going in circles since we were fourteen years old." I drink my soda until it slurps at the bottom of the cup.

"What now?" he sits back and crosses his arms over his chest.

I change the subject. "Is Smitty really dating that Margo girl?"

Clearing his throat, he drops his arms to the table. He rips the corner of a napkin. "She's just a girl."

I roll my eyes and laugh. I shake the ice in my paper cup. "Jackie said she saw them at the mall."

"They hang out." He piles all of our trash together and gets up to toss it out.

I follow with his rescue can. "Where did she come from?"

He rubs his face with the palms of his hands. "She's here for the summer. Staying with some family in Toledo. It's not a big deal."

We walk back to Becka in awkward silence. It's stupid, but I feel like he owes me more. He should have told me about this before Rebecka had to hear it from someone else.

When we get back to the beach, his best friend is with mine. She stands a few feet in front of him waving her arms around and wiping sadness away from under her sunglasses.

"Who is she?" Becka cries. Tears fall down sun-pink cheeks from behind her dark lenses.

Smitty shakes his head and crosses his arms, exhaling as his cheeks fill with air.

"Hal," she cries harder, pushing his shoulder. "Use your fucking words! Who the fuck is she?"

A few passers-by watch the confrontation. Mothers move their kids along while others stop and whisper and point. I walk faster, but Oliver reaches them before I do.

"You're a punk, you know that?" She tries to hit Hal, but I catch her arm.

"He's with her, Leigh." Her tone edges hysterical. "He's been with that girl and he won't even tell me."

"Becka," Smitty tries, sounding wounded.

"Get the fuck away from me!" she shouts.

He walks and Oliver goes with him.

CHAPTER
forty-three

July 14th.

It's Thomas's nineteenth birthday.

"We should go there, right, Bliss? I have to get more clothes anyway." Becka turns on her side in my bed and faces me.

With my blanket over her head like a nun, she's snuggled up safe. Her toes find mine under the sheets, and I remember painting them last night: razzmatazz red-pink for me and pale-turquoise for my girl. We shaved our legs and plucked each other's eyebrows. We recolored her hair, pink again, with dark violet tips and a little bit of green in her bangs. She even let me pin empty soda cans in her hair to see if it would curl.

It did, and it was beautiful.

"We should go," I encourage, pulling the sunrise-colored sheet over my shoulder. "You should see your mom. You haven't been there in four weeks."

"She's probably drunk," Becka says.

"She's sad," I remind her.

"Me, too." She sighs.

"Me, too," I say.

After we shower, she dresses in a pair of yellow shorts and a plain white tee shirt. I slip into a pair of black side-fringed denim cutoffs and a white button-up cami. I blow dry and curl my hair. She leaves her hair voluminous soda-can-curly.

Mom comes in without knocking and picks up our towels from the floor in my bedroom.

"Where are you guys going?" she gently pries.

Eyeliner in hand, I stop applying it on Becka's eyelid to say, "I can clean my own room."

She's happy I spend so much time at home. It took her a couple of weeks to realize that Becka and I need to do our own thing and back off, but she still hovers.

"It's fine, baby. I like doing this for you." She pats the top of my head. "So, where did you say you were going?"

"I didn't," I state evenly, returning to Becka's half-lined eyes.

"It's my brother's birthday." My girl speaks up. Her breath smells like Crest Fairies toothpaste.

"He's back from his road trip?" Mom's tone is questioning. She brushes some sand out of my bedsheets.

Becka turns her head to look at my mom. She has one eye lined and the other bare. "You look really pretty today, Mrs. McCloy." She turns back to me with a blank face.

Mom blushes. She smiles. She's really too easy.

"Okay, but not too late, Bliss." Mom stands with an armful of dirty clothes.

"Okay," I say more than cheerfully.

When we're ready to go, Becka and I argue over who's going to drive. After an entire morning of keeping my feelings on the back burner, my best friend sets me on fire when she sounds just like him.

"You're acting like a child, strawberry-blonde."

All at once, so fast, too hard, his absence hits me like a brick wall.

I would double over if she wasn't standing here.

Pain gnaws at my ribs from the inside. It burns through my veins, thick and rich, from head to toe. It laughs at my expense—stab, stab, stabbing—until I want to scream and stab back. At something. At everything. At him.

I clear my throat and put my sunnies on, separating a few of my berry curls to keep my hands busy.

"I'll drive." I leave my hair alone and search through my handbag for my keys.

A few tears I can't help settle on the frames on my sunglasses. I groan and drop my bag.

"Shit, Leigh. I'll drive. Calm down." Becka picks up my bag and heads toward her Jeep.

I chase after her. "I can drive."

My chin quivers, but I don't let her see. I have my keys in my hand. I jiggle them in the air. "I'm already starting the car."

She looks over her shoulder at me.

"I have the top down," I say optimistically with a forced, fake smile. "You know you want to."

She finally gives in and jumps into the Rabbit. I accelerate a few miles over, the speed limit and shift into third gear. Sweet summertime-scented air sweeps through my hair fluttering it around my head, giving me clarity I crave. Becka's sherbet-colored waves fly higher in the wind. We shake our heads and relish the sunlight. When I have to stop at a light, we take quick pictures with our phones.

A small part of me hopes to see the Continental in front of their house. I know it won't be, but I'm still disappointed when his space is empty save for an oil stain from a leak the Lincoln had a while back.

Tommy's Mercedes is in front of the garage. Lucas isn't here.

I park on the side of the house.

"We shouldn't stay long," Becka says, leaping out of my car. "Let's go get those corn on the cobs from that vendor at the beach. Extra butter. All the cheese. Super-hot chili."

I walk around the trunk of my car. I kick a rock, and my toes get dirty through my t-strap sandals. Becka takes my hand.

"Say yes," she says.

"Yes." I smile.

We take the steps hand in hand up to the porch. I keep my eyes away from the swing where Thomas and I first made our rules.

Becka walks right in and the smell of brewed coffee and Tommy's perfume sinks right in, giving me goosebumps. Everything is the same, utterly. The placement of the furniture, the pictures on the wall. I expected it to all look different. Be different.

The only thing out of ordinary is the atmosphere.

He's not home, and I can sense his absence here more than I have the entire time he's been gone, and I want to turn and run. I don't want to be anywhere near this place. His things. His room. His bed.

Tommy's in the kitchen. Her hands are on the island countertop where a mug of coffee steams in front of her.

"Hey, Mom." Becka walks in ahead of me. She pulls out a stool across from her mother and sits.

Tommy's head lifts up. She walks around the island, takes her daughter in her arms, and hugs her.

"This is exactly why I didn't want to come home." My girl doesn't mean it. She returns the embrace.

We move to the dinner table. Tommy brings the coffee pot and three mugs.

"I don't know what I'm supposed to do. Was I supposed to buy him a cake in case he comes home?" she asks, not necessarily looking for an answer.

"Mom." Becka groans.

Her mother continues, "What if he shows up and thinks none of us give a shit about him because I didn't buy a fucking cake for his birthday?"

"He's not coming home." Her daughter picks at her nail polish.

"That's why I didn't buy one. Your dad wants to toss all of Thomas's shit out on the lawn."

I'm not surprised.

"He talked to him," the woman of the house says nonchalantly.

Mine and Becka's heads snap up. My girl sits forward and asks, "When?"

Tommy sips from her mug. "A couple of days ago. Dusty called and your dad answered."

"What did he say?" Becka asks.

"What the fuck does Thomas ever say, Rebecka?" She runs her hand through her damp hair. "He told your dad to mind his own business and hung up."

Becka's shoulders fall. "He called dad to tell him to fuck off?"

"I don't know why he called," my boy's mom answers sharply.

Tommy's aged five years in a month. Her usually perfectly colored hair has roots, and a few grays are showing. She isn't wearing any makeup, and her manicure is less than stellar.

There's dust on the dinner table and dirty dishes in the sink. There are empty wine glasses on the counter, and the trash is full. No one is running up and down the stairs. No one is laughing. Baseball bags aren't by the front door. The TV isn't on, even for noise.

One delinquent changed the dynamic of this entire house.

"Your dad told him he was going to trace his credit card, and the conversation ended."

We head up the stairs, and his bedroom door is closed. Self-preservation isn't a concern, and I no longer want to run. I think about opening his door to crumble onto his bed. I debate whether or not it would make me feel better or make this that much worse. Touching his sheets. Lying my head on his pillow. Being inside of those walls. Our dividers.

I go in with Becka and jump on the bed.

"Does it feel good to be here again, or what?"

I sit beside her. "Yeah." Lie.

"It's weird without him here, right? I'm not fucking crazy for feeling this way, am I?"

I shake my head. "No."

Not a lie.

"DID YOU call Oliver?" My girl lifts her flat black and hot-pink beach cruiser into the trunk of my Rabbit.

"Yeah," I slip in behind the wheel and start the car. She tries to shut the trunk, but the bike is too big. "It's fine. Leave it. I'll drive slowly," I call out.

She jumps in. "Are they there?"

"Yep." I put the car in first and drive forward, away from Dusty's empty parking spot.

"Do you think Margo is there?"

I bite on my bottom lip. "Not sure."

She nods and sets her elbow on the door, gliding her hand up and down through the wind in waves. "If she is, I'm hitting her over the head with my board."

I roll my eyes and turn up the stereo, letting this week's annoying, can't-get-it-out-of-your-head pop song play too loudly.

The wind whips and tangles our hair while the trunk of the car bumps along the bike. We sing the lyrics in our most out-of-tune voices, and at a stop light, a man and his wife in the car next to us laugh while we get the words wrong and pretend we know what we're singing.

Top 40 isn't usually our thing.

This is the first time in years that I've just been Rebecka Castor's best friend. I'm Thaddeus and Teri McCloy's only child. I'm just a girl in a car singing shitty music. I have nowhere to be, nothing to hide, and no secrets in my pocket.

I'm just Bliss.

The air smells like salt water and sand as we curve around the mountainside, and in the distance, the ocean looks like diamonds. Wildflowers and shrubs decorate the world around us, and the sky is beautiful, spotless, and pristine. The sun is high, and cars are parked anywhere and everywhere. We pass surfers walking with their boards and paddles under their arm, their destination: the Pacific. We drive by families, tourists, and people riding their bikes, and kids with beach balls.

Life goes on.

With both hands on the wheel, I say, "I don't know what I want to do after high school."

She waves me away with a scoff. "So fucking what? We'll study stupid shit like Botany or Meteorology."

I smile. Not a lie.

"Logic," I offer.

Becka laughs loudly. All of her teeth show, and she holds her hands over her stomach. "Yeah, we'll major in logic since neither of us seem to have any."

"Folklore and Mythology!" I say with a giggle.

My girl stops laughing. "That's a good one."

She's dead serious.

I LEAVE my phone in the car.

"Do you think Smitty will be mad we're here?" I ask, straddling Becka's bike.

She drops her board to the ground and holds it still with her bare foot. She gathers pink and violet together into a ponytail at the top of her head. Her greenish bangs hang over her right eye.

"Who cares? This isn't his beach." She jumps on her skateboard and pushes away. "I don't see his name on it."

I pedal slowly behind skateboard virtuoso. She bends at her knees and holds her arms out at her sides for momentum. Most people move out of her way, but a few complain about her being on the sidewalk.

We roll down the beach, and my girl spots the corn man and stands straight to point. Her wheel gets caught on a rock.

Becka glides through the air in a mess of pink and green and purple and screams. She hits the sand with a loud thump, and her board flips end over end until it lands on the other side of the sidewalk. I skid to a halt and jump off the bike.

"Stop the corn guy!" she yells, holding her wounded elbow.

"Becka." I sigh, helping her up.

She claims her board and jumps right back on. Sand sticks to her knees, and her right elbow drips blood down her forearm into her palm. Instead of going straight to the vendor selling the Mexican corn, I follow her to the same concession stand Oliver bought me fries and a soda at a few weeks ago.

The girl behind the counter takes one look at us and freezes.

"Can I have some napkins, please?" Becka turns her arm over to get a better look at her injury.

I stare at the girl, who's nodding, and I know she knows who we are.

The brown-haired, freckle-faced girl watches until we sit at the dirty, been-carved-into plastic table with the cheap red umbrella over it.

"Awesome." Becka dabs her bloodied wound.

"That's her." I steal one of her brown recycled-paper napkins and help clean off her arm and hand. Some of it won't come off, so I lick a clean spot of the napkin and rub some more.

"Who?" Becka pulls her arm out of my grip but keeps her cut covered with her hand.

I sit back in hard plastic. I shake my head. "The girl at the window is Margo."

"Are you kidding, Bliss?" She turns toward me with hysteria behind her eyes.

I collect the blood-soiled napkins. "I saw her when I was here with Oliver, but he didn't say anything."

"How do you know?" She searches for the one who stole her not-in-a-relationship-boyfriend.

I'm about to shrug and say that it's probably not her, but fate is an evil bitch—spiteful like the suffering in my chest left from my boy. They probably work together, fate and suffering, changing expected outcomes and killing teenage dreams, rupturing hearts and hopes.

Fate steals the disappointment in my chest with suffering and then slaps Rebecka right across the face with it.

"Let's go." My heart is a hummingbird, fluttering nervousness.

Unaware of our presence, Smitty's suddenly at the window in his orange shorts and white tee, talking to freckle-face.

He sees Becka staring at him and his new girlfriend and moves away from the food window. Margo disappears from sight, only to reappear when she exits a side door and starts walking toward us.

A tear falls from the corner of my best friend's left eye, but it's not from sadness. She ripples with anger.

Smitty approaches us, and Rebecka takes a few barefooted steps in his direction and knocks the rescue can out of his hand. His expression is uncharacteristically put off and bothered. He picks up his can and shoves it under his arm.

"I'm not talking to you about this here," Smitty says lowly, but loud enough for me to catch.

"You're with her? Out in the open, everyone knows ... You're with that girl?" Heartbroken points toward Margo.

"I have to get back to work." His eyes meet mine as he tries to walk away. I know he hurts and loves Becka, but being a second choice is not easy.

Becka pulls on his shirt, and it splits at the neck.

The sound of stretching and tearing cotton gives me chills. I've done that same exact thing many times—pulled and tugged and torn and ripped until love finally faced me.

Smitty turns, carefully placing his hand on his not-girlfriend's hurt elbow and guides her from the crowd to the sand. I watch him verbalize with his eyes while she screams and points. She kicks sand and punches him until he holds on to her wrists and speaks so lowly I can't even read his lips.

I don't need to read Becka's.

"I fucking hate you," she sobs. "You're doing this, not me. Not me, Smitty!" He shakes his head.

Too frustrated to stay quiet, clearly enough for me and everyone else to hear, he says "You're fucking Petey."

Becka smacks him as Margo rushes past me.

I hurry toward my friend. Smitty tries to keep them apart, but Becka's unhinged and Margo's limbs are too long.

Rebecka manages to get past Smitty and hit Margo in the face, but freckles has at least a foot on her height-wise. No effort at all is made when the brunette pulls her fist back and lunges forward, decking my best friend in the mouth.

Becka falls on her bottom, and her busted mouth bleeds down her chin, onto her white tee.

Gasps and screams come from the crowd of people who have circled around us. Down the sidewalk, security guards on their bicycles make their way over. An older man in bright blue swim trunks points in our direction.

Becka spits blood into the sand. Smitty bends down to her, but she pushes him away as she stands and sprints toward the enemy. I step forward to help, to do something, but my wrist is pulled, and I'm pushed back.

"Are you fucking kidding?" Oliver says as he runs past me.

Some grown-ups break up the fight. An old man holds my girl back by her forearm. With a busted lip, she tells him he's hurting her, but he doesn't let up.

If the boys were here, this would never have happened.

Smitty and Oliver stand with two security guards and Margo. Her hair's pulled and knotted, and her arms are crossed over her chest. The left strap of her tank top is torn and there's blood on it. They ask her questions, and she points at Becka but shakes her head.

Smitty sighs and shrugs and says, "It was a misunderstanding."

The man holding my girl finally lets her go when one of the security officers beckons her over.

"I'm going to kill that bitch," she mumbles under her breath as we walk.

"What happened?" Brad, the bicycle security guy asks us.

While she explains, I notice Margo's wandered back to her job. The person who must be her boss has met her by the side door and is wiping his hands off on his white apron, looking over at us.

"What's your name?" Brad asks me.

I look away from treasonous boys and toward the fake-cop. "Leighlee McCloy," I say hesitantly.

He takes his sunglasses off to get a better look at my face. He has raccoon eyes. "Judge McCloy's daughter?"

My shoulders fall. I'm going to be in so much trouble if he tells my dad. "Yes."

"Get out of here before I call your dad to come get you," he says.

Becka and I straighten up. I smile widely. She squeezes my hand.

Brad points a finger in my face. "I don't want to see you here for the rest of the day."

We take off running through the sand, past disloyal boys, toward Becka's skateboard and my bike. I stand up with my feet on the pedals and the salty, sandy air breezing through my strawberry-blond while my bleeding best friend pushes and rolls, pushes and rolls.

I pedal ahead of her so she can grab the back of my seat. People move out of our way unhesitantly. I look back and she's smiling.

I swerve but correct myself. "Your tooth is chipped again!"

"What?" She holds onto the cruiser seat with one hand and touches her mouth with the other. "No!" she yells with a smile, all chipped and swollen and bloody-ruby under tangled emerald bangs.

My beat-up girl rolls off the curb and kick-pushes toward the car. By the time I get there, she's in the front seat, checking out her grill.

"I can't believe this happened, Leigh," she whines, kicking her feet.

I laugh and unlock the trunk, trying to figure out how to fit the bike in.

"Becka—" I call when Tanner comes out of nowhere and takes the cruiser from me.

"Need some help?" he asks.

"Thanks," I say, taking a few steps back.

Tanner maneuvers the bike into my trunk even better than Becka did the first time. He's wearing a hat, but his blond hair sticks out from beneath it, sun-bleached and sea-thirsty.

He has a scar on his eyebrow where Dusty hit him last year.

"Good?" he asks, closing the trunk as much as he can.

"Thanks, Tanner," I say. I smile as I open the driver's side door.

Becka turns in her seat. "Hey, have you seen my brother around?"

I close my eyes and take a breath.

"Nah," he replies, lifting his hat and running his fingers through beachy blond hair. "I saw Pete at the gas station with Ben, though."

My girl practically stands in the seat. "Petey? He's back in Newport?"

Tanner laughs. "I guess."

"Thomas wasn't with him?" My heart pounds hard and fast. I can feel it in the tips of my teeth.

"I haven't seen Castor in a while." He steps away from the car. I open the door with heavy arms while Becka flips onto her butt and types away on her phone.

"Come to my house tonight." I shake my head, about to decline when he says, "I'm having a party. Cruise by. Free beer."

"We'll be there," Becka speaks up from inside the car.

"Sweet," he says before jogging off.

I slip into the car and stick the key into the ignition. "Really?"

She shrugs. "We can ask around about my brother."

I shift into reverse and sigh. "Where to?"

"Let's get ready at my house." she answers, back to typing on her phone. "Your mom is starting to freak me out."

THE STREET Tanner lives on is bumper-to-bumper parked and stuffed, and there's no missing which house is his. Small, red, lit up, and loud, his home overflows with a crowd. There are people all over his lawn and in the street. They barely move out of the way so I can roll by.

I look for the Lincoln, but don't see it.

Ben's Benz is here. So is Valarie's piece of shit Sentra.

"Park on the fucking sidewalk." Becka laughs.

I find a spot at the end of the block as my girl digs through her purse. She presents an orange prescription bottle and shakes a few pink pills into the palm of her hand.

"They're my mom's. She has anxiety or whatever," she says, dry swallowing.

I lock the doors and meet my girl on the sidewalk. She has a bottle of her dad's rum in one hand and holds her other out for me. My heels tap on the concrete. It's uneven in places, but I'm good in heels. The humidity in the air from the sea being so close dampens my skin and flattens the little bit of curl in my hair, but it feels nice.

I'm nervous.

Two houses down from the party, Becka stops and screws off the top to the bottle, tossing it over her shoulder. She takes a larger-than-her swig and passes it to me. I sip.

I recognize a few people on the lawn and smile, but I don't stop to talk. Heavy beats and low-slick lyrics fill the stifled air. Inside the house smells like spilled beer and burning bud. People are too closely crowded, and I have to push my way through.

"Do you see anyone?" she yells over the music.

I look over my shoulder to find her eyes already hooded over and high-slanted. She's smiling like an idiot and looks more like her brother than ever before. She passes me the bottle. I swallow a mouthful.

Stopping in the middle of what must be Tanner's living room, I look around. This is the youth of the nation: torrid, displaced, slutty, and drunk. It's the same people doing the same thing every weekend, promising themselves they won't grow up to be like their parents and swearing that one line won't change shit. This person fucks that person, only to sleep with their best friend next weekend. Disease spreads, physically and mentally. Their laughs are corroded and their skin is melting.

It's boys in men's bodies and girls doing grown-up things. We're all clueless and seeking, taking too many chances.

I hate knowing that Thomas is the epitome of these choices. He's the motherfucking king of this lifestyle.

Right now it's fun—*fuck it, we're young*—but when things get serious, when it's time to grow up, then what?

Thomas won't be the king of shit, and Valarie will be the girl who fucked her way through high school. Mixie will always wonder about the baby she didn't have, and Casper will have to live with the guilt of introducing all of these kids to the big, bad, scary world.

I press the palm of my hand to my forehead.

Where the hell are you, Dusty?

I'm a different kind of monster than these people. I'm crafty. I'm sneaky. I don't fuck around, but *I fuck around*. These people rot from the outside in; I'm the opposite. My insides are made of tar and oil, blended with a little love for my boy. My heart lacks compassion for everyone but him, and when we get older and these lost people need to be found, they'll probably come to a person like me for answers. I'll be their therapist or their doctor … I'll be their judge, when all along I was the girl who sat back and let it all happen.

"There's Tanner!" Rebecka yells over the music.

I head in his direction. Someone spills beer on my shoe, another almost burns me with a cigarette. Every foot of this house is occupied by someone, making it nearly impossible to get to the kitchen untouched.

I take another drink from Becka's bottle of sorrow.

There are as many people in the backyard as there are in the front. I thought I recognized a few faces, but they're starting to all blend together. Everyone looks the same. Acts the same. Sounds the same.

"Who are all of these people?" I bend down and ask in my girl's triple-pierced ear.

She shrugs before taking another swig. She cringes and speaks, "Who knows."

Tanner spots us from the other side of the kitchen. He calls my name and waves us over, but Kelly and Mixie run into us first.

"What are you guys doing here?" Kelly's hair is longer and less silk-like. Her dress hangs too loosely, and her eyes are dose-open and beamy. I haven't seen her all summer, and like everyone else, this season has aged her.

"We were invited," I say. Someone bumps me from behind.

"Have you seen my brother or not?" Rebecka's unsteady on her feet.

"Not." Kelly looks bored.

Mixie pulls apart her split ends. She looks the same as she always has: washed-up and bittersweet.

"You should ask Dolly," Kelly adds.

Mixie rolls her eyes and drops the ends of her hair. "Let's find Cas," she says.

"Who the fuck is Dolly?" Becka asks. She steps in front of me like she subconsciously knows I'm going to need to be guarded from this conversation.

But I already know. I've always known. I'll always fucking know.

Kelly steps up on her tippy-toes and looks around the small house with a silly smirk on her face. "Over there," she points to the other end of the house.

In a blue-and-white striped bandeau and navy high-rise matelot shorts, her hair is long and dark, and her skin is pale. With a beer in one hand and a cigarette in the other, this girl looks lost like everyone else.

"Are you Dolly?" Becka asks, entering this girl's circle with me in tow.

"Sure," she says. Her voice is low and even.

"My brother is Thomas Castor. Have you seen him?" Becka blinks too many times.

Her face is so static and unaffected that it's hard to look at her. She's pretty, but kept away, like looking through a veil. She is seduction and shame.

She's just like him.

"I haven't seen that dirty boy. Who are you?" she asks.

Someone bumps into me again.

"I'm his sister." Becka moves a little closer. I grab her arm.

"Can't help you."

"You fucked him, but you haven't seen him since?" Rebecka yells. She drops the bottle of rum and tries to shake me off.

My best girl's outburst grabs the attention of everyone near us. They're all looking, waiting, and I've already been in one fight today. I don't think my body will even work on command right now.

The girl points her beer bottle at Becka and says, "Get the fuck away from me."

Pill-careless and alcohol soaked, Becka pulls down on my wrist until I let go. She turns away from me and bumps right into Petey.

He holds her at arm's length. "Hey, pretty in pink, getting into trouble?"

I've kept every secret, told every lie … I do everything for Thomas, and this is where I am: alone and resentful in a room full of monsters.

I'm full to the brim and decaying.

Tears pour down, unconfined. I don't make a noise or move. I just let them slide down my warm cheeks.

Dolly laughs, and I want to pick up the rum bottle and smash her face. I want to ask if she felt it while Thomas fucked her, because I feel it every single time he fucks me.

In my chest.

In my lying soul.

In my eyes and my arms and my kneecaps. I feel it in every single fiber of my being.

I wipe cries away and look around searching for nothing. What I need isn't here. What I need is doing his own thing without me. What I need didn't care enough to take me with him.

He wants me to stop loving him. Fine.

Done.

I'm done.

Ben's suddenly touching my elbow. I pull my arm away from him as I turn. He looks concerned, and I detest him for it.

"What?" I ask, trying to sound indifferent. "Where have you been?"

Petey rubs his thumb under Becka's lip, checking out her tooth.

She broke it, fighting for Smitty, I want to say. *She doesn't love you wholly, Pete,* I want to scream until my lungs bust. *Fucking beware.*

The truth is not easy.

My truth: I love a lost cause. I love a failure, and I lost myself in him when I was nine years old.

"You shouldn't be here," Ben says. He hands me his beer, probably just to get me to do something other than stand and stare at how black his eyes are.

I drink the whole bottle.

Jammed and pressed against people, I can't breathe. The back of my neck sweats, and I search the room on my tippy-toes, over heads toward the open front door. I'm about to make a run for it when Valarie pushes her way between me and Ben.

"Does your mom know you're out so late, little sister?" Val asks mockingly. She reaches for Ben's hand and laces their fingers together.

"Be nice," he tells her with a smile.

Any calm Rebecka regained with Pete around vanishes the second she catches sight of Casper behind Valarie.

Pete tries to pull Becka by her oversized black shirt, but she shoves him away.

"Where's Dusty?" she demands.

Casper looks around, waiting for someone to tell him this is a joke.

"Am I his babysitter?" he asks.

"No, you're his drug dealer." Rebecka spits in his face.

Petey forces Becka behind him with a shove.

"She's drunk," Pete says with heavy breaths and tensed arms, prepared and willing.

Casper wipes his face off on the sleeve of his shirt. He breathes out of his nose and smirks at Pete.

"I don't know where your brother is, Becka."

He's lying. A liar knows a liar.

I don't wait around for an explanation or reenactments once Casper walks away. I turn and leave, and it's Petey who chases after me through the door and out to the lawn. He hugs me, and I hug him back. I don't worry about appearances, because there are none. I am totally stripped of everything but the complete agony I feel.

My phone starts to ring. I know it's him.

"You going to answer that?" my guy's best friend asks, taking a step back from me.

I wipe my face with the back of my hand and slip my singing phone into my pocket. "It's probably my mom or something."

"I can take Rebecka home if you need to go." He reaches forward and wipes my eyes for me. "It's sad when little sisters cry."

My phone starts ringing again.

Petey and I share another smaller hug, and then he walks.

With my heart in my throat, I drop my car keys twice before finally getting the door unlocked. I shut myself in and sit in silence for a few seconds between Thomas' call going to voicemail and the time it takes him to dial my number again.

I pull it out of my pocket and look at the screen.

Accept or decline.

I know what I need to do and say to him. I just have to do it.

"What?" I pick up. "What do you want, Thomas?"

"Where the fuck are you, Leigh?"

"Tanner's," I answer.

With the phone on my ear, I drop my forehead to the steering wheel.

"I can't be this person anymore," I say.

He laughs.

My heart shatters.

"We're not good together. And you don't think enough about me." I cover my mouth with my hand and sob.

"Leighlee—"

"I can't anymore, Thomas."

"Don't fucking do this," he insists. "I'll burn that whole motherfucking town down."

His attempt is hollow and falls on surrendered ears.

EVERY MEMORY I have worth remembering can be tied to Thomas. Everything I've done has revolved around our relationship.

I spent time with Rebecka to be with him. I went to school to be near him. I stayed on the phone all night to talk to him. I told my dad I accidentally broke the lock on the back door, but it was actually my boy. He lit my sparklers, he played hide-and-seek, and he gave me my first sip of alcohol. Thomas showed me why three joints are better than one. He was the first boy I ever slept next to.

He was my first kiss. My first love.

Memory after memory plays like an old film behind my closed eyelids— broken, scratched, and not completely clear. One after another. Good and bad.

I can't deal.

I jump out of bed and open my closet. I dig through all of the clothes on the floor until I find it, the first present he ever really gave me.

My favorite thing ever.

With half-shut eyes and tired tendons, I take the hoodie downstairs. After all of this time, smoky-vanilla and uncheckable-trouble lingers on washed-worn cotton.

I miss him so much more.

I open the washing machine and shove the hoodie in. I twist off the top of the detergent and pour half of the bottle on the navy blue baseball hoodie. I turn the water on. I set it on heavy.

But I can still smell him in the air.

The washer fills up with hot water, and I keep waiting for the smell of cigarettes and mint gum and disorder and crazy love to go away. It's pore-deep in my skin, though, and thread-tied in wet cotton.

I unscrew the bleach and pour the entire bottle in.

The fumes choke me, but that doesn't stop me from looking into the tub just to make sure midnight blue turns patchy-purple-pink-white. I cough and my eyes painfully start to run. I reach into the washer drum and submerge the sweater completely. Hot water and bleach pierce my broken cuticles. Tears slide off my nose into soapy liquid. When it's full, it begins to spin.

With dripping, burning hands, I turn off the washing machine and pull out my sweater. I fall on my bottom with my back against cold white metal and hold Thomas's hoodie against my chest, bleach spotting my black romper, and I cry.

I can't smell him anymore.

Two DAYS later my fingers still smell like bleach.

"Do you need my help with breaking down the basement?" I ask, putting the orange juice back into the refrigerator.

Mom ties her hair into a ponytail before pouring herself a cup of coffee. She's dressed in one of dad's old flannels and has excitement in her eyes over the gym they're going to build down there.

"It's okay." She passes behind me to get the creamer out. "Where did you get that dress?"

She slips her finger under the halter. I step away from her before she spills black java on my white eyelets.

"I bought it a while ago." Lie. It's from Tommy.

"It's pretty. Do you have plans?" She takes a hesitant sip from her mug.

I shake my head. "Not today."

"If you need me, your dad and I will be down below all day." She waves over her shoulder on her way out of the kitchen.

I take my orange juice up to my room and lie stomach down on my bed and am taking the "How Do You Know He's The One" test in Seventeen Magazine when I hear the familiar engine's rumble.

My heartbeat flies. My cheeks redden. My skin tingles. My shoulders straighten.

I know.

Dusty's here, ready to burn everything down.

CHAPTER
forty-four

"When did you get back?" I run my fingers through my mother's willow tree, keeping my voice low and my head down. Long, green velvet leaves tickle my arms, and chills rush from the tips of my fingers through my elbows.

"Just now," he says, walking behind me, peeking between the willows. "I came here first. I haven't been by my house."

I glimpse over my bare shoulder, chancing a look. Thomas' eyes are tired and his skin is colorless. His normally short blond-brown hair is long and dirty, curling slightly over his ears. The black jeans his legs are in and the gray tee shirt his thinner-than-usual chest is covered with are brand new.

He looks disgustingly beautiful. Perks of a sinner who has money.

"Leigh, I said I was sorry," he apologizes, swatting at tree branches.

You always are.

"It's not like you're my girlfriend."

I turn around and Thomas is closer than I anticipated. He's almost touching me, surveying my movements with hopelessly dark, apologetic eyes and slumped shoulders. There's a cigarette behind his left ear, and I know he carries a more disgraceful addiction in his pocket.

"You're right," I argue. "I'm your victim."

"I'll always want you," he whispers, brushing his nose along the ridge of my jaw.

His sudden proximity is overwhelming after time apart. I don't have a moment to adjust before he takes my hand and presses my palm against the pulse point in his neck.

"Do you feel that? Do you feel how fast it beats?"

I do.

"You make my heart flutter, princess."

I feel it.

He's further gone than he's ever been, and his eyes are imperceptible black, but love's pulse is as sure and quick under my touch as it's always been.

This, I know.

Thomas removes my hand from his neck and kisses my knuckles. He flashes his curved smirk, turning my butterflies to pins.

"You're high," I whisper.

"I am."

He smiles.

I move away from him, extending my hand to tickle the willow. "Were you with her?"

"With who, Bliss?" he asks, losing the grin.

I laugh. And not because this is funny, but because this is pathetic.

"Don't call me that," I say, shaking my head in disbelief before turning away.

Unimpressed with my built walls, I feel him studying my every move and detail trying to find his way in. It's surreal to be able to smell him again: dank green grass and Doublemint. I've tried hard to forget this scent, but I used to love it on my own clothes, in my hair, all over my skin. I used to savor it.

That was before.

I close my eyes, imagining for a moment that my heart isn't broken, that he loves me as much as I love him. I try to convince myself behind shut eyes that Thomas doesn't continuously choose drugs over me. I play myself a fool by believing one day it will only be him and me.

"What do you think?" I cry, brushing tears away as they fall.

His silence slaughters.

"What do you want to hear?" he finally asks softly. Thomas reaches out, claiming me. "Who do you want me to be?"

Whispers of forever and outcome touch the spot below my ear with his lips. "When you turn eighteen, everything will be different, Leighlee."

Excuses.

Like he never left.

But he did.

"You look pretty in this dress. Let me take it off and love you," he begs, declares, and promises. "Let me be with you."

I know he loves me. I never doubt his love. I doubt his intentions and respect. I distrust his motives and allegiance.

Love?

I smother in dictating love.

He's love's traitor.

"My parents are home," I say.

Thomas leans down and kisses the side of my throat, running his hand up the back of my white dress. He tugs the hair at the nape of my neck. "What did you do while I was gone?" he asks, his voice calm as tension rolls through him.

I laugh sorrowfully in his arms. "You mean, who was I with when you took off for over a month?"

Thomas groans in my ear, pulling my hair a little harder. He tightens his fingers into a fist and presses his nose to my jaw. "I swear to God." He breathes. "I'll kill him."

I grip onto his arm and dig my nails into his skin. The bricks stacked higher every night he was gone, and like that, I crumble.

"No one," I say, moving my hand underneath his chin. Forcing him to look at me, I hold Thomas by his face.

This isn't the boy I grew up loving; this is a man who brings me along for his ride.

"Because I love you." I refuse to allow fear into my voice. "Because I love you, nobody else will ever touch me. Even though you are constantly touched."

He closes his eyes, shaking his head with a small smirk. We're still pressed near. I can feel his words on my skin. "I haven't been with anyone."

My heart cracks, and I hate him for this.

His eyes open, and I miss blue.

Thomas' grip on my hair loosens, but he gathers me completely to his chest. I'm held until everything I've heard and felt, wondered and worried, decided and become in his absence, dissipates. He holds me until there is nothing between us but my dress and his shirt.

Love is fucked-up, but love is all there is.

Thomas flattens his right hand against the small of my back, pressing and keeping me close. He drags his nose slowly up the side of mine and kisses my top lip.

"Come with me," he whispers.

I breathe in his words, and when I exhale my reply, it's easy.

"Okay," I say.

And it doesn't feel a thing like falling.

THOMAS WAITS in the Lincoln while I run inside, grab my shit, and lie my lies like nothing ever changed.

Only now I walk out to him in the daylight.

Relaxed behind the wheel, long-gone-love has his arm stretched across the bench seat as I approach. He smirks when he sees me and makes me open my own door.

"Where are we going?" I ask, getting in.

Starting the car, "Portland," is all he replies.

Suffering in silence that's too close and only broken by coke-cold sniffles, I stare out the windshield while Thomas drives.

It's maddening.

At least love has an excuse for being unbearable. He's spun to the fucking sun, but at least he knows where we're headed. I got into this car without any real idea. I may have just seen my parents for the last time. Adrenaline fueled by the thought that we maybe just left for real courses through me, anxious around a heart that beats for the boy across from me despite all his self-centered sins.

Slow and steady, I focus on the pattern I taught myself the first time Thomas left me while he merges onto US-20. Regrets impend and homesickness for him yearns under my skin. Frustration and hesitance peck like an impatient vulture at my backbone and my reason, my nature, the point of all this won't even look at me.

I roll my window down.

Holding white eyelet cotton in place with my left hand as fresh air blows through, I force my nervous heart down into my chest with years of practice, hiding it from the person it's flying high on. I have no idea what's waiting for us almost three hours away, but I settle in.

Because knowing hasn't ever changed anything.

We're just past Corvallis when my phone vibrates in my purse.

One new message from Oliver.

Hey.

In the corner of my eye, Thomas leans back slightly. Loosening his grip, he drives carelessly with just the heel of his right hand, and arrogance stifles the space between us. He rests his free hand over the bitch in his front pocket, and I fight back below the belt.

Hey, I reply.

Just after one o'clock, sunlight surrounds us on all sides.

We've been on the road an hour and a half, and Dusty's leaned back, brushing his fingers back and forth through his unwashed hair. It's grown long since graduation, but I stop that train of thought in its tracks.

I don't look directly at him. I refuse to give him my eyes, but in the corner of my vision, the stretch of muscle and skin and bone from his elbow to his wrist is smooth and touch-tempting. His jaw is hard-set and so are his black eyes, and for a second, the thought that he knows what's waiting wherever he's taking me is a comfort. I consider turning and facing him, trying to talk, but it's gone the second he sniffs.

It's a pathetically small sound, and I hate it with the deepest parts of myself, because that's Her showing off her grip on my boy. That sound is deficiency and subjugation and weakness because she's destroying love, and the parts of me that don't hate him want to reach over and brush his dirty hair back. I want to ask where his hat is and kiss up-all-night-for-too-many-nights eyelids, and comfort this person with the cool softness I know he needs.

But then he sniffs again.

I cross my legs away from love and lock my eyes on moving trees.

Because all Dusty does is misuse my heart.

And there are still parts of me that want nothing more than to make it better.

SUNLIGHT BURNS bright as we exit into busy downtown Portland.

I've been here a few times, but never with Thomas. I recognize some streets and buildings as we pass them, but my stomach knots with that endless, terrible-anxious feeling that only comes when you're lost.

And my addiction still won't acknowledge me.

Blowing out a breath and measuring another one in, I comb my fingers through wind-blown curls while he switches lanes. My legs are tired and my feet are asleep from being in a car too long. My composure wears thinner with every mile, but I'm not giving in. When fight-or-flight kicked in under the willow, I picked fight and I meant it.

I chose this battle and I can hold my own in it.

Nerves are nothing I can't handle. I'm fine.

Until my phone rings, and the sound it makes for Becka fills the Continental.

Fear of the unknown, and guilt from lies on top of lies fade, weak compared to the shame that crushes my shoulders. All I can think of are blanket forts and un-bought birthday cakes, a house that's nothing like a home, and how much the boy I'm running away with hurt my best friend.

"Answer it," he says casually.

He knows it's her, and as I look from the pink sherbet and bright sunshine smiling through his absence on my phone over to abysmal-black eyes still locked on the road, my heart sinks for miles. My throat closes while my voice sticks in my windpipe, and love-born pain and anger throttle me.

I can't do this, I want to tell him. *How can I do this?*

How do you this?

Thomas turns right down a street I've never been on. His voice sounds hollow and irritably edged when he speaks again.

"Answer your phone, L."

Weighed down with years of breaking, my heart plummets. My toes curl against wedges and my fingers clench up. My arms tense so tightly they ache, and I close my eyes, straining for every bit of calm I can piece together. I force the phone to my ear, because my girl is calling, and she was by my side every second love wasn't.

"What's up?" I answer.

City miles breeze across my face and then leave me smothered as I roll my window up, hoping to hide the sounds of traffic.

"Hey," Becka says. "What are you doing?"

"Getting dinner," I lie. "What are you doing?"

"Watching a movie. I'm bored. Let's go to the beach."

Behind my eyelids, I can picture her clearly in my mind, hanging off her mom's sofa upside down, the purple ends of her hair brushing thick carpet. I wonder if she's still drinking out of straw glasses.

"I can't." Not a lie. "Dad has some alumni friends in town and we have to go to this banquet thing."

Thomas doesn't make a sound. He doesn't stretch or shift. He doesn't even sniffle, but I feel his temper heat the small space around us. Bitterness fills the enclosed air and sticks to my lungs like the scent of hot asphalt.

Breathing stings.

"Oh." His sister sighs on the other end of the phone, and I silently beg her not to ask any more questions. "Lame," she continues.

I'm deplorably thankful.

"That sucks. Call me tomorrow?"

"I will."

"I love you to the moon and back, Leighlee Bliss." Best-friend-confident, the smile in her voice rings through wireless waves making a tear roll hot and fast down my cheek.

Every day Dusty was gone, we were together, and now he's sitting where she should be. I might not ever get her back, and he doesn't even care.

Two more tears fall, and I swipe them away.

Love is the ruthless opposite of everything fair.

Choosing love will not be forgiven.

"I love you, girl," I tell her.

I lower the phone to my lap after we hang up, and resentment chokes my lungs. Forcing my tears to stop, I bite my lip and breathe through wanting to strangle the stranger next to me. He's close enough that I could touch him if I reached over, but in reality, I'm totally alone now.

Even at my very lowest when he was gone, I never felt as alone as I do right here.

With every cautious breath, my grip stumbles along a dangerous edge. Reality becomes a place more than a state of being, like sanity or insanity are steps I could take. Coming unhinged would be easier at this point than snapping my fingers.

Inhaling as deeply as I can, I hold it until calm touches my heart again and composes impulsive hate.

The car slows simultaneously, turning, and then stops. Opening my eyes, I squint through too-bright sunshine to find Portland sidewalks busy with late afternoon life. Black suits with briefcases stroll alongside hipsters in cardigans and cutoffs. Parents dole out ice cream cones and friends giggle over cell phones. Shops and restaurants line the block, and at the corner, The Hotel Andra stands nine stories tall.

I know without a single word and countless new questions, it's where we're heading.

Silent as he's been for hours, Thomas gets out. His gait is indifferent, his posture careless, and his eyes avoidant as he walks around the front of the car. The wind blows, and I can see the shape of his body through his shirt. The top of his ribcage stands out under black cotton, and I want to cry.

Pressing my lips closed, I hold it in with everything else as he comes to my side of the Lincoln and opens the door.

Love doesn't offer his hand.

I don't wait for him to.

FOLLOWING THOMAS through the glass double doors, into the low-lit lobby, I feel the concierge's eyes on me, but my boy doesn't stop at the desk. I follow him straight to the elevators, and even though we're not rushing, it feels like everything is happening really, really fast.

Couples and small groups talk and laugh quietly as we pass. The whole place smells like cherry maple, mahogany and rosewood, gardenia candles and new money, and reality—the fact that I have no fucking idea what's about to happen—grows exponentially heavier. The ride here was uncomfortable in the extreme, but this place is completely foreign.

I enter an elevator behind Thomas, and when the doors close, he sticks his hands in his pockets and looks up. Clasping my own hands behind my back, I remain just as quiet as my monster while numbers chime with every floor we pass. My head spins with how we got here. I think about prom, and I remember drinking from a cup I knew was spiked without hesitation because it was from this person. I think about sitting on his lap while he smoked joints and following him into streetlamp light when I was thirteen years old.

My choices with Dusty have always been risky, but okay because I was with him. I could trust him.

And here I am, still following him, trusting him over my own judgment.

But he's a legal adult now.

Love's graduated from punk-hoodlum to actual criminal, and I'm more than a hundred miles from home. I'm a matter of steps from following my heart into some hotel room without a single clue who or what is inside. It occurs to me for the first time that maybe Thomas' friends don't know where he's been, and the thought of strangers, lurid and dirty and grown with their habits spread out behind some locked door, sends terror crawling through my veins.

The elevator stops on the top floor and the boy who usually can't keep his

eyes or hands or any part of who he is to himself around me steps off without missing a beat.

I don't fight the pull when my feet follow without order from my brain. I double my wedge-steps to keep up with crooked devotion.

Softly glowing lights line both sides of the hallway, tinting walnu-colored carpet and ivory-hued walls dusty gold. Everything looks antique and extravagant at the same time, and it's thickly quiet. The whole long corridor feels laden with secret-keeping.

Ahead of me, Thomas' steps are unrushed and impassive, but his black-on-black low-tops don't drag. His stride is indolent, but aware and unswerving. I try to ignore my nerves as we pass door after door. I trade fear for imagining what it might cost to stay here a night.

But I can't.

Wondering who or what waits for him, for us, eats at me. Fear spins pupil-black, coke-white dizzying scenarios through my head, filling my apprehension with blank stares, greedy hands, and powder. Everywhere.

Finally at the end of the hall, I stop as trouble does, and he tugs his wallet from his back pocket. For the two seconds it takes him to pull a key-card out and unlock the door, I can't breathe. My heart can't even beat.

Don't be afraid, I pray.

My pulse doesn't pick up again until Thomas pushes the door open and stands back waiting for me to enter what I know is an empty room.

I step inside on tired legs to find no strangers or unwanted faces, just my boy's Yankees hat on the floor. One of Ben's hoodies is draped over a lounge chair and there's a phone charger on the table mixed with half-crushed cigarette packs, headphones, a pen, and empty coffee cups. I breathe in, and the room smells like linen, recycled air, and hiding. There's music coming from the iPod dock in the far corner, and a voice layered over foreboding notes supplicates and solicits through our silence.

It's Radiohead, but I don't know the song.

Dusty's phone rings. I glance behind me as he answers it and closes the door, but he speaks too softly for me to hear. He walks to the opposite side of the room while dismal and disjointed minor chords creep louder through the air. Provocative and ominous lyrics echo dark foreshadows in my ears, and unease trickles from where my conscience exists. It seeps into my bloodstream in cold little drips as I lay eyes on the unmade bed across from me and my backbone slips a tremble.

I keep it straight as I step forward.

With gutting curiosity, I walk a straight line to the mess of heavy navy blankets, stark white sheets, and messy pillows. A spiral notebook that looks like it was tossed on the corner of the king-sized bed catches my attention and I look over my shoulder at Dusty. His back is to me and he's still on his phone, and it all makes sense.

He didn't come home today.

He might not have known if he'd return to this room with or without me, but he didn't fucking check out of it. He didn't take any of his things. He didn't even stop the music.

Turning back to disheveled covers that my secret's probably disintegrated and diminished into more than slept in, I grab the notebook I've never seen and flip it open. While he speaks in disquiet tones, I scan the pages and let sick truth spread through me. His script varies, and there are scratched out phrases and places where his words stray from light blue lines. I stop when I see *love* and *can't* and *baby*, but I'm unable to make out too much before my eyes close, fighting tears so hot they burn.

My heart hardens like stone behind iron ribs, and my blood courses like boiling mercury. Sadness sharpens into pure rage, and a relentless, insistent ache for the source of all this agony to hurt like I do.

I turn again, and my presently-absent soul still has his back to me. He laughs and there is nothing warm about it.

Gritty organ-key tones, too many drums, and incensing guitars cloud louder as I step forward over scattered pieces of sullen, selfish love. I step on his things, and every step feels like walking wrath, like I am patience lost.

Intent to be heard and to hurt, I snatch the iPod from its dock and fling it as fast and hard as I can at Thomas.

Time stops in the second before plastic technology hits the wall next to him and shatters on impact. It makes a tiny mark on the wall and split-apart shards hit my boy's shoulder. He doesn't duck, but a rush I've never experienced flows through me.

Thomas doesn't take the phone from his ear, but he's stopped talking, and when he turns around, the smug set of his lips enrages me. Vengeance burns the back of my tongue, filling my throat and mouth with wrath so strong I could spit fire.

We're finally here.

There is no love in this room.

Locking my eyes on nothing but black, I pull a breath, and when I speak, I don't recognize my own voice.

"Hang up the phone."

Thomas doesn't move, and I burn into fury faster than I can blink.

"Hang up the phone!" I shout, hurling his notebook at him. It doesn't fly as fast or straight as the iPod. Thin pages flutter through the space between us and land in a pile near new Converse with a muffled and pathetic thump.

Watching me with preying eyes, Dusty licks his lips.

"I'll call you later," he says into the phone, disconnecting the call. He steps forward slowly and I steady my feet.

"Why did you bring me here?" I ask, louder than I mean or need to while I search his eyes for anything to make sense of.

The smirk I've always loved curves into a condescending grin.

"You want to have this fight now, little girl?"

My lungs smolder and my brimstone heart seethes hateful, jilted beats while this boy spits acid through a smile I used to dream about.

"Come on, sunny side," he taunts. "We just got here. You don't want to have a little crybaby breakdown first?"

The flames in my chest raze and burn deeper.

"Didn't you miss me, Bliss?" he asks, his voice depleted and mean as he steps closer. "Don't you want me to hold you?"

"Don't fucking touch me," I warn, shaking my head as I step back.

"Don't touch you?" His laugh is depraved. "Okay," he says. "Did you bring your fucking crayons?"

"Why did you bring me here?" I demand so loudly it fills the room.

Dusty doesn't raise his voice in the least. He smiles so sincerely my heart splits, and he fastens dope-open, honesty-filled eyes on mine.

"Why'd you come with me, baby?"

"You asked me to," I remind him spitefully.

He shakes his head. "No."

"Yes," I insist, furious that he's so far fucking lost he can't even carry a conversation. "You did. You said to come with you—"

"No," he interrupts, his raspy voice a little sharper, a little louder now. "Tell the truth, Leigh. Why'd you get in the car? Why did I just watch you throw everything good in your life away?"

Fire swallows me whole.

I fall, and there's nothing to hold onto.

There's nothing but the darkness of knowing he's right.

I scream.

And scream.

And strain to keep screaming until my throat's scratched raw.

Opening my eyes, I see red.

My fate stands tall across from me in shades of blood and black. He hasn't advanced, but I realize as I look that I've lifted my hands at some point. I'm holding them up, palms out, telling this person without a word to keep the fuck away.

"What am I supposed to do?" Tears pour from me. I sound failure-filled. "Am I supposed to stay here and watch you do this? Be soft and sweet to you while you snort your life away?"

I can't breathe. I've opened an inferno inside myself.

"Am I supposed to take you back again? Be your girl? Am I supposed to ask my dad to walk me down the aisle so you can put a ring on my finger between lines? You want me to hold your hand while you kill us both? What the fuck am I supposed to do, Thomas?"

Fire spreads into an ocean and love—

Love never taught me how to swim.

He taught me how to cling to him, and all I want in this moment is to pull him under with me.

"It doesn't matter," I cry, hatefully alone. "You're never going to change. No matter what I do or where we go, if we're together or not … you're a loser, and you're never going to stop hurting me."

What's real falls on a boy that doesn't budge. Tears spill from my eyes while his don't even blink, and this is it.

Love is sinking, and it's taking us both.

Love is knowing this is just as much my fault as his, because I allowed it. I invited it when I pushed his patience at every turn. I made love lie. I made love a secret when he begged me not to. I betrayed love.

Pins that used to be butterflies stick through my heart and lungs, and I choke.

"You left me." I point my finger between cries. "I've loved you my whole life, and all you do is leave me."

My chest caves in.

Thomas' black eyes glass over as I catch my breath. His breathing is unsteady too. He swallows, and I see his Adam's apple and all the muscles around it work. I swear I see his pulse writhe for every beat. He looks like unstable, impending devastation, and when he steps, he moves with a grace only hunting can bestow.

"I fucked some girl," he says, emotionless. "Last October, the night before I came home."

My entire frame shakes, out of control, but I'm stuck, frozen in flames. Stepping closer, Thomas bears down with wild black and drops the pitch and volume of his voice.

"I couldn't pick her face out of a lineup."

Red, heart-shaped sunglasses and a veil of pale and putrid gentleness burn the backs of my eyes. I'll never forget her static-screened face, and the one who chose her wouldn't know her if he saw her again.

I swallow everything but bitter hate. "I heard."

Pure volatility's temper spikes. He steps closer, and I step back, and as we circle, I can feel his anger in the air like a living, enmity-breathing being right here in the room with us.

Pushing with his words like he's pushed me with his silence, he says, "I don't even know her name, Leigh."

I don't move, but I'm aware suddenly that I can. Standing taller and glaring up, I close my hands to keep from striking out.

"I do," I say, and it's more than just a trigger for this person.

It breaks his back.

In a matter of seconds, Dusty flips the desk and speakers go flying. Drawers fall and crack open and the legs break loudly. I stagger back as he stalks forward in the chaos, black eyes lost and darting around the room before locking on mine.

Keeping my hands up as I move, I protect the only thing that's protecting me: distance.

He sniffs, and all I see is Her all over him.

Filled with his nearness, my pulse pounds a storm from my chest to my ears. I tremble from the inside out in dangerous proximity, because even though I keep stepping back, he remains constantly close enough to reach out and grab me.

But he doesn't.

He maintains my space and searches my eyes high and low, pushing me with incurable black, and when I don't back down, he pushes harder.

"I fucked Valarie for years," he says, gutted and tormenting. "I fucked her, and I got into bed with you."

Disloyalty pulls like a millstone around my neck.

"I lied to you," he pushes. "Over and over."

Instincts cut up my spine, telling me to leave and never look back. That's what this boy wants, but I'm cleaved to this fight with all that I am.

Self-centered and life-taking pushes harder.

"I use you," he says. "Just like I used her."

"Tell me something I don't know," I spit.

Turning away from me, Dusty pulls breaths like fumes through his nose. He clenches and unclenches impatient fingers, stepping from our fight and turning. He's shifty-unsteady and I know he wants to break something. This is killing him, and the distance I'm making him keep is hell.

I breathe shallow and quickly. It's nothing like how I've taught myself to, but steady between fear and ire as my broken heart paces and turns. Showing me his profile as he faces the only exit, he drags a hand down his face, thinking.

He sniffs.

He blinks.

He sniffs again.

Dusty breathes, and I can see him deciding and rethinking, and his look makes me nervous. His black softens with hopeless warmth as he turns straight to me. Hands in his pockets, all endless eyes and mournful shoulders, he makes the bottom of the ocean burn.

Love seeks, but it's too late.

He speaks words he can't ever take back the same second I realize saving us means saving myself.

"I had sex with her for the first time after that day on the porch swing with you."

My soul unravels.

I don't want this truth.

Memories choke me as I try to speak.

"You … That day—"

I close my eyes, and my own dirty feet and Dusty's brand new shoes, side by side on his mother's front porch swing four years ago, crumble to a thousand pieces in my mind.

"Rule number one is that you have to always smile when I'm around."

"Fine, but I have a rule, too."

"What is it?"

"You have to always tell me where you're going."

"No."

"Yes."

"That's not even the same, Leigh."

"It's still a rule, and rule number three is that you have to follow rule number two, always."

"I told you where I was going," Thomas says, opening my eyes.

But I look at him, standing still, and all I feel is gone.

Love is what nightmares are made of, and when my bad dream speaks, his voice is so hushed and hollow it barely enters my ears.

"You're not smiling," he pushes, two tears rolling fast down each of his cheeks.

I can't do this.

I can't live this moment.

Shifting my feet to run, to leave this state of being, I step back, and it all happens fast. I don't know if the give is in my footing or the floor, but my heels stumble and I lose balance. Thomas reaches to catch me, but I'd rather fall.

The second his hands close around my arms, I strike. I hit his chest, his shoulders, his jaw, everywhere I can.

"I hate you!" I cry out, hysterical and beyond. "I fucking hate you."

Past unyielding, gathering fistfuls of my hair and my dress, his hold swallows me whole while he digs his nose into the bend of my neck. He opens his mouth and I close my eyes, begging God for strength because I feel everything I can't deny. My heart, my hurt, every sense of self-preservation and all my hostility and distrust, want this person.

Dusty's the source of everything in me that aches and hates, and all I want in the whole world is for him to hold me closer.

Our feet stumble as we struggle, and I clutch onto him for life.

"Why are we like this?" I cry. "I don't want to be like this."

Broken breaths burn my skin as love clings every bit as violently tight to me.

"Tell me to leave you alone," my boy begs, drained and dying. "Tell me to let you go. Tell me you don't love me."

I lie well, but I can't say those words, and this time when I hit Thomas, I grip onto his layers and he chokes out a sob as I gather him recklessly and completely to myself. I fight to get him closer and I can feel him, breathing and fighting and holding on too, and all I can think is here he is.

This is my soul.

Right here.

This is a life that exists just for me, and I closed my hands in hatred and raised them against him in anger.

Drowning, I strain and struggle to stay with Thomas. He shifts and I panic, but love covers my hands with his own.

CHAPTER
forty-five

His touch is heavy and slow and all I want in the world.

It started a minute ago, or a few, or some seconds. It's hard to say. I don't know how long I've been asleep, but the scent of clean linen and stolen smoke surrounds us, and Thomas holds me close, brushing his thumb along the bottom of my stomach.

Exhausted under the weight of waking, I stretch for comfort.

With my back against his chest, he brings me firmly to himself. Swift between my shoulders, his heart beats as he drags his nose along my neck, breathing me in. He presses where his fingers were just brushing, and my chest tightens. My eyelids burn from crying and breathing takes effort. Everything aches, dull and awful and raw.

Sliding his hand between my legs, love doesn't let me hesitate. He slips under my dress and covers me with his palm, and everything that aches warms under his touch. My pulse fully wakes, thrilling my veins as I open for him, knees bending and wedges I still wear sliding along hotel sheets. Burying my face into pillows that aren't his but smell so much like him, I lift my hips and love that split my spirit rubs my softest place with quick, capable fingers.

Persistent through cotton, he's much wider awake than I am. From the pattern of his breathing to the measure of his touch, he's concentrating and purposeful. I reach down, chasing the fires he's lighting with every circle, and he curves our fingers together, making me touch at his pace, and it's so good I sing for him.

Shifting quickly, Thomas kneels between my legs. Dizzy and disoriented, I blink my eyes and make them adjust. Early sunset paints the room dark gold.

It falls across my boy in long slanted lines from blinds that were closed and are now parted by something thrown or broken.

Unstill, Dusty's a shifting blur of bronze-sunlit blond hair and a stretched out, torn up gray tee. He buries his face in my neck as he sinks against me, hips to heart, and gives me all of his weight. Unsparingly hard between my legs, he moves with intentional and unapologetic rhythm that makes my dress ride up and sparks open behind my eyes. He brings my hand to his neck, and under my touch, the heart of love beats heedlessly, making my own pick up.

My blood trembles and hums as I lift, close, so close.

"Come on," he whispers, rough and deep, thick with insistence under my ear.

Gripping with both hands, I arch so hard up and into him that my body leaves the bed. My cries come undone and I cling to the person taking me apart.

When my shoulders and back touch blankets again, I feel lighter, lifted. Breathing comes easier with Thomas like this, surrounding and in between, above and beyond, all over me, but heavy love moves quickly in my haze.

I clench my fingers into my dress as he reaches under it, pulling cotton out of his way and sliding me open with his fingers like he's searching. Biting my lip through his ungentleness, I take him in.

Sundown-glowing and caught up, Dusty's beautiful this way.

He touches me without shame or uncertainty, pressing and sliding inside and all over. It's indelicate but so wanted, and when he shifts his other hand under my back, making me arch higher and open wider, I bend like I was born to. Trouble holds me in place like the natural, unavoidable phenomenon that gives weight to all things and presses so deeply my hold on everything shakes.

Low and coarse, his whisper covers me.

"It's going to hurt more if you're not ready."

Flutters dip and tingles tighten while heartbeats crowd my throat. I tense up and push at him while panic and need fight inside me.

I can't—

Sliding deeper, Thomas strokes fingers that know where I'm most nervous and desperate, and I strain against him, pleading with my whole body.

"Come on," he whispers again, so low it sinks into me with his touch. "Come, baby."

I can't help it.

Breathtaken and lost, I'm still spinning when Thomas leans up abruptly. Pulling cotton away, he takes my hands and presses them between my legs, pushing my fingers where his just were, inside.

"Keep your hands right here. Just like this," he says, sliding his fingers along mine, showing me how he wants me to open and touch.

Following his heavy pressure and quick rhythm, I open my eyes as Dusty leans onto his knees. He reaches for my left foot but watches me, and lust flickers under my skin while shame swims through my bloodstream.

I blush so hard I burn, but I don't stop.

While I circle and slide and profane for this boy, he unclasps my shoe with nimble fingers and tosses it aside. Yearning, I bend my leg around him and rub my bare foot along his denim-covered calf while he reaches for my other ankle. Black eyes shift between my own, my hands and back to my eyes, making intimacy I've only ever felt with love bloom sweetly through me as I push deeper, giving in to need with curved fingers and obscene fervor.

Broken beyond repair doesn't look it as he works the other little white buckle open. Assertive confidence hardens the contours of his face while light and dark fall across him in stark lines. Dusty looks sure of himself and stronger than just nineteen and two days, and reality claws at me. I don't stop touching, but my chest tightens painfully, and I close my eyes.

In the same second my shoe leaves my foot, Thomas throws it, and the thump against the wall pulls my eyes open just as quickly as if he'd told me to.

Fated and filled with dark, his look enfolds a wave of panic over all my passion.

Grabbing the bottom of his shirt, he pulls it up and off. It leaves his dirty hair sticking out in every direction while sunset and shadows slant across his bare chest, and between tightly pouted lips and tighter drawn brows, it's all too much. I reach up as my disaster reaches for his belt and he smiles, sad and daring.

"You think you're going to stop me, L?" he asks, unbuckling right under my hands.

Bearing down on me with loaded irises, he gives me an insubstantial fragment of a moment to reply. When I don't, when I tighten my grip on his wrists, he reaches under my dress again. Only this time, he doesn't touch where I'm slick and aching.

Gripping my hips, Thomas lines me up directly beneath him.

"I can't even stop myself," he whispers, pressing his hands into my thighs until I'm more open and bare to him than I've ever been.

With my hands still around his wrists, my heart pounds against my chest, shaking my whole body with the force of each beat, but not in fear. The weight of love is tremendous, but I'm not afraid of this person. I want all of him. I've always wanted him.

Eyes locked on Dusty's, I lift my hips to feel where I need him most, but his hands are in the way. Rough knuckles slide where I'm most tender as he undoes the first button of his jeans.

"Do it," he says softly, undoing another button while my eyes close and I arch higher.

"Come on, girl," he half bids, half begs, his voice a solemn shade of the sound I fell in love with.

Undoing another button, he moves his hand. Mostly undone and irresistibly hard, he rocks against me.

"Tell me to stop."

But he feels so good my head falls back and I revel in the contact.

The bed shifts and embittered love snatches me up, tugging and tearing my dress away. Still in his undone black jeans with his belt hanging open, he tries to lay me down in my never-more-nakedness, but I wrap around him and hold fiercely tight because in the split second he flipped from broken to resentful, so did I.

After years of *no, baby,* and *we won't be like that,* this is it how it happens?

Digging my knees into his sides and my nails into his neck, I fight this liar until I draw blood and he groans.

Like my difficulty is nothing, Dusty presses me down into the bed, and he's the one that says it.

"Stop."

The harshness of his tone and the force of my pulse throttle all my nerves. I push and pull harder for control of what I want most, lifting my hips eagerly for it, and the boy who sets my heart free is no gentleman. He lets me fight him as he pushes his clothes down, but then he's there—not within, but between and heavily against—and pinning my hands under his.

My inhale shatters in my throat, and I close my eyes, curving completely up and into this person as he slides slowly, soaking himself. He drops his face to my neck, covering my skin with warm breaths and a sound that comes from lower than his chest. As he moves, my entire body opens. Every push-slide makes my whole world part to accommodate him from between my lungs all the way out to my legs, so wide it hurts.

But it's home-welcoming.

My fingers and toes curl, and my pulse drops deep into the heart of my aching. Every inch of my skin tingles for every inch of his, and I feel like I'm going to burn into pure light, but Thomas stops mid-slide and moans into my neck as he presses the head of himself against me.

Love is pressure so hard it feels impossible.

His entire frame shakes.

I open my eyes and see the tremble in his shoulders that I feel in his arms. All heart and sinew, he looks down at me and his black overflows as he starts to push. Sound drops out as he enters. Pressure becomes acute and overwhelming, but I lift into it.

Love pushes with weighted hips and everywhere goes dark. I'm swallowed by the same black that surrounds him and I cry out, but there's no room for my voice anymore. I'm too small for what I need most, and it makes everything hurt.

Above and everywhere, Thomas sinks to a place inside me I've never felt, and the darkness I'm in glows purple around the edges. Cries turn into tears. I need him deeper, through and past and under all the pain stinging me. I want to wrap my arms around him so badly and bring him closer, but instincts keep my hands on his shoulders because I feel like I'm all that holds him up.

Barely breathing, ragged and sharp and immeasurable, buried in my body-space stays still long enough for me to breathe too.

Seconds pass.

Maybe minutes.

I don't know.

Under and around love like this, there is nothing but hot and dark and full.

I open my eyes, but my head's tilted back. All I see is ceiling, and when I take a breath I can't help the little sound that comes out of me, because I feel him when I inhale. Thomas groans against my chest and it echoes warm and deep around my heart, but I feel pinned. I feel brimming, and red, and I need him to move.

Trying to shift, to adjust and accept, I slide my hands from his shoulders to his neck, into his hair. It brings back shakes he just got a handle on, and I can feel control slipping from his breathing.

Love is suffering through going slow.

He's dying to sink into me.

He needs to fuck.

Already-fullness aches and pressure stings around a spike in his breathing, and I swallow hard as he takes my left hand in his right.

Blinking, I think maybe he's going to pin it down again, or place it over his pulse, and this thought makes my corresponding beat flutter sweetly through the pangs of parting.

But he doesn't.

He brings it down instead, between his hips and mine.

I'm confused that there's space for our hands, and at first all I feel are flames.

Then he places my hand on myself, and my heart convulses.

I feel how tightly spread and stretched my body is around his, and fear rushes renewed and twice as strong through me as Thomas brings my fingers up, placing them at the base of himself, showing me.

He's only halfway.

I can't breathe again.

I can't be still again or open enough again. I can't again. There's so much of him left. I can't—

Love without end brings my hand back up and places it over his wild-flying heart. He palms my inner thighs with his other hand, spreading me further for himself.

"Be still," he says lowly.

Looking into me, his black runs over, and I give myself to it. I lose myself in Dusty's oblivion and watch him watching me as he presses down on my leg, making me open so much wider.

When he pushes this time, I feel my soul split.

Helpless, my lids drop and I will every part of myself to open, open, open.

Thomas pushes and pushes, and I try to breathe through it, but I can't.

Until he drops his forehead to mine and his air is on my lips, and then breathing is all I can do as he braces his body against my own. He pushes all the way into me, and I break to make the shape forever takes.

My eternity moves deeper without missing a beat, and it burns like open fire, but I hold on.

Be soft, I think. *Be easy for him. Be open for love.*

Rocking his hips forward, Thomas moves my entire body. I wince, and he brushes his lips across my cheek.

"Shh." He kisses me with soft lips and softer breath. "Shh."

I don't know if he's trying to comfort me or himself or both of us, but it works. When he rocks forward again, there's a swell of satisfaction around the sting of him, and I blink my eyes open again.

My boy's blurry this close, but even out of focus I can tell he's aching. His eyelids are closed tightly and lips I crave are pressed thin with endurance. His skin burns against mine while his strung-out heart surges with a madness I know all too well. We're in a room, in a city that feels nothing like home to me. We're further gone than I ever imagined we could be, but this beat, this dangerously swift rhythm under my palm is natural to me.

"Shh," he whispers again, kissing the side of my parted mouth as he rocks deeper.

And just like that, I melt.

Between softly-assuring murmurs and love's hard-beating heart, I surrender, and I know my sunken-soul feels it, because he starts to move.

Not fast.

Not rushed.

But so heavily.

Closing my eyes and opening my lips, I ride every push he drowns me with and let him hear new cries. Little and innocent and delicate and deep, notes I've never made fill my ears and grow longer, sweeter, as Dusty starts to truly move.

More than all the way inside, he pushes deep into me, and the way he moans lights my whole body up.

With one hand around my side, he slides his other through my hair, tilting my head back as he fills me with sworn and purposeful rhythm. He drags his lips down my cheek, over tear tracks and back to my neck where I feel him, trying to kiss but his lips won't close and his breath feels so good on my skin. Moving like he wants to cover me completely with himself, he kind of pants and moans as he starts to say something, but it's too low. I can't hear it at first.

Pulling back to fill me deeper, Thomas curves his fingers through my hair and tilts my head to the side. He brushes the shell of my ear with his thumb as he strokes with strength I feel everywhere. It's overpowering and unavoidable, and this time I hear him.

"I knew it," he whispers, pushing permanently deep. "I knew it. I fucking knew it."

I feel his words more than I understand them.

I know with every pound of my heart and drop of his hips that nothing will ever be the same now.

It sends a spark through me that unhinges my boy, and he's moving again. He angles my hips to take more, and I cling to him, unashamed of how much I love his loss of control.

Because I do.

I love this person reveling and fulfilling, all-consumed and unconstrained in passion. I love him falling into me, and I love the hurt that comes from securing myself to him because that's how I know it's real. I cherish the way my chest feels ripped open every time he breathes in, and I'm enamored with his sounds, lost and conflicted and steeped in unbearable need. I die for his suffering muscles and his barely-withstanding bones, and the blood beating so hard through his veins I feel it under my fingers means more to me than my own.

Dusty loves me too hard, too deep, too far, but it's the kind of madness I crave. It hurts but it's familiar to me and comfortable like home, because loving this person has hurt for as long as I can remember.

It's how I know I'm doing it right.

When he can't get any deeper, when love is as all the way into me as he can be, he digs. He works himself unfathomably into my world, and he makes my marrow quiver and my tingles sing.

I look up to find his black dripping as he moves. Low lashes are wet, but his eyes are fixed. Every push is enlivened and purposeful. He's not going to stop. He can't.

He digs and his heartbeat abounds while mine throbs to the same abandon and with every beat, he fastens us. Prodigious love carves me out with every thrust, creating a space inside me solely for himself. I'll never get back the pieces he's taking away, and only he will ever fit.

I slip.

I feel like I pour.

I want to come, but the physical flames that burn with every slide are too tight, too sharp, and Thomas slows like he knows, but he doesn't ease. His strokes are just as long and heavy and unchaste as before, but he moves with lush intent now. Strained shoulders square and gorgeous lips pout, and I swear I feel his pulse where we're connected.

He's close, and I know it.

And I've never wanted anything like I want this.

Slowing further, this boy slides with deep ease and basks in filling me. His jaw drops and his mouth hangs slack as I lift into him, asking for more with my hips. Rocking soft little circles where he's inside me, I open my lips right under his and hold his face in my hands.

"Dusty … " I whisper. "Dusty, Dusty …"

Love falls hard.

He fucks me.

He fucks so fiercely, so utterly without constraint that I cry out loud, and he digs his teeth into my chest, biting and pushing and pulling as he comes.

It's warm.

It burns like capturing and completing and forever, and I don't let go.

I can't.

My soul floods apart inside me and doesn't stop after he gives me everything. It's slick and full and overwhelming, and opens nervous uncertainty in the back of my mind because I can feel everything about who we are changing.

I sting and pulse and flow with love, but the boy with my heart in his teeth keeps moving.

CHAPTER
forty-six

I'm tender under Thomas but can't bear the thought of stopping him.

The moon's glow and city night light cut through the dark, outlining the boy who's as naked as me now. Narrowed brows and too-long hair that won't stay pushed back stand out in shades of ivory and ink and silver as he moves.

Tireless love presses his weight along me with steady rhythm and I close my eyes, basking.

He's not inside, but he's making me feel wet all over, like we're rocking in a pitch-dark, swelled-full raindrop. I think of summer storms and the ocean in June, and I hear his voice burn low around me.

"Let me," he whispers, pressing my shaky legs apart with his hands, spreading and sliding against my softest, sorest place.

I have nothing to compare this or him to, but it's been hours, and Dusty's still so hard.

Digging his fingertips into my skin as he slides his hands to my hips, he kisses under my ear as I bite my lip.

"Bliss," he says heavily, like my name is a rule in itself. "You have to let me."

I'm scared of the sting and the stretch and the pain, but I crave the intensity, and love slides slowly, showing me how badly I need him too.

His swift, even, dead of night pulse encompasses me as he lowers his chest to mine. He leans close, so that his lips are by my ear and mine are by his as he presses into place, and I gasp so sharp, so deep it hurts.

Love pushes a note from the center of my soul, and it comes out of me in a cry I can't control. He moans for it and his proud sound sinks into my skin with his breath.

"Fuck," slips from him and feels like it drips down my neck.

Wrapping my arms around him, I brace myself for the fullness of forever-love and with a smoother, deeper drop of his hips, Thomas gives me everything.

I cling to his arms and grip fistfuls of his hair as he moves. I dig with my nails like he digs with his pace, and he curses and groans when I break flesh, but it makes him move harder.

"Baby," he groans.

"Leigh," he moans.

"Fuck—"

Dusty handles me, making me take every push, but I can feel him losing himself in me, and as he moves with inexhaustible need, little aches and tight tingles pulse together around him. I don't come, but I meet every surge of his hips with my own, and I feel the shake that starts in his wrist. It climbs up his arms as he fucks me, and it makes his shoulders shudder. His stomach lifts and falls unevenly against mine with his shallow breaths and all of his muscles flex. He comes so hard I shake too, and as love makes me whole again I cry.

I can't help it.

CHAPTER
forty-seven

"Relax," he tells me, up on his knees and holding my hips, rocking right against my hands.

I don't want him to stop, but he's been building this lush, bottomless ache in me for hours, and it's killing me. My head is gone. My heart's worn-out and I have no idea if this is normal.

I don't know what normal is for sex.

Thomas has slowed down, but he hasn't stopped. He's just feeling me now, moving with deep adoration and shameless strokes, and it's torturous—

How good it is.

Feeling Dusty.

Inside me.

"Leighlee," he calls quietly. His voice sounds like I feel: indulged.

I open my eyes to beautiful black and find lips he can't un-pout curved up.

"Relax," he says again. "Stop trying to push me out."

His smirk as he says it sends me flying, and I fall back. Shifting closer, disordered hair and bare-bones divine, delicious for my eyes and glorious to my heart, tireless love presses my knee into the bed, making me feel all of him. He works and overworks both of us, and I roll my hips for what I can't get enough of either.

I finally have all of this boy, and he—this part of him, our sex—is better than anything. My lips quiver and my legs shake. Every part of me squeezes and tingles and wants, and new euphoria dismisses everything else. Our sex dizzies and demands. Thomas and I aren't just connected; we are connection undivided. It's addictive and it's staggering.

When he groans, I feel his body echo the sound.

When he's all the way within, I feel every heedful beat of his greedy heart.

When he breathes, I breathe.

And when he can't—

I tense tightly as endlessly insistent love holds me where he needs me most and pushes us to a place so sweet I cry. I cling to him, desperate for relief, but the deeper and heavier he moves, the deeper and heavier the ache grows, and I can't help it.

"Thomas," I plead with my whole body, pressing my lips together between words to keep my shaky grip. "Please, please …"

"Open," the flame making me ache says, lids low as he rocks above me. Bringing his thumb to my mouth, he presses on the corner and drags it along my lips and teeth, making me part. "Let me hear you."

My jaw falls slack, and I sound as low and lustful as I feel. I sound bare and beyond, and the person who gets this from me, the only one who's ever had me picks me up so he's all that's touching me in the world.

"There," Dusty whispers, on his knees and moving with all of me wrapped around him. "There, baby."

My head falls back as reason and meaning and purpose take me apart. My soul guides me from the inside to fulfillment I was born for, and I burn into contact with his.

Love is mind-numbing and vision blurring.

It's divine and lush, enticing and surreal and so real.

I sing for love, and I am the most myself I have ever felt.

Everything's waves of almost-dawn light and overflowing forever as Thomas lowers me back to the bed. He's everywhere at once, moving hard and moaning so lowly, so scraped-hollow sounding I think he's hurt, but his rhythm goes wild. What sounded like pain warms into the sexiest unsteady breathing pattern ever as he chases himself into me, and when he comes there's no air. He pushes everything but himself out of me and turns all perception into sensation.

I cry rapture.

I taste red.

We fall under together, both of us in so deep over our heads I barely hear myself.

"Don't stop, don't stop, don't stop …"

Dusty bends us so close I feel his arms and legs shake. Pressed to mine, his stomach rises and falls with the effort of breathing and his chest and shoulders are flushed hot. There's sweat along his forehead when I brush his hair back and hold onto disarray, but black eyes are locked and his body is deeply persistent.

Rolling his weight into me, wholehearted love whispers:

"Never."

CHAPTER
forty-eight

S unrise pours through broken blinds, stinging my waking eyes. I turn to hide from it without thinking, and my whole body aches through that mistake.

I bury my wince and turn my face into pillows that smell like love.

Everything throbs.

My thighs and between them radiate soreness so strong they pang with my heartbeat as I pull twisted blankets over me and curl up. I blink my tired eyes open on where my boy should be, but find a closed bathroom door instead.

The line of soft light underneath it is cruelly bright, and the small sounds behind it are muffled, but I hear them.

The two of them.

Tap, tap, tap.

Together.

Sniff.

I close my eyes and I can still feel Thomas, inside and all over. I swallow, and the sullen-selfish boy who carries my life in his lungs has dug himself so deeply into me, I swear I taste him on the back of my tongue.

Tap, tap, tap.

But love has made me weak.

Sniff.

I let him have Her.

CHAPTER
forty-nine

My cheeks are pinker than they've ever been.

Leaned against the bathroom counter, I lick my kiss-bitten lips. They tingle and I blush harder. Fogged around the edges from the shower we took together, the mirror in front of me reflects a brand-new girl. Under soft and un-made-up lids, my eyes shine and my pupils look deeper. Sensitive skin glows against thick white terry cloth and love's marks are fresh-red on my chest.

I smile. I can't even help it.

I look younger and older at the same time, cherry-strawberry blond and so alive. Under the hotel towel, my curves feel more curved and my bones hum. My muscles ache, and all along my hips and thighs are supple blue-violet impressions of abandon. My legs are weak from opening and allowing all night long, and between them, I'm carnation-turned-scarlet, swelled and so sweetly sore.

I feel florid like the word galore.

I feel like pure, organic allure.

I feel like truth and fulfillment have sturdied my backbone with strength I didn't have before this, and it's a good thing, because when I step out of the bathroom, daytime has painted our hidden den in startlingly unforgiving light.

Our bed's a disaster and empty cigarette packs and old coffee cups on the table stand out. Broken desk parts and shattered iPod shards litter the thick carpet, and when Dusty turns to face me, he's tucking his affair into his right front pocket.

While I was admiring all the ways love changed me, he was spreading his slut and getting off right outside the door.

I allow this, too.

Showered clean but dope-dirty, the only boy I know for a hundred miles stands tall in yesterday's jeans and a new tee, and I might as well thank him.

I should get down on my shaky knees and show my gratitude for giving me the exact thing I asked for when I knew without a doubt that nothing was going to change, and I surrendered anyway.

"Hey," he says, smirking and devastating.

"Hey," I say back, looking around the room for my dress.

Blown-black eyes follow me as Thomas pushes a hand through clean dark blond hair.

"Your parents think you stayed with my sister, right?"

Glancing up, I can practically see cocaine all over his posture, arrogant and taunting, and I want to break his fucking nose.

"Yeah," I say, spotting my dress. Draped over the back of the chair in the corner, it's the one thing in the room that isn't where it fell yesterday.

My legs burn as I walk. My thighs throb and resent every step, but I hide my pain from the one who gave it, and he tosses my phone into the chair I'm approaching.

"Tell them you'll be home this afternoon," he says.

Resisting the urge to pick it up and throw it back at him, I grab my dress.

"It's ripped," love says behind my back. I don't have to look to know he's grinning smugly. "The strap's torn."

Of course it is, I think. *You tore it. Just like you tear everything.*

"So buy me a new one," I snip, turning to the sound of flicker and flame.

Dusty's smile grows as he blows smoke toward the ceiling and when he looks at me, the bitch in his eyes glints. I drop white eyelet cotton back onto the chair and take a few careful steps to my left, refusing to let my aching show. I'm not giving him the satisfaction.

But as I crouch down to grab my underwear and pull them up under the towel, I can't contain the sting. I wince and hiss and bite down cursing, and across the room, filthy love exhales smoke with a proud sound as I stand up. Cracking open dresser drawers, I find the perks of a sinner with money he couldn't care less about. I pull on basketball shorts and a tee that swallow me and gather my wedges and purse.

I leave my dress and Thomas grabs only his notebook and Ben's hoodie.

We don't speak on our way downstairs, but hardhearted measures his stride to match my hindered little steps. He opens the door for me, and when he offers his hand outside, I take it.

PORTLAND'S FULL of stores, but the one we're in is fairly empty. There are a few shoppers and two sales ladies and too-loud pop music playing, but I'm focused on one thing as I look through the racks of dresses.

Dusty's eyes lie heavy on me from a few feet away. They're hidden behind pitch-dark RayBans, but his regard is palpable. I've felt longing-love in his look for years, but there's newness in this focus. Instinct and possessiveness have grown so strong that when I look toward the dressing rooms, he looks in the same direction.

I glance to the exit and his eyes follow.

Love's attention is shameless.

I could step in any direction and this boy would follow.

I literally have sway.

Making my way to the next rack, I feel my pulse in my palms and fingers. It flows down both arms and fills my chest. My boy's boldness gives me confidence and his close-keeping footsteps make my heart soar. Grabbing the first dress I find in my size, I head toward the fitting rooms with trouble perfectly in tow.

The attendant holds her hand out for the dress as I approach, and I pass it to her with a courteous smile.

"How are you today?" she asks, something sort of like unease or hesitance in her tone. She glances over her shoulder as she leads the way to a hall of small rooms.

"Well, thank you." I nod politely and wait a few steps back as she unlocks a door. Thomas and I aren't touching, but I feel him just a few inches behind me.

"Okay," she says, eyeing us. "My name is Helen. If you need a different size or anything, just let me know."

As she opens the door and steps aside, I tuck air-dried, loosely-curled hair behind my ear and step forward.

My monster follows me right in.

"What are you doing?" I ask with a laugh.

Dusty shoots Helen a smile and closes the door.

"What?" he asks, feigning innocence.

"This is a *girl's* dressing room, you know."

I look up and my heart flutters as his lips part and he smiles higher, showing his teeth.

"Go ahead," he says, nodding behind me to where Helen hung my dress.

As Thomas leans against the wall, I turn to face a sundress printed with tiny rosettes, but there are mirrors on two sides of us and all I see is him watching me.

"What?" I ask, tugging the drawstring of his shorts from my hips.

Tall, dark, and derelict covers me with his look as I let them fall, and when I pull his shirt from my shoulders and stand in nothing but pink cotton bottoms, he grins like I just told him the best secret.

Stepping forward in the small space, he reaches behind me and tugs the dress free, letting the hanger fall loudly to the floor. Smiling as I lift my arms, I let him bring the dress over my head and as he guides it down my sides, he brushes his fingers less than gently over my tender hips and turns me around.

"You think everyone doesn't know?" His voice is quiet and his words are warm along the top of my ear as he brings me back against him so we both face the mirror. His lips are hot and his strength surrounds me.

"You think everyone doesn't see how you're smiling, Bliss?" He slides both hands down my sides and over my stomach, pressing his touch into me through thin fabric. His arms flex control as he rests his palms low, low, low, right over a thousand tightly-tingling little knots.

I lean my head back and bask in possession.

"The way you move …" he whispers. "You think you can hide what your body knows now?"

With my lip between my teeth and my pulse between my legs, I peek up at our reflection. Thomas' face is turned against my cheek, half-hidden by my hair, but I can see the sharp corner of his smile.

"You can shower," he tells me, kissing the shell of my ear. "You can put on new clothes. You can take the smallest little steps, baby, but I see you."

I grip addicted hands and lean into tried and true muscle.

"My sex is all over you, girl."

My legs and lips and breaths all shake, but I push at love's touch, asking for more. He slides one hand up over my wild-beating heart and drags his other down between my legs. Under the dress and under thin cotton, he slides his fingers along sore, so-needy softness, not inside but all over. It's too good, and not enough, and he knows it.

Sure of himself, Dusty chuckles against my neck. It's all breath and it makes me feel like melting as he holds me to himself by my strongest muscle and my most delicate place.

"Is there anywhere you can't feel me?" he asks, dauntless and provocative and so fucking certain.

It makes me bold, too.

Shifting, I turn in his arms and step onto his feet to make me taller. Gripping his shoulder for balance, I lift his sunglasses to his head so I can see his eyes when I say it.

"Is there anywhere you can't feel me?" I ask, watching him blink a few times, adjusting to the light. It looks like it hurts, but dope-devoured black softens slowly around the edges, and I love that I can do that. I love that I can see him go mellow and sweet for me, so warm with trust and adoration that onyx almost glows.

"No," he whispers.

Bending to kiss me, open and falling, Thomas picks me up. Mirror glass is cool on my back and when I gasp he kisses me deeper, and just like that we're shifting again.

"You'd let me, wouldn't you?" he asks, stepping into me, pressing me into the glass and covering every inch of my body with his. "You'd let me fuck you right here, just like this."

Wrapping my legs around his waist, I answer by pressing my hips up into his, knowing he'll push against me for it.

He does, and I grip his hair, making him groan and push harder.

"You'd let me," I tell him, circling up. "You'd let me fuck you right here, just like this."

Beaming darkness, Dusty rolls his hips so hard I cry out. His hand covers my mouth quickly, and he laughs so low I feel it between us. It sounds like gravel and light, rolling around together in the bottom of his throat.

"Excuse me—" Helen's knocking impatiently on the other side of the door. "Is everything okay?"

"No." Hard between my legs and looking right at me, mischief smiles wide with his hand still over my mouth. "Bliss is about to fuck me and you're interrupting."

When rushing out before the cops get called kills my legs, love carries me on his back.

The laughter in our lungs is high enough to float on.

It's HALF past three when we merge onto I-5. The windows are down and the sun is high. I'm in stolen dress. Trouble's lighting a joint, and we're heading south.

Back to Newport.

Taking a deep breath, I brace myself. We still have a summer to finish, and my senior year, and then what?

I flip the radio on as Thomas switches lanes. Most of the stations are static and the few that aren't are all sports and news. Popping the glove box, I search for CDs since I destroyed his iPod. There's only one, and I slip *Attack and Release* into the stereo to fill the void of questions I don't want answers to.

Slow guitars and a single, laden-heavy drum beat start around us.

"Ain't it just like dyin'?" The Black Keys ask. *"Except you can still feel the same?"*

Looking over, I find my boy smiling. Driving with his left hand loose on the wheel, he drapes his right along the back of the bench seat, opening and inviting. I slide across and sit in the middle spot, and each time he smokes, his arm curves around my shoulders smooshing me to his chest and making me giggle. I take a couple hits he holds to my lips as the miles pass and he kisses the top of my head.

Love's closeness comforts me long after the CD ends and the joint is out, but the unsmooth vibrations of the road under us wear on my sore thighs. Seeking a different position, I uncross my legs without thinking and it makes me wince out loud.

"Baby," Thomas murmurs, shifting in his seat. Turning slightly toward me, he places his hand on the inside of my thigh and carefully soothes sore muscles.

I close my eyes and lean back, measuring in a slow breath.

Love's touch works the ache out. He switches to my other leg, and when that burning hurt is gone too, he shifts again.

"Come here," he says gently. Back behind his shades, his eyes stay on the road as he guides me toward him. "Come up here."

Glancing at the highway, I hesitate for half a second before rising to my knees. I duck my head as I climb up, and he wraps his right arm around me, helping me settle onto his lap. I hide my face in his neck and am unburdened by the feel of Dusty's heart and lungs working so close to my own. I yawn and when I breathe in, we smell the same, like hotel soap and the joint he just finished, new clothes and vintage love. July sunlight warms my back while summer wind blankets us both, and the sound of the running engine and passing cars relaxes me.

My boy tilts his face toward mine every now and then, not to whisper or kiss, but just to brush his cheek against the top of my head, and I feel high on him. While he's spun on more than one illicit substance, I'm soaring on my own drug of choice—the same one I've always chosen—us.

When I looked out my window yesterday and saw irredemption, too thin and so pale leaning against his Lincoln, I didn't know what to expect. His posture was contrite under the willow, but his words were anything but, and his eyes were fit for a funeral. I had no idea what to expect when I got in the car, and now—

I brush my fingers back and forth over the double-stitched collar of his tee shirt. While he drives us back to secrets and lies and sneaking and not touching, the sun shines in and I look up at him.

Peaceful in this moment, Thomas is beautiful. His eyes are relaxed and his nose doesn't remind me of his selfishness. It's just a perfectly shaped bit of cartilage that takes air to lungs I treasure and keeps him breathing, alive and here with me. What draws my attention most though is the scruffy stubble across his chin and jaw, and I'm smiling, but I can feel tears gathering behind my eyes.

Somewhere, at some point in the middle of everything, this boy started shaving.

And I missed it.

And now it looks like he's gone weeks without caring to.

Since he's cared about anything but Her.

Swallowing my broken heart, I pick at his collar.

"What would you have done if I hadn't come with you?" I ask, close enough that I see all the tiny little muscles around his eyes tense.

"I don't know," he says. "Make you regret it."

Letting the words sink in, I rub my fingertip along white cotton stitching and under it, over more-prominent-than-when-he-left collarbones.

"Did you miss me?" I ask, hating how small and self-conscious this hurt makes me feel.

My weary soul doesn't miss a beat.

"Every minute," he whispers, gathering me more near.

Pressing my nose to his neck, I let my eyelids fall as he turns his head to kiss mine. He rests his cheek on my crown and some seconds pass.

We breathe.

We touch softly and bend closer.

We whole-heartbeat and as seconds stretch into minutes, I know with every mile that we're closing the distance between who we are and who we have to be for me.

Guilt constricts spitefully around my heart, tightening my chest. Sadness stings the backs of my eyes. Stress-anxiety drops my temperature and knots my stomach, and knowing I won't survive him leaving again sends panic coursing through me.

"Will you come over tonight?" I ask. "Will you stay with me?"

Thomas' legs shift underneath me, and he nods.

"I will," he says. His voice is just above a whisper, but there's perseverance and purpose there. "We'll make it work."

It helps, but I'm slipping fast.

Helpless and hopeless in love, I kiss his neck. I use both hands to pull his collar out of the way and I kiss over his pulse. He grips my hips to still me, but I can't. There's nothing else in the world for me but getting closer, knowing we're supposed to be closer than this.

Cursing, Dusty sniffs as he shifts, turning the wheel and killing the engine. He grabs me and turns us, but nothing happens fast enough.

Wind blows through our rolled-down windows and the Lincoln rocks as cars rush past us while fated and fucked-up love lays me down on the bench seat. He pulls cotton away from me hastily as I tug at his belt and buttons. I push at his clothes as he comes down on top of me, but nothing clears or calms until I feel him press where he should, and nose to nose, parted-beautiful pout right over my open mouth, he pushes inside.

I cry out as love stretches and brands and makes himself fit. Inundating my heart and overwhelming all my senses, he completes every painfully deficient part of me and consumes like fire.

Dragging the top of my dress down, he reopens new bite marks and covers the source of my life with his teeth and groans. He digs deep and unflinchingly, pulling us both all the way into to the place in me only he can reach.

CHAPTER
fifty

I linger in the shower for almost an hour. When I get out, I want to crawl into bed, but not as badly as I want to avoid the third degree.

Plus, I'm starving.

Fresh faced, I put on my comfiest sweats and most oversized sweater, and head downstairs. Dad's sitting at the kitchen table with paint in his hair, on the phone with his father. He smiles when I walk in, but I don't miss his nosy eyes questioning my middle-of-the-afternoon pajamas.

Hiding hurt with every step, I smile back and grab some leftovers from the fridge. I take them with a bottle of water and my phone, and flip on the television in the living room. With a glance over my shoulder to be sure I'm unseen, I sit down as slowly and carefully as I've taught myself to breathe.

Even after the longest shower, every part of me aches. Teeth-cuts on my chest and bruises on my hips throb with every beat of my pulse. The muscles in my thighs pang heat in dull hums and between them, inside, I miss love sorely.

Flipping channels with the remote, I pop open a Styrofoam lid and have never been so happy to see cold pizza. I'm two bites in when my phone vibrates.

One new message from Becka.

I hate him.

Thomas and I got back a while ago. Either he just walked in or she's just now texting me, and I resent how disavowed the second option makes me feel. I start to type back a message to ask what's going on, but another from her comes through.

He's high as fuck.

I stare at the words and don't know what to say. My stomach churns between hunger and guilt.

Want me to come over? I ask.

But her next text takes a few minutes.

I'm not the one my girl wants, and I'm kind of doing the same thing to her, but it's different.

It's whatever, she says.

"WHAT HAPPENED?" Mom asks, sitting down next to me and brushing my hair back.

Lying to her is ten times easier than misleading love's little sister. I tell her about a night at the roller rink that never happened while she adjusts my blanket.

"Becka and I bumped into each other." I laugh as I say it. "I fell right on my ass."

"Leighlee!"

It works. She's too caught off guard by my word choice to even consider doubting what I actually said.

Ignoring aches and burns, I unbend my legs and rest my feet in her lap. I cuddle-bury my sock-covered toes in her warmth, and it secures my story.

"I'm okay," I tell her. "Just tired."

I DON'T know what time it is when I wake, but I feel like love is early, like I just texted him and barely closed my eyes.

Blinking for focus in my dark room, the first thing I see is Thomas' hand leaving my door. I think maybe the sound of him locking it is what woke me.

Sleepy but so eager, I sit up and pull my sweater off.

Clean-shaven and shower-fresh, all low-tops and soft cotton, trouble's golden-lit by my nightlight and so high I can see his pulse. Wordlessly turning and tugging me to the side edge of my bed, he talks to me with his hands around my knees and I listen with my fingers under his tee, pushing it up and off. I whisper to him with my sting-burning legs curving around and pulling him close, and he whispers back by giving me contact so sweet I could die. It sets my heart rushing when he comes down onto me. It's too good, too needed to bear silently.

Gasping sharply, I grip Dusty's sides as his palm covers my mouth. He presses me down with more of his weight and I push up into him with my whole body.

Please, please, please, my heart sings.

Pushing sheets and shorts away, we touch and I bend, and my eyes squeeze closed in the glowing dark as this boy parts my body to hold his. I curve and burn and shake and circle, trembling-needy and pinned beneath undeniable love, and when he presses down on my leg, making me open all the way, it's everything I want in the world.

But I can't help crying out under his hand.

All the way open isn't enough when I'm too tender.

Slowly sliding his hips, not inside, just slick and hard and against, Thomas uncovers my mouth.

"Shh," he whispers, lips to lips like a kiss. "Shh."

I try to.

I will myself to be quiet and still and softly strong enough. I feel him sliding and pushing and trying too, but then he presses right where I ache the most for him, and it's too much. I want him so badly but I can't physically handle what love needs.

Cutting a breath that tastes like copper, I shake my head as Thomas angles his hips, rolling slowly along me like a burning wave.

"Stop, stop, stop," I whisper, reaching up to hold on.

On fire under my palms, his pulse burns insistence and capability, but Thomas stills. His eyes close and he swallows a drawn, yearning sound as he digs his grip into my bedding and my pressed-down leg.

He needs me and it hurts.

"Let me," I tell him quietly, reaching between us.

His forehead and eyebrows draw tightly, and his breathing is unevenly shallow. He's gone from the relief of feeling found to stifling lost sounds, and seeing him need me like this floods me with heartbeats.

Touching him carefully with both hands, I watch his breath catch and I feel his arms strain.

"Shh," I whisper like he did.

With my left hand on his hip, I wrap my right around him. I love this boy with one slow stroke, and when I reach his head and rub him longingly against where I can't open enough, his entire frame tenses. He moans, and I kiss him to cover the sound. I bring him closer with my legs, and when I stroke his body down to mine again, he moves with my touch.

Barely holding himself up, Thomas lets me guide him until he starts to shake. His rocking goes from smooth to instinctual and tight little hurts pang through me as I press my knees as wide apart as I can.

"Love, love, love," I whisper and beg and encourage, stroking and palming and sliding sweetly.

Airless above my lips, Dusty falls, hard and warm and everywhere.

"He walked right by me."

Love is shirtless in his shorts and I'm naked under sheets, and his voice feels so good on my skin.

"He hasn't said anything at all?" I ask as he lays his head on my chest.

"No." Thomas brushes his thumb around my belly button while he fills his heart with the sound of mine. "That's where Becka gets it."

Wrapping my arms around him, I know what he means. His sister's tongue gets sharp sometimes, but not like his or his mother's. My best friend has her father's temperament. A turned back is how they say fuck you, and being disregarded by your family has to hurt, but love worked for it. There's no surprise in his tone as he talks about them.

The prodigal delinquent sighs and his breath is warm over his marks in my skin. Brushing my fingers through clean-cut hair, it's insane to me that hours ago we were a hundred miles away, and no one has any idea.

"It doesn't matter," he says, turning onto his back, resting his head level with mine. He bends his knees and pats his shorts where there are no pockets, but he wouldn't smoke in here even if he had his pack.

Turning to my side, I tuck my legs under where his are bent while he stares up at nothing in particular. He's here, curving his left arm under his head and touching my skin with his right hand, but he's inside himself, and we're quiet for a long time. When he draws his fingertips over the bruise on my hip that's the same shape as his thumb, I don't wince. His with-me-but-not-with-me touch is so light it almost tickles.

Almost.

"I told them I'd go to Springbrook, Leigh." Drawing a slow circle around his mark, love gives me hope I don't want.

Two hours away in Springbrook, Oregon is a rehabilitation center called Hazelden that I've heard Tommy and Becka talk about. I've scrolled through pictures, and it looks like a fancy cabin meets a renovated church, but results are promised between mediation, stress management, shame resilience, and treatment plans.

My head spins with words like *transition, motivation, and stabilization. Prevention, dependency, development of a sober support network* dizzy me with nervous uncertainty and stupid optimism.

More than anyone, I want Thomas clean, but his blue has been gone so long that just the thought of it feels unfamiliar and inaccessible, and what if he does straighten out? Then what? Aside from being together, he's given less thought to the future than even I have.

Curving closer, I wrap both arms around him and lay my head over his heart.

I try not to hope, but he started it.

TWO NIGHTS later, it's almost three in the morning and love is wide awake in his anxiousness.

"Springbook's only half an hour from Portland," he threatens. "You know that, right? You know how easy it would be—"

I cut him off by bringing the blunt back to his lips.

In the back of the Lincoln, we're in pajamas and jeans with holes in the knees. We're bare, violet-tipped toes and old Etnies, sleepy blue-greens and restless blacks. We're pressed together palms and fingertip touches, and kisses— so many unsteadily given forehead, cheek, and chin kisses that ask for any and every assurance.

"You know I can't take my phone?" he pushes. "I can't even take reading material that isn't *recovery related*."

Bitter around the last two words, my boy looks away and shakes his head. I climb into his lap.

"I know," I tell him gently.

"Do you? You know it'll be at least a month?" He meets my eyes, and I can see his frustration tipping, nerves and bad habits and his mood all flipping too quickly.

"It's not like …"

He stops.

"I can't take my fucking phone, Leigh."

Cupping his face, I brush my thumbs under his eyes until he looks up at me. "I'm not going anywhere, Dusty. You'll never be without me."

Black eyes seek and plead. Dusty looks young and lost.

"Can you do it?" he asks, searching my face. "Can you live on nothing for that long?"

Lost and caught between *I don't know* and *haven't I already*, I'm more scared of feeding love uncertainty than I am of his absence.

Pressing close to keep him with me, I fill my eyes and heart and voice with confidence.

"We'll make it work."

HOURS LATER, sitting at my dressing table with a song about home and burning reminders turned up, I tap my feet to piano beats and dust shimmer across my eyelids. Dad's at work and Mom's at the library with her book club. It's a little after ten a.m. and I'm waiting for Becka to call like she said she would.

The Castors are making the two-hour drive to Hazelden together today. They're going to pick me up on the way.

Pulling a pink petal skirt up my legs, I grab a white tube top and tug it high enough to keep secret marks covered. I let my hair air-dry because end of July heat is going to have its way regardless, and I rock to my tiptoes as I cross my room. My thighs still tingle-sting a little, but the ache in the rest of my legs and in between is getting better while the hope love put in my heart caresses every part of me.

I've lived without Thomas before. I've survived his runaways, and this is different. It's for something good, and I want to try.

Downstairs, I grab organic powdered sugar and dip strawberries from the garden right into the bag one at a time for breakfast. I think about calling Becka

and asking what the holdup is, but decide to just head over there instead. This is a family thing and I'm invited because I'm family. Driving myself will save them the trip here and make my nervous boy smile.

Setting the bag of sugar down, I grab another strawberry and head upstairs for my shoes and phone. I only make it a few steps before I hear the low rumble of trouble outside.

My heart skips a double-beat. My stomach flips and turns with confusion. I'm not sure why Becka didn't call or why they're letting Dusty drive the Lincoln, but I grab my keys from the post near the stairs and continue up the steps for my things.

Knuckles knocking on the other side of the door stop me again and my heart flutters triple.

Love is reckless when he's nervous. He's one-tracked, and I should probably be more wary of his inconstancy, but it's him. I sort of crave it. I kind of cherish it.

Heading back down with my keys in my left hand, I set the strawberry I'm still holding between my front teeth and open the door.

Wayward and willful stands tall in brown cutoffs and a faded black Used tee shirt from when he was sixteen. He starts with cut-short-again hair, new sunglasses, and a clean shave, and ends with old low-tops, sockless, and untied. Showered-fresh and coke-straight, Dusty open-mouth laughs as soon as he sees me.

Remembering the strawberry between my teeth, I roll my eyes and bite down, tossing the green top past rebellion in all his glory.

"Hi," he says, pressing his hands into the doorframe on either side of me. He leans down but still has to bend his knees more than a little.

"Hi." I smile.

"Hi," he says again, leaning his weight into the frame. With his lips barely parted, slick pretending to be innocent kisses me just once.

I like my lips. They taste like my strawberry and his Crest, and it's almost too sweet.

"What are you doing here?"

Thomas nods behind me, toward the stairs and steps inside, making me step back.

"Come on," he says, cool and relaxed, leaving his shades on. "Go get your shoes."

Turning, I start up the stairs as he shuts the door and follows. I remain a few steps ahead, but his energy and proximity radiate.

"Where are we going?" I ask, glancing over my shoulder as he follows me into my room. I buckle a sandal as he looks around my sunlight-filled space.

"Albany," he says casually.

My heart drops into my stomach with the weight of what I should have known all along.

Thomas picks up an eye shadow compact while I slip on my other sandal. He looks it over while I stand on one foot trying to buckle the stupid buckle, but I'm frustrated now and I can't get it. My leg wobbles, and I hop to keep my balance, but I still can't get the stupid thing, and this hoodlum punk with his stupid sunglasses and his stupid grin, all selfish and disappointing and out of place in my girlie-girl room, laughs.

I grip onto his arm for balance, and he holds my hair out of my eyes so I can buckle my sandal.

"What's in Albany?" I ask, refusing to keep resentment out of my voice.

Thomas hands me my sunglasses.

"Absolutely nothing," he says with a sharpened edge.

Setting my sunnies on top of my head, I grab my purse and even though I don't understand, I take his hand when he holds it out. With our fingers together, he continues.

"Miles and miles," he says as we take the stairs, "of bullshit, small town nothing."

I close my eyes and swallow sunken hope, but biting back my anger is harder. By the time we get to the front door, I stop walking when he opens it. When he turns to face me, I pull my hand from his.

The letdown in my heart hurts, but it's how fed up I feel that is so consuming I can't even find words. Raising my brows and glaring up, I demand answers with my eyes, and when he doesn't answer I cross my arms.

In true Thomas Castor fashion, cynicism curves his smile into a smirk, and he doesn't have to lift his shades for me to see his impatience. Stepping toward me, he takes my hand back.

"Linn-Benton," he says. "Community College, that's what's in Albany."

Love gives my hand a tug.

It's light, a pull I could easily resist, but I don't.

Locking my parents' door behind us, I drop my sunnies to my eyes and follow my boy to his car. He opens my door first, and I reach over to open his as he walks around. As he turns the key, I'm torn as usual between my guilty conscience and my trouble-loving heart, but the second he drapes his arm across the bench seat, closeness invites and overwhelms.

"What are you going to tell them?" I ask as he backs out.

Thomas shrugs. "The truth."

I buckle my seat belt.

ALMOST AN hour later, we've stopped for Slurpees, agreed to disagree on music, and taken two wrong turns. The boy behind the wheel laughs, but it's bent and sort of brackish, and it doesn't escape me that just because this isn't rehab, it's still not his first choice.

Thomas is sticking around for another year because he can't let me go and I don't want him to.

Even if he had checked into treatment, who's to say that was going to last longer than this? After my initial anger burned off into the breeze, I remembered that everything with love is a risk.

He's staying.

He's trying.

And at least this way he gets to play ball.

Thinking about the future in any capacity always sets me on edge. Becka's, my own, Dusty's, ours—we can all make our own choices, but there's so much we can't control. It's all dependent on more than just our own dreams and needs, and loving someone only increases those variables.

This is becoming clearer to me every day.

My best friend wants me to go to California because that's what's right for her.

My parents want me to go to Oregon State because that's what's easiest for them.

If Thomas had his way, we'd keep driving right now and never look back.

The only person taking any actual interest in what I want, in what's right and best for me, is Oliver.

Instead of thinking about lounging on the beach with Becka between folklore and mythology, or getting lost for hours on end in French poetry in some far away library, I think about what I could be that would make the most money, because facts are facts and they're moving fast.

For a teenager, Dusty's inheritance was huge, but there's no way it's going to carry us. I have no idea what he wants to do. So maybe this whole college-classes-for-a-year thing isn't just okay. Maybe it's good. Maybe it will open ideas up that neither of us has had yet.

I look over as we turn onto Linn-Benton's campus. We spot the main office, and I unbuckle as he parks. Cutting off the engine, incorrigible love leans back. He rubs his nose with the backs of his fingers, and he sniffs. His smile remains, but he's unsteady.

While my optimism has been growing, right next to me, his anxiety's been increasing.

Bending my leg underneath me, I face him as he pats his pockets and takes his legal habit out. He taps the pack against his palm, but cigarettes aren't what he wants.

She's in his other pocket.

She's calling him.

She's crying for my boy's attention so loudly I want to tell her to suck *my* dick.

Blowing out a breath, I look around the semi-crowded lot and weigh my pros and cons in silence. If Thomas doesn't use, he'll be twitchy, distracted, and quick to flip both his middle fingers. If he uses, he'll be detached, condescending, and all the more audacious. Both options are twisted sick, but we can't change who we are now, and if I, sober, can't tell him which choice is better, how can I expect him, spun, to know what's right?

My addiction stares out the window while he continues packing his cigarettes, and I smile softly, truly sincere.

This decision is his, and either way, so am I.

"I'm going to go in and grab a number or a place in line or whatever," I say, loyal-hearted and willing to stand by love in any condition as long as he shows up for me to stand by.

"I'll see you inside?" I ask. "Unless you want me to wait?"

Finally looking over, Thomas smiles tightly, like he wants to, but doing so is effortful.

"You're okay," he says.

I kiss his cheek before I get out.

Nine minutes, six excuse me's, and one clipboard sign-in later, I sit in a lobby with my legs crossed and my purse in the orange plastic chair next to me. I swing my dangling foot sort of nervously and unwrap a roll of SweeTarts.

I feel my heart before the double glass doors on my right open.

Walking toward me, leering at skirts and ties as he passes, Dusty doesn't unlift his shades or unsmirk his lips for anything. I don't need to see his eyes to know, but when he moves my purse and sits down next to me, I reach for his sunglasses anyway.

He lets me, but as I nudge his Ray-Bans to his crown, his cockiness tightens up. His jaw tenses a little and his eyes narrow.

Black.

Black.

I take a good, long look.

He didn't bail, and maybe that's small, but it's something.

"We're number twenty-four," I tell him.

"What are they on?" he asks in turn, low-toned and stretching his legs.

"Fifteen," I say, hoping the wait isn't long.

Thomas slides his fingers down my arm and takes my hand.

It's only been twenty minutes, but you'd think we've been sitting in these cheap chairs for hours.

The secretary just called number twenty-two, and crooked love is ready to walk. His knee bounces while his heel taps the linoleum. Shifty in his seat, he traces my knuckles, my cuticles, and the lengths of each of my fingers like maps, but his touch is absentminded. Blacked-out-blues dart and wander, and his breathing is anything but a pattern.

But we're so close.

"Hey," I whisper, covering his skin-and-bone-blueprint-tracing fingers with my own.

Dusty tilts his head toward me but keeps his face forward. His eyes don't focus and his knee doesn't stop. I trace his knuckles like he's been doing to mine, and he rearranges our fingers, interlacing them together: him over me, over him. Leaning in so I can whisper softer, I get close enough that my nose and lips brush his shirt.

Love smells like Tide and vanilla and warm summertime.

"Do you remember when I didn't know you were in the bathroom and I opened the door?" I ask quietly.

His fingers trace and his heel taps, but he turns his head. He gives me his ear, but I need him to really hear me. I need to keep him here.

"You pulled me in with you, remember?"

The corner of his smile twitches, and I know he's remembering setting me on the counter and touching my knees, stepping between them and tugging at my dress, feeling his way up my legs and warning me to stay away from the most harmless kid ever.

"I knew then," I tell my love quietly. "I didn't understand, but I loved how it felt to be with you. I wanted that."

His heel keeps tapping, but he leans back a little in his chair.

"I didn't know what to do with my hands," I whisper, touching his. "But I wanted you."

Sitting up, Thomas pushes my right leg off my left, uncrossing them. I keep cool, but he squeezes my knee, and I know I'm playing with fire.

"Twenty-three," the secretary calls, prompting a mother and daughter to stand and shuffle.

Black eyes close and my boy's heel has stopped tapping, but under his hand, my own knee picks up where his bouncing left off.

SEVEN MINUTES later, we're called back to fill out paperwork, and then sent down the hall to a computer lab. We sit down together, but all Thomas cares about is my hair and my arms and my legs. I'm trying to enroll him into the next year of his life and all he's doing is pulling at me.

"Look," I say insistently, moving the mouse across different entry-level classes.

Leaned forward but toward me instead of the screen, he doesn't take his eyes from where his fingers curl around my summer-blond ends.

"This is important, Dusty," I tell him, pointing to the screen. "What do you want to do?"

Half-sly and half-completely careless, he smiles. He looks up, but not at the computer. Black eyes are all mine.

"Be with you," he says, dropping his touch from my hair to my back. He slips the tips of his fingers under my top and my heart flips. My focus wavers and the precious place between my legs feels no pain.

I pull away from his hand.

"English?" I ask, looking back at the screen and ignoring my pulse.

"Sure," he whispers, bringing my chair closer. Moving my hair, he kisses my neck and his warmth surrounds me. His lips are soft and his breath is softer, and he knows it.

"Be serious," I say, selecting some class and scrolling down the page for another.

Thomas kisses under my ear, and I feel him smile. His hand wraps around mine in my lap, and I hear him breathe in before he says it.

"Marry me."

My heart swells in my chest and I forget how to breathe.

Love turns my chair completely toward him against everything experience has taught me, wishful hope blooms. He's about to say something else, but he sniffs before he speaks, and I remember exactly how to breathe.

"Algebra?" I point out. "You'll need that if you want to transfer—"

"Sure," he interrupts, slouching back and looking down. "Whatever you want, Bliss."

I HAVE no idea how we make it through the rest of enrollment, but Dusty's had his fix.

I need mine.

Between merciless sunlight and soul-baring black, I spread like an open flame in the back of the Lincoln. Needful and greedy and eager, I lift and grip as this boy makes me give him the sound he covets most. I cry out, and crude possession takes over. Yearning consumes. Compulsiveness demands, and totally hopeless brings both of my legs over his shoulders.

It hurts.

It's everything.

It's too hard, too fast, and not enough.

Stripped and sharp and struggling, the sound that comes out of Thomas as I dig my nails into his skin and pull his hips into me cuts through to my heart, but that's where I need him. I want him all the way deep, all over every beat.

Even through my cries, I feel his moans from inside.

We fuck until I'm burning up and begging to fall, until I'm screaming for it and his hand is over my mouth, and someone has to have heard us, but I can't care. All of me curls and burns around all of him. Flickers tingle through my veins and tighten in my chest. Everything glimmers and throbs with my pulse, and I want it back—

That feeling he gave me in the enrollment room before She snatched it away.

The way I felt the other night in my bed when he told me he was getting help.

That wishful little thrill love is so good at giving me lately—

Hope.

"Ask me again," I manage between breaths this rush leaves no room for.

Half-undressed and buried from beginning to end squeezes his eyes tightly closed. His rhythm falters but he's lost, unheeding and blissfully subjugated in feeling. He keeps moving.

Cutting my nails into his sides, I slack my hips. Dusty mourns the loss of contact with a pained sound and presses harder, chasing me back down. I lift my voice and whole body up, helpless for more that's still not enough. He fucks with all his weight, and breaking skin, I bask in my heart's abandon and soul's struggle.

"Ask me, Thomas," I tell him with my teeth under his ear.

Love drags the force of himself through me, and I lie back, higher than the sun shining light all across us. The muscles in his neck and shoulders strain and frustration digs between his eyebrows every bit as strong as he digs for home inside me.

"Give me your hand," he says, his voice just as devoured as the rest of him.

Lit, I bring my fingers from his sides to his face. I hold his cheeks and touch his hair, and he's perfect like this, but he shakes his head.

"Your life, Leigh."

Gravity drops out and significance rushes through me. Dusty presses his right hand over my chest. The muscle under his touch rises and reels, and it's too much.

"I want this," he says. "Give me this."

My heart pounds, and I want to scream but there's no air.

"Marry me," love finally whispers, deep inside, all over my pulse and moving hard.

It's all I hear before I cry and he starts to shake.

CHAPTER
fifty-one

Tommy handles her son's choice to go to Linn-Benton instead of rehab with more wine and new prescriptions. Lucas deals by spending more time at the office, but their daughter, as usual, does not accept, nor does she pretend for anyone that she does.

"Cocaine," she says, declaratively disgusted and loud enough that I know her brother down the hall hears her.

"Seriously?" she asks louder, her volume increasing with caustic sarcasm.

It's the first of August and a few minutes after noon. The air conditioning is set to freezing, but we're in swimsuits under shorts and long sleeves. Sitting on her unmade bed, I'm consciously aware of keeping my summer cardigan buttoned over my marked-up chest while Becka sifts through mail at her desk. Tossing issues of Spin and AP to the floor, she drops everything except for a large, white envelope.

"Seriously?" It chimes this time, every bit as loud, but excitement filled now.

The envelope she tears open is stamped with UCLA's emblem, but it's not thick enough to be an acceptance packet. Jumping up from her chair as she reads with wide blue eyes, my girl beams.

"Oh my fucking … Fuck … Yes!" She sits back down to read it again, but her knees bounce. She radiates pride and excitement, and she should.

Rebecka slaughtered her way through AP and IB classes. This isn't the first scholarship of its kind, and it won't be the last. For all of her decadent wildness, baby-pink is brilliant.

"It's not nearly enough," she says, smiling wide. "But it's a major fucking start."

I'm genuinely happy for her, but I know what comes next.

"Have you filled out your application yet?" she asks, turning to her laptop, click, click, searching and clicking some more. "Actually, if you apply to all of them, we can just choose one together."

I pick up a Rolling Stone off her floor.

"Not yet," I say, lying back on her bed, opening the magazine above me.

"Baby," she admonishes.

"I will. I promise."

Not a lie.

I will.

I'll fill out applications to huge West Coast universities for her, but I'll do so knowing I won't get in, and knowing further that even if I do, I'll never be able to afford it—and even if I could, I wouldn't be allowed.

My mind wanders to the boy down the hall, and I cross my legs to feel the sting.

Love is finding comfort in love-made soreness. Love is assurance in a familiar ache.

Love is still feeling loved, days later.

"Okay, but like, soon," Becka says, looking at me. Seriousness sharpens her voice. "Like, the sooner the better," she continues. "As in, let's do it right now."

Rolling my eyes, I laugh.

"I thought we were going to the beach," I remind her as I sit up. Tossing the magazine aside, I press my fingers to little cardigan buttons to be sure they're still together.

"The beach isn't going anywhere, princess kid. This is our future."

No, this is your future.

"Are you …" She starts to ask something, then stops mid-question and gets up from her chair.

"What?" I ask, confused and more than slightly anxious as she walks toward me.

Reaching, she tugs at my buttons and pushes my swim tank down, and panic replaces all of my blood.

"Becka, stop!"

Pushing her and pulling at my clothes, I flip out, wincing through every sting that struggling with my best friend brings. I end up on my back with every defense I have up, fighting frantically to cover the marks over my heart, but I can't, and she laughs.

Jaw-dropped and fierce, she pulls her hand from mine.

"Are you fucking kidding me?" She jabs her pointer finger so spitefully hard into the bruise in my chest that I scream.

"Rebecka!"

Kicking, I push her forcefully away and sit up. I pull both sides of my stretched-out sweater together and wish I could wrap it around my whole self.

"You lying little freak," says the kettle. She laughs and it's real, but there's bitterness underneath it, and distrust burns through her blues as she tugs at the edge of my cardigan like she's looking for more.

I pull away. Dusty's mark throbs and burns. I feel violated.

"Are there more?" she asks. Her blues widen, incredulous. "Are you fucking Oliver?"

Swinging my legs over the side of her bed, focusing on that hurt, I scoff. "No."

"It's okay," she says back, her tone softer, a little apologetic. "You can tell me. I won't be mad."

She's so much like trouble.

"I'm not." I should be thankful we're not talking about the future anymore, but now I just want to go home.

"You really can tell me, Bliss," Becka insists, smiling. "The truth shall set you free, you know."

I don't hold my breath waiting for her to tell me she's been blowing Petey for who knows how long.

"Truth," I say flatly. "I'm not fucking Oliver."

"So, DO you have some ideas?"

Miles from fucking, Oliver and I sit at my mom's kitchen table with our laptops side by side.

Between spending my days with Becka in the sun and my nights underneath hard-spun love, I've managed to splinter off a few minutes for just myself over the last couple of weeks, and I do have some ideas.

"I found some I think I like," I tell him, opening my notebook. There's a list on the first page and only three schools are on it, but it's not nothing.

Subtly stylish and ever good looking smiles. Summer as a lifeguard's been good to him. Tan and fit, he smells like the beach and makes me want to lean.

"What about majors?" he asks.

I shrug. I have no idea, but unlike with my parents or Becka or Dusty, I'm not scared to admit that here.

"That's okay," Oliver says, extending his hand for my list. "You don't have to know yet. It's okay not to know."

I focus on the ocean-blue and grass-green paint streaks on his black cutoffs as he types the first school on my list into his laptop.

"You can go in undecided. Just start with whatever interests you in any way and go from there."

His tone is as patient and kind as usual, but I like it better with music in the background. Opening a playlist on my screen, I scoot my chair closer to his and we take virtual tours together. Linfield and Willamette are pretty, and I like that they're smaller, but they're not as far from my parents as I'd prefer. Mayhurst is farther, and gorgeous, but crazy expensive, and that's when Oliver suggests the Art Institute in Portland.

"They have a ton of scholarships," he says. "And their programs are amazing."

I don't doubt these things, but it's only two hours from here—which is close enough that Thomas could come visit whenever, but so could my parents.

"Are you going there?"

Quietly cool smiles with kind of, sort of shy pride.

"No." He shakes his head. "I got into Pratt."

"Wait." I narrow my focus. "What? Oliver, in New York? Pratt Institute, Pratt?"

He laughs a little and says, "Yeah," but that's it.

"Do you want to stay in Oregon?" he asks.

I shrug again, and when he brings up The University of Puget Sound on his screen, I'm awed not only by how pretty it is, but by possibilities.

"Tacoma isn't too far from home," he says. "But enough to get a little free."

I only half hear him as I reach over and start clicking.

MOM WAS excited when I brought up Puget Sound.

"It's private, right? Small? Isn't it affiliated with a church?"

When she said she wanted to make plans to visit, I wasn't lying when I said I'd like that.

I haven't decided, but I think I like it, and I have yet to tell Rebecka any of this. I will when the time is right, and today is not that day.

It's her father's birthday,and her mother is going all-out as usual. She's throwing a huge party and my Mom's letting me go on the condition that be I home for breakfast Sunday morning.

Whatever.

Ben's leaving for school next week. Pete spends all his days at Easy's garage. My boy drives to and from Linn-Benton week-daily, and I start my senior year the day after tomorrow. It's been weird not seeing them all the time, and it's only going to be stranger when school starts and they're nowhere to be found in the halls.

Standing in front of my closet, half-dressed with curlers in my hair, it's hard to shake apprehension away.

Pushing dresses around, I wish I was getting ready with Becka. We've spent so much time together lately. It's different, but it's hard not to miss. She hasn't brought my marks back up, but she's more possessive of me and our time so I'm surprised she still hasn't replied to my text from this morning.

Jealousy and resentment burn through me, but I swallow hard. So what if she's with Petey? Maybe she's good for him. His eyes are clearer than Dusty's lately.

Stepping away from my closet, I grab my phone.

Tell me something good, I text love.

I sit down at my vanity and reach for bronzer. Not a full minute passes before he replies.

Come over.

THE CATERING van is parked across the street from the Castor house. Lucas and Tommy's cars are in the garage, but Becka's Jeep is nowhere to be seen.

I pull in next to the Lincoln.

Smoothing down my sundress as I get out, I push my curls over my shoulders with one hand and carry Luke's card in my other. It's a little after four and still hours before the party starts. End of August heat sticks to me, but the sky's cloudy and the breeze blows through soft peach-pink cotton as my Candie's sandals click across the driveway.

I let myself in when I get to the front door, and inside, the house smells like warm bread and fresh flowers.

"Hi, sweetheart," Tommy greets. Carrying two gift boxes, she smiles a smile that could melt ice caps. "Rebecka isn't home yet, but Thomas is around here somewhere."

Nodding, I look around on my way to the stairs. No dirty dishes or paperwork clutter the counters. Nothing's piled up or unclean. It's all spotless-perfect, just like it used to be.

With the exception of gourmet delicacies in the kitchen.

Love can wait for chocolate.

Stopping before I head upstairs, I pop open a little box to find tiny nonpareils, and I feel him.

I've always known when Dusty's close, but it's stronger than it's ever been. It's more than just my heart now. From my fingertips to my toes, my entire body senses his presence, and I smile to myself as I take a piece of chocolate and let him come to me. I listen closely and get a little rush on the simple sound of his approach.

Enclosing trouble doesn't lift his heels as he walks. He takes his time across the tiles. His steps sound like an at-ease siege, and each one fills my veins with anticipation. When I turn to face him, lawlessness on long legs looks far too good in a plain white tee and dark slim denim. His eyes are lightless, but they're zeroed in. I'm all he can see and his focus grips me like I know his pocketed hands want to. His regard covers me and his look is just like his kiss.

Territorial.

Spreading.

Dirty.

Closing our distance with a sense of certainty and pride not even a god could get away with, Dusty smirks, and I know I'm in too deep. His walk alone lays my conscience out and strokes deeply into it with every step.

Smiling, I meet his black dead-on.

"Hey, swag."

Lips I crave curve into a full grin, and for as different as so much feels, this person is the same as he's ever been when he looks at me. All disorder and daring and barely abided longing, he's still mischief, wrapped up and too bound to stay away.

Playfully lowering his lashes over shameless proof of his habit, my hoodless-hoodlum tilts his head over mine.

"Hey, sway," he says quietly.

I smile sky high.

A couple hours later, my boy's boys have joined us, and after a blunt in his room, we're back in the kitchen because I'm dying for more chocolate.

Petey opens a beer while Thomas and Ben pour shots. I've got half a truffle in one hand and the other half in my mouth, and I want milk. At the same time I pull the carton from the fridge, the front door opens.

Stoned-golden and giggling low, we all four look around the corner as Becka steps inside with sweat on her forehead and her board under her arm. Purple and pink and wind-tangled hair that's fallen from her ponytail sticks to her and her baby blue eyes gleam heavily.

"What are you doing here?" she asks, looking right at me.

Unable to hide and too high to care to, I eat the other half of my truffle.

"I was bored," I say. "Where have you been?"

"Just riding."

Maybe it's the pot, but everything feels awkward.

Then this girl walks to me and steals the carton of white milk from my hand. She sips straight from it and Petey fakes being disgusted.

"I'm going to shower," she says, handing it back and wiping her forehead with the back of her arm.

I pass the carton to Pete and take off after my girl.

"I'm coming too!"

Back on Dusty's floor, we're sore-cheeked and smoke-surrounded.

To my left, Thomas leans against the foot of his bed like he used to. Pete's across from me with another blunt, cracking up so hard he has to pause the story he's telling every few seconds, and Ben's on my right laughing twice as deep and blushing even deeper. He falls over, covering his amusement with both hands.

Between my boy's nightstand and his bed, I'm in the spot that's always been mine and I'm laughing too. We're as close to how we used to be as we can get, and I don't want things to change any more.

As if sex and drugs haven't done enough to stunt and deform this togetherness, Becka's here. She's squeezed between me and love, laughing just as hard as Tweedledum and Tweedledumber, and I hate how spiteful I feel.

"Wait, wait, wait," she says, pulling from the bottle and passing it to her brother. "Remember that morning when we were getting ready for school, and Ben called to tell you he got his first pube?"

I laugh because everyone does, but the grudge in me tightens.

I need this, and she's in my space.

"Oh, oh!" She turns to me, tapping my leg as I hit the blunt. "Remember when you screamed? In the bathroom? And Dusty came running up because he thought there was a spider?"

Petey and Ben snicker, but I don't laugh. I hold smoke deep in my lungs and concentrate on not screaming.

"That wasn't funny," Thomas says, and I blow smoke toward his ceiling, exhaling slowly, steadily, and practice-perfectly.

Love saved me, but his sister isn't fazed.

"Okay," she says. "You're right. That wasn't nearly as funny as when she asked me what a blowy was."

I force myself to laugh along, but hostility bites the back of my tongue.

"I figured you'd know."

Pink and purple and in the way laughs like she's forcing herself too, and when I pass her the Philly, she smiles.

"Don't be bitter, princess kid," she says, curving her ankle around mine. "You know I love you."

CHAPTER
fifty-two

"Shh," Bliss whispers with her finger pressed to her kissed-too-hard lips.

"There's no one here," I say.

Baby turns away from me and walks toward the front door of my house. Her heels tap on the wooden porch until she removes her shoes and waits for me on the welcome mat with bare feet. Soft yellow porch light above her shines through Leigh's hair. Her curls are loose, and her cheeks are fucked-too-long pink.

"I know," she whispers. "I don't want to disturb the fireflies."

"You weren't thinking about them before," I say into her ear, slipping the key into the lock.

Bliss turns the knob and leans back with the door, catching her footing right before she slips. She tiptoes into the house with her shoes dangling from her pointer and middle finger, as if we have to sneak around.

My pops has business in Los Angeles, and my mom and little sister went with him. Becka wants to check out the schools and taste the beginning of her so-called future.

I come up behind my girl and kiss the side of her throat. She smiles and curves into me, dropping her shoes beside the couch. I set my hands on her hips and push my already-hard-again cock against her. Leigh nibbles her lip and hums, tilting her neck for my mouth.

"We have all night?" she asks, whispering. Chrome-white moonlight from open drapes brightens half of her face.

I can taste my love on her skin, combined with salt from making her sweat. I know I'm still inside of her, drying between her thighs. Leigh wears my bite marks on the tops of her shoulders, over her rib bones, and on her ankles. I've kissed her purple, and overstretched her muscles and tissue.

"Yes," I say against her temple, leading her toward the staircase.

I slip my hands under her shirt and push the tips of my fingers into her low-toned sides. She places her hand on the rail and sucks in a breath.

"Can you?" I ask, moving my right palm over her soft stomach.

She nods. "Yeah."

I dip my hand into the front of her jeans and feel where I was not even an hour ago. She's hot and swollen and wet from earlier, like I knew she would be. She whines, tender and sore, but her mouth shapes up, loving this sensitive proof of crazy as much as I do.

This girls loves when she can feel me long after we're done, when all she has to do is press her palm between her legs to feel our ache.

When we finally stumble into my room, I can feel my heart pulse in my dick … and in my pocket.

Love me first, my bitch haunts.

I pull off my hoodie and drop it to the floor reaching for the hem on my girl's shirt. I kiss the dip between her collarbones while Leigh drags her deep purple nails down my biceps. Baby bites my ear as I reach back and unstrap her black B cup.

She doesn't love you like I do, cocaine continues, deep in dark denim.

I lead my girl toward my bed—our safest place. She falls forward onto her hands and knees before crawling to the center of the mattress. I hook my hand into the waist of her jeans and pull until they get stuck on her thighs. She turns to her back and leans on her elbows, kicking her feet until her legs are free and skinny blues are over my shoulder, joining my sweater.

Come on, baby, this addiction whispers.

Topless in cotton underwear, baby sits up and stretches toward me. Amid her open knees, she smiles high while unbuckling metal from leather. Jingling with every pull and tug, my belt sings in her hands. My girl goes for my button, easily opening me up with the flick of her fingers.

Don't let her touch me, the demon in my pocket pleads.

I pull my hips away and push Leigh back, curving my hands under her thighs and pulling her bottom to the end of the bed. Trying to ignore my habit's desire, I drop to my knees and kiss from Leighlee's knee to her bitten ankle.

"Stay like this." I stand to my feet and press my lips to her knee cap.

Leighlee sighs.

She knows. You know she knows.

Slipping my finger into the elastic of her underwear, I say, "Take these off."

Green eyes daunt and strike, screaming everything she'll never say again with her own voice—*loser, you left me, I hate you.* Those were a one-time deal.

"Go," Leigh snaps. She kicks my hip with her just-been-kissed foot and rolls onto her stomach.

I tickle the bottom of her foot, trying to make it better, but it's too late. I sniff and rub my eager nose. My gums tingle and my palms prickle. My body stands here, but my attention is already in the bathroom with my slut spread out and waiting, all lined up and vindictive.

Hurry up, she laughs.

I turn and go.

My mind is one step ahead of itself. I'm closing the door, and I already know I need to flip on the light. I'm flipping on the light so now I need to empty out my pockets. I'm emptying out my pockets, envisioning myself cutting lines.

I catch my reflection in the mirror.

Look real hard, motherfucker. That's you and me.

Black eyes, black heart, black blood. I need a shave and a haircut. My nose is red. My nostrils slightly flare. I sniff.

I toss my vindicator on the counter and turn the sink water on and let it flow to hide this noise from Leigh. After pulling off my shirt, I cup my hands under the water and sink my face in.

Breathe in and drown yourself, pussy, cocaine pushes. *It's the only way you'll ever be able to stop.*

With my palms on the bathroom counter, I look into the mirror again. Water drips from my chin and nose, and my hairline is damp. Faint purple-blue colors collect under my eyes, proving how tired my body really is.

My form suffers, failing, withering away—diminishing—while my insides jump to their own altered up-tempo pace. My brain, my heart, and my energy run strong, fast and undying as long as I give in. But my eyes, skin, and complexion tell a different tale.

Hmm ... loser?

No. That's too nice.

Expected.

I squeeze my eyes closed.

She won't always understand. She won't always accept. But I will, baby.

I pull a towel from the rack and dry my face and hands. Then I pour this nagging bitch out onto the counter and cut her up with the razor I keep hidden behind the mirror. I let Her in with a rolled up twenty I hide under the trash can.

She fucks quick and hard, steady as She goes. One, two ... three. It takes no effort anymore. I'm good at this. Exceptional. Phenomenal.

I tilt my head back and rub my nose with the back of my hand, and I chill while everything falls into place. My spine straightens and my heartbeat evens out. It's too fast and rocking, but so much better. I roll my neck and crack a few knuckles before I chop Her into four more lines.

So fucking swift.

This time when I catch my reflection, I don't give a fuck.

Compelling and unbeatable, I'm confident. My eyes burn darker, and I hold my head higher as cocaine weaves and bonds Herself into my muscle and bone. Marrow is traded for lost inhibitions, and when I flex it's pure strength.

I turn off the water before switching off the light and opening the door. Baby Bliss is dressed in my hoodie, sitting on my computer desk with her legs crossed and the window open, letting late night October air in. Her lips hint blue, but her eyes are all determination.

Slipping a cigarette between my lips, I light up and sit in the chair at her feet. I place them in my lap and smirk between drags. "What?"

Leigh tries to pull ten little toes away, but I hold onto her right calf.

After one more pull from my smoke, I toss it out the window over her shoulder and blow white fumes out to the side. I stand up and push my girl's legs open stepping in between, digging my fingers into her thighs, pulling her to the edge of the desk until she can feel me against her.

"Kid," I tease. "Little girl. Pretty princess."

Her nails break the skin on the top of my hand. "Let me go."

I brush my lips across her cheek and sigh. "Baby, baby, baby."

She pushes her fists into my chest. "Get away from me."

I rock my hips against her, and the entire desk shifts and bangs against the wall. My pencil holder falls over and different papers scatter. Leigh's hands move to the edges of the desk beside her. Her head falls back, and her lips part, letting out the sweetest little moan.

She moves against my cock. I push back. The computer monitor falls over and paint chips off the wall. Leigh wraps her legs around me and whispers, "Come closer," between little cries.

The hoodie comes off easily, and she clings—lips to lips, chest to chest, stomach to stomach. I lift up and turn away from the window, surefooted and aware. I can hear and feel and smell and sense all. Thanks to seven white lines and strawberry blond kisses.

Love is vivid.

We fall to the mattress in a breathless hurry of open mouths and lifted hips and pulled cotton and pushed-down jeans. Leigh tries to slip me inside while I'm kicking my pants off. She groans in frustration when I pull back.

But she gets the tip and loses her mind.

My girl can't wait, so I fuck her with my socks on.

"Right here, baby," I whisper, tilting her chin toward the side of my face, near my ear. "I want it here."

My girl knows, and she nods.

I pump my dick a few times before I line up and settle on my elbows so I can get what I want. When I slide and push in as deep as I can, Leigh gasps right into my ear.

Long and hard and loud, Leigh cries out. There is nothing more bittersweet than the first sound she makes. While she drags her fingers down my shoulders, I bring her right leg up. It unites us a little more, but not as much as we need.

While I stroke deeply and fully, moving my hips with intent, I feel her nails inflicting damage to my already harmed skin.

"More," I groan into the side of her neck. "Harder, baby."

I won't be satisfied until she splits me open and touches me on the inside. I want her fingertips to dance on vertebrae, and I want her arms to get tangled in veins and arteries. It'll be enough when she's elbow deep, coated in my life source. I need this girl to break apart rib bones and puncture lungs to reach for my heart. I want her to rip the right ventricle from the left, just to feel the very center of where my heart beats for her.

"That's you," I'd say. *"That's where you are."*

I dig my feet into the mattress for leverage and posture. My left sock slips down my foot and the sheets gather beneath us, starting to come undone. Leigh's hands fall from my back to my bed, and her nails press into gray cotton. Her back arches, and I push in harder, pressing my pelvis against her clit. I lick her partly open lips. I whisper things I don't even understand.

I pull out and turn her on stomach. Leigh laughs lustfully, pushing her bottom up so I can slip in.

I come, but I fuck through it.

THE WORLD is static and clocks are dead. Stars are gone and the moon drops from the sky, leaving us in complete darkness while the sun is stuck in the east, unable to rise. The trees surrounding the house burn, and the walls from the house fall flat. My girl cries, "God, God, God. Please, please, please," but even He has left us.

We are the only people left in this universe.

We're alone, faithless and sinning. Love begs, pleads, and demands The King of Kings to hear her. She makes deals with Our Creator. "Give me this and I swear … I swear!"

But love is losing religion, and there is no God here.

Baby comes, tight and quaking around my cock. I press her to the mattress until she's flat and I'm on top, slowly leading her through her namesake.

She cries. Leigh always does.

We keep going and hours have passed. All of the sheets have fallen from the bed, and my socks are long gone. I sit against the headboard while baby rides my dick. Her eyes are barely open and I keep slipping out because we're too wet.

"I'm so tired." She smiles lazily.

Leigh's arms fall slack at her sides, and her shoulders slouch. She falls into my chest and softly kisses under my chin.

Carefully leading my girl to her back, I pull away from Leighlee and she shakes her head.

"I'm okay. Keep going," she says breathlessly. Her legs fall open, and I can see how too-loved her center is.

We should stop, but we can't.

So I lift her hips and slip a pillow beneath her lower back.

"Better?" I ask, settling between her legs again.

She smiles with closed eyes and nods her head, dropping her knees completely wide. Then I'm inside again, fueled by obsessed love, and Her.

WE'RE LYING on my floor with the blankets and pillows. Baby's in one of my shirts with her feet up on the bed, and her red-yellow hair fanned around her head. She's focused on the TV while I'm centered on the bruises I've put on her body in the last two days.

Nothing slips my mind. Not a single thing is overlooked or forgotten. I ate her childhood and molded her into this person—cold and calculating and bitter—everything she shouldn't be.

The simple smile she used to get when she saw me and the excitement our secret used to create is lacking. I miss cream soda floats and snow boots that saved the world. I miss being on the phone with her talking about nothing at all. I miss the times when she melted over my touches simply because she loved me—only because she loved me.

All of that has been replaced with this need to prove that we love each other and need each other the most. It never stops.

Leighlee's suspicious of everything: clingy, needful and defeated. She's always touching me, binding us together however she can. It's a pinky hooked in my belt loop, her toes touching my ankle under the dinner table, her mouth around my cock.

We're holding on, but I know that one day our grip will slip.

I sit up and open the top drawer of my nightstand, reaching in for my bag. Baby turns her head to see what I'm doing but looks away just as easily—unaffected.

"That's not normal, you know?" I say, holding a half-smoked joint at the corner of my lips.

I light a match in my right hand and use my left to protect the flame. My eyes squint as trees catch fire, and I inhale, deep … deeper … so fucking deep. I breathe until my lungs are full and burning.

I exhale.

"This should be good," she mumbles, rolling her eyes.

"You shouldn't be untouched by this," I say, spinning my bad habit between my thumb and pointer finger. "It should bother you."

She sits up. "*That* should bother me? That's never bothered me."

I press my lips to burning paper and pull. With my lungs full, I say, "Because I fucked you up."

Bliss gets up, and small, precious fingers move around my ankle and slowly up my calf. "I'm good for you, though, right, Thomas?"

I smoke and nod, dying under her hands. The racing in my head slows down just enough to allow myself to relax. Baby moves her touch under my kneecap now, kneading her fingers, forcing the right side of my mouth to tilt and smile.

Then, with her lips right below my ear and her body between my knees, she says, "If I made you choose, would it be me?"

I laugh, blissed out on the weed and my girl. "Yeah," I say.

"Good," she says.

Then she's up, and she's gone.

And I know.

I try to catch her ankle, but Leigh knew what she was doing when she was touching me hypnotized. By the time I'm up, she's already in the bathroom with the door shut and locked. I pound on it, and the wood trembles under my fist. It splinters and deforms, but it does not open.

"Leigh," I yell, "don't fucking do it."

The bathroom trash can hits the door from the other side, and she's opening and closing the cabinets.

"Open the door!" I cry like a man who's about to lose everything.

Then I hear baby open the toilet seat.

The user in me overrides rationality and my body moves on its own, beating the door until the frame separates from drywall. Chalky pieces of plaster snow down on me, but the lock does not give and the door holds.

The toilet flushes.

I wail out like a beast, raspy and scratchy and writhing. "Open the fucking door, Leighlee."

Slamming my fist into the fractured barrier between me and my girl, my knuckles split, rupturing old scar tissue and bleeding out between my fingers and down my wrist.

"Stop!" Baby pleads with terror in her tone.

I raise my fist to hit again, but she unlocks the door. With my swollen, blood coated hand, I turn the knob and push it open. My girl is in the small space between the toilet and the counter with her chin raised high but her arms out in front of her.

Bliss screams, pressed against the wall. I step to her and slam the palms of my hands into the flat surface at each side of her head, splintering sandy colored paint and wallboards underneath.

"What the fuck did you do?" I seethe.

Baby doesn't lower her hands. They push against my chest as she stares straight up into my eyes. She refuses to answer, and I hit the wall knocking the mirror from its nail.

This girl steps into me, and when I don't back up, she pushes harder, forcing me away from her. Just a step—a step I take right back from her—but she did it, she moved me.

I smile maliciously through wrongful tears. "You think I can't get more?"

She pushes my arm away and stands unbowed, trembling but firm. "I don't care."

I laugh and move away, turning on the sink. I dip my wounded hand under cold water and watch it turn light pink from blood.

"You're disgusting." Bliss walks out of the bathroom.

"I'M GOING to wear this today," Leigh says, pulling my dark gray hoodie from its hanger. She brings it to her nose and inhales. "Rebecka won't be there, and nobody else will know it's yours."

She makes me re-hang the bathroom mirror so she can get ready for school. I sit on my bed afterward and watch love curl her hair. She has mascara and hair spray, and whatever-the-fuck else spread all over the counter. Baby stands on her tiptoes to get a better look at her reflection. At one point, Bliss isn't paying attention and leaves the curling iron in her hair for too long. Strawberry-blond starts to smoke and Leigh blames me.

"You'll be the end of me, Dusty," she says, smiling through the mirror.

I want to drive her to school, but we'd have to explain to my parents and Rebecka why her car's parked on the side of the house. I don't give a fuck.

"Tell them," I say.

She pulls her curls out from under the borrowed-from-me hoodie hood and says, "We've gone this long, what's another couple of months?"

Everything.

When we leave the house behind, she turns one way down the road and I turn the other.

I'm in class now, slouched in my seat, tapping my pen against my folder. The constant noise annoys the girl sitting beside me. She crosses and uncrosses her legs, flips her hair, and clears her throat while staring at my hands.

I don't even know what class I'm sitting in. I was under the assumption I was only doing this until she graduated, but things changed when she sent in an application of her own.

University of Puget Sound.

I feel it hanging over our heads, just as looming as our secret.

Our plans were never concrete and far from practical, but I love the notion of Bliss and me leaving town the day she graduates. Eighteen or not, she's supposed to be mine after this. That's been the deal all along.

She's ruining it.

Portland is close enough to be held responsible for the last seven years. It's close enough for weekend visits and family holidays, and too many fucking expectations. It will be near enough to feel the disappointment of everyone who will be hurt by our lie.

"Be real," she keeps telling me. "We can't just run."

I think we can.

I tap my pen a little louder, a little faster. Tap, tap, tap, tap.

I sit up straight and clear my throat. The girl next to me gives me a dirty look before pretending to write notes.

I check my phone. Leigh should be just out of third period, and I have ten minutes before I can leave.

I'm coming to get you, I text.

She replies right away: *can't.*

I get up and walk out.

With an unlit cigarette between my lips and my phone at my ear, I push through the double doors and walk across the lawn toward my car. I can't be still. I can't be in that class with that girl and my thoughts.

"Hello," love answers.

"Why can't I come get you?" I ask, holding my phone between my ear and shoulder to light my smoke.

"You start baseball today, remember?"

"Yeah, that." I smile and blow contaminants into the air.

"I'll call you after school," she says.

We hang up, I grab my folder, and I head to my next class.

Whatever it is.

THE SUN is in my eyes—running, squats, push-ups, and lunges—I finish my last sprint and slow to a walk with my hands on the back of my head.

"Want to hit a few?" Coach asks me.

"Whatever," I answer.

I trade my hat for my batting helmet and tap the bat against my cleat before I stand in position beside home plate.

"We're only practicing, Castor. Go easy," Coach says from the side. "Keep swinging until I tell you to stop."

The pitcher pitches, and I swing and miss. I spit and reposition.

The pitcher pitches, and I swing a hit.

The ball flies out somewhere. I don't give a shit where it went. It's not here, that's all that matters. My body tells me to run. That's how the game is played. Stand, swing, and run. It doesn't change because the coach tells me not to go. I hit the motherfucker, I'm going. We're going.

The pitcher pitches, and I swing and hit again.

I drop the bat and run.

"Castor, swing again. Swing until I tell you to stop!" Coach yells out.

I jog back and sweep off home plate with my left foot.

"Stop hitting so hard, Castor. We're only practicing your swing. Warm up," Coach says. "This isn't the real deal. It's too early for that shit."

The pitcher pitches and I swing and smash the motherfucking ball.

Because that's the fucking deal.

I drop the bat and run, and I make it past first base. But coach steps out from behind the fence and yells, "What part about it's too early to run do you not understand, Castor?"

I stop between first and second, breathing too hard, thinking too hard—stuck. I shrug. "I don't know," I say, out of breath. "Habit."

"Get up to bat," Coach says, placing his hat back on his head.

The pitcher pitches and I swing and miss.

My elbows are high and my knees are bent. I watch the ball until it's right in front of me. I swing, and I miss.

"You were swinging too hard before, Castor. Now your swing's off," Coach yells. "You're tired. I told you it was too soon."

I take a practice swing off to the side. I step up to bat. I watch the ball, and I tell myself to be careful, swing lightly, and don't run.

This shit is natural. It always has been.

Bliss always will be.

The pitcher pitches, and I swing and hit.

I drop the bat, and I run.

I'm not one of those people who learns from his mistakes, and there are always consequences when I slow down and walk.

"You need to do what's right for this team, Castor." Coach's tone and obvious dissatisfaction pulls me off the field. "This isn't only about you. She's counting on you to do your part."

My heart jump kicks, beating and fighting to keep up with adrenaline. "What?"

Slowly and sarcastically, coach repeats, "Your team is counting on you to do your part."

I rub my eyes with the palms of my hands and take off my hat, tossing it near my glove on the dugout floor. I can't think straight. I can't function. I can't be here with her in my head like this. It's becoming inescapable.

I need a line. I need Leigh.

I need to do what's right.

"Got it," I say dismissively. I sit on the bench and hang my head between my shoulders.

"Whatever you have going on, kid," Coach continues, "get it figured out and come back tomorrow. We'll try again. Fresh start."

I head over to Pete's. He opens the door and offers me his open arms.

"You're all clay-dirt dirty, big-time college ball player," he jokes, letting me by.

I feel like I haven't spent much time here lately, but everything is absolutely unchanged. Same dirty carpet, couch, and walls. It smells like bud and booze, with the slightest hint of vomit, courtesy of Rachel. A working TV is set on top of a broken one. An old blanket covers the front window, and Ben's sitting at the kitchen table, packing a bowl.

It's just the three of us, and it's exactly what I need to clear my mind.

After a couple of hours with my boys, I've finally mellowed out and sunken into the couch beside Ben, who's in town visiting from school. With a beer between my knees, I have my girl on the phone.

"Where are you?" she asks, disharmonized and let down.

"Petey's," I answer, undercover-like because we're still this big fucking hush-hush. Maliciously, I add, "Mom."

"It's my birthday on Saturday. Don't be gone on my birthday." Leigh sighs into my ear. It sounds like she might be crying, but it's the way she always sounds now.

Love is knowing you did that to her.

"I'll be home tonight," I say.

"It's three in the morning, Thomas," she says.

"You're right." I smirk. "I'll be home tomorrow after my fresh start."

I hang up and slip my phone into my pocket.

"Family problems, or what, Dusty?" Pete sets his empty bottle on the table we were just taking lines off of, the same table that's been here since we were kids sneaking cigarettes out of his mom's purse.

"Something like that," I say.

He keeps my gaze, and I return his look from earlier. He isn't so sly, and I'm not so convinced. I could say it right now—you're fucking my baby sister—but I don't, because he doesn't say it either.

Ben scoots over and sits closer to me, thigh to thigh.

"I love her, Thomas," he says, and then he starts to cry. Just like that, fucking waterworks.

I think my boy's gone crazy, but I feel the same way. It has to be the bowl we smoked earlier. It has to be the drugs. This shit was bound to start killing brain cells eventually.

I try not to laugh, but when Ben says, "So don't fuck her, okay?" I lose it.

Laughing, I fall to my side on Pete's ugly fucking couch. It smells like dust and cigarettes. Has he been with my sister on this piece of shit? Uncontrollable laughter causes stomach cramps, and I can't breathe. I laugh until I'm crying, too.

"I know she's all slutty and shit," Ben explains, "but she's a good person, Dusty. I'm serious."

I sit up and wipe my eyes. "What are you talking about?"

"Don't fuck Val anymore." He moves his hand from my knee up to my shoulder. "I love her."

Pete takes the bowl from Ben and hits it.

"Sure," I say. "Congratulations on that … I guess."

I clear my throat and chew over whether or not I should tell him it's been over a year since I've been with Val. It's been about a year since I've been with anyone but Bliss.

"Bros before hos," he says, and I start to laugh all over again.

"It's not like that, Ben," I guarantee with a smirk.

When our moment is over, he calls Val and asks her to come over. She's on her way with Kelly, Mixie, and Katie. When the girls arrive, Valarie sits on Ben's lap and looks at me with eyes like saucers. She bites on her thumb nail and messes with her hair, and not much has changed about this girl, except now she's loved.

I get up for another beer, and Kelly and Petey are in the kitchen. She cries at the table, splotchy faced and brokenhearted, and he leans against the counter that's covered with old fast-food containers and empty booze bottles, pushing back a piece of linoleum with the toe of his shoe and speaking in low, regretful tones.

I mutter an apology for interrupting and open the fridge. The handle is loose and the inside is empty, with the exception of beer and a half-gallon of milk.

"I don't know why you're doing this," Kelly cries. With her elbows on the table, she covers her face with both of her small hands.

I screw off the top of my brew and toss it in the sink. "You good?" I ask Petey.

He doesn't look at me and continues to kick the lifted floor.

I kind of linger between the kitchen and the living room. I don't want to sit beside Val and Ben, and I don't want to listen to Pete call it quits with Kelly, and I definitely don't need to be near Mixie or Katie. It's not until my phone starts to ring again that Petey finally turns and gives me his eyes.

"It's my sister," I say, just to see what he does.

He smiles. It's four o'clock in the morning, and he's the only one talking to Becka at this time anymore.

Then Mixie slides beside me. "You holding?" she asks.

"Yeah," I say, glancing down.

She bats her lashes like it's pretty, but she looks like what she is: strung out. "Want to share?"

I down the rest of my beer and say, "Sure."

Mixie and I walk toward the back of the house, and I feel Pete's eyes on me the entire time.

Behind the closed bathroom door, she sits on the edge of the bathtub and opens her legs, lifting her hot pink stretched cotton dress around her waist. She's wearing a thong and it's fucking disgusting.

"For old time's sake," she says with a giggle.

I separate our lines and keep my eyes to myself. My phone is still ringing.

"No thanks," I mumble.

"Are you sad?" she asks. "Are you sorry because Valarie's with Ben? Is that why you won't fuck me?"

I glance over and she has her finger under lace between her thighs. In a gross attempt for my attention, she moves it over and shows me her run-through pussy. I laugh and lift my eyes to her face, to her dirty hair, to her skinny arms. Mix used to be kind of, sort of beautiful, but that was before she was chewed up and spit out. Youth is absent from her downcast face now, superseded by lowness and rejection.

I do my lines and leave the rest for her and meet Pete in the kitchen where he's bagging up the trash that has accumulated this week.

My phone keeps ringing.

"What was that about?" I ask, silencing it.

He uses his arms and sweeps everything off the counter into the bin. "Answer your phone, Thomas." He kicks the can back against the wall. "Little sisters only call if they need you."

THE SUN isn't up yet, but it peeks between clouds over the east. Streets are empty. Houses are dark, and businesses are closed. I'm the only one at the stop light, waiting for it to turn green, and my phone has finally stopped ringing.

As I turn onto her street, I slow my speed and flip on the heater. I reach in the back for the blanket I leave in here and drop it on the seat next to me.

Four houses down, I call her and switch off my headlights. I cruise until the Lincoln is nothing but a quiet rolling rumble and stop in front of the willow tree.

Leigh runs from the back, barefoot and bare legged. She tugs on the hem of her oversized white sleep shirt covering her most precious parts. My girl tiptoes up to my car and gets in with a rush of cold wind.

"Oh my gosh, it's freezing," she says happily, like I didn't keep her up all night with my absence.

Leigh sits across the seat with her feet in my lap and the blanket over her body. I puff on a joint while she tells me that Smitty and Becka don't talk anymore, and I think about telling her about Pete because I know she knows, but I don't.

"She got mad at me because I was sitting with Oliver." Leigh half laughs, half yawns, like it's no big deal. Except, with that motherfucker, it always is.

I blow on the end of my spliff before taking another hit, fighting the urge to push her feet off me. Baby takes notice of my discomfort and sits up.

I hate the sleepy purple beneath her eyes.

"Don't start," she defends.

I laugh. "I didn't say anything"

"You don't have to," she answers defiantly, suddenly awake. "He's my friend."

"Who you tried to sleep with," I reply sarcastically and intentionally to hurt her feelings.

I take one last hit and blow smoke out the window before starting my car. "I have to go."

"No." She shakes her head.

"Take the blanket with you. I'll see you later."

"Thomas, no."

I scoff and sit back, dropping my hands from the wheel. "What?"

"Don't be mad at me," she says.

She's so small and wrapped up warm in a blanket that smells like our sex, but this girl is the only person who can cause me to swell with rage so quickly. I want to punch the windshield out. I want to fuck doubt out of her.

Anybody I touched before Bliss meant zero—*they're* nothing, forgettable, and inconsequential. No names, no faces, no feelings. But Oliver, the only other boy she's ever put her lips on, is a legit option and a constant presence. I can tell by the way she says his name—smooth, with a small lift of her lips.

"I'm not," I finally say.

I hurt you, you hurt me … I love you more. This is what we've become.

So I skip one habit for the other. I go home and cover myself in counterfeit passion.

Love is saving her from me.

CHAPTER
fifty-three

The continuing detachment between my sister and Bliss is unmistakable. When I get home the next night, Leigh's sitting on one couch and Becka's on the other. They're arguing about school ... again.

"Nothing will change, Becka," my girl says evenly. "Why do you keep bringing this up?"

"Because we had a plan!" my sister shouts.

"No," Leigh corrects her. "You had a plan."

Clipped short by my arrival, the girls try to act like nothing is wrong, but their hurt lingers in the air.

"How was baseball?" Becka asks, let down by the end of their conversation. She sits back with the remote and absentmindedly flips through the channels.

I drop my equipment bag and shut the front door. "Fine," I say, looking between them.

Baby takes a small glimpse at me and sees the dope sickness. She rolls her eyes, and tears that may or may not belong to me slide down her cheeks.

Like I don't have enough to worry about, her look says.

I haven't slept in two days and can't deal with her concern right now. Opening the fridge for a bottle of water, my mother makes me sit down.

"Eat. You look like shit." Mom drops a bowl of pasta on the table in front of me.

"Thanks," I mumble, digging in with my fork. I force myself to take a bite but push my bowl away when Alfredo sauce hits my stomach.

"You're not going to eat?" Mom asks.

"I'm not hungry," I say. I push my seat back and get up.

I kiss her on the forehead as I try to pass, but she holds on to my sides and keeps me close in her mother-strong hold.

"Please, Dusty," she whispers.

With unsteady hands, I remove Mom's fingers from my shirt and walk away. The forkful of food in my stomach makes me ache. I'm nauseous and dizzy, and the slut in my back pocket is the only fucking remedy.

I'm in the shower, but I don't remember climbing the stairs. Hot water beats down on sore muscles and joints, but my skin is so tender it feels like needles. My stomach rolls and my head pounds. With one hand on the shower wall, I bend over and heave.

Drying myself off hurts more than the water did, so I don't. I dry heave some more but manage to brush my teeth.

Just one line. Only enough to make this go away.

In my room, I can't find my pants.

They're on my bed.

And this feels exactly like falling.

"Open your eyes."

She touches my chest, my arms, and my face.

"Please, please..." Baby's crying.

I open up, and Bliss is above me with tiny little tears wetting her cheeks.

Those are all mine, I think to myself.

I'm on the floor beside my bed, naked and unheated, and I know this is messed-up. I know I should move, but before I can form a coherent thought or make my body work, my stomach retches. Leigh helps me roll onto my side. It's a lot of pain and a lot of noise, and I only scare my girl.

"You're okay," she says softly, moving hair away from my face.

She sits beside me and rubs my back while my empty stomach kicks me from inside.

I grab for her, and she lets me. She allows me to pull her down and hold her under and does nothing to fight back. Leigh, halfway tucked beneath my weight, hugs me just as strongly as I'm clutching her.

"Tell me what to do," she says.

"It hurts," I groan between clenched teeth.

"I know it does," she whispers, wiping sweat from my forehead.

With my cheek pressed against her chest, my tears soak through her cotton shirt. I grip and force and overpower and cry. "I need it. I need it."

"No more, Thomas," she pleads so softly with so many tears. "Just try."

I'm asking her to get my pants, inside my pockets. "Please find Her," I whine.

Leigh doesn't get up, and she doesn't hesitate to say no.

I ask over and over and over again, and I'm being too loud, and I'm hurting her. I literally crawl up her body, scratching and bruising, ignoring her evident pain.

"Okay. *Shh*—be quiet." Leigh tries to move away from me, but I pin her wrists down and slide between her legs.

"Don't leave. Don't leave me!" I'm crying, and my stomach, and my skin ... I want to close my eyes.

"I won't," she says. "I would never."

WE'RE IN bed and I don't know how she got me off the floor. I try to open my eyes but the room spins.

I'm too hot and too cold and crying and itching and uneasy. I want to crawl out of my skin. I feel like every bone in my body was broken and re-set wrong. The rush in my blood hurts. My open pores ache. My teeth are sore. Breathing stings and pangs. Being awake isn't an option.

Leigh's behind me with her chin on my shoulder and her arm over my chest, making this manageable.

"For me, Thomas," she whispers in my ear. "Try, for me."

I nod, even though I don't completely know what I'm agreeing to. But as soon as I do, cocaine screams inside me, twisting and pleading her case.

I DON'T leave my room the next day, but I'm unstill.

I'm under the covers. I'm on top of the covers. I'm on the floor. I'm in the shower. I'm smoking a cigarette. I'm smoking a bowl. I'm on the phone with Bliss, frustrated. "Why the fuck are you making me do this?"

I'm calling her back, apologizing.

I'm in my clothes. I'm out of them. I'm hungry. I can't even think about eating.

I feel better.

I feel so much worse.

I throw my phone because it won't stop ringing. I tell my mom to leave me the fuck alone because she won't stop knocking. I put my phone back together because my girl might be calling.

I look for Her, because I know She's here somewhere.

I come undone and turn dresser drawers upside down and search the pockets of every pair of pants I own. I look through my shoes and my shirts and my hoodies and my backpack. I toss papers and lift my mattress. I'm in the bathroom, and I know—I fucking know: Bliss flushed my slut again.

I'm on the floor, crying and struggling. I'm alone and gutless. I'm torn. I'm powerless. I'm in love.

One more time.

Just one more time and I'm done.

I look for my phone so I can call Casper. I come up with excuses to give Bliss.

My phone rings before I dial, and it's sunny side, and I have nothing—no justification.

I hear her voice, and it's almost as good as Her.

"I'm thinking about you, you know," she says calmly.

I cry, but baby doesn't mention it. She just talks.

"I wanted to leave school so bad," she says, this time with a smile in her tone.

Her voice soothes me.

"And I'm probably a bad friend, because I hardly said two words to Becka all day." Leighlee sighs.

I think I hear a car door close outside, but it's hard to tell through everything else.

"Then she tells me she won't be home tonight," Leigh says softly. "She has plans."

Shirtless, I lie back on the bathroom floor and the cool tiles feel so good on my overheated skin. I put Leigh on speaker and place the phone on my stomach and listen.

"She said she was going to Portland with your parents, and they won't be back until tomorrow morning."

I rest my arms at my sides. I close my eyes.

"So, after school, I called my parents," Leigh says.

Tears fall down my temples into my hair.

"I told them I was staying the night with my best friend," she whispers.

My bedroom door opens.

So do my eyes.

And she's here.

MY EYES are the cleanest blue they've been in a year.

I step over clothes and trash, and I can't believe I did this to my room again. I put on a pair of boxers and check my phone. Ignoring anyone that isn't Bliss, I check her messages first.

Hey, sleep-all-day boy, she sent. *I wore your sweater to school. It smells like you.*

It feels like you, says the one after that.

I can't wait until it is you.

I sniff, clearing my still-raw passages, and out of nowhere, longing hits me like a train. My mind turns one-tracked, and I can taste Her in my throat and feel Her in my sinuses. One phone call is all it would take to get the most cravable kind of disgusting.

I open the top drawer of my night stand and toss my phone in. I smoke and it alleviates some of the urge.

To drown out cocaine's calling, I turn up Nirvana. I clean my room. I slip my dresser drawers where they belong and fold every shirt, pair all of my socks, and toss whatever doesn't fit me anymore into a pile in front of my bedroom door. I go through my closet, and I clean everything out from under my bed. I trash all of the junk from my computer desk and pull my bedding from my mattress.

I feel lighter once it's all done, and when I look at the clock, a couple of hours have passed and the craving is nothing but a rustle.

With an armful of sheets, I finally leave my room. I pass by my sister, who didn't go to school today. She's lying on her bed, talking on the phone. I can't hear what she's saying, but her too-bright smile is a dead fucking give away.

The girl we've been lying to is a liar, too.

Down in the laundry room, I fill the washing machine with detergent and water and shove my bedclothes in.

I head to the kitchen and grab an apple from the fruit basket. I still feel like I'm recovering from a really bad hangover, but everything is quieter, slower, and calmer. The urge to run is quiet.

I bite into the green apple and the sour taste waters my eyes and curves my lips. At the same time, the washing machine begins to make a loud knocking noise.

"Dammit, Rebecka!" Mom yells, turning toward the laundry room.

I follow her down the hall since she didn't see me. I cross my arms and lean against the door frame. Mom opens the washer and the spinning stops. She reaches in and pulls out my dark gray sheets.

"What the—" she whispers, dropping them back in.

I clear my throat. With wet hands, she turns and looks.

She *really* looks.

Mom's shoulders sink, and her defensive posture eases. She was gearing up for a fight, but instead she sees blue eyes.

"I did some laundry," I say.

The left side of her lips lift in a small smile, but she turns away and starts pulling pillow cases and blankets out of the tub. "You can't put so much in at once."

"Sorry," I say.

Mom drops wet bedding in a laundry basket and closes the washer lid. She dries her hands and says, "You didn't go to school today?"

I shake my head.

"Are you..." she starts, unsure.

But before she asks anything I'm not ready to answer, I cut in. "I have some clothes that need to be dropped off at the Goodwill. Can you do that for me?"

Mom stands tall. "Yes."

As the rest of the afternoon and evening pass, the cravings come and go—some stronger than others. I keep myself occupied. I smoke. I clean my bathroom. I make plans with Leighlee, and I talk to my sister.

"You might not get into a school in California," I say. I'm lying on her bed, and she's in front of her mirror, putting Neosporin on her cut-up-from-skating knees.

Becka rolls her eyes. "I worked too hard *not* to get into California, Dusty."

"Where did you even apply?" I ask.

"Everywhere," she says, like a dream.

The conversation turns to Bliss, and my sister's unease about my girl really shows.

"She's so fucking small-town," my baby sister says. "And, like, how am I ever supposed to trust her?"

"She's your best friend, Becka," I say.

"Yeah, and best friends aren't supposed to lie. Best friends aren't supposed to make plans and ditch those plans." She shakes her head, and I get it, because Leigh abandoned our plans, too.

"We were just … supposed to go," little sister says, tossing the ointment. "But she's so fucking—good."

"You've never lied to her?" I ask, but I already know the answer.

Her cheeks blush. She's not as good at keeping her secret as Bliss. She can't look at a person and lie like Leigh can. Rebecka is shifty and nervous, but my girl, she's a flawless liar.

"Not the point," she answers. "But no, not really. Not about this."

"Maybe we're just too different. I mean, it was fine before, but now … it's just not working out." She picks up a magazine to keep her hands busy.

Liar. Her position screams untruth.

But she's right. They're too different.

A LITTLE after eleven, Leigh calls me to say her parents are in bed.

On the drive over to her house, I'm accompanied by a nervousness I'm no longer used to. I park down the street, but after I walk away from my car, I walk back and park one block over.

I don't remember the side door of her house ever squeaking before, but it does now. I stop, halfway in the kitchen and halfway out, and when I don't hear anyone, I step in as fast as I can and close the door as quietly as possible.

I bump into the kitchen table.

"Fuck," I whisper, barely catching myself.

I'm a troubled wreck, and it's like the walls are closing in. My heart beats in my throat, and my hands sweat. One wrong move and Thaddeus will open his bedroom door and shoot my fucking head off.

The stairs creak and when the ice-maker drops ice, I almost lose my cool, like I'm some fucking pussy.

By the time I make it to Leigh's room, my heart beats loud enough to wake the neighbors.

Then I see my girl and I'm okay.

LONG BEFORE her parents are due to wake, I get out of bed. Baby wants to walk me to the door, but her tired heart and too-rested muscles keep her eyes from opening completely.

"Don't leave. Stay for my birthday." she whispers through the dark. She smiles, but the rest of her remains sunk and sleepy under cozy blankets and sheets that smell like us.

"Your birthday is tomorrow. I'll be back for you later," I say quietly, pulling the comforter over her shoulders, covering where I was just a second before.

I can hear the rain through the window and smell it through the vent, mixed with dust and the slightest hint of natural gas. Warm, artificial air gets rid of the chill and makes it so homelike in here.

I walk past the judge's door and don't think twice about him and his wife sleeping on the other side. I take the steps down to the living room like I normally do, and I don't bump into the kitchen table. The side door squeaks, but I'm outside walking around the side of the house before anyone inside would even realize they heard anything at all.

Love is confident.

With my hands in my pockets and my hoodie-hood up, I'm drenched by the time I reach my car, unseen and missing my girl like crazy.

As the day progresses, I go to school, and I go to baseball practice to master my swing—slow and steady. I'm patient, accountable, and still.

"Practice makes perfect, Castor," Coach insists.

"I already was," I joke.

He chuckles and pats me on the back. "You damn kids don't know shit."

Bliss calls on my drive home.

"I'm ready. I'm so ready!" she says. We've waited all week to celebrate her birthday together.

I laugh, driving into Newport's town limits. "You don't think it's too cold, baby? We could—"

"No!" she shouts. "We're doing this."

Forty minutes later, with a clean hoodie and a Yankees hat tugged over damp hair, I pull up to the front of Leigh's house as she runs out with her pink pillow and white backpack. She's wearing my hoodie under her black jacket and a pair of yellow skinnies that aren't warm enough for how cold it is.

She gets into the car and tosses her things in the back. My girl kisses me all over my face and whispers, "Drive," over my lips.

I take us to the grocery store on the outskirts of town. I don't think it's far enough away to get out of the car together, but my girl can't go all night without sugar. She'll die.

I hand her some cash. "Just go in, babe."

Leigh covers her head with her borrowed-from-me hood and pulls the strings tight, tying them in a bow. Red-blond bangs damp from the rain stick to her forehead. She's all eyes and nose and smile, and kind of, sort of hidden, but not at all.

"No one will even know it's me." Bliss laughs.

I look down at her feet. "Yeah," I say with a smirk, "because wedges in October give nothing away."

She wiggles her toes under black leather and brass buckles. "It's my birthday," she teases, smiling under too much cotton.

I turn off the car and unbuckle my seat belt, saying, "It's not your birthday, yet."

She opens her door as I open mine. "No one will see us."

With my hands in my pockets, I keep my hat low and my eyes down. Leighlee's at my side, not skipping a beat while my heart pounds in my fucking throat. She stops to ask some lady who's loading her groceries into the back of her car if we can take her cart. She hands it over with a smile.

My girl runs ahead of me with it. Its wobbly wheels zigzag while they roll too fast. Baby jumps on and glides all the way to the automatic double doors, holding on tight. I up my step to catch her, and when I do, I turn her around and she kisses me.

I want it so bad.

This.

Out in public.

"You're crazy, sway," I say, taking the cart.

The store is brightly lit and warm. The air smells like cinnamon apples, welcoming the fall season. My hands sweat on the cart handle, and I can feel my cheeks heat red.

After stopping in the cereal section, I take off my cap and push my hair back. "Get what you need, Bliss."

She looks around, still tied in a bow. "I don't need anything here."

I lean my forearms against the cart and drop my head. "I'll wait."

"Thomas, no one here knows us," she says lowly, but surely. Her soft little hand touches the back of my neck. She scratches teal painted fingernails under my hat. "And who cares if they do?"

I look up and meet green eyes full of uncertain determination. "You do," I answer.

"We can leave. Go through a drive-thru or something," she says in an annoyed tone, looking at each cereal box.

"We're already here," I say, exhaling.

She walks away.

"Leighlee," I call after her, but she keeps walking.

When I catch her at the end of the aisle, I circle my arms around her stomach and press my lips to the side of her neck.

"You can have a chocolate milk," I bribe, lifting her up. I set love inside the cart and tell her to stay down while I push. "Hide."

My girl drinks a Yoo-Hoo out of a straw and tells me what she wants as we go up and down each aisle. Boxes of junk food and juices pile at her feet. I take baby though the produce section and she makes a face. I throw in a couple of apples anyway.

"That stuff will kill you," she jokes.

By the time we make it to the register, I'm no longer worried about being seen. The check-out lady scopes me and Bliss like we're crazy, but my girl is sitting in the cart up to her knees in trans-fat, so I don't blame her.

"You'll never eat all of this," I say on our walk back to the car.

She searches through the bags and finds her box of Whoppers. She opens the seal and pops one in her mouth. "Watch me," she says with a wink and crunches chocolate malt between her teeth.

THE SUN goes down as we drive toward the beach, and the momentarily clear sky turns blue, then pink, then purple and orange, before fading to black. By the time we park, clouds cover the stars. The scent of rain is heavy in the air, tied with ocean salt and sand.

We're the only ones on the shore and it doesn't take a genius to guess why. The wind chill coming in from the ocean is bone-shivering, and the echo of thunder in the distance guarantees more rain. There's electricity in the air, and it's not only from Leigh and I.

Thaddeus and Teri McCloy's blissful wonder is supposed to be sleeping safe and sound in my sister's bed tonight, not catching pneumonia under the clouds with a secret she shouldn't be keeping.

Leighlee unfolds and lays our blanket flat onto the sea-sprinkled dock, the same aged boat port that's been our stomping ground since we were old enough to get away for a while. This wood knows us. It carries our names carved in its panels. It's heard our conversations, seen our bodies, and kept our secrets.

Baby unbuckles her shoes and takes them off one at a time, dropping each one on a different corner of the blanket so the breeze doesn't lift it. Then she zips her jacket up, but leaves the hood down. I give her my hat and hope it helps a little. The bill falls over her eyes, and she looks pretty when she peeks at me from under it.

"If you get sick and die, I'm killing you," I say.

She pushes my arm and scoffs, but her eyes are forgiving. "It's not that cold, overprotective boy."

Leigh sits between my knees with her back against my chest and uses my coat to cover her legs and bare toes. The wind has died down and the air doesn't seem so cold, but rain is near and thunder is loud. Waves hit the rocks under the lighthouse with more force, and the sky is pitch-dark and taunting, promising a downpour.

"Do you remember when your dad had that charity thing here?" she asks, falling deeper into me.

I remember Bliss under street light, lying to me about where my sister was. I told her we didn't pull wings from butterflies.

"You made me smell your shirt." She laughs, looking up at me.

"You had Oliver's sweater on," I remind her, kissing the tip of her nose.

Baby rolls her eyes with a disregarding simper. "You were grass and vanilla-scented—*trouble,*" she says. "You've always smelled like difficulty to me, Dusty."

I rub my lips across her right cheek and whisper in her ear, "That was a long time ago, princess."

"Nothing's changed," she says. Leigh sits up straight, crossing her legs. My arms fall from her body, but I pull her back. She can't take herself from me.

She couldn't then, and she can't now.

"Watch out for bed knobs," she says. Her eyes fill up, but she doesn't cry.

"What?" I ask, holding a little firmer. She might run, but I have her. She won't get far.

"You wrote it on Becka's shoe." Leigh tries to free her arm from my grip, but I won't be undone.

I hook my arm around her stomach and press her entire body against mine. With one arm around her middle, I use the other to pin hers at her sides. Leigh tilts her head back and turns her face into mine.

"I wanted that so bad," she says, like the memory slices her throat. "I wanted bed knobs. I wanted something that was just ours. So I went to your room."

My hat falls from her crown and lands on the blanket. Red-blond hair sticks to her forehead. She tries to shift her way out of my arms, but I'm not letting go. She elbows me in the stomach, but I only grip closer. With her back completely against me, she arches but gets nothing.

I kiss the side of her face. "Stop, stop, stop …"

"Your pillows used to make me sleepy," she says. "Those sleepy, trouble-sweet pillows."

She twists and jerks and turns, but I give her nothing.

"Thomas," she groans, but doesn't panic. "I can't breathe."

"I can't let you go," I say, under the thunder. I don't even know if she hears me. "I can't. Just stop."

Leigh uses her legs to try to lift and bites the side of my neck. She thrashes and screams into the so-close-to-storming night. But when nothing works, she gives up, and I'm still here, holding her down with heavy love.

"I made so many excuses for you. *It's a Thomas thing.*" She scoffs. "When everyone finds out about us, do you know how stupid I'm going to look?"

My betrayals surface: Valarie, Mixie, Katie, Dolly … so many more. Some I can't remember. Most I don't remember.

Her.

"I'm sorry." I kiss Bliss' cap-creased forehead. I kiss over her watery eyes. I let go of her arms and grip her chin so I can turn her head and kiss her lips.

She kisses me back.

Lightning strikes and cracks, and the entire world turns silver.

Baby's kissing to deflect. She forces my arm away from her stomach and she turns in my arms. On her knees between my legs, her lips are so fucking soft and cry-salty from her … from me.

We kiss with our eyes open, and hers tell the story of us: dependence, lies, and misery.

I kiss over and under her lips, licking her teeth and sucking her tongue. I slide, glide, linger, and slip. I kiss her until she can only breathe out of her nose. I kiss her until she can't breathe at all. I kiss her until the corner of her mouth splits.

I kiss her until her eyes close.

"I love you," I say against swollen lips.

"I love you more," she whispers.

"I loved you first."

"I love you always."

I smile against her cheek. "I love you crazy."

IN THE backseat of the Continental, the windows are foggy and the cab glows orange-yellow from the street light we're parked beneath. Rain comes down in sheets on the hood. Lightning strikes and thunder rolls, but it's nothing compared to my girl. She's alive and raw, lost in the middle of our own storm system.

"Love me," she moans, arching her back and tilting her head. "Love me. Love me."

Under this light, Leighlee's hair has never been so red and her eyes never so green. Her voice has never been this bare, and her words never this honest. She pours legitimacy and roars trueness.

She rolls her hips, riding my cock and rough-handling my heart.

"Did any of them fuck you like this?" she whispers in my ear with an unmistakable edge in her tone. "Did it feel like this?"

Baby's nipples harden and brush my chest as she strokes up and down my dick. She places her hand on the side of my neck and moves her lips from my ear to my mouth.

"Could you not even stop yourself every time you were in someone that wasn't me?" she asks.

With my left hand holding hard on her hip, I push my right up the length of

her spine until my fingertips touch the nape of her neck. I tangle and grip and pull, locking my fingers in her hair. I hold until she cries out and rides deeper. I guide her head back, and when her neck is completely exposed, I sink my teeth into the made-just-for-me place right above her collar bone.

I bite until I taste princess blood and she moans my name, battling the fucking thunder for power.

I stroke hard, and I stroke full; I fuck her until my cock and my love are the only things in her world—until her mind is blank and all that is left is me.

With one last, long moan, Leigh goes slack. I don't stop pushing and hold her weight, stroking mine into her. As I pull her neck away from my mouth, open teeth marks bead the tiniest bits of blood. I lean forward and lick them away.

Baby circles her arms around my neck and keeps us close, forcing me to slow. Lighting hits the ocean, illuminating the car, turning yellow-orange light chrome.

Leigh's eyes are back on mine, but they tell a different story now. One that splits my chest and bares my soul: belonging, happiness, and sacrifice.

"How could you give this away?" she whispers through tear-coated lips. "How could this belong to anyone but us?"

I gently hold her closer, shaking my head with can't-be-told-with-words disagreement. I brush my fingers over teeth marks and apologize over and over and over.

"Can you feel me?" I whisper into her skin. "Can you feel what you do to me?"

Baby wraps her legs around my lower back and her arms tightly around my neck. She cries out, nodding her head. Our sticky-wet bodies push and rub and press together.

Pressure builds. Fire rages. "Fuck," I barely breathe.

I shake. I always do.

She has no concept of how much I love her. To mark her this way—the only way one person can mark another from the inside. To fill her up and know that after, I'm still there.

Only ever me.

"Never," I say. "Never like this, Bliss. ... Only you. There's only ever been you."

FARTHEST TO the right in my backseat, I sit against the door with my girl coiled up beside me. Her head rests on my lap, and her hands are prayer-like under my left thigh. Late night passes and early morning has arrived. Bliss might have fallen asleep for a little while, but I've been wide awake and repentant, questioning my authenticity and hoping I'm strong enough to do what baby needs me to.

Because it doesn't feel like it.

And I can feel *everything.*

All of it.

She's still in me, under my skin, scratching at me from inside, ripping me up. She chews on veins and kicks my heart, demanding, *listen to me!*

I press my hand over my life-beat and push pressure until Her bombardment stops.

With a change in tactic, my dirty habit sweetly tiptoes on bones, pleading false promises.

Don't abandon me, she says. *Let's go get high.*

I sit up and clear my throat. I run my fingers through my hair. I sniff.

Leigh reaches for my hand and holds it over her heart. It helps.

Slightly.

I press my cheek against the misty window until the glass warms by my heat. I pull my hand from Leighlee and reach for my jeans. My pack falls from the back pocket.

I can't find my lighter.

I groan.

Leigh sits upright. "Here," she says, handing it to me.

Without meeting her storytelling eyes, I take it and light my smoke.

Cocaine plays with my heart strings.

Leigh slips my hoodie over her naked body and curls her feet under her bottom. I roll the window all the way down, needing the icy October air on my face.

"Are you okay?" she asks carefully.

He will be.

I take another drag and smile at my girl. "Yeah," I say.

Baby settles in next to me. She extends her legs and stretches before propping her feet on the back of the front seat. Still sleepy, she yawns, and it breaks my fucking heart.

Because she shouldn't be here.

I try to remember the last time I looked at my girl through non-addicted eyes.

I've been lit through each I love you, spun through each touch, and drunk-wasted through each don't ever leave me. All the affection I've ever shown this girl has been habit-stained and guilty. She never had a chance against a monster like me.

I can make this go away, Dusty.

"Bliss," I whisper with a throat lodged full of regret. I shake my head in an attempt to clear too many thoughts.

"Hey," she says soothingly, brushing my too long hair away from my eyes. Baby smiles and my insides constrict. "Tell me," she says.

"Princess," I say, brimming with anxiety and regret and self-disgust and *how could she let me love her like this?*

Leigh moves in closer. My body turns toward her and submits to her touch. Now I have my head in her lap, but my hands are not pray-like. They clutch and grab, and push and move.

She rubs my back and speaks quietly. "Tell me, Thomas."

So she turns my head with her hands on my face, forcing me to be still, giving me no choice but to look at her.

But looking at her is too hard.

It's all there, on every part of her … It's her heart speaking to mine.

It's in me, able to ignore all of it because I've been too fucked-up to care.

I cry.

"I'm clean."

CHAPTER
fifty-four

She's salty kisses and sandy toes.

My girl sits behind me with her legs draped around my waist, and her arms around my stomach. With lips pressed into the back of my cotton-covered shoulder, baby's eyes barely peek over the top. We're watching the sky, waiting for the sun.

It's ten past way too early in the fucking morning—six or seven maybe. The car got too small, so we got dressed and got out. It's warmer today than it was yesterday. The wind is gone and the sky is mostly clear. Last night's storm left the sand packed and firm, keeping our footprints stamped until it dries. Driftwood litters the shore and the waves stole our blanket but left Leigh's shoes on the dock.

We're still the only ones on the beach, but it won't be this way for long. Every weekend this place hosts a town-wide flea market. Soon, it will be filled with people looking to sell, trade, and buy, and we'll have to go.

She's silent and sweet as the closest and hottest star rises. Leigh rubs the back of my neck and twirls my hair around her fingers. She whispers things in my ear like, "You were so fucking sexy last night," and "Do you know what your smile does to me? It knocks me out. It sends me flying."

So I do it. I smile.

She doesn't fly, but she stands up and wipes sand from her bottom. "Take me over there and buy me something for my birthday, knockout."

Barefoot and morning-messy, we get a few funny looks. The birthday girl's wearing my basketball shorts and sweater while my jeans are rolled up and my tee shirt's pulled out at the neck. She's covered, but my kissed-purple neck is showing, and these people know.

Two knit beanies, a scarf, and an Indian blanket later, Leigh's stomach growls, but she doesn't want to eat here. On the walk back to the car, we pass a vendor selling vintage jewelry. My girl doesn't pay it much mind, but I call her back when pearl and pink catches my eye.

I point it out, and Bliss smiles.

"What is it?" I ask the vendor, touching the heart pendant.

An older man with dark, wrinkled skin and all gray hair stands beside Leigh and me. "Pink Jadeite—the stone of Heaven."

"Can she try it on?" I ask.

Leighlee holds her hair up as I fasten the necklace. Pearls lie softly on pale skin, and the pendant touches right below the hollow point between her collarbones.

"It's too much," Baby whispers as we walk away with the symbolism of love and compassion around her neck.

I drape my arm over her shoulder and say, "Never."

WE'RE PLAYING with fate, but I stop at a small diner on the way home and park the Lincoln in the back. I put my hood up since Bliss is wearing my hat again.

"Do you care if I smoke?" I ask. She knows I'm not talking about tobacco, and I know she wants me straight.

She shrugs. "I'll go get us a table."

I light up and in the far back of my mind, I know this doesn't make me drug free. I can't give it all up at once, so I'll take it easy. I'll deal with one habit at a time. Slowly.

Yeah, right, cocaine whispers.

After I smoke, I walk into the restaurant and a bell on the door rings, signaling my presence.

"I'll be right with you," the waitress behind the counter says, holding a coffee pot. She has a pen keeping her hair up.

I spot my girl in the far booth. Watching me with relaxed eyes and a small smile, Bliss sips on chocolate milk. I sit down across from love, placing my back against the window. Leigh gets up and slides in next to me, settling between my knees. She leans on my chest.

"I ordered marshmallow swirl and peppermint sprinkle cupcakes," she says.

"You're going to get a stomach ache," I say, kissing the side of her head.

"I've had one for years." She takes my hand and kisses my knuckles. "You smell like pot."

"Like trouble?" I ask, turning the coffee mug on the table upright.

"Just like trouble," love says softly, leaning her head back onto my shoulder.

The waitress delivers the cupcakes and pours me some coffee before walking away. I wipe frosting from baby's chin, and she takes bites that are too big. She asks me if I think she's fat, and I tell her to shut the fuck up. She points to her soft stomach and I put my hand over it.

"It's mine," I say. "And I love it."

"Some of my jeans from last winter don't fit."

"I'll buy you new ones." I clean marshmallow fluff from the tip of her nose.

"Becka told me I have cellulite."

I roll my eyes. "Becka's a fucking liar."

Leigh stops laughing, and her smile breaks. "She is, right? She's lying to me."

Allegiance to my boy seals my lips. He hasn't told me, but I know—I've known. So does Bliss. Neither one of us wants to acknowledge it. But it's not the same because we've lied longer and heavier.

"Yeah," I answer, turning my back on my best friend and opening up even more to the only person who matters. "She's lying."

Leigh nods, crumbling some of her cupcake between her fingers. "Do you think they'll tell us?"

"I don't know."

She picks at the rest of her sugar, and I take one more drink of my coffee before I give it up. Our server comes around checking my cup a couple of times. On her third time by, she drops the check on the table.

"Do you want to go?" I ask.

She has a birthday party today, so she told her parents she'd be home early. I wish I could pack her into my car and just drive. I'd put her in the fucking trunk until we were too far to turn around. I'd keep her.

But I can't.

Sometimes love is doing what's right.

You know what to do, dirty boy.

She's too good for you anyway.

You've ruined her. Look.

Look at her.

Look.

Leighlee moves to the spot beside me, and I pull out my wallet and leave the cash on the table for the waitress. Leigh sits back and sighs.

"Be birthday happy, birthday princess," I say, doing my best to keep my voice even.

"This time next year will be so different," she says with peppermint twinkles on her curved lips.

I want a line. It's so fucking bad right now.

Can you taste me? She taunts. *Can you?*

"Hey." Baby pushes my shoulder back. "Hey, listen to me."

My lips curl. They can't help it. I love her weight on me.

"Knocked out," Leigh whispers, referring to my smile. "Flying. Every time."

Sunshine brightens her face and dances on her lashes. Her eyes are sugar lit, and her lips are stained light pink from frosting. Her touch is my cure, and everything else falls away but this cupcake girl.

"Be my boyfriend," she says, laughing softly, catching me by total surprise.

With my hands on her sides, I push her back far enough to see her face. Baby's cheeks are just-say-yes red, and her eyes are tale-telling again: love, love, love.

She holds my face in her hands, serious now. "Do you know what it does to me when you leave?"

I keep my eyes with hers.

"It kills me," she says. "It feels like dying."

"Sunny side—" I'm about to apologize, but she puts her marshmallow and peppermint scented hand over my mouth.

"Don't say you're sorry." She smiles more. "Just, be my boyfriend."

I smirk under her hand.

"Don't make me wait any longer, heart-buster. Be my boyfriend already," she says softly.

I move her palm away from my mouth and kiss her.

This time, she melts.

AFTER I drop my girlfriend off at home, I drive to my house. Mom doesn't bother to ask me where I was, but she does ask about Becka.

"Haven't seen her," I say, dropping my keys to the table.

"She better not miss Leighlee's birthday, Thomas." My mom looks up at me after she ties a pink bow around the white wrapped box.

I take a few steps toward the stairs. "She wouldn't," I say with my hand on the rail.

"I never know anymore." Mom sighs.

Once in my room, I fall on my bed face-first and slumber in a dreamless sleep for hours. When I do wake up, heavy-headed and more rested than I've been in a while, my mom's sitting beside me.

"I love your face when you sleep, Dusty." She runs her fingers though my hair.

I close my eyes and dissolve under the tender touch only a mother can offer.

Then she sees the marks on my neck.

"Who the fuck did you let do that to you?" she asks, completely taken back and obviously disapproving.

I cover my face with my pillow, frustrated. "I just woke up. Get out."

The woman who gave me life stands up and walks over to my closet. "You need help, Thomas. How long is this going to continue?"

She tosses a pair of jeans and a red tee on my bed.

"I can get myself dressed, Mom," I say from under the protection of my pillow.

"Did you even buy Leigh anything? Are you going to fuck this up too?"

I point to the box with baby's sunnies on my computer desk.

"You didn't wrap it? You saw me wrapping earlier, Thomas." She takes the gift and leaves.

Now I'm back in front of Leigh's house, and I'm nervous.

My girl is in there. My girlfriend. My life.

I can't fuck this up.

I cannot fuck up today.

But here I am, looking at my phone again. It's calling my name, I swear. I almost threw it out the window on the drive over.

I should have.

While I'm at war with my phone, my sister's Jeep drives by. She pulls behind the judge's sedan in the driveway, and I see my best friend in the passenger seat.

They're going to do this.

On her best girl's birthday.

I grab the sunglasses, lift my hood with no intention of lowering it, and get out of the Lincoln. I walk up by the willow tree, and my sister stands at the top of the driveway with her arms crossed and her eyes rolled.

Her navy blue shirt reads in white letters: *You Mad, Bro?*

And his says: *I Ain't Even Mad.*

"I tried calling you," Petey says. His clear eyes are guilty. My boy has his hands in his pockets and his head low.

I light a cigarette and blow smoke in the air.

"I wanted to tell you…" he starts.

I flick the cigarette butt into the street. "But what?"

"I feel bad," he says.

I smirk. "So do I."

My best friend is hooked up with my little sister. Lies and unfairness aside, it's twisted on principal alone.

I walk past him, through the grass and around Rebecka.

"Don't be a dick," she says spitefully.

I knock on the McCloys' door and wait for someone to answer, but Becka walks in first. Leigh's in Thad's recliner with her bare feet up. I hear my mom's heels tapping around in the kitchen with Teri, and the judge walks down the stairs to my side. He offers me his hand before I can extend mine first.

"How's it goin', kid?" he asks, deep-toned and semi-threatening. He's always been a huff and puffer.

Leighlee's eyes lock on her best friend.

I don't stand around and watch their pretend-innocence crumble. I set my girl's present on the gift table and walk into the kitchen.

Leigh's mom practically throws food at me. "Try this," and "I made this," and "I'll give your mom the recipe for this."

While Teri cooks, my mom helps, and Thaddeus picks and oversees. The conversation flows easily until my girl walks through the kitchen with my sister behind her. Leigh opens the back door and lets it slam into the wall on her way out. Everyone jumps, surprised by the birthday girl's anger. I'm only stunned she isn't doing a better job at keeping it under control.

"Girls," my mom says with a wave of her hand. "Becka probably ate Leigh's last Twinkie."

My heart splits, but for love's sake, I make myself laugh with mom. Teri and Thaddeus are in the dark and have no fucking idea that their daughter's most treasured friendship is falling apart.

I excuse myself once conversation starts up again. Since the girls went out the back door, I head toward the front.

I sit down in a lawn chair with an unlit cigarette between my lips. I have my cell phone out again with my thumb on the power button when my oldest friend comes outside. Pete stands beside me and sympathy and regret linger between us.

"I haven't told anyone," he says. "But you could have told me, Dusty."

I smile with spite and look up at my boy. I pull the cigarette from my mouth and hold it between my middle and pointer finger.

"So you can be there for me?" I say sarcastically, placing the smoke back between my parted lips. "You have no fucking idea, Pete."

He walks to the end of the porch and cracks his knuckles before turning back and opening the front door.

"Go get her," he says evenly. "I'll find Becka."

Then he's gone.

I don't get a second to process my thoughts before Leighlee runs out from the side of the house. Shoeless, baby's hair is windblown, stuck to tear-sticky cheeks, and her makeup is smeared, running down her face.

My unsmoked cigarette falls from my lips and tap dances on the porch before it settles and rolls. I stand and put my phone in my back pocket, ready to go to my girl, but she runs up the steps first. Upset and hurting, she drops to her knees in front of me.

I do the only thing I can do.

I drop, too.

"It's so unfair," she cries out, holding onto my sweater.

Pulling her to her feet, I walk my girl around to the side where no one can see us. I push strawberry-blond away from her face and hold the back of her head with trembling hands as I kiss her forehead. "You need to calm down."

Are you looking now? cocaine asks. Do you see her now?

"She gets him, and I have to wait for you. It's not fair, Thomas," she shouts through her tears. "After all this time, she just gets him!"

"Leigh, Leigh—baby ... Listen to me, girl." I hold her face up. Tears run over my thumbs. "You have to stop."

"I don't care anymore," she says sadly, but so unwavering.

I smile through terror. "Yes, you do."

My heart double-beats in anticipation for what we've spent so much time avoiding, and anxiety chews through me. If someone comes looking for the birthday girl, we're fucked.

You've been fucked since that banana Popsicle.

"I should probably go, Bliss," I say, struggling to keep my tone level. "We can't walk into that house together."

"No, don't leave." She stops to think. "Go to the store. My dad forgot the candles. I'll tell them I asked you to get some."

I unhook her fingers from my sweater. "Just—you have to calm down, Bliss."

She holds on to my neck. She pulls me down. She bites my chin, my jaw, my earlobe. "You know what it does to me when you leave. Go get candles and be back."

I press my forehead to hers and take a deep breath.

"Don't leave me. Please, not now."

"Okay," I say.

I turn my phone on when I get into my car and it lights up just like I knew it would. I rub my nose, and without checking any of the messages Casper's left, I delete everything but his number.

Baby calls on the way to the store.

"Hurry," she says.

I walk up and down the aisles until I find the candles, and when I do, there's pink and white candles, glitter candles, long candles, striped candles, polka-dot, sparklers, candles that look like numbers. I grab the one and the seven. I grab the glitter candles, and the pink and white ones.

I walk away but go back and take one of each.

While I flip through some bullshit fashion magazine in line, trouble finds me.

"Hey, Castor," cocaine's main man beckons.

My habit comes to life with a deceitful smile and greedy hands.

I toss the magazine with the candles and turn, but I don't look and reach in my back pocket for my wallet. I will my posture steady.

"Hey," I answer.

Casper sets a liter of Mountain Dew and a Slim Jim on the conveyer belt behind my items.

"I've been trying to call you." He pats my back and squeezes my shoulder.

"My phone's broken." I pay what I owe, take the receipt, and collect my bags. I walk away, and he doesn't call me back.

Casper follows me out to the Lincoln.

"I got some new shit," he says quietly, just between us.

I finally turn and face him. "Not interested, Cas."

I have one foot in the Continental and the other on the pavement. I'm losing my patience with this guy. Casper is no friend of mine. He's dirt—he's a fucking predator, and if he doesn't back off, I'm going to lay him the fuck out.

"Come on, Dusty." He leans in closer, untruth and waste personified. "Take a sample."

I spit on the ground.

My very own bag boy looks around, checking his back before reaching into his pocket and palming Her.

My heart soars. I can feel my cheeks warm …

"Don't just stand there." Casper shoves the bag to my chest. His eyes are worried, like I might not accept it.

This is who we are. Casper and I are the youth of the nation. We lack credibility and significance. We run in circles, saying the same shit, fucking the same girls, using the same drugs. We're a bunch of broken and bent motherfuckers, destroying our minds, overindulging, looking … seeking, but never finding.

We run, avoid, and dodge. We live off excuses. We live to die young.

I clear my burning throat.

I face facts.

It's *in* me.

The fucked-up factor.

I'm insignificant and uncredited. I run in circles faster than any of them. I fucked all of those girls before anyone did. I invented bullshit excuses, and I use *all* the motherfucking drugs. I'm no better than Casper. I'm dirt. I'm waste.

I don't live for Bliss. I live *off* her. I drain her. I take. I lean. I use.

I love.

I *love* her.

I do.

So fucking much.

Bliss is love to me.

But sometimes …

Love is not enough.

Baby has my heart, but this, Her—cocaine—She tied, sealed, and bolted freewill. She overtakes and overrides. She lives through me.

I look around and shake hands with Cas, taking what he has to give.

"Call me," he says, walking away.

I sit in my car. My end burns a hole in my hand.

I don't even wait.

I empty the grocery bags onto the floor and use the magazine I bought for Leigh to spread this cunt. I part Her into sloppy, uneven lines. I split Her wide open.

Choose your last words, cocaine whispers seductively.

I fuck her fast and hard. Lines blend and slide and fuse until I'm snorting a pile. My hands shake. My knees bounce. My heart—not me—my heart cries, *no, no, no.* It fights me. It makes me choke. It makes *me* cry.

When I've fucked all of her, I push the magazine to the floor and sit back.

I breathe through clenched teeth while tears falls from my so-open eyes, down my cheeks, off my chin. I punch the steering wheel until my knuckles crack and pour. I scream.

Fiends scream.

We do.

We yell.

I told you, cocaine sings. *I told you you'd do it.*

I run my hands down my face and wipe my tears away. I start the car. I back out of my parking space. My heart beat, beat, beats while black stretches my pupils, and I can feel it. I can feel Her filling the voids Her absence made. I sit taller. I feel better. It's like fucking magic.

Something's different, though.

I ache. I feel. I regret.

I know.

My surroundings are liquid. My vision is tilted. My motions are a second ahead of my focus, and my focus is fucked.

I shake my head. I swerve. I almost hit a sedan. They honk. I don't know which way to go. I pull off the road.

I hold onto the wheel with blood dripping hands. I breathe too fast. I cry more. I yell more.

Nothing helps.

She's staking claim. She's marking me the only way one can be marked from the inside.

She's living off me. She's draining me.

Unable to move, my head falls back and hot tears pour from my eyes. I can feel myself solidifying into succumbing. It's unstoppable and too fucking late.

With what little control I have, I unseal my heart and let love run.

"Tell me a secret, Thomas."

"*I love you.*"

With my arms useless at my sides, I close my eyes.

You fucked her, my sickest sadness tells me. *You fucked up.*

"You fucked up. You fucked up," I whisper over and over.

It was me.

It was always me.

There is no Her.

There's no She whispering in my ear, chewing on veins, kicking hearts.

There's only me.

All along.
I'm the tempter.
I'm the sick sadness.
I'm the cunt.
It's my deal.
A dusty delinquent.
Mini-foul to full on filthy.
A monster.

CHAPTER
fifty-five

Unlocking the front door of her parents' house, Bliss steps inside furnace-heated, pumpkin spice scented shelter. She takes off her scarf and warms as she walks toward the kitchen where fresh bread cools on the table next to a note.

Baby, it says. *If you get this, I'm at Apple Fest.*

There's a heart around a smaller heart.

All my love, Mom.

Bliss breaks off a corner of bread, flushes it down the garbage disposal, locks the front door, and climbs the stairs at a steady, normal pace while I beat as best as I can around numbing hurt.

My blood doesn't flow smoothly.

It stops and starts around my breaking.

Every opening and closing of my valves aches.

Her pace isn't rushed, but Bliss has been waiting for this. When she gets to the bathroom and stands alone in front of the mirror, seeking me, I make it everything but easy for the girl who forced a grudge into my chambers.

Breathing purposefully, she stretches her fingers all the way out. She forces air into lungs that surround me and glares into eyes that are red-rimmed but painfully dry. She hasn't cried since she pulled it together for love that was supposed to come back four days ago and didn't.

Low on strength and weak with absence, I beat poorly, only because in doing so, I harbor hope that maybe, just maybe, she'll think of him.

Bliss washes her face and closes her eyes. She hasn't eaten in days, and when she braces her hands against the counter and leans, she's noticeably undernourished.

Cry, she pleads with me. *Please.*

Give me something. Anything. Please.

I fight beating.

This is her fault.

Closing her fingers into fists, Bliss screams as she slams them against the counter.

He left you, she digs at me. *He doesn't want you.*

Hate him.

She scratches cuts into her palms when I don't listen, and I feel the sting, but it doesn't register anywhere else. Out of pure protection, her mind refuses Leighlee Bliss any more hurt.

Fucking hate him, Bliss demands.

I pulse his name through her veins, half out of fear of being buried deeper and half in hope that she'll give me something in return: a single thought of blue eyes, what his laugh used to sound like, anything.

Swallowing hard, love's false witness fulfills my fear. She withholds air violently tightly in her throat, and once upon a time, I'd have protested such a punishment. I'd have beaten faster and fought her for the oxygen that our entire body is dependent on, but this fight is old and too common now. I know every step too well.

They're numbered with as much awful simplicity as one, two, three.

Try.

Fail.

Carry on.

Be merciful, I plead. *Say death.*

But Bliss is merciless.

She swallows hard and locks me down, all the way deep where only Thomas has ever touched—where only he can reach—and leaves me to relinquish alone.

It's been a week and one day.

Love made his choice and now, he and I both get nothing, because nothing is what hurts the very most.

Drained and weary from surviving, Bliss sinks into a hot bath up to her ears. I can feel her listening, trying to hold on to my flawed rhythm, and I let her.

I'm weak from living without too, and I know she's searching for him in me.

The first memory that's clear enough to make my pulse skip is his voice.

"Here."

It's feeble and pale in comparison to the real thing, but as the rest of Thomas comes into focus behind her closed eyes, my beats fill with love.

She remembers him walking toward her with a gift bag while she sat up in his bed, grinning like crazy. I remember glowing.

She remembers the smell of home and the feel of the softest cotton, *"Is it dumb that I gave it to you?"* and blue eyes looking at us for just a fraction of a moment longer before he turned around so she could take off her dress and put on his sweater. She remembers him offering his hand and how she held it until she fell asleep, and nothing hurts, because I remember him touching her fingers all through the night. She remembers waking up with his arm around us for the first time, and if I had wings I'd flip and flutter and fly.

Pulling a deep breath, Bliss opens her eyes, taking me from memory.

I despise her, but she gave to me.

Fair isn't fair, but it's how we work.

Trembling, I open up and let precious hurt out.

Wincing in the water, she curls in on herself, suffering, and I give her another beat. A small, choked sob slips from her, and tears pour down her cheeks.

MINUTES TAKE hours that last for days, and each morning finds Bliss the same as the one before it.

Sore, chosen over, and left behind.

Not strong enough, not good enough, never enough.

Gutted and stuck and fucked in love.

Sorrowful down to her sinew, she wills sluggish muscles and slender bones into submission without waiting for eyes or ears or lungs to adjust against the cold wall of waking. She washes over diminishing aches from the last time she held love and dresses in clean clothes that hang loose over his fading marks.

I beat blood toward every one of his impressions, longing for all that's left of our boy to stay while she makes perseverance look effortless and youthful.

School is difficult because it means seeing a girl she used to know get out of Petey's classic Caprice every morning. Blond again and smiling without a single care, Rebecka reminds us both so much of the one we love most, and it makes my work so much harder.

Frail and alone and running on empty, I'm only a heart, and in truth, I'm half of that.

DAYS STRETCH into nights that last for weeks and find Bliss crying at four in the morning. It's tapering off because it begins to take effort, and I'm as harrowed as she by what life has become.

Perishing.

Curled in the middle of her bed, she's near passing out when the pull overwhelms us. Sharp, more like a jerk, our soul's sudden presence is all-consuming.

Sore fingers tremble and curl. Chapped and tender from crying lips tingle and part. Aching arms and knees shake, and cold toes bend against neglected blankets. Pupils swell and tiny ossicles strain to gather every sound from the air as Bliss jumps out of bed.

My agony is nothing in this moment.

Thomas is here, and I'm wild to get free.

Desperate for his hands, I flutter toward her throat, and at the foot of the bed, her phone vibrates.

He's here, I pound against our ribs, delirious with love's proximity. *He's here. He's here. He's here.*

Her phone stops just to start again, but she moves toward the window instead of her bed so that she can see what I already know.

One floor down and moonlight lit, shifty love waits at the door Bliss has kept locked every night since he left. Hood up, he has left hand in his pocket, covering his killer while his right holds his phone.

The girl I keep alive turns from the window and sits at her desk. She watches as one voicemail becomes two, then three, then four, and checks them with her fingers barely wrapped around her phone, holding it out, inches from her ear.

"Open the door." Dusty's voice is strong, but bitten back, controlled. "Leigh—"

For a few seconds there's nothing but wind.

"Leighlee, come open the door, baby."

One after another, his messages incense.

"Let me in, Leigh. I swear to fucking God—"

And degenerate.

"Do you want me to die out here?"

Pleas and demands echo between threats and ultimatums whispered violently with claims and counterclaims.

"I'll set this house on fire, Bliss."

She closes her eyes.

I beat like I'm dying.

"Princess." He sniffs. "Please ..."

I shake the curved bars of my cage.

Let him in, I cry. *Don't do this.*

Bliss sets the phone down after the fifth voicemail. It's ice-cold angry.

"You're doing this."

She concentrates on a single, slow breath, and I clamor and pound like the beast she's turned me into. Flaring up, I pump too fast to get enough blood into each beat. It shortens her inhales and makes her vision gray around the edges, but Bliss contends. She pulls shaky legs up and rests her throbbing head on brittle knees, and when I still don't calm, she presses the heels of clammy hands over her sternum, into my septum.

I strive and agonize and grind beats against her, but she doesn't let up. Thomas doesn't leave another message, and when he walks away, I split open cuts in my tissue that are shaped like back-scratches from another. I rip mostly-healed scars that he cut into me years ago, the very first time he made us cry. I burden her shoulders and break her resolve with *"I wasn't with Clarissa."*

"I've never been with Mixie or Katie."

"I wouldn't lie to you."

"Get the fuck out if you don't like it."

I don't have arms, but I bear them. I dig teeth and knuckle and raw hurt against this girl. I make her feel everything.

Hate him if you need to, but call him back here.

I flood her with savage, ruthless beats, and as she moves back to the window, I overrun her with first-time fast, backseat-crazy, and unlocking-the-front-door-in-a-thunderstorm beats. I work more forcibly than I ever have, praying at the top of our lungs for her to lift the glass separating me from love.

Refusing another breath, Bliss curves her fingers into fists so tight her knuckles ignite.

Dusty's turned away, but he hasn't left. He paces and shakes his head and smokes. His cigarette sticks between his lips when he faces us again and bends his right leg, kicking the door so hard the porch beams quake and the window we're looking out vibrates. The dogs next door bark, and down the hall, Thaddeus sits up in bed with Teri clinging to him, both of them waiting to hear something more before they move.

Fear freezes through my veins, but Bliss is not about to look away now.

Pulling up the hood that fell back, Thomas doesn't kick the door again. He doesn't run or hide or make any attempt to hurry away. He simply turns his back and walks right through her mother's yard, flicking his cigarette into the flowers as he goes.

WEEKS WEAR on me.

Bliss plays her part well, but she's a shadow of a ghost walking behind who everyone thinks she is, and Oliver doesn't make that any easier. He looks closer than anyone else, and all I feel under his consideration is tender, heavy, and spiteful.

"Hey." His pupils dilate as he looks at her, and her buried need to lean yearns toward him. His steps lighten and his fingers curve the slightest bit tighter around his backpack straps, but there's no change in this person's pulse. Even as her steps fall in line with his, Oliver's heart says nothing to me.

"Hey." Bliss smiles back. It doesn't go as deep as his, but it's not completely contrived. Some of the tension in her shoulders relaxes and some of the stiffness in her neck eases as she takes his offered arm. There's relief in his reliable kindness, but his heart simply lubs and dubs.

While the rest of our girl finds a solace, I wane in disregard.

But I'm what keeps us going.

Even when I hate her for it.

I REMAIN contentious as the end of November freezes into winter, but I'm wearing out. I keep our blood flowing, but it's too thin. It isn't only love that we're starving for anymore, but actual sustenance.

While our wasteland of a girl sleeps without dreaming, she fills our lungs with air and each life-forcing beat takes all my strength. Wind muffles most sounds outside, but even between it and my enfolding debilitation, I recognize the low roll of the Lincoln from down the block.

I wake up widely.

The sound of his car door opening and steps that are steady with intent are music to me. I hammer against our sore chest, pummeling blood through our drowsy veins, but it's the sound of Bliss' phone vibrating that helps me wake her.

She silences his call and doesn't know it, but one floor down, love turns the handle on the side door. It's locked as usual, and I endeavor frantically in the dark. Sitting up in bed, bending legs that burn to run to him beneath her too-light weight, she refuses his second call and listens to the first message.

"Let me in, L." His voice is thick in his throat like he hasn't used it in days. "You said I'd never be without you. You'd never take yourself from me, remember?"

All ten of her fingers clench as she pulls the phone away, resisting the urge to throw it and scream until everything gives out.

He calls again.

And again.

Forever, I remind this fool. *You said forever.*

Throbbing life through our limbs, making our fingers and toes pound with my potential, I push pressure through rhythm until her vision blurs and her hearing clouds. I make her mind resound my cry, and it forces her to move.

The second she's to her window, love looks up, and I weep beats.

I recognize this person, but Bliss can't.

He's all ours, but he's pale and sunken around eyes like dice that were always loaded.

Dusty's lost.

Turning her back, Bliss walks away and shuts off the light. She gives love the same darkness she gives me, and sits frozen on the edge of her bed while marrow boils and pops inside her bones. Her joints scream and her stomach twists to turn inside out. Every inch of skin cries for closeness and contact, and under all the throes of prodigal reprisal, I hear what I ache for more than anything else.

Our boy's heart is faint, an echo of an echo almost lost to cruel wind, but I hear it seeking me.

Love?

It's cutting tears.

Love?

Calling home.

Love?

I fall, and as Bliss closes her eyes to keep control, I scrape and swear against her.

I curse.

I hate.

I beg.

Please.

Don't do this.

Tiny blood vessels around her eyes break under how tightly she fights.

Let go, she pleads back at me. *Please, let go.*

I drop beats like bombs while Bliss sheds red from our palms. I rise higher and she fights harder, and in the middle of all of it, glass smashes and breaks outside.

The neighbor's dogs go insane, and more glass shatters.

Rushing downstairs, we make it just in time to see Dusty through the lace curtains that hang in the bay window of the living room. Baseball bat in his left hand, he heads back to the Continental door he left open and gets in without a glance back. He doesn't peel out or speed off. He just starts the car and rounds the wheel with one hand, driving away half a second before Thaddeus rushes down the stairs.

In a tee shirt and boxers, with his gray and black hair going every direction, the judge heads straight to the front door. His socks are pushed down from sleep, but his shoulders are squared and his heart rate is accelerated, but steady as he unbolts the front door. Prepared and willing to go to any extreme to protect what's behind him, he lifts his arms, and we see the gun in his hands.

"Leighlee—"

Grabbing her daughter from the window, Teri pulls her behind herself, and they hide around the corner of the room. Bliss holds on out of shock, and after a few minutes, her father returns.

"It's okay," he calls.

The heavy sound of his gun being set on the table next to the door resounds louder than his voice as Teri goes to him. Bliss follows, pretending to be the kind of scared they expect her to be.

"What happened?" her mother asks. Reaching back, she takes her miracle by the hand and brings her close, stroking strawberry-blond hair.

"Somebody was driving off when I opened the door, but I couldn't make out the plates or the car," Thad says, looking only at his wife. Reaching out, he gently disconnects her from Bliss.

"Come out here," he says, his tone assuring as he leads her toward the door and leaves his gun.

Bliss refuses to be disregarded.

"What?" she asks, stepping forward, trailing her parents. "What is it?"

Her mother turns strict eyes in our direction and her father finally looks at us.

"Alright," he says. "Come on."

Outside, Teri gasps and covers her mouth.

We heard the glass.

We saw the bat.

But the Rabbit's smashed out headlights are more than an unforgettable sight. They're a sign, a message, and I thrum love's name like a victory march, because I know.

He'll be back.

"It's LIKE, six miles away. Don't make me be the only senior that's riding with her parents."

Bliss will fake-cry if she has to.

"Just to school and back," she says, then softer, "It's not like I have anywhere else to go."

"Just for today, Bliss."

Starting the day negotiating simple freedom isn't easy.

Seeing Petey visit Becka at lunch time is harder.

Keeping her facade up becomes an undertaking for every step and breath, and when Tanner's best friend Bryan falls into step next to her, it only gets worse.

"Hey, Leighlee," he says with a too-sly smile and boy-slick intentions. "How goes it?"

Pressing her fingers into skinny denim pockets, she's polite to him as fabric stings her wounded palms.

"Hi," she replies coolly.

Bryan Turner's heart pumps blood to places she has no interest in while he licks lips she'll never consider.

"What are you up to tonight?" he asks, nodding his head when one of his friends calls his name.

Bliss shrugs, and I detest her wholly.

Tell him, I urge her. *Tell him you're going to wait until your parents are sleeping and then we'll make a twisted trade—memories for hurt. Tell him you're torturing love. Tell him you're going to curl up into a pathetic ball and wish like hell you had the guts to shake the yoke of inauspicious stars from your world-wearied flesh, you fucking coward.*

"I don't know," she says. "Why?"

"We're all going down to Cobble beach," he answers with his eyes on our girl. He looks, but not like Oliver, and nothing like Thomas. "Me and Tanner, some friends from somewhere, Molly …"

Bliss digs her hands deeper into her pockets, focusing on stinging hurt instead of the overwhelming want to scream.

"Isn't it a little cold for the beach?" she asks.

Bryan laughs a little as we approach the French room. Bliss unpockets her fingers to tuck hair behind her ears.

"Molly'll keep you warm," he replies, and without any trouble, he takes her hand and writes his phone number on the top of it.

"Call me," he says before walking away.

Love's traitor thinks about it.

All through French and then all through calculus, she considers what might happen if she called Bryan, went to the beach, popped X at some party with people she doesn't really know, and Dusty found out. She torments me and wears herself out imagining trespasses and consequences, and as the day finally comes to a close, she can't bear the thought of going home—facing interrogating eyes and being in a bedroom she's shared too much with love.

Texting her mother, she promises to be home before dark and heads the school library. She spreads books out but does no real work, and as hours pass, exhaustion catches up.

When the sound of librarians cleaning up wakes her, she's the only student in sight. Packing her bag, she buttons her coat and wraps her scarf around her neck. She puts on gloves over palm-cuts and Bryan's number, and pulls up her hood, bracing for the December wind. It greets her cheeks like a slap as she steps outside, and Bliss moves quickly toward the senior parking lot with nothing on her mind but getting to the car and out of the cold.

Between the freezing breeze and skinny snow flurries, just before we turn the corner of the building, the heart of love steadily hums my name in the frostbiting air. Our chest expands to accommodate my joy, and Bliss' legs almost give out from under her at the sight of our boy.

Leaned against the front of the Lincoln, which is parked right next to the Rabbit, Dusty has his hat pushed back and his hood off, not hiding any part of his face. Black eyes lock on Bliss, and hands that I long for are loose in the edges of his pullover sweater pocket. Faded and emaciated in dark slim straights, he's got one foot in the grave and the other kicking the bucket, but his old black and white Vans are tied neatly tight.

He doesn't move an inch as Bliss approaches.

Love, his heart calls, needing and reaching. *Love?*

Love, I call back, needing and reaching, too. *Love.*

Bliss resists the pull our entire body feels, and with another step, she notices two shiny new headlights have replaced broken empty spots.

Rolling her eyes, she walks to her car and opens her door. She wants to get in and drive without a word, but I pulse direly. Leaving her door open, keeping us half behind it, she turns to face the boy with bloodshot eyes and dirty, too-long hair.

Sky-high and so-unwell looks at us, but doesn't move. She lets him stare until I feel more alive than I have in months, and then cuts fire straight through me.

"My dad almost shot you," she says, crossing her arms and stifling the song I'm calling to our soul.

Love doesn't lift his eyes from her lock. Desperation disguised as carelessness, charading as courage, pretending to be cocky, keeps his posture straight and his stare impervious. His second choice is all over him, filling him with black and covering him in white.

"Let me be put to death," he says without a flinch.

Bliss turns away.

"I'm fucked-up, baby," he says louder, the pitch of truth in his voice compelling her with starving undertones.

"No shit," she spits, taking off her bag. One of the straps is caught on her scarf or her coat.

"Bliss, I tried," he continues, standing straight up, disconsolate and irreparable sounding, suppressed against his will, brittle and abused and destitute.

Past hope.

Past help.

"I was there. I just wanted to go home, but you wanted your fucking candles—"

Tearing her backpack strap free, she rips her scarf.

"Open your eyes!" she shouts, turning around.

Undoing her ruined scarf and opening her coat, she bares her frame against him like evidence. Faded red-blond hair whips her cheeks and cold wind stings unwell skin. Bliss isn't gaunt, but her clothes hang, and in natural light, she knows he can see the bruises under her eyes. Relentlessly aiming the effects of his choices right at him, she pulls the shoulder of her shirt aside and exposes collarbones that have never shown until recently.

Love's heart beats my name in apology and regret and mourning as he looks. He reaches for her, but she gets in the Rabbit and closes him out.

I fight as she drives.

I constrict my atria and strangle my ventricles, and she chokes around how I make her cry, but I don't stop. She drives and drives with nowhere to go and finally pulls over at the end of her street.

She has to pull her shit together, and I'm not letting her. I hold beats until she hits the wheel the same way he does. Screaming, she digs the heels of her hands into her eyes.

Stop, stop, stop, she sobs.

Unable to catch a breath, she pushes her fists into her chest, crushing me and refusing to breathe until gravity wavers and her vision narrows into a dark gray tunnel, and I have no choice.

I beat.

FINALLY AS helpless as me, Bliss is awake and waiting with the door unlocked.

Just as drained as she after being forced to work against my will, I flutter only feebly as he turns the handle.

She sits up as he approaches her room and rises to her knees as he enters, and there's no hesitation. Nothing has harmed either of them as deeply or unmitigatedly as the other, but as they fall together into her bed, everything calms.

There are no apologies or threats as they gather together. No questions or assurances pass between them, and no clothes come off. There's only closeness, clutching on and clinging tightly all through the night.

Drugs don't let Dusty rest, but he finds assuagement in Bliss' breathing. It evens out his own as she sleeps, and he slides his fingers through her hair.

Love, his pulse whispers, found and safe and unceasingly grateful.

Love, I whisper back in soft symphony.

Love.

HE LIFTS himself from us before her parents wake, and when they do, she leaves to spend the day with Daisy.

Lie.

She drives straight to the dock.

I'm here, she texts.

She drinks coffee to stay awake through waiting, and not half an hour later, he pulls up. Sunglasses hide both of their eyes as she gets out of her car and into his, but his heart reaches for me the same time his hand brings her across the seat, right to him.

Love.

Love.

We rest in harmony while he drives away from the Rabbit, but when he turns onto his parents' street, Bliss lifts her head warily from his shoulder.

"They're at a charity banquet for the weekend," he assures her hollowly. "Your secret's safe."

There's spite in his voice, begrudging that singes wounds in her that haven't even begun to heal.

"Ours," Bliss bites back as he parks. "Our secret."

Thomas shakes his head. "No."

Promises flow between his heart and mine in their silence. She slides out his door after he gets out, unwilling to let go of his hand even in their contention, and follows him inside.

Behind his closed and locked bedroom door, they take off their coats and shoes, and Bliss looks around a little. His curtains are drawn, but even in the mostly dark, she can tell nothing's been touched in too long. This place doesn't smell like smoke or Tide, and when they get into his bed with their clothes still on, his blankets and pillows don't hold any vanilla or trouble. There's nothing to smell at all, until he brings us close.

Relief lies in the bend of his neck and against his chest. Where Dusty is warmest and I feel him best, he still smells exactly like himself.

Her rest is deeper than his, but he drifts, too. They spend all day in his bed, and when night falls, they only curve closer, and real sleep finally finds our boy.

It's there, in the same bed they've shared so much in, while the bodies that carry them relax deeply into dreaming, that I hear his heart clearest. Its rhythm is weaker than ever and his blood is thin. Systole takes too much effort, and dependence clenches every beat.

As Leigh shifts, nestling her nose along his skin and he strokes the small of her back, bending his neck to unconsciously curve more near, I listen closely to his run-down tricuspid and mitral valves, and it hurts.

Addiction is a fist around Dusty's heart.

And all I can do is beat.

Love, his pulse promises, defenseless and vulnerable, nervous.

Love, I whisper back, made of it and aching.

Love.

LEIGH AND Thomas are more stolen than ever now, a ghost and a shadow, half-alive and even-less, but it's not like before. Our girl eats enough to sustain me while unsubstantial death wears away at our boy, but they don't stay away any longer than they have to. Their voices go unused more often than not, but my beat and his weaker one never treat each other with silence.

The coming end of December covers everything with snow, and Tommy calls on Christmas Eve.

"We miss you, baby," she says, cry-hoarse and chardonnay-tanked. Her attempt at good tidings splinter apart. "You know you're still welcome here anytime."

Bliss spends the holiday fake-smiling and counting the hours until love shows up with snowflakes stuck to his hair. His thin cheeks burn with cold when she sneaks him in. His teeth chatter and his hands shiver, and not just from the winter. Our entire soul trembles, inside and out, and no matter how tightly she wraps around him, it's not enough.

No matter how hot she runs the shower, it's still not enough.

No matter how closely she presses herself when she steps inside, fully clothed with him, it's never enough.

Love's strung out at the end of his rope. He shakes all the way to his bones and crushed under dependence; his heart stumbles just as badly as his words.

"Don't fucking leave me," he stutters, discordant in the steam and breaking under the stream. "Why are you always leaving?"

"Shh," she whispers, holding on with every ounce of love we're made of. "You have to be quiet."

Thomas groans too deeply.

"Get off me," he tells her, gripping bruises into her sides. "Let me go. Let me fucking go—"

WE SPEND New Year's Eve at a party with Daisy, Bliss, and me. Too drunk to do right, she presses her mouth to her friend's when the clock strikes twelve and kisses her deeper when everyone around them cheers.

She's that girl now, and I'm drowning.

In the middle of the party, she pulls her phone out and dials love.

"Bliss," he answers, but it's too much.

She wanders outside and stumbles a crooked line down the middle of the street in just her dress. She calls him again and again and can't see through falling snow and champagne tears. The Lincoln pulls right up next to her, and she doesn't even realize it.

Stopping in the road, Thomas gets out and pulls her roughly inside. It's warm, but Leigh's frozen, and love curses at her.

"What the fuck is wrong with you?" He sounds regret-filled and angry, but far away to her ears. He presses his hands over them and rubs her scalp and shoulders and back. He unbends painfully-stiff fingers with his stronger ones, and when he brings her close enough to cup his palms around her mouth and breathe heat across her blue lips, it's too much again.

Bliss pulls on our boy, and lips that haven't touched hers in months taste like Jameson and broken rules. He kisses her back, but it's desperate and stricken, nothing more than every effort to go backward.

JANUARY IS twice as cold as December, and February feels no warmer.

Dusty's gone more, and Bliss grows closer—as much as any half-alive liar can—to Oliver. She gives in to his dependable strength, and love can always tell when she has. Her shelter brings her flowers on Valentine's Day, and her storm brings only black eyes. When he sees the bouquet on her vanity that night, his heart weeps behind cocaine's grip, but his fingers dig and his teeth sink.

"Do you think he's better than me?" love asks Leigh, pinning her down, cutting off my circulation in her arms. "Is that what you want?"

She shakes her head.

Lie.

"You could have it," he tells her, letting me flow.

Love? His heart chokes, closer to death than life. *Love?*

Love, I never stop promising what Bliss can't. *Love.*

LEIGHLEE AND her mother spend the last weekend of March at Puget Sound. They tour the campus and fill out enrollment paperwork.

Thomas doesn't come over when she gets back. He's gone forever, and when he finally returns, they touch but don't speak. They kiss eye corners and elbow bends and sternums, but not lips. They make codependence and comfort, but not love. Dusty and Bliss have squandered love. Their words have twisted it. Their hands have marred it, and their choices have poisoned it.

All that's left of love is whittled down to knowing.

And it's only ours now.

As SPRING warms the world, Rebecka turns eighteen on the first of April.

"Happy birthday," Bliss tells her as they pass in the hallway.

"Thanks." The girl who used to be our best friend doesn't even look at us now.

TWO WEEKS later, there's an acceptance letter and housing packet from Puget Sound waiting for Leighlee McCloy on the kitchen table.

Smile lines creased with pride, her mother cries.

Bliss fills it out, seals and stamps it to send in the morning, and when Thomas sees it on her desk, he breaks her skin. He wants to break her bones. He pushes and pulls and bites so hard I think his teeth might finally sink into me, and I know this mark will last forever, but I'm not afraid of love like this.

Dusty might hurt the girl that carries me, but his heart would never. His heart is the best heart. It's brave and strong and blessed-special. It talks to me, and it needs me, and I'm dying for it.

MEASURED BY pitiful tears, too-little-too-late beats, and hands that once held every part of one another, a thousand years pass over the course of the next few weeks.

May shines too warm to feel so dead.

The day before Saturday's graduation is overcast and humid. At school, Bliss plays the part of a normal senior on her last day. She smiles high and hugs friends and signs yearbooks, but inside, she's beyond burned out.

Overexerted and overextended, she doesn't want to face this.

The end.

If she had it her way, she'd sleep through the next twenty-four hours and wake wherever she's meant to be with the choice made for her.

If she trusted me, we'd end up exactly where we're supposed to.

Mishandled and past cure, I run on beats made of anxious anticipation as she sits down to dinner with her family.

Her father's parents are here for the big day tomorrow, and Bliss plays it up perfectly. She acts the part of the good daughter, but her stomach knots around food she forces into it. Her tendons and ligaments tense, and I'm so crippled with worry and missing that I'm beating unevenly without meaning to.

But I'm buried so deep now she can't even feel my faltering.

We're both still steadily disappearing, just as we have been since last October: slowly, secretly, and alone. It doesn't matter that we're surrounded by people. No one notices.

Until her phone vibrates, and everyone looks.

Keeping her expression casual and her posture at ease as she silences love's call, she stands with her phone in her hand.

"Excuse me," she says, leaving the kitchen for the hallway.

He doesn't leave a voicemail, but a text comes through.

Come out.

Teri's less likely to say no when Bliss asks for something in front of company, and there's no guilt in our girl as she does exactly this. There's no hesitation in lying straight to all their faces and there's not a single slip or crack in her demeanor.

Shameless and refined, the ghost of Bliss is every bit as flawless as she always was.

"Not too late," her mother calls.

Rolling her eyes behind her sunglasses, Leigh nods.

Outside, she sits in the driver's seat for a moment, fingertip-smoothing out what's left of today's makeup. She puts the Rabbit's top down and pulls clammy-damp and air-flattened curls up into a bun. Sitting back, she breathes out and concentrates on breathing in, but I can't slow my swiftness.

The black cherry Continental is waiting for us when we pull up.

Leaning against the trunk, Thomas is in black jeans and a black tee. No hat. No shades. Just a hopeless dusty delinquent smoking a joint while he waits.

I listen for his heartbeat as she gets out, but it's hard to focus when he looks at her like he is right now.

Even after she's locked him out and turned her back and ignored his call, even though she's made every plan to drag him through perdition for another four years, even with a tomorrow that's supposed to be theirs hanging uncertainly over their heads, his eyes see all that she is, and he looks with nothing but love.

Blowing smoke upward as she approaches, he offers her the joint when she stands in front of him. He flicks it when she shakes her head and I listen hard for languishing beats, but I can't hear anything over the ocean.

Looking up, Bliss meets eyes that are drug-dark, but his clothes and skin and hair are clean. Love's high, but he's not stumbling or slurring. He's not calm—there's chaos in his black—but he's composed, collected, and in control.

Turning and walking around, he opens his door and follows her into the Lincoln.

Only then, finally, with the rest of the world shut out, do I finally hear his heart.

Love? It seeks and pleads, weak as an anemic newborn. *Love?*

I all but fall apart as the two of them fold together.

Love, I whisper soothingly. *Love.*

There's no sun to watch go down, but Bliss and Dusty hold on as light fades to dark. They wrap around and press together, surrounding one another while the breeze blows and waves lap outside. His fingers trace her palms and she rests her head over my favorite sound, and for the first time in forever, hours pass too quickly.

Half in his lap, half curled up with the steering wheel behind her, she shifts a little, trying to work the pins and needles out of her arm. Not wanting to move, she settles back into place, but love knows. Brushing his fingers between her shoulders, our boy looks down as we look up.

"Let's get in the back," he says quietly.

They climb over the bench seat one at a time and lie together, heart to heart as the sky darkens.

Love, we beat, soft over skinny, and strong together. *Love.*

He wraps her closer, loosening the tie from her hair as she curves her leg around his waist. Bending and unbending his fingers through strawberry-blond curls, he commits the feel of her to memory. He slides his thumb along her temple and cheek, and brushing his lips across her forehead, he lets his eyes close in what's Heaven for him.

In the softest and stillest and most silent part of the night, deep in the sacred solace of shared diastole, I'm calm in our harmony, and I hear love's heart, talking to this boy the way I sometimes talk to Bliss.

It's just as strangled by addiction as my own name is, and I don't know if Thomas understands it any more than I know if Leigh understands me, but I understand this whisper with searingly sharp clarity.

I tremble, and her fingers curl into his shirt. His arms bring us closer, but it's no comfort to what I'm hearing.

Love? Terrified and unbelieving, I'm the one asking now. *Love?*

Love, his pulse vows as sincerely as a prisoner can. *Love.*

But I hear it.

In between every stifled beat of my name, I hear Dusty's heart telling him to let us go.

CHAPTER
fifty-six

I t's here.

The end of the countdown.

The day our secret isn't a secret anymore.

The day we're not supposed to give a fuck.

Finally.

No regrets.

No second thoughts.

No reluctance.

Just go. Just drive.

Be gone.

Don't look back.

Never look back.

Runaways.

"Are you nervous?" the girl behind me asks.

I look over my shoulder, but not at her face. She's swearing black flats, and I can't help but think that they're not nice enough for this occasion. Meanwhile, my metallic heels sink in the grass.

I pivot and look forward, dismissing her.

I ignore everything but the line in front of me.

Even him.

Especially him.

Because, one person at a time, I'm moving closer to my future.

"My heart is beating so fast," the girl whispers, trying to keep conversation.

Thankfully, the line proceeds as more names are called.

Three more until it's my turn.

I take a few more sinking steps.

Two more.

I place my hand on the rail and set my right foot on the first stair, finally reaching the stage.

As I stroll up—ready, smiling, faking—I can hardly feel my heart.

MOM PUSHES me one way, and Dad pulls me another. Mom wants me to take a picture with these people and those people, and Dad wants to show off his only daughter to the entire Portland judicial system he forced to come watch.

Grandma's in my face, touching my cheeks with her cold hands. She's so proud of me. She knew I'd be great. She remembers the day I was born.

"You truly are Bliss," she says.

"Thanks," I say back.

Grandpa insists on squeezing my shoulder, like I might forget he's standing right beside me. He smells like muscle rub and too much cologne. It's giving me a headache. My father's father slips me a twenty dollar bill and tells me not to use it all in one place.

Then he squeezes my shoulder again.

Jackie and Daisy come over and we exchange sincere goodbyes, as if this might be the last time we see each other.

It might not be.

We may have the whole summer.

Mom calls my name again, requesting another captured moment with my fucking French teacher.

I slip under the arm of my educator and sigh.

As my mom holds the camera up in front of us, Madame Ancel asks, "In a hurry, young lady?"

I shake my head, leaning a little. "I just want to get home."

The woman who taught me the language of love holds me a little tighter and softly quotes Jane de La Fontaine. "*Rien ne sert de courir, il faut partir à point.*"

There's no sense in running; you just have to leave on time.

"Smile!" Mom squeals, taking the photograph.

I see Petey before I see Becka, and I see Lucas and Tommy before I see Dusty, who's walking at a slower pace with a half-smoked cigarette between his lips. Ben and Valarie are behind him, and further back, Mixie, Kelly and Katie follow.

Becka has her blue commencement gown, completely unzipped showing the white dress she's wearing underneath, and her cap in her hand. Her hair is entirely blond again, and she's wearing a bow, but it's there because someone told her to wear it.

I know.

Her cream-colored wedges are in her hand, leaving her feet bare. Pink-polished, her toes dig into the muddy grass as she walks faster, coming right for me.

Kicking off my heels, I meet her halfway.

We collide, and I hide my face in her neck to ignore the boy I know isn't ignoring me. We cling and cry, and I give my attention to the person who should have had it all along.

"Bliss," Becka says softly.

Like old times, she smells like cookies and feels like sticky sweat. I kiss her with wet lips, and I whisper, "I'm sorry. I'm sorry."

With this girl's face in the palms of my hands, I see Thomas behind her. He stands back with eyes hidden behind Ray-Bans and hands sunk in pockets.

His cigarette is gone.

Beside him, Lucas and Thaddeus are cordial. They gracelessly congratulate one another on raising a high school graduate.

Tommy cries, but she tries to hide it.

Ben wipes her eyes with the sleeve of his white button up, ignoring the smudge of makeup it leaves on his cuff.

At our side, Kelly ignores Petey, and Petey looks uncomfortable being avoided. Valarie wants to leave. Mixie wants to get high, and Katie's waiting to do whatever the others tell her to.

"Come on, girls. One more before we leave," Mom motions for us to move closer and pose.

Becka and I smile at one another while my unrested heart kind of, sort of buckles. We can stand here all evening and cry. We can say whatever we want, but this friendship has already passed its expiration date, and there's no going back.

"It feels like we broke up," Becka says, wiping my tears away with her thumbs.

I don't do the same for her.

"Don't break up with me," she says. "Things can be the same."

Lie.

Catching me off guard, Ben picks me up, and Petey playfully pulls my hair. I cherish them. I love them. Ben and Petey have always been around.

They're The Boys—my boys.

When we were little, Dumb and Dumber made Sleeping Beauty cry, and as we got older, they made it known little sisters are off limits, and showed me why three joints are better than one.

They're my defenders, my saviors … My friends.

"Little sister," Valarie says in passing, running her hand through my hair like she has many times before.

Then I'm in Tommy's arms, and I bury myself in her red hair and hold on like she's my own mother.

"I'm proud of you, pretty girl," she whispers.

From Tommy, I go to Lucas. Tall and dignified, he's as intimidating as he was the very first time I saw him after his son stole my nail polish all those years ago.

"Princess," he greets me like he did then. The attorney slips me some money, and it's much more than the twenty bucks my grandpa gave me.

After love's father kisses the top of my head, there is nowhere to go other than to Thomas.

I'm not ready for him.

I probably never was.

He pulls his hands from his pockets and lifts his sunglasses to the top of his head. As a consequence of the night we spent, his eyes are swollen and red. My boy's expression is an assortment of unhappiness, denial, and determination. I recognize unpredictability in his posture and volatility in his stare, like he can change the inevitable.

Recklessness takes a few steps toward me, and Mom snaps a picture. I keep waiting for my heart to leap, but it gives nothing more than a low thump. Even when he pulls the end of my blond-red curl, its beat remains feeble.

Love is killing us softly.

"Congratulations, sunny side." His straight smile swerves with my hair between his fingers.

My pulse should be pounding, pumping blood to my cheeks, but it struggles.

Giving up or giving in … I don't know yet.

After a moment, Thomas hasn't backed away, so I smack his hand and warn him with my own sleepy-swollens. *Too close, boy.*

He drops his sunnies back over his eyes, and when he smiles this time, he's allover hoodlum with awful purpose.

And still, my heart is thin.

Thomas leans in, taking my wrist in his hand. "Don't look at me like that, Bliss. You're breaking my heart."

My pulse drops to a low beat while the rest of my body searches for his smell, his touch, his affection. My senses look for something to pull my heart back up. But as we die, everything slows.

Thomas smells like laundry detergent or his brand of shampoo. His touch is not much more than a touch, but he's trying, fighting fate. His affection is lacking, self-satisfying and self-seeking, but it's still only for me.

His grip on my wrist is not genuine, but cautionary.

Stick to the plan, his hold says. *Now or never.*

I let the front of my body press against the front of his, expecting to light fire, but it's only a hum.

"I love you," I whisper.

His arms circle around my shoulders, and mine secure around his lower back. I hear my mother's stupid camera clicking, and Tommy say, "She's like a sister to him."

My boy holds tighter, and so do I.

"Tell me," I say like a breath, smiling so no one knows this is torture. "Say it, Thomas."

He turns his head into my neck and whispers, "I love you."

Digging my fingers into his back is all I can do to keep the earth below my feet. I close my eyes and cling to what we have left, hoping it's good enough, intending to make sure it is.

When I drop my arms because we've been hugging for too long, Thomas doesn't let go.

"We can leave, Bliss," he says like a prayer.

I grip onto his sides and try to push him from me, but I can't get away. His hold on me is reliable and proves failing-hearts faulty.

"The car's right there. Just get in," he whispers like it's ending him.

Then his lips are on my neck, and the tiniest pinch of my skin is between his teeth. Before I have a chance to think, my hands pull him closer before shoving him away.

Like a shot of life, my heart picks up and my cheeks warm as Thomas steps back. His smile dares.

It says, *"Play it off or play it up, girl."*

I half laugh, overwhelmed. "You're such a jerk."

His smile falls.

I place my hand over my chest where my heart pulses in spite of me. It pumps blood through my veins and arteries and lungs, keeping me alive, giving me no choice other than to live through this moment, which is everything it was never supposed to be.

With less enthusiasm and uneasy posture, Mom announces her wishes for a group photo. I want Thomas to put his arm over my shoulders, and I want to put mine around his waist, but he stands emotionless beside his sister.

Pete stands next to me, so I circle my arms around him instead of his best friend. Ben sneaks between Rebecka and I, and he leans his head on top of hers.

Mom's not satisfied.

"Come on, girls," she says kindly to Katie, Kelly, Mixie, and Val.

Awkwardly, the Sluts stand in a row on the other side of Pete.

"Closer," Mom says, looking at us through her camera screen.

My boy shifts impatiently next to his sister, patting his pockets like he does when he's ill-fitted. As Valarie moves herself between Ben and me, I hold onto Petey as tightly as I can. Kelly moves to his right, and he puts his free arm over her shoulders. When I look up, he grins madly.

With Katie and Mixie at Thomas's left, we squeeze in as tightly as possible to fit in the frame.

With proud parents on one side of the camera and the disparate youth on the other, Mom shouts, "Say cheese!"

In unison, like an opus, we do.

And it takes no effort at all.

After a couple of flashes, we gap and separate, and the moment of simplicity is gone.

With only a couple of feet between us—twenty-four inches that feel like five hundred eternities—Thomas shakes his head with a sad half smirk, keeping his eyes away from me.

When Pete asks him if he wants to take off, I watch him walk out of my direction and get into his Lincoln.

And I watch him drive away, without me.

"HANG OUT with me, like we used to. Spend the night. Spend the weekend," Rebecka says before we leave this school for the last time. "It's only right we're together. You're still my best friend."

"Maybe I'll call you after dinner," I say, unable to meet her eyes.

"You better," she says.

I stare out the window on the short drive home, watching the same shade of green pass—the same shades of mud and wet and moss and gray. My dad has music on low, but nothing registers. Nothing is distinct. Everything is flat, fixed, and bland.

Until Dad pulls the car into the driveway and asks, "What the hell was that, Leighlee?"

Settling back into my role is seamless, but not facile. With years of experience, I sit up straight and force my voice out.

"What?" I ask.

He meets my gaze through the rearview mirror. "Thomas," he says.

"It was nothing."

"We don't like it," Mom chimes in, with implication in her tone.

With my hand on the door handle and my stare on the back of my mother's head, I say with a little more aggression than I should, "There's nothing for you not to like. I'm his ..."

"Little sister." Dad finishes my sentence, cynically.

Grandma knocks on the car window, ending the conversation for now.

I SIT at the kitchen table picking blueberries out of a muffin I have no intention of eating, in my graduation gown I have no will to take off. My nail polish is marred, and my cuticles are inflamed. I roll my wrist and extend my fingers and think, *these are the hands of a desperate girl.*

"It's not Leigh I don't trust," my dad says, opening and shutting the fridge.

I breathe though my nose and sit back, pushing my mother's homemade effort toward the center of the table.

"She's a seventeen-year-old girl, Thad," his mother replies, winking at me, taking my side.

Like I care. Like anything being said matters

"He kissed her because he knew he could. He took advantage of her." Dad opens a bottle of water. "And she's going to college—then what?"

They're fucking ignorant.

I know exactly how to survive on my own.

Thomas taught me about drugs and villains and everything else my parents keep in the dark. I've seen assaults and witnessed drug deals—I know the pusher. I can roll a joint with my eyes closed. I know the difference between kush and ditch weed, and what cocaine looks like.

I roll with criminals and addicts and sluts and alcoholics. I know a girl who had an abortion, and I know a whole group of girls who have fucked for drugs.

My boyfriend is white trash.

So are all of my friends.

And I'm just like them, but in prettier dresses.

Because of them, I'll be fine.

With Thomas, I will be fine.

Mom grates cheese for the enchiladas, the meal she thinks is my favorite.

"Maybe she can live here for another year and go somewhere closer," she suggests, like I'm not in the room.

A month ago, she framed my acceptance letter to Puget Sound, and now she's acting like my opinion doesn't matter.

When Dad agrees and suggests they buy me a new car so I can commute, I finally say, "Do you think I've never been kissed?"

Grandma laughs, but Mom scowls, and Dad warns, "Leighlee."

Excusing myself from the table, I walk away from this sorry excuse of a graduation party and head upstairs. What I really wanted was my friends to come over, with music and food and laughs and some sort of truth, but Dad shot the idea down.

"How would that look?" he said. "What would the neighbors say?"

It was easier to act like I wanted enchiladas.

In my room, I dig through my purse for my cell phone. While it rings my boy, I open my closet door and search through hangers for something to wear.

My call goes to voicemail.

"Dusty." I sigh and hang up.

After lying on my bed until the sun goes down, I pull a red cotton and lace dress over my head and brush my hair over my shoulder. I rescue pink Jadeite from under my bed where I threw it months ago and fasten it around my neck where it belongs.

As I sit at my vanity, his name is on repeat inside me—

Thomas.

I pin my bangs back, and I wipe off this morning's mascara with a cleansing towelette until my eyes are clean from black but still last-night-red.

Thomas.

Once my face is concealer free, I stare at myself in the mirror: freckled and blemished and purple and swollen. The new-in-love, fresh-faced child no longer stares back at me. Like my hands, this is the face of a girl who struggles.

Thomas.

Breaking the spell, my phone rings, vibrating and singing a tune. It's not Thomas, but instead of being disappointed, I'm indifferent.

"Hello," I answer, impassive.

"I'm coming to get you," Becka shouts over music. "Ready to get your party on, Bliss baby?"

I sit back down at my dressing table. With my phone between my shoulder and ear, I dot foundation onto a sponge and cover war wounds.

"Sure," I answer.

She shrieks happily. "Pack a bag!"

"Okay," I say before I hang up.

Instead of setting the phone down, I set my sponge down. And instead of calling Becka back and telling her I have no desire to be anywhere near her, I call Thomas once more. When I get his voicemail again, I hang up and call Oliver.

He says my name.

Like a whisper.

Like a dream.

Like a fucking charm.

"Bliss."

I just ask, "Becka wants to go out tonight. Are you?"

"I want to see you," he says.

Circling my brush in blush, I say, "I heard something about Tanner having a party."

Oliver clears his throat. "Yeah, that's what Smitty said."

I apply pink to my cheek bones. "I'll see you there."

He's quiet, awkwardly. He has something to say, but he doesn't. "Okay."

Pussy, the single thought breaks the chant momentarily.

With my makeup polished perfectly and my hair re-curled, I text Thomas because he hasn't called me back. I slip my feet into a pair of wedges and don't bother packing a bag. I have no aim with Becka. I'll be in the Lincoln by then. I'll sleep in Dusty's clothes, on him, under him, beside him.

As I gather my purse and my phone, checking my hair one last time, I realize I wouldn't give a shit if I never stepped foot in this room again. It was part of a routine and a path that brought me closer to the desired result: a life with Thomas.

And I almost missed my cue.

Downstairs, my dad and grandfather sit in front of the TV. My mother pulls food from the oven, and my grandmother, the first person to notice me, sets the table for dinner.

"Going somewhere?" she asks kindly, folding a napkin before placing it down.

Mom drops the pan of enchiladas on the counter, splattering cheese and sauce and green onions and black olives.

"Where do you think you're going?" she questions, tilting her head, scoping out my clothes and shoes.

"With Becka," I answer.

"Leigh, I made this dinner for you," she replies harshly.

With frizzy hair and a dirty apron, she's acting as if enchiladas are some feat. Like they took all day to make and not an hour.

Like my very own loaded gun isn't out there, under the impression I don't want him.

"Can we eat now?" I ask, instead of arguing.

"No," Mom tosses a dirty spatula in the sink.

The clink, clink, bang grabs my dad's attention.

"What's going on in here?" Dad asks, deep toned and stern. He has a red stain on his white shirt, from dipping into dinner too early.

He looks at me, but my changed outfit and purse ring no bells. In his eyes, I could never do anything to disappoint either of them. I'm perfect, idyllic Leighlee Bliss. So blissful. So bliss-filled. I'm a little ray of Bliss.

Held tight Bliss.

Secured Bliss.

She'll-never-be-too-far-from-home Bliss.

"Your daughter," Teri says, giving me a pointed look before turning her eyes to her husband.

Dad rubs his stomach, briefly flashing his eyes in my direction before staring down his wife's cooking. "What about her?"

"She wants to go with Becka," Mom unties her apron. "But she went out last night."

When my father looks at me, he finally notices my hair, my makeup, and my outfit.

"No," he states.

Satisfied with his verdict, my mom hangs up her apron, hands Grandma the plates, and grabs a clean serving utensil from the drawer. My parents talk about marinated chicken and sour cream and using the good wine glasses because tonight is a special occasion.

Softly but severely, amid their commotion, I say, "I'm going."

Dad looks up from the plate Mom is helping him serve. "You're not," he answers, dismissively.

I stand straight. "I am."

"Let her go, Thaddeus," my grandma says. "She looks pretty."

Dad shakes his head, but I lift my chin.

"No, Mom," he says. "It's risky on a night like this."

Grandma backhands her son on the arm playfully. "Oh, stop. You can trust Leigh."

Right on time, headlights from Becka's Jeep shine through the front window. She honks, and I shift my footing, ready for anything.

My parents share a look, and when Mom nods, I know I'm free to go. Without a word, I turn and leave. They probably think I'm so excited, like they're giving me a taste of life. A little dose of freedom. A real teenage experience—two nights in a row.

Lucky me.

REBECKA IS lit out of her mind.

My used-to-be best friend has her hair in a messy ponytail, and her eyeliner and lipstick are smudged. She won't stop bouncing her knee, and she's chewing gum with her mouth open, too fast and too loud.

I feel like I'm sitting next to a stranger.

Slowing to a stop at a red light, Becka presses her palms into her eyes. "I took some shit, and I'm fucked-up, baby."

I sit back and roll my eyes, mentioning nothing when the light turns green, then yellow and back to red. This girl and her mother's pills are nothing compared to Thomas and cocaine. Becka's such a fucking girl.

When the light turns again, I get out of the car and walk around to her side. I open the door and tell her to scoot over.

"I'm driving," I say.

She moves, but her foot gets stuck on the seatbelt, and she bumps her head on the window, and she drops her phone between the seat and the center console.

"Fuck!" she yells.

I get in and go.

The closer we get to the beach, the thicker the air becomes. By the time I park a few houses down from Tanner's, my curls are limp and my eyeliner's blurred. My skin is sticky, and my attitude isn't much better.

On top of that, this girl is still digging for her phone.

I move her hands away and help her look. "What did you take, Becka?"

She sits straight and pulls down her visor, flipping open the mirror. She rubs black pencil out from beneath her eyes and shrugs her shoulders. "I don't know. Something new in my mom's cabinet."

I have to reach deep down, but with my pointer and middle finger, I manage to secure her phone and pull it out.

She takes it from me before kissing the screen. "Thank you, thank you, thank you, best friend ever!"

"You're welcome," I say, reaching in the back for my purse.

Then she says, "I'm waiting for Smitty to call."

And I ask, "Smitty-Smitty?"

She sits up and slips her phone into her back pocket, nodding her head. "I miss him."

Out of the Jeep, hand in hand, Rebecka and I head toward Tanner's house.

Less crowded than usual, everything else is the same.

Dolly's in the corner with her boyfriend. Valarie and Ben are in the kitchen. Casper and Mixie are kissing in the hallway. Kelly's taking shots with Tanner and Katie. Oliver is at the keg, and Smitty's right beside him.

Everyone's here except Thomas and Petey.

I turn to Becka. "Where's your boyfriend?"

With glossy eyes and a blank expression, she shrugs. "I haven't talked to him." And a second later, "There's Smitty!"

She tries to pull me, but I walk, and she lets go.

When I catch up to them, she's smiling, and he's smirking. She's blushing, and he's arching his eyebrow. She's sighing, and he's crossing his arms. She's turning her head away, and he's tilting her chin back.

He knows she's high, and he hates it. His disappointed eyes say so.

But she's a Castor; she doesn't give a fuck.

"Beer?" Oliver bids, holding out a cup for me.

I gladly take his offering and drink most of its contents in a single try. Oliver whistles at my attempt, and when my lungs feel like they're going to burst, I pull the cup from my lips and wipe them with the back of my hand. When he goes to get me a refill, I push my way through the kitchen and out the back door.

A bonfire burns and crackles in the center of the yard, surrounded by beach sand and the rest of the party. I sit beside it in a spot by myself, and after a few moments, my cheeks warm, and the tip of my nose stings.

Oliver approaches and takes a seat in the sand beside me. I peek up and love the fire on his skin, but its reflection off his dark hair is my favorite.

He elbows me playfully. "What are you looking at?"

I lean my head on his shoulder. "Nothing."

After a few moments, the silence turns awkward, and I can practically see his words taking shape in the smoke in front of us.

I lift my head. "Out with it, man."

Oliver lowers his eyes and shuffles the sand between his knees through his fingers. "We didn't get to talk at graduation—"

"I know," I say quickly. "My mom wanted a picture of us, but—"

"Bliss, I saw Thomas kiss you."

My heart beats.

It pounds.

It fights inside my chest cavity and struggles to get through my breast bone.

"Leigh—"

Closing my eyes and say, "Oliver, don't."

But he says, "Bliss, I know everything."

I cover my mouth with both of my hands and open my eyes. Staring at the sand in disbelief, I shake my head as the world around me begins to crumble.

Shuffling from the sand, I stand on unsteady feet and Oliver follows. He reaches for my arm, and when I try to shove him away, he pulls me closer. As tears stream down my face, I give this boy one more chance to mean something more.

This boy sees through my veil and notices dark circles, collar bones, and chipped nail polish. Oliver knew it was Thomas on the other side of the text messages in the middle of class. My skater boy watched me closely when Thomas caught us kissing, and he knew then that deep blushes were only shame and guilt for kissing a boy other than my best friend's older brother.

I circle my arms around the back of his neck and run my fingers through his too-busy-skating-to-cut hair. I let him kiss the side of my face. I stand a little closer because I love his warmth. I love his skater boy scent: grass and sun and summer. But there's nothing more.

"I have to go," I mumble, wiping my face on his sleeve.

I turn away from the boy who let me wear his sweater when we were thirteen and bought me Fun Dip on Valentine's Day a year later. The person who touched my leg while I slept through a storm. Oliver, who draws me a card every year on my birthday. The only friend I have who lets me lean instead of leaning on me.

With his kiss on my cheek still warm, burning like a trespass, I say, "Oliver, you can't tell—"

Indifferent like I've never known, Oliver crosses his arms over his chest before he looks at me, but his eyes skip and lock over my shoulder. His posture changes from jilted to guarded.

The hair on the back of my neck stands up, and my fingers twitch. Blood calls truth's name as it flows, and joints and muscles, ligaments and tendons, all work together turning me away from the fire toward the house. A chair gets thrown. A girl gets knocked down. Glass breaks. There's yelling from the door, and an entire group of people trying to hold someone back.

Love is knowing who it is.

I know before I hear Petey yell, "Thomas, back the fuck up!"

I know before I hear Becka ask, "Why do you even care?"

And I know before Oliver says, "This is what happens when you keep secrets."

My eyes meet Thomas' as soon as the crowd falls apart.

Go, my heart beats.

Love takes one more step toward me before Petey and Ben both pull him back by his flannel.

I turn from my spot in the sand and run toward my boy, hearing the whispers as I push my way through bodies.

"What's going on?"

"Thomas and Leigh?"

"What?"

"Really?"

"No fucking way!"

Trouble is a shell of the boy he used to be, cocaine-brittle and heart-failing, but love gives us both incomparable strength. He breathes through his nose, working his hardest to get his best boys off his back. He gets one arm free and tries to come forward, but Ben pulls him by the neck of his shirt.

It rips.

Petey whispers in his ear, low and smooth under the chaos. "If you love her …" his lips say. "If you love her …"

But these people want to see Thomas do what Thomas does when he's crossed, so they instigate.

"That's your girl, bro?"

"He was kissing your chick, Dusty?"

"I thought little sisters were off limits."

Near love, the circle tightens as Oliver heads for him, and I get elbowed in the chest, pushed back, and pulled away. I don't catch my footing and fall into the side of the house, scraping my arm on stucco. I try to run back into the cluster of people, but nimble arms circle around my waist and turn me from the struggle.

Pushing down on arms without caring whose they are, I kick my legs and scream, "Let me go!"

"Leigh," a voice I know well whispers in my ear. "Stop."

I dig my fingernails into Valarie's hands, and elbow and squirm and stomp and yell, but the girl who had Thomas first does not waver.

I watch the crowd move and move and move.

I watch Oliver step up and reach for my boy.

I watch Ben and Pete release Thomas.

And I watch love and confusion fall to the ground.

Through legs and arms and spaces between people, I watch my boy inflict and endure pain. For every blow he gives, he takes. But there's years of anger in his fists—years of watching me be with Oliver, years of me saying no, and years of drugs, hiding, disappointment, anger, hurt, and neglect.

The party responds to each hit, each kick, each cut lip and busted nose. But in true Dusty form, after a few minutes, it gets frightening. Girls scream, but not a single one of them is louder than Rebecka. My boy's boys exchange looks, wondering if they should break it up.

Tanner kind of, sort of moves forward like he might, but he knows better firsthand.

I turn in Valarie's arms. "Val, please! Let me go."

Her eyes shift from my face to the fight, and she releases me and takes a step back. I run for Dusty, and this time people let me through.

Oliver struggles beneath my boy, bruised and bleeding. His knuckles are raw, and the neck of his shirt is ripped. His shoes skid and push and dig into the concrete underneath him, trying to gain leverage, but Thomas is ruthless. He'll bleed to death before he gives up.

Cocaine has Dusty's back.

Finally on his feet, Oliver pulls his torn shirt off and throws it to the side. "Come on, motherfucker."

Dusty's blood-coated, and his eyes are wild. He spits and wipes his cut lip with the back of his hand before rushing Oliver. They collide and fall into the sand around the fire pit. Embers and smoke and ash swirl together above the flame while the party instinctively follows.

Ben, Pete, and Smitty finally jump in and pin Thomas to the ground, giving Oliver a chance to get up.

The fight is over, but the party's shocked. This is usually the part where Thomas says or does something to ease our anxiety, but that's not happening this time. He thrashes and struggles in the sand to get free. Tears run from his eyes into his bloody hair, and this is reality. This is my boy's life. This is my life.

This is truth.

This is our deal.

CHAPTER
fifty-seven

People love Dusty's invincibility. He's a king, and when they're around him, they feel like royalty, too. His swagger gets girls wet, and all of these boys want to be just like him.

Thomas Castor will never fall.

Thomas Castor will be forever young.

But this is what drugs have done to love.

Indestructible Thomas Castor is being held to the ground, crying like a child, fighting off his best friends, begging for his freedom.

Is that what kings are made of?

"Pete," broken and addicted groans, his tone thick with tears. "Get the fuck off."

In the corner of the yard, Oliver's shirtless and raging, throwing lawn chairs and shoving the ones who hold him back. He paces, tearing up the lawn in madness.

"Get the fuck up!" Oliver shouts. "Come on, motherfucker. You want to bruise somebody, bruise me!"

I stand in the pathway between love and friendship.

Based between two different worlds, over the yelling and the struggling and the crying, I notice everyone's eyes are suspicious and questioning.

Val, with my scratch marks down her arms, stares at the person she thought she loved before looking over at me with questioning eyes. Tanner rubs the raised skin on his eyebrow.

Smitty, struggling to remain in front of his friend, stares at me while Oliver shouts, "He busted her fucking headlights," and points at Thomas. "Remember? At the beach? When Bliss was crying?"

"She's not worth it," Smitty spits, turning away from me. "She's just a slut, Oliver."

Moving Katie and Kelly out of my way, I get closer to his fallen majesty.

"Let him up," I say.

"Get her the fuck out of here," Petey shouts, keeping his grip on Dusty's wrists.

Kicking up sand, I pull on Petey's shirt until he falls, and when he tries to move back toward Thomas, I climb onto my boy and hold my hands out to keep him away.

"Stop, Pete," I cry. "Just stop."

Leaning against Thomas' kicking legs, with my arms extended and my eyes brimming tears, my heart beats harder than it ever has.

I feel it.

Every lie was merited. Every secret meant something. Every stolen moment and hidden kiss and scarf covered wound came down to this. Fuck their looks and fuck their questions. Fuck Becka, and Smitty, and Oliver. Fuck my parents, and Thomas' parents. Fuck college. Fuck cocaine. Fuck the whole wide world, because he's mine.

I choose him.

I choose Thomas.

He stands up, and so do I, and I expect him to see me, but he looks past me with hollow and forever-black eyes.

"You want to kiss someone?" Thomas says to Oliver, stepping forward.

He shrugs his shoulders, circles his neck, spits, and squares up. I hold out my hands against his chest and ask him to stop, but he walks right through me.

"Kiss me, motherfucker." Love smirks, reaching for Oliver. "Come on, kiss me!"

As Thomas steps by me, I grab onto what's left of his shirt and close my eyes, expecting to be pulled.

I'm not.

Thomas stops and forces my fingers from ripped cotton. He holds my arm up, glaring at me. Rather than cowering like anyone else would, I stand tall.

"I want to go," I whisper.

My boy cracks a sarcastic smile as his fingers tighten impossibly more. "Now?" he asks.

"Yes."

My heart pounds

"Yes."

His lips curve. "Look around, sunny side."

I don't.

"There's strength in numbers, girl."

My eyes shift away from love for a half second. Becka's strung-out blues are wide and watering. Oliver stares right at me, pleading silently. Smitty won't face any of us, and even Ben runs his hand through his hair, looking up at the stars.

"I'm ready," I say with my heart in my throat, returning my eyes to my choice.

Thomas straightens out his shirt and rubs his face in his hands, and when he drops them, his hopeless expression gives me a head rush. I thought love was lost in all our bullshit, but it's here. He's right in front of me, all fucked-up and weak.

I'll take the bad, because there is so much good. For every busted headlight, there's history that cannot be duplicated by a person who draws me birthday cards, or a friend who kissed me so she would be my first.

Dusty would die for me, and I totally fucked him.

He spits more blood on the concrete. He turns to Oliver and says, "Go near my girl again, and I'll fucking kill you."

With the music from the house and ocean waves as our backdrop, love turns and laces his fingers behind his head and walks. I follow.

As I pass Rebecka, she grabs onto my wrist and jerks me back. I pull my arm, trying to get free, but she doesn't let me go. Her eyes scream accusations, and her defensive stance confirms her suspicions.

She knows her best friend was never only her best friend.

"Rebecka, let me go," I say.

Like my touch is poison, she does.

I run after love, through the side gate, out to the front of the house. I spot my boy right away, walking to his car at the end of the street.

"Thomas," I call out.

I run across the lawn and hurry under orange street lights and trip over a crack in the sidewalk. I wipe my eyes on my forearm and shout again. "Dusty!"

Beside his Lincoln, he finally turns. I stop running, struggling to breathe between gasps and sobs. He pats his pockets, pulls out his cigarettes, and lights up a smoke.

The closer I step, the better I can see how swollen and wounded, black-and-blue, and cut he is. His knuckles are raw and bleeding red, and his eyes are bleak.

There's no trace of Thomas in them at all.

"You can't leave me," I say, approaching his body space.

Thomas blows smoke into the sea-salty air and flicks his cigarette onto the neighbor's yard. Love leaves me on the sidewalk and walks around to his car and unlocks the driver's side door, scrutinizing me with cocaine-blacks, taunting me with a smug smirk and a condescending wink.

My boy starts the engine and presses on the gas, shattering silence. He flips on the lights and leans over to open the passenger door.

"Get the fuck in the car, Leighlee," he demands, righting his position.

Cream-colored leather is cool on my bare legs, and my spot in his car feels foreign to me. Breathing in vanilla and the lingering smell of pot, I tug on my seat belt, but it's locked. I pull and pull, but give up as I'm blinded by tears.

I cry in my hands.

"What are you crying for?" Thomas asks.

"I can't get my seat belt on," I say, filling my palms with sadness.

"Put it on, Leigh," Thomas says sternly, but all I can do is cry. "Put your fucking seat belt on, Bliss!"

I don't jump. I don't flinch. I don't do anything but scream into my hands.

Thomas reaches over and pulls on the belt. Plastic cracks as he forces the nylon loose.

After he locks me in, he drives, not bothering with his own.

Thomas's cell phone rings as we pull onto the highway. He ignores it, driving with both hands on the steering wheel. The Lincoln's headlights fill the route in front of us, shining bright on the trees. I watch the dashed yellow lines between the lanes, counting them as we get closer to home.

Thomas doesn't talk, and I don't expect him to.

Unable to keep them open any longer, I let my eyes close.

I don't open them again until the car stops.

When I do, I get one moment's peace. I'm with my boy, and he's looking at me with his hand on my knee. His touch is gentle, soothing, and even though his eyes are blueless, they're consoling.

"You have to go," he says lowly, sitting back in his seat, looking straight ahead.

"Why are we at my house?" I ask, tipping hysterical.

I look over at my wrecking ball, but he won't look at me. I clutch onto his flannel and claw at the neck of his torn white tee.

He's crying. Slowly, quietly …

"Thomas?" I question, ripping his shirt further.

He takes control of my wrists and holds them in his hands up to his split lips. He kisses each and every one of my knuckles and closes his eyes. Love's long eyelashes are wet, and he sniffs.

"No." I fight against his hold. I sit up on my knees and move closer to love. "Thomas, no."

My kneecaps press against his thighs, and my tears drip onto his denim. His almost swollen shut eye looks pitiful as he cries. He bites nervously on his bottom lip, reopening his cut.

"Don't make me stay here," I beg.

"Leighlee …" His chin quivers.

As blood circulation slows in my hands, they lose sensation, but it doesn't matter. None of it matters unless I have him.

"I'll go with you," I say, twisting my wrists so I can dig my fingers into him. "Don't leave me. Not again."

"Bliss, stop," he chokes. More tears stream down his cheeks. "I can't—we can't …"

I cry out, hiding my face in his neck, forcing myself closer. "Please."

Desperation moves me on his lap, and I kiss the side of his crying face while he keeps his grip on my wrists. Thomas' eyes are closed and his lip bleeds, but it doesn't stop me from biting it until his grip loosens. When I have my arms free, I circle them around his neck with no intention of letting go.

His body molds to mine, eliminating space, connecting us completely. His lips press into the side of my neck, and his voice whispers in my ear, "I'm sorry."

I clutch while Thomas takes us somewhere other than here, and I cry until the car stops in front of his parents' house.

The Castor home is lit only by the silver light from the moon. My boy opens the car door, and the wind chime from their porch sings us a slow, sad song.

I touch my wedges to rocky pavement, listening to tiny rocks grind under my shoes. Love gets out of the Lincoln behind me and shuts the door, sending an echo through the forest surrounding the house.

"Do you think she's here?" I ask, following him past his sister's Jeep.

"I don't know," he answers quietly, unlocking the front door and stepping aside for me to enter before him.

He steps past me to the kitchen and flips the lights on. Squinting against the sudden illumination, I notice Tommy's redecorated since the last time I was here. Winter colors have been replaced with summer, and there's a larger glass coffee table where the old wooden one used to be in the living room. New throw pillows sit on the couch, and a rug I've never seen lays on the floor.

Dusty opens the freezer and pulls out an ice pack. As he holds it against his eye, I join him in the kitchen and lead him to the table so I can get a better look at his wounds. He tilts his head back without argument, and lets me press the cool compress to his injury.

Love starts to cry again.

Between his knees, with his hands on my hips, love does nothing to hide his hurt. He cries openly and loudly. He pulls me closer, until my knees buckle and press into the edge of the chair. Holding on with one hand, I run my other through his hair, breaking up blood and knots.

"Tell me, boy," I say, kissing his forehead.

Straddling his thighs, I curve to suit him and hide us behind a curtain of my strawberry-blond hair. The tips of my wedges brush the kitchen floor. The ice pack drops.

He kisses the side of my throat.

Under my chin.

The corner of my mouth.

"You and cocaine make me crazy," he whispers over my lips.

His shredded fingers touch my face while he kisses each freckle and each

tear track. Thomas slides one hand behind my neck and moves my hair out of our faces with the other. Love forces my head back so he can kiss across my collar bones.

It feels like goodbye.

Salty liquid stings already-sore eyes, and already-tender fingers grip at the front of his shirt. With his mouth near my ear, I press my wedges into the floor and push myself up my hoodlum's legs until where he hasn't been in so long feels what needs him so badly.

"Stay," I whisper through teardrops.

I circle my hips.

"Stay with me," I cry again, clutching onto cotton.

My boy's mouth doesn't move, and his hands hold my arms. He breathes uneven breaths right below my ear, and I feel it when his sadness drips onto my bare shoulder. But no matter how hurt he is, he can't keep his body from reacting to mine.

Love knows.

Plagued with years of abuse and misuse, my heart jumps as our mouths make the best kind of love.

Nothing tastes better than Thomas' mouth, bloodied and slashed, defending what we are. I savor the battle through his split lips, like justification. The swelling feels like protection. Each bruise looks like declaration.

It's messy and hard, and it hurts, but we open our mouths wide and our tongues reach so far back. Our teeth collide and his lips bleed against mine. I brush my fingers through his hair instead of pulling, and Thomas circles my hips instead of holding.

I bring my head back and stare up at the ceiling, gasping for breath.

"Not here," he says, pressing his face over red cotton, between my breasts. His hand slips under my dress. His fingernails scratch up my thighs. His palm slips inside my underwear.

Without warning, my purse that was on the couch in the living room hits the leg of the chair Dusty and I are on together. When I look over my shoulder, I see my betrayal in the eyeliner running down Rebecka's face.

When she walks away, I've absolutely lost my best friend. I feel her void as her Jeep speeds out of the driveway.

Slipping my fingers from Thomas's hair, I cover my mouth and close my eyes. I try to breathe, but I can't inhale.

"You knew," Thomas says lowly, pushing my hair over my shoulder. "We always knew, Bliss."

Grief rocks through me in waves—immense rises and rolls.

Love's whole stance shifts from easy to firm, and his touch changes from comforting to controlling. He sits up straight and moves me down his lap. He wipes wet eyes in the bend of his elbow and clears his throat, and his already-so-open pupils stretch even more, swallowing up any vulnerability he was showing just a moment ago.

"I should take you home," he says.

My boy crosses his arms and stares over my shoulder, purposely avoiding my eyes. His cocaine-blacks are so fucking taunting, teasing me.

Drugs are killing him.

"Where will you go?" I plead.

Thomas gets up, but I sit back in the chair and refuse to move. I'll climb the walls. I'll burn this motherfucker down. He can't make me go without him.

"Isn't this enough?" he pleads. "What more do you want, Leigh?"

"You're not leaving without me," I yell, standing up and kicking the chair we were just sitting in.

"Kick it again, princess kid," he provokes.

I do.

Thomas laughs.

His knees bend.

He holds his hands over his stomach, and he tilts his head back.

His teeth show.

Outraged, I pick up an orange from the fruit basket on the table and throw it. My boy dodges my effort easily, so instead of throwing the basket of produce one at a time, I pick the entire thing up and launch it.

I toss the cookbook next, the garage door opener, and a half-full water bottle.

When I've thrown everything but my purse and my cellphone, I reach for both, but he gets to me first. With my back against his chest, Thomas holds my arms down and forces me out of the kitchen. I trip over apples and glass and his legs, and thrash, fight, and pierce my nails into his arm.

I bite his wrist.

"Stop!" he yells. "Calm the fuck down!"

My boy shoves me from his grip toward the steps.

"Get upstairs," he demands, turning me around and pushing me forward.

Lightheaded and desperate, I place my hand on the banister and take a slow step up. Impatience steps around me and walks into his room before I've even made it upstairs. Upon entering our safe spot, I can tell he hasn't been here in a while. The room smells closed off and closed up. Everything is too tidy—too long untouched.

Guided by the moonlight he lets in through the window, Thomas walks back and forth, shirtless. He's thin, and his skin is pale. His shoulders are scraped up and his ribs are bruised, and he has punctures from my fingernails in his hands.

"Are you going to stand there all night?" he asks.

I close the door with a soft click and force oncoming tears away. Carefully reaching under his ivory lampshade, I pull on the cool metal chain and light the room with a dull yellow

"I need to change, and then I'm taking you home," my heartbreaker says, opening his closet door.

I go to him and press my lips between his shoulder blades. Love's skin rises, and whether or not he realizes it, he leans into me. The unbeating half of my heart turns in my grip, and my hands slip from his sides to his belt.

Dusty's eyelids close over chemical black irises, and he covers my hands with his, but I still tug black leather from its brass buckle and hook my fingers in his belt loops. Carefully stepping back toward the bed, I bring Thomas with me.

When the back of my legs hit the mattress, I fall back and lift my dress up, opening my knees to bare it all.

"Bliss," he says like a breath, looking at me under wet lashes.

"Please," I cry, about to give up. I close my legs and lower my dress.

Love inhales a shaky breath and leans on the bed.

Thomas turns me on my stomach and kisses the back of my neck softly. Holding me like I'm a bubble and not the girl he's been with since he was thirteen years old, he's unhurried and gentle, like I might break.

He pushes my dress up and kisses my lower back as he pulls down my underwear, leaving my delicates at my knees. He palms my thighs, opening me up enough to see, and then sinks his teeth into my bottom, just before I feel his mouth on my center.

His lower lip touches my clit, and he licks between my folds and pushes his tongue inside me. I feel his teeth and his chin and nose. I feel his breath, and I feel his voice when he pulls back and moans *"Fuck"* against part of me that has only ever been his.

Then he opens me wider and kisses me deeper … firmer.

My boy trades his tongue for his fingers, sliding them in and out of me slowly while he kisses my inner thighs.

Teardrops fall onto the tops of my hands. Elbows I refuse to let slip ache in hurtful protest. My hair sticks to my cheeks as I trap desperate cries behind clenched teeth.

Unzipping his pants, Thomas climbs onto his bed behind me, hard between my thighs. He sinks into me, burying his face in the side of my neck. It's slow going and more painful than it should ever be.

It feels like the last time.

"I love you," he whispers, breathless as he fills me. "I love you, girl. I love you."

Letting my head fall forward and to the side, I give him more of the skin he adores, but I can't stop looking at our hands. With none of the usual selfish regard for his own need, he moves his hips slowly, making sure I feel all of him.

Smooth and sensual, his lips brush across the back of my neck, and his fingers lace with mine.

My boy is making love.

With my hands still pressed into the mattress, I push my hips back, forcing him to fuck me.

Thomas groans into my neck. I feel his entire body tense up.

"Do it," I say, muffled by his comforter. "Do it, you fucking—"

"Stop," my soul taker begs helplessly. "Let me."

He guides me from my knees to my stomach and covers every inch of me with so much of him. I feel his lungs expand on my back. His hips press against my bottom, and I feel the outside of his thighs against the inside of mine. He pulls my hair, but only enough to make me moan. Thomas uses his teeth, but they barely brush the surface of my skin.

He loves me patiently.

He loves me kindly.

He loves me like this should have been our first time.

Overcome and overwhelmed, I sink into the bed and let go. The weight of his body pushes me into the bed, but the weight of his despair slaughters me wholly.

As he rides me, love's movements shift from measured to unconcerned. Guided strokes become negligent thrusts. Gentleness gives way to crudeness, consideration to mindlessness.

He gives me what I wanted.

Only now that I've had what love can really feel like, this is a sick sadness.

The love I know is gone. I have his body. I have his lips. I have his hands. I have his voice, but the energy is missing. Our ever-present-until-now intensity is forced. He tells me he loves me, and my heart drinks it up, but his words are empty.

I'm soaking up and down my thighs, and he's slippery between me, but I wrap my legs around him and let him fuck me through what I know is right and wrong like I always do as my heart shatters and I go numb.

"It's okay," he tells me, aching.

Coming is unhopeful and renders me helpless. My knees fall open and my arms drop to the mattress, and in this moment where I'm supposed to feel closest to the one I love, I feel utterly alone.

"Love stays, girl," he says as my eyes close and the fire burns out.

CHAPTER
fifty-eight

Looking over at Thomas while he smokes a cigarette behind the wheel of his car, it's hard to believe he's the same person who told me he liked my hair color on that first day of school.

That was the beginning of us—a princess and a troublemaker.

I trusted him then, but now that's gone.

"Thomas …" I start.

He kills the engine and leaves his hands on the steering wheel.

"Promise me," I say with my heart in my throat.

My boy breathes through his nose before turning his body toward me. "I said I'd be back."

"When?" I ask, turning my eyes down.

"I'll call you," he replies, patting his pockets.

His pack is on the dashboard.

"Come inside with me. It doesn't matter anymore," I say, finally looking over just as he turns the end of his smoke cherry-red.

Nicotine fills the cab of the car. He cracks his window.

"It does matter," he says with tobacco-filled lungs.

I shake my head. "Dusty—"

"Leigh!" he cuts me off. He forces me to look at him and studies my eyes, my nose, and my mouth. "I'll be back."

With tears that feel like fire, I pull my face free from his grasp and open my door. My house is as dark as it should be at three in the morning. I thought I might not come back here; I'm disappointed I was wrong.

As I exit the car, Thomas grabs my elbow and pulls me back in. There's a rashness in his expression that wasn't there a second ago.

"What?" I ask.

"I love you," he says, clearly. "Only you, you know. I love you only."

I pull my arm free and get out of the car.

He sniffs.

Before I close the door, I lean in so he can see me, and say, "I love you too, boy."

TWO HOURS later, the sun's come up, and I've torn my bedroom to pieces.

By the grace of God, my parents didn't hear me come in. They didn't hear the Lincoln drive away, and they didn't hear the neighbor's dogs.

I might have kicked the fence as I snuck by.

Fuck those dogs.

Everything I own is thrown across my bed and spread across my floor. I choose pieces at random, tossing cotton and silk and lace and whatever-the-fuck-else will fit into my bag.

Once I'm packed, I leave my room before my parents come in. The house smells like coffee and syrup, and the local news is on the television.

Mom, still in her nightgown, leans against the stove. My dad, who's sitting at the kitchen table, stabs at his healthy version of pancakes. He looks up and nods his head, shoving a whole grain mess into his mouth.

I come in and sit down across from him.

"What time did you get home?" Mom asks, looking over my shoulder toward her husband, awaiting her backup.

I pick at my already-chipped-polish under the kitchen table, and shrug. "About one."

Lie.

Dad points his fork at me, swallowing his bite. "I told you to be in early, Leigh."

I shrug again. "Sorry."

I leave before they ask any more questions, and after retrieving my cell phone from upstairs, I grab a blanket and wrap it around myself before curling up on the couch.

My parents try to call me back into the kitchen. My mom even comes into the living room to glare, like I fucking care.

"This is why we don't let you out, Leigh," she says. "You won't be one of those kids who disrespect their parents."

I ignore her and text Thomas instead.

I'm ready.

He doesn't reply before I fall asleep.

I'M WOKEN up by my mother trying to reach under the blanket for my cell phone. It's clutched not-so-snugly in my hand, and she already has her fingers on it. I tighten my grip around the only way I have to get a hold of my boy and pull it deeper into the blankets, away from her. I slip it between my thighs and hold onto red fleece with both hands so she can't get in.

"It was ringing," she says, like she wasn't trying to invade my privacy.

She begins to clear off the coffee table, stacking together a few loose magazines. She wipes away some dust with her open hand before brushing it off on the jeans she changed into.

"You know, Leighlee," Mom says, restacking copies of *Home and Garden*, "you've never given me any reason not to trust you …"

I sit up and clear my throat. I can't be still. I can't be down here at all.

"But after last night," she starts again.

With the blanket still over my shoulders and my phone in hand, I stand and head upstairs. I don't listen to what she tells me as I go, because no matter what she says, neither one of my parents has ever trusted me a day in my life.

Halfway up the stairs, I stop. "Where's Grandma and Grandpa?"

Mom scoffs but answers, "They left."

When I get to my room, I close my door and drop the blanket. I shove clothes I don't need any more from my bed to the floor and sit down with my phone.

It's already after noon, and I don't have any missed calls.

I tell my speeding heart to calm. I bite on my bottom lip while I slide my finger across glass, unlocking my phone. I check my text messages just to make sure my mother wasn't lying and hope that maybe Thomas sent something while I was sleeping and she read it first.

My inbox is empty.

I scroll through my call history.

She said it was ringing, but the last call I received was from Becka, yesterday before the party.

She lied.

I pull my legs onto the bed and cross them while I sit back against the headboard. I press Thomas' number and watch until the call goes through and I hear it ring. I twirl and curl on my hair until some of it pulls from the root right as Thomas' voicemail picks up.

I don't cry.

I call him again.

When his voice mail picks up a second time, I still don't cry.

I call a third time.

And a fourth.

The fifth time it goes straight to voice mail. He's turned his phone off.

Instead of panicking, I lie flat on my back and stare up at the ceiling with my cell on my stomach, and I wait.

And I wait.

He'll come for me.

I know he will.

I've been lying in bed for over an hour, staring at the walls, motionless. I don't breathe too hard or roll up and cry like I want to. I keep my arms at my sides and my head on my pillow and stay silent so I don't miss his call.

During my quietness, I consider packing up my car and leaving. I could go to him instead.

But what if he's coming here as I'm going there?

"Please, please, please—" I whisper achingly as I dial him. "Please answer."

It rings.

And it rings.

And it rings.

When his voice mail picks up, I crumble and hide under the safety of my blankets and sob into my pillow. I dig my toes into my mattress and pull at my bedding. I cry until my lungs burn and my face tingles, and my body goes numb.

I cry until I sleep.

When I wake up, my room is exactly as I left it. The radio plays some random station, and a song I'm still not listening to belts its chorus. My curtains are open and my window lets in the breeze. The sky isn't gray anymore, but pink and orange and purple, coloring my room with its setting sun.

I'm buried by my blankets, and my sheet is bundled underneath me, tangled at my feet. My pillow is wet from my crying.

The only difference:

My bedroom door is wide open and my mom is standing in its frame.

I blink a few times, trying to clear my head. I reach for my phone, but I already know he hasn't called.

It's a little after seven, and my heart sinks when my phone proves me right.

"Are you going somewhere?" Mom asks, her tone partway condescending and partway afraid.

She steps into my room and picks up a dress from the end of my bed. She kicks my packed bags with the toe of her shoe.

I don't answer. I don't know what to say.

The person who gave me life walks around my room. She looks inside my empty closet and stares at my bare vanity. Mom brushes her hand over the corkboard on my desk that used to have tons of pictures of me and my friends pinned to its surface but now stands bare. She opens the top drawer of my dresser, but says nothing when she discovers it's not filled with my socks anymore.

"You've been up here all day ..." She picks up the smallest of my three bags from the floor. She unzips it and looks in. "It's a little early to be packing for school, don't you think?"

I shake my head.

"No?" she asks angrily, raising her voice.

She drops the bag to the floor. Some of my things fall out.

"Get out of that bed, Leighlee," she orders, more upset than I have ever seen her.

I immediately start to cry again, but I don't get out of bed. I don't even move.

Her feet pound on the carpet as she storms over to me. Mom pulls the blankets off of my body and grabs me by my left wrist, sitting me up. "So help me Leigh, get out of—"

I cry out, and she lets go.

She takes a few steps back, and I know what she sees. My wrists are discolored and swollen, and I'm holding the one she grabbed against my chest.

I go for the blankets, but my mother reaches them first, pulling them completely off the bed. She runs to my bedroom door, and with her hands on both sides of the door frame, she yells for my dad. "Thaddeus!"

I lie back down, still cradling my hurt arm against my body. Mom comes back and forces me to sit up, this time by my shoulders. She clutches my chin and moves my head back and forth, searching me for more injuries. When my dad comes into the room, she has my hands in hers.

"What's going on?" he asks, taken by surprise.

Mom turns my arm over and finds my elbow.

Dad takes a few more heavy steps into my room.

"Who did this to you?" Mom asks, down on her knees in front of me.

"Answer her, Leigh," Dad's deep voice echoes off my bedroom walls.

I shake my head, pulling my hands from my mother's. I wipe my nose. "It was nothing," I lie. "There was a fight, and I got pushed into—"

Mom falls back on her heels, and she looks at me like she never has before: suspiciously.

"You're lying," she says, her voice eerily calm.

Our eyes meet, and she sees through me, staring every lie I ever told her right in the face.

I look away first.

Mom stands and holds out her hand. "Give me your phone."

I hold it tighter. "No."

She looks at my dad, whose ample and daunting presence makes him look more like a judge and less like my father. His arms are crossed over his chest while he watches how I react, looking for evidence to prove my untruth.

"Ask why her bags are packed," Mom suggests, looking back at me.

Dad's entire body stays as it is, but his eyes move. They notice the same things my mom did when she came in: my closet, my vanity, my dresser—all packed up.

The only familiarity in my dad is in the same eyes that roam over all of my things. They're soft light brown unlike my green, and unwrapped. While his chest fills up with a frustrated breath and his arms drop to his sides, his eyes are unwilling to believe what he sees: the evidence he was looking for.

"What's going on?" he asks me, clearing his throat from any real emotion.

"Dad," I say softly, looking away from him.

"The truth, Leigh. Now." His voice is firm.

Meanwhile, my mother opens everything, searching through my things. She opens my makeup bag and dumps it out; pink Jadeite falls with my lip gloss and blush.

"Give me your phone," she demands once more.

I hold onto my cell, turning my knuckles white.

"Leigh, don't make me—" she starts, but Judge McCloy cuts her off.

"Teri, enough!" he finally yells. "Tell me what the hell is going on, Leighlee, or I will turn this whole room upside down."

He's not lying, and they'll find out eventually.

I look up at him and as calmly as I can, through steady tears and shortness of breath, I say, "I'm leaving."

"What?" he asks with an unbelieving tone.

"I'm leaving … with Thomas."

I've never taken much consideration into the way my parents look. My mother has always worn her hair the same way, and my dad will never shave his mustache. They look just about the same to me as they did when I was two, or five … or ten. They're typical—they're my parents.

But if it's possible to age a person with words, I've done it.

Like lifting a veil, they're seeing who I am for the first time. The light from both of their eyes dulls. Wrinkles I've never noticed on my mother's face suddenly appear. My dad's hair looks more gray than black. Their shoulders sink and their expressions change, making them seem less alive, wary of everything.

"You're not going anywhere," Dad says, like he's not sure.

"Dad," I begin, sincerely sorry for how I've hurt them.

But I knew.

I always did.

As hurt as they are, and as bad as I feel, none of it makes a difference. They will always be my parents, but a life without Thomas wouldn't be living at all.

"You're not leaving this house," my dad speaks loudly, making me jump.

As my family breaks apart, my cell phone finally rings. I don't answer it, but I look down and see his name and picture.

Then I hear his car.

So do my parents.

All three of us look toward the window, but my mom is the only one who moves.

With her hands on the windowsill, Mom leans out. "Thaddeus, go down there now."

He's already halfway down the stairs.

When the front door opens, I rush off the bed, but my mom's arms act as barricades. When I try to push past her, she has no problem pushing me back.

"You're not leaving this room, Leigh," she says with tears finally falling from her eyes.

My heart beats against the inside of my chest. I feel it in my throat and in my bruised wrists. It races in my stomach and under my fingernails. It echoes between my shoulder blades and under my kneecaps.

I turn away from her and run to my window. The curtains have fallen closed, and instead of pushing them apart, I rip them down.

Wearing what he wore when he dropped me off, my boy stands at the end of the driveway with his hands in his pockets and his head down. Dad walks straight for him, and even though I can't hear his words, I know he's forbidding and threatening.

To anyone else, it may seem like my dad has the upper hand. He's bigger and older and louder than Thomas. He's a judge. He's a father. He's feared and respected, but love has never had much respect for titles. This is his world. Thomas doesn't have to shout or cuss or hit to get his point across unless he wants to.

As my dad speaks, stepping closer to my so-obviously-high boy, Thomas finally looks up and smirks.

It sends my dad over the edge.

Gripping my upper arm, mom pulls me away from the window. I twist until her grip slips and I'm let loose and take the stairs down two at a time. The front door is partly open, but when I reach for the knob, my mom comes from behind me and slams it shut.

I manage to open it again, but she's stronger.

"Get back to your room," she demands with a shaky voice. Her eyes are glossy, and her cheeks are red, but she isn't crying anymore.

I turn and run through the kitchen instead of fighting with her. The back door is unlocked and open by the time she catches up with me, and I take off through wet grass and over rocky gravel. I run past the barking dogs and around my car. I outrun my shouting mother, who's trailing behind me, nowhere near as fast as I am.

As I circle around the house, the sun is almost all the way down, lighting the front yard in dark purples and heavy blues. The street lamps have turned on, and the front porch is lit by a 40-watt bulb.

Thomas and my dad have moved from the driveway to the lawn. My boy sees me as soon as I come into view, but my dad's back is to me. Love's dark eyes linger, and he holds his hands up, as if surrendering. He shakes his head. He looks down.

Dad pushes him.

I'm caught off guard, and my mom runs up behind me and locks me in her tight grip. I scream until what's left of my voice goes out, tugging and trying to jerk out of her arms.

It's not until the next door neighbor comes out of the house to see what's going on that Mom lets me go.

With both of my hands free, I call the first person who comes to mind.

While the phone rings and my mom tries to explain to the neighbor that everything's okay, I hurry away from her and run toward my boy.

Halfway across the lawn, Petey picks up my call.

"Hey, princess," he answers easily.

My dad pushes Thomas again, and this time love laughs as he stands back up.

"Petey!" I cry into the phone.

"What's wrong?" He's frantic now.

Before I can answer, the phone's knocked out of my hands. As I bend down to get it, my mom circles her arms around me and spins me around.

"Mom!" I cry, pushing against her chest. "Let go!"

"What's wrong with you?" She forces our legs out from under us. "Settle down, baby."

Between her knees, with her arms wrapped around mine and her cheek pressed on the top of my head, I can't answer. There are so many things wrong with me. Everything's fucked-up.

Our neighbors from across the street have come out of their house, too.

"Should we call the police?" they ask, standing on their porch.

Dad has Thomas backed against his car, but steps away from my boy long enough to answer. He holds his hand up and manages to speak without yelling.

"Everything's okay. You can go back inside," he says.

Unable to move, I keep my focus on love. His black eyes are wide, and his face is still busted-swollen from his fight with Oliver. My dad's questioning him, and he's pacing. He wants by, but Dad won't let him pass.

"I need to talk to Leigh," Thomas tells him.

"You're not going near my daughter," Dad replies, shoving Dusty back as he tries to move past him again.

Mischief looks at me and spits in the grass. He straightens out his shirt before meeting my father face to face.

"You think you could keep me away from her?" he provokes. "You haven't done such a good job so far, Judge."

Dad grabs Thomas by the front of his shirt and flips him onto his stomach, shoving his knee into love's back like he would some criminal. With the wind knocked out of him, Thomas goes down hard.

"Don't make me hurt you, Dusty," the man who gave me life says, detaining fate.

I dig my heels into the ground and push back until my mom falls. Her hold on me loosens, and I'm able to get onto my knees before she pulls me back down. She grabs my wrist, and I scream.

"He didn't do this!" I yell, cradling my hurt arm to my chest.

She lets me up, and I try to go around her, toward my boy who is still under my father's knee, but she blocks my way.

"I don't even know who you are," she says lowly, brushing hair out of her face.

"You can't keep me here, Mom."

Her head snaps in my direction. "You don't think so? You're seventeen, Leighlee."

"I don't care."

Before she can say anything more, Petey's black and white Caprice pulls into the driveway behind my Rabbit. He's alone, and he doesn't even bother turning off the car before he opens the door to get out.

I run straight to him.

"Leigh!" Mom calls after me.

I run right into Petey's arms. Embracing me for a moment, he pushes me back by my shoulders, looking at my face.

"We're leaving … We're going, and he showed up. My dad keeps pushing him, and my mom won't let me go."

"You need to slow down. I don't understand a fucking—"

He's cut off by the arrival of the black Mercedes I know so well screeching to a stop right behind the Lincoln, facing the wrong way in the street. Tommy gets out first, running around the front of the vehicle. Lucas exits the car next, as collected as he always is, rolling up his cuffs as he walks up the driveway.

"You called them?" I ask Petey.

He nods.

"Get away from my son, Judge McCloy," Lucas demands with the slightest hint of rage in his tone.

Standing back with Petey, I watch as Tommy heads toward my mother and immediately starts arguing. My mom points her finger like she always does, and Tommy listens with her arms crossed, stunning, even now. As my mother continues to explain what's going on, Tommy's defenses fall and confusion takes their place. My second mother looks at me from over her shoulder before giving her attention back to a woman she could never really stand.

"Did you know?" my mom asks madly. "Did you know about them, Tommy?"

"Maybe, but not like this," Tommy answers.

"I trusted you with my daughter." My mom says with tears in her voice. "I trusted you to take care of her."

"I did!" Tommy defends. "I did. We love her, Teri ... I would never hurt her."

On the other side of the lawn, Thomas is upright, expressionless with a grass stain on his shirt. Our fathers are not having a much different conversation than our mothers, except my dad is noticeably upset, and Lucas is less so.

"You think I'd allow this to happen under my roof if I knew?" the attorney asks, eyeing his son with nothing less than rage.

Dad shakes his head, but his tone eases. "Do you know about anything that goes on under your roof?"

Lucas takes a step forward. "What are you trying to say?"

"Nothing that you don't already know, Luke. Look at your boy."

And maybe for the first time in forever, Dusty's father actually does.

CHAPTER
fifty-nine

We're two kids who fell in hopelessly in love.

Our intentions were never vindictive. We're selfish, not malicious. All we wanted was to be together, but addiction and dependence made true liars of us and turned our innocent love into crazy love.

Somewhere along the line, Thomas and I shifted from hopeless to helpless.

While our parents talk things out, Thomas and I look at each other through the chaos. Broken, busted, and scarred, my heart beats for him—my life.

The beginning.

The end.

But he needs the kind of help I can't give him.

I walk across the grass, and Dusty meets me halfway.

He cries, slowly and silently. Love's lashes are wet, and his black eyes are soft, as caring as cocaine can be.

He reaches for me, sliding one hand to the back of my neck and placing the other on the side of my face. He pulls me in close and leans down until our foreheads touch and our noses brush.

"*Baby, baby, baby...*" he whispers. His tears fall onto my cheeks.

"Let's just go," I insist, clutching the front of his shirt.

Thomas smiles sweetly. His eyes are all mine.

"I remember the first time I ever saw you, Bliss. I think about that shit all the time." He presses his lips together before continuing. "I loved you then, you know."

His touch falls from my face to my shoulder and slides down my arm. He takes my discolored wrist and holds it up, showing me.

"I'm looking at you, girl," he cries around his words.

"What are you saying?" I ask, pulling on him.

He closes his eyes, and I see the shadow of the boy he used to be, lost behind pale skin and addiction. He hides behind Dusty, declared mini-foul before he ever had a chance to be anything else. He's mixed with the purple under his eyes and the cut on his lip. He's in the sweetness in his smirk and the kindness of his touch.

I haven't forgotten him.

I haven't given up.

"Bliss," he says under his breath.

"Thomas," I break, pulling him down.

He hugs me and kisses down the side of my face with wet lips. He cries against my skin, holding nothing back. He sobs. He shakes. He whispers love.

"I wish I could take you with me," he says, pressing his lips to the corner of my mouth.

I shove him away and stare, trembling with a thin heartbeat and misunderstanding.

"I am going with you," I insist.

He looks over my head toward the willow tree that means more to me than he'll ever know.

With his fingers tied up in his hair, he shakes his head. "No, you're not."

Refusing to believe what my heart already knows, I ask, "When are you coming back for me?"

Love's hands drop, and he wipes his eyes on his forearm. "I don't know."

His face is expressionless, like he's turned everything off. The black in his eyes has shifted from soft to hard and all too consuming. Tears fall, but he can't help it. He can't turn that truth off.

"Don't lie to me," I answer without air.

He clears his throat, patting his pockets. He breathes in through his nose, flaring his nostrils as he looks at me.

There is no light in him when he says, "I promise."

The breaking of my heart is unlike anything I have ever felt in my entire life.

It's being put to death with no life to give.

It's being full of dread, but feeling entirely empty.

It's being completely still when all I want to do is collapse.

Heartbreak is having every moment play before my eyes like I'm dying.

It's pink spinning wheels and soccer balls, cake in baggies, and teachers that smell like peanut butter. It's zombies and princesses. It's clothes that smell dirty and butterfly tattoos. It's finding the dock at the lighthouse and kissing for the first time. It's accidentally saying I love you, and *"If you were here, I'd probably eat your elbow."*

It's seat belt bruises across his chest and being a gentleman. It's when he kicked my backpack across the empty room, and *"Tell me you're with Oliver so I can lay that motherfucker out."*

Heartbreak doesn't feel a thing like falling. It's a decade under the influence and *The Fault in our Stars*. It's saying no every time he asked and staying up all night until he got home. It's *"Tell me a secret, Bliss. Come on, tell me something."*

It's remembering the way his face looks when he's inside of me. The way his lips part and pout. It's feeling him between my legs and around my body. Heartbreak is the memory of his muscles under my palms and his breath on my lips. It's his hair between my fingers and, *"I knew it. I fucking knew it."*

It's Sluts and Boys, secrets and lies, cocaine and peppermint marshmallow, and love is a traitor. It's birthday candles and gray bed sheets. It's creating dozens of rules to break and one to keep so it can never be broken.

"Rule number six: no promises."

"Okay."

"Promise?"

"Promise."

"And that's it."

"That's the only one."

My heartbreaker lifts my chin, pushing hair away from my face. "It's okay. It's better … it is."

I grab the collar of his shirt and pull. I cry like I've never cried before. I fight like I have nothing to lose, because I don't.

The worst part is he lets me. This life taker just holds on while I tug and punch and yell. I rip his shirt. I re-split his lip. I scratch his face. I pull his hair. I take us to our knees.

"You can't leave me, Thomas."

Our eyes meet and they stay for a moment—remembering, loving, memorizing.

Thomas reaches up and twirls a lock of my hair between his fingers. He watches strawberry-blond dance in his hand before letting it fall.

Then we're being pulled away.

CHAPTER
sixty

The next morning I tell my parents everything I think they should know, which is just enough to stop the questions. They assume the story I tell them is a half-truth of what the last eight years really were anyway.

My parents blame Lucas and Tommy. They blame themselves and Dusty. They don't come out and say it, but they blame me, too.

The only thing we can all seem to agree upon is that Thomas needs help.

As days pass, the bruises around my wrists fade, but the ache in my heart remains. Dad puts new locks on all of the doors without giving me a key, and Mom has our home phone number changed. I haven't seen my cell phone since the day the truth came out. I'm made to sleep with my bedroom door open, and to leave the house is out of the question.

Mom goes through my room, confiscating anything she recognizes as a gift from the Castors. When she finds pictures of me and Thomas, she cries to herself quietly, but doesn't take them all.

I let her have the hoodie that was already ruined with bleach, and I don't say anything when she carries my computer and iPod away.

I keep pink Jadeite hidden.

As days turn into weeks, Mom and Dad have no problem reminding me that I won't be eighteen for another four months.

Their house, their rules.

I don't care.

Time doesn't mean much.

Nothing does.

I'm just a girl with a broken heart, half-alive.

Without him, that's my deal.

CHAPTER

sixty-one

I t's the fourth of July, and Mom needs two more eggs to finish something else that's going to solve all our problems. I'm not surprised when she takes off her apron instead of asking me to run to the store like she would have before.

"Let me and Bliss get it," Grandma speaks up, back in town for the summer holiday. "Some fresh air will be good for us."

Aimless, too heavy to even drift, made of wreckage anchored by a heart that I hate for keeping me alive, I go along. Unwashed and unmade up, I follow Grandma outside. She winks as she starts her car and opens the roof to let light in.

"There's vitamins in sunshine you can't get anywhere else, you know," she tells me.

I'm silent as she drives.

At the store someone stops her to talk, and I amble inside. Grabbing a carton of eggs, I turn the corner of the aisle and walk right into the last person I ever expected to see again.

The eggs don't crush, but Valarie smiles, and everything rushes over me in a wave.

The girl whose lighters and hair ties I found on Dusty's floor when I was too little to even be in a boy's room smiles a little. She still looks older than her age, but fuller, clean. Diamonds stud her ears and black is all gone from her green eyes. They gleam brighter than they ever did under streetlamp light, and she's ditched cigarettes, holey jeans, and Chucks for white shorts, flip-flops, and hummus.

She's the most stunning girl I've ever seen all over again.

For the first time in months, I laugh. It's small and hoarse and mostly air, and nothing really, but I do it without even meaning to.

Naturally, cool as ever, so does Valarie.

"Hey, little sister." She beams. "Long time no see."

I have a fleeting, ridiculously intense and intensely ridiculous urge to hug her.

"Hey," I say, and as I go to tuck hair behind my ear, I feel my deficiency in every dirty strand. I look down to avoid looking at her, but my own flip-flops are old and their color is dull. The paint on my toes is chipped and the ends of my sweats are stepped-on and frayed.

"What are you doing here?" I ask, looking up and around the store, scanning faces.

Same as always, she runs her fingers through her dark tresses. Even in the corner of my eye, her hair looks healthy, split-endless and satiny, nothing like my own.

"My mom wants to cook for her boyfriend of the week or whatever. I wanted to help."

I glance at the package of sun-dried tomato and basil humus in her hands, and she rolls her eyes.

"I'm kind of addicted to it," she says, looking me over. Her smile stays. "What are you up to? How are you?"

Stuck between fate and suffering, I look up and don't know what to say.

Valarie and I are not the same, especially in this moment, but we're more similar than we've ever been. We've both put obsession before wellbeing. We've both fucked ourselves and other people in search of love. We've both been chosen over and left behind. The difference between us is how she stands. This girl has always walked with her shoulders back and her chin high. She owns who she is, broken pieces and all.

"Shitty," I answer honestly. "Kind of … yeah, really shitty."

She laughs and it's weirdly relieving.

"Yeah?"

I nod. "Yeah."

"Pete said he tried to call you."

"Yeah." I nod again, bitter inside with my parents, Thomas, the world, and myself.

"They took my phone," I explain, tapping my thumb against the egg carton. "Not that anybody wants to see me anyway, but you know."

We're quiet as a family walks by, and I think I should maybe stop talking, but I don't want to. The truth sucks, but honesty feels good. Getting it out feels good. I suddenly want to tell her all the worst parts of everything, but I don't know where to start.

"Hey," I start over, shifting the eggs to my hip and standing straight. "How's Ben?"

The girl who scratched love up while I was teeth-chattering over hot chocolate smiles. Like a teenager, like exactly her age, she ducks her head and peeks at her toes while her cheeks go pink, and she truly smiles.

"He's good," she says, and I know the sparkles in her ears are from him. None of the rest of us stayed any kind of together, but Valarie and Ben did. "He's coming home tonight."

There's a sting in my chest. Jealousy and hunger and soreness stretch the hole between my lungs wider open, but it's not this person's fault.

"That's good," I say.

Not a lie.

It's quiet again, and the urge to pour my broken heart out grows, but I see my grandma at the front of the store. Following my eyes, Valarie glances over her shoulder.

"Hey, here," she says, handing me the hummus. She digs through her purse and retrieves her phone. "What's your number?"

My iPhone was the first thing my parents took away, but then they didn't want me going to school without one. My replacement phone is little and cheap and not smart, and I literally never use it. I don't have a single number, and don't even know my own without looking it up.

But I don't want to lose the only person who knows something real about who I am, and still has a smile for me. Reaching into my back pocket, I open my phone and turn it on.

"Sorry," I say, waiting for it to load before I can read her my digits.

"Cool." She smiles after giving me hers. "See you, Bliss."

For the first time, I don't hate it.

WHEN WE get home from the store, I clean my room. I shower ,and I make an appointment to get my hair cut.

I go for a walk, and I walk until the stars come out, and when fireworks open up above me, I let myself cry.

THE NEXT morning, I take another shower.

I shave my legs and put on clean clothes and mascara.

Dad's at work, but Mom's making coffee when I get downstairs.

"I want my iPod and my computer back," I tell her.

THERE ARE some songs I can't listen to, but it's not because of the lyrics. Certain specific combinations of beats, bass, and guitars take me right back too clearly to summertimes that were too innocent and are still too raw. But the world is full of new music, and old music that's new to me, and I keep it going.

I cry to it.

I dance to it.

I shower to it and walk to it and trade it back and forth with Valarie. I pack up to it, and when my future roommate and I start emailing back and forth, and she wants me to tell her about myself, I sit down at my desk with it. With gently layered guitars touching and holding me from the inside-out, I start a new playlist and consider the idea.

Of me.

Myself.

It still feels like it started with him, like I began when purpose introduced himself to me when I was nine years old. But in truth, I was born before then. And despite half of my heart tearing itself away with his absence, it still beats.

I'm still me.

Nothing about him entering or leaving my life changes the fact that I have my mother's eyes or my father's nose. I still crack my toes when I'm nervous, and my freckles still come out in the sunshine. But there are other pieces of me that I know came from knowing this person.

Both because of and in spite of Thomas Castor, I'm a strawberry-blonde with collarbones that show. I'm a monster, but a soft one, and my favorite color is clear blue.

I can double Ollie on a skateboard, drive a stick shift with my eyes closed, and make Slushee art like a champ. My French accent is to die for, and I know what it means to talk with your eyes, and exactly how to toast the perfect marshmallow. I can curse in Italian, and I can have exactly two shots of anything before I feel it. I know which wine to cry into and which to celebrate with, and who to find if I ever need a lawyer for anything.

I've suffered alone in a bathroom stall, died in the shade of a favorite tree, and come back to life in a hotel bed. I've looked up at Heaven from a grocery cart and blacked out walking down a snowy street. I have a sweet tooth like none other, one girl's number in my phone, and a scar on my chest from a boy that once loved me stronger than the ocean is deep and hotter than fire burns.

I always eat the middle bite of peanut butter and jelly first, and I will never, not ever pierce my belly button.

Maybe I won't ever feel again the way I did with Dusty. Maybe I shouldn't. Maybe our deal was enough for one lifetime, and that scares me because it's all I've ever really known.

But I remember that it's okay not to know.

I'm broken, made of pieces, but my pieces are made of more than just love.

Adding songs for all of them, I send the newest piece of my life a playlist as my reply.

IMPARTIAL AND unapologetic, the sun doesn't care about anything but shining.

It pours down on me just the same as it always has and just like it does across the road and all the other cars on it.

The Rabbit's top is down, and my skin tingles and hums with the start of a burn that will probably hurt tonight but feels good right now. As miles roll by, my shorter than ever red-blond hair flies around my face. Freshly-cut soft strands tickle my neck and cheeks in the late summer heat, but the wind caresses me with salty-sweet ocean air. My parents are behind me with boxes and bags that wouldn't fit into my car, and I have music up, up, up.

Despite waking up too many mornings wishing I hadn't and every indolent effort on my part to waste life away, it's happening. I'm driving to college that's more hours and miles from home than I've ever stayed, and spinning at the precipice of being more free than I've ever been.

Live, my heart beats steadily in the pause between songs. *Live*.

My lips curve into a smile as my new favorite comes on, and I turn it up a little louder. In my lap, my phone vibrates with a new message from Val.

Good luck today, little sister.

It's her way of saying love.

Maybe it always was.

Glancing between the freeway and the screen, I send glad gratitude back and drop my phone in my lap. With my right hand easy on the wheel, I move my left with the breeze out my window and sing along about dust and bones and darlings and falling.

When my phone vibrates again, the feeling in my chest is utterly distinct.

I used to measure everyone and everything in my life against the pull I feel between my lungs and all through my veins right now. I only knew who I was in relation to it—to him—but that wasn't fair or right or smart or good.

Bad choices, I think as I look down at a number I don't recognize, but know. I'm not an innocent kid holding a yellow Popsicle anymore, but I'm still young, and I've learned a lot.

Chances are meant to be taken.

Rules are made to be broken.

Smiling higher than the first time I couldn't help it, I accept the call and bring the phone to my ear.

"Hello?"

MARY'S
Acknowledgements

I have to start this off with a special thank you to the team of people who helped make this book available for the world, Arijana Karčić, Debbie Rios, Maxann Dobson, and Melissa Jones. Thank you for your part in making my dream a reality, and for teaching me a thing or two along the way.

To my best friend Ashley, my sister-in-law Jennifer, and my sister Christina, words cannot explain the appreciation I feel toward each of you for the loving and unconditional support you've each given me as I made myself crazy breathing life into Dusty. You each played a huge role in keeping me semi-sane, and I thank you for that.

To my mother, who never seems to understand how much I love her, thank you for your sacrifices.

Jason, you have given me a life I never imagined living. Your support is invaluable.

To my children who are still too young to hold this book, I love you.

Silvia and Dee, thank you for being there when I needed you the most.

Catherine Jones, you've become such a vital part of my writing process. Because of you, Pickup Truck and Low exist. Because of you, I am a better author. Thank you.

Natalee, Cjay, Kelly V., Mandy, Sam, Samantha, Heather O., Peta, Amber L. Johnson, Charity Pierce, Sarah Pierce, Jeanne McDonald, E.K Blair, Debra Anastasia, Willow Aster, Teresa Murmett, Thaigher Lillie, Valentine S., Brenda and the crew at the salon, my aunt Angela and everyone who threw me the party, Dionne (Thank you for taking a chance on me), my puppy, OGs, Dusty Lovers, the Dusty Street Team, every blog that had ever featured my books, anyone who has taken the time to reach out to me, and THE READERS—THANK YOU!

And finally, to anyone who is or has lived through the cycle of addiction. Know that you are not alone, and there is an end to the madness if you want it bad enough.

Don't live life being a victim. It's not worth it.

The heart is deceitful above all things and beyond cure. —Jeremiah 17:9

SARAH'S
Acknowledgements

To Brand New, William Fitzsimmons, APES, The Mowglis, Damien Rice, Taking Back Sunday, The Used, Imaginary Cities, Blink-182, The Violent Femmes, Mumford and Sons, The Silversun Pickups, The 1975, Lykke Li, Live, Nirvana, The Head and The Heart, Our Lady Peace, Marina and The Diamonds, Jimmy Eat World, Tyler Knott Gregson, Tom Petty and Stevie Nicks, HAIM, Shakespeare, Kundera, Nabokov, Lindelof, Waheed, and Wilde — you continue light my dark. Thank you for all that you've shared. I love all of you.

To Catherine, thank you for correcting my commas and for your time and energy spent with Dusty. It means a lot to me.

To Sammi, thank you creating dustyislove.tumblr.com and giving us such a beautiful place. You're truly supercalla and such a wonderful friend and I love you.

To Ari, Pico, Panda, Jac, Karla, danikool, Crystina Falero, Lauren, Erika, Peta, Mildred, mericuh, Rosalinda, Mandy, Melissa, Mollie, Bree, Berta, Stacey, my mimosa, my carebear, Anahi Lacey, Riley, Nicola, AnaLisbeth, Cerece, Sophie, Jamie, Stephanie, sariedee, nicoluscious, Amber Sachs, fragilecloud, dayzee, adoublea, Natalee, Ernest, Katy, Ray, Sherry, Heather, Palin, Michaelbear, Frederico, Emily, Zero, Sam, Mister Jones, Eli, Johnna, and tater tot — thank you all for sharing with me, for listening, for laughing, for shelter, thoughtfulness, inspiration, sincerity, wine, music, hearts, tumbles, flutters, hugs, so much love, and for continuing to show me where the good goes. Thank you for being a part of this and a part of my life. I love all of you.

To Frenchie — tell your mother that I do mean you, Ariel. I love you and I'm thankful to and for you.

To Sam, please, have some cinnamon rolls! Thank you so much for being one of the first to read and love this story. I love you.

To Diane Rinella, Jennifer Theriot, and tbird, thank you so much for making Houston a thousand times cooler than I could have imagined. I love you guys.

To my darkling, my KRG, my brightheart, and my Bunny, my love for all of you is beyond compare. Seneca said that one of the most beautiful qualities of friendship is to understand and to be understood. I've found that on so many levels with each of you and I'm thankful with all of my heart to call you my friends.

To Max, for giving love in my heart your time and focus, late nights, patience, care, and support. Thank you for all of your help and kindness. I love you.

To Moses, thank you for being a person I truly and wholly admire, a friend in the deepest meaning of the word, and a girl I always feel so fucking cool with. I love you more than small silver wreaths and iron lungs.

To my grandmother who I love and miss so much. Thank you.

To Karin, for sticking with me during what have been the hardest seven months of my entire life. Thank you for being the person I share everything with and want to for always. Thank you for loving my heart and for filling my cup, for trail mix that keeps me from dizziness and for helping me feel not alone. Thank you for reminding me what to focus on and for voiceletters and your gasp and the way you sound when you smile and for loving him too. So much, thank you for loving him too. Thank you for careful help with this and all my work, for late nights and for looking up and opening things I can't. Thank you for being my good morning and the bombardment I look so forward to and my goodnight. Thank you for being my person to turn to, no matter the reason. I love you more than the sun and the moon and all the stars, more than books are good and more than coffee coffee all the time. Je suis nee pour elle aimer.

To Bishop, for sticking with me just as strongly for these last seven months and our whole lives. Thank you for videos that make me laugh when I'm crying (apparently) and for killing that wasp in my bed netting. Thank you for suggesting words and for sharing ideas. Thank you for helping me wake up on time and for bear assistance. Thank you for hugs, and for the way you love Ziggy and Sawyer, for mini-feasts and for letting me play life with you and for flying with me and for sitting beside me at that table and for letting me sit by you at the movies today. Thank you for being the coolest person to share Houston, and so many of my days with. I love you, all the way down to your blood and bones and guts. I love you so much. I love you, goddammit.

To you, the reader, thank you for giving not only this delinquent and his princess a chance, but all of the people in this story. Thank you for giving them a place in your heart-memory. Our time is one of the most precious things we have to give, and the fact that you've given yours to this incarnation of love means more to me than I know how to say. Thank you doesn't feel big enough at all to convey that feeling, but from my heart and soul, sincerely, thank you.

To the little buffalo fast asleep on my toes and keeping them warm, I love you more than the sunrise. Thank you for letting me lay my head on your heart when I couldn't get a grip on anything else. Thank you for being there when I go to sleep and when I wake up. Thank you for being one of my very favorite parts of this life. I love you.

And to trouble, how is it that almost five years feels like a few too-short seconds right now? I'm sitting in my quiet room and it's this moment that's finally here and with everything that's hurt, all I want is for *this* moment to last forever. Thank you for loving me. Thank you for Paris and for walking with me, for courage and validation and for being the only reason I need. Thank you for taking my gun away. Thank you for your trust and your truth and the reckless, helpless way your heart beats and beats and beats. You are Heaven-sent, and I won't dare forget.

I love you.

ABOUT
Mary

Mary Elizabeth is an up and coming author who finds words in chaos, writing stories about the skeletons hanging in your closets. Known as The Realist, she is one half of The Elizabeths--a duo brave enough to never hide the truth.

Mary was born and raised in Southern California. She is a wife, mother of four beautiful children, and dog tamer to one enthusiastic Pit Bull and a prissy Chihuahua. She's a hairstylist by day but contemporary fiction, new adult author by night. Mary can often be found finger twirling her hair and chewing on a stick of licorice while writing and rewriting a sentence over and over until it's perfect. She discovered her talent for tale-telling accidentally, but literature is in her chokehold. And she's not letting go until every story is told.

For more Information on Mary's solo work, including her upcoming project True Love Way, set to release in January of 2015, and Closer in 2015, follow her on:

Amazon:
http://www.amazon.com/Mary-Elizabeth/e/B00MW8Z81Y/ref=ntt_athr_dp_pel_pop_1

Facebook:
https://www.facebook.com/pages/Mary-Elizabeth-Author/1431640340382601

Goodreads:
https://www.goodreads.com/author/show/7496678.Mary_Elizabeth

Twitter:
https://twitter.com/TeamSmella23

And you can also visit her on her website at www.MaryElizabethlit.com

ABOUT
Sarah

Love's listener works from her heart.
She did this for Dusty.
For more information on her past and future work, visit:

http://www.littlegreypages.tumblr.com/

http://www.facebook.com/littlegreyache

http://www.twitter.com/littlegreyache

http://www.goodreads.com/author/show/7496682.Sarah_Elizabeth

This paperback interior was designed and formatted by

www.emtippettsbookdesigns.com
Artisan interiors for discerning authors and publishers.

Made in the USA
Monee, IL
26 August 2020

39896328R00180